I0587714

Detective Hodgins Victorian Mysteries

Books 1, 2, and 3

Nanci M. Pattenden

Murder Does Pay, Ink

Published by Murder Does Pay, Ink
Ontario, Canada
www.murderdoespayink.ca

ISBN 978-1-7750491-4-2 print
ISBN: 978-1-7750491-5-9 e-book
10 9 8 7 6 5 4 3 2 1 0

ACKNOWLEDGMENTS

I'd like to say a great big thanks to Omar and Ashley, owners of Cardinal Press Espresso Bar in Newmarket for providing a wonderful environment in which to work. They have a lovely big room in the back of their coffee shop, creating the perfect place to call "my office."

As always, thanks to my editor, MJ, of Infinite Pathways, and Chris, my graphics guru.

THANK YOU

Detective Hodgins Victorian Murder Mysteries

Body in the Harbour

Death on Duchess Street

Corpses for Christmas

Body in the Harbour

A Detective Hodgins Victorian Mystery

Book One

CHAPTER ONE

Danny stretched out on his belly half way up Conner's Wharf watching the ice swirl, while Michael stood at the end of the wharf, throwing snowballs at the seagulls as they flew overhead, screeching their displeasure. Waves thrashed the pilings of the wharf, churning chunks of ice around Toronto Harbour. Several pieces surrounded something soft, grinding against it; pushing it further into the hard sand along the waterfront.

"Hey Mikey, what's that?"

Michael walked over to Danny and knelt beside him. He turned his head, following Danny's outstretched arm, and shrugged. Danny scrambled to his feet. "Looks like someone threw out some old clothes. Let's go see."

Danny ran back along the wharf with Michael following slowly, not terribly interested in a pile of clothing. Jumping down near the shoreline, Danny slipped on the rocks. His shoe hit the cold water, instantly soaking his foot. Michael hurried to his brother's side and helped him up.

1

Making their way towards the shoreline, Michael stopped and grabbed his little brother's arm.

"It's not clothes," Michael said.

Danny pulled away from his brother's grip and moved in for a closer look. "I never saw a dead man before," he said reaching out.

Michael grabbed hold of the back of Danny's coat. "Don't touch it. We'd better get Dad."

They scrambled to the road, and ran up Lorne Street to the Queen's Hotel on Front. The doorman smiled and gave his usual greeting to the two boys who'd become regulars at the hotel over the Christmas break.

"Good day Master Daniel, Master Michael."

Instead of stopping to chat, they headed straight to the front desk looking for their father, Ben Grove, manager of the hotel. Between gulps of air they told him about the man on the shore. Ben had trouble understanding, but once they calmed down and got their breath back, he had them repeat everything. He found it difficult to believe his sons had actually stumbled across a dead body, but their wide eyes and shaky voices told him something was definitely wrong.

Two of Ben's oldest friends were in the dining room arguing about the local politics and enjoying the hotel's signature dish, Fillets of beef a la Rossine. Ben took Michael and Danny over to their table.

"Sam, Charlie, sorry to interrupt, but I need your help." Ben repeated the boy's story. "Can they sit with you while I fetch the police?"

"You sure he's dead?" Charlie asked. "Might be some drunk still celebrating the new year."

"No, I don't think so, Mr. Kelly," Michael said. "He looked like the dead fox we found by the pond last summer." Michael looked at Danny and made a face. "Except the man didn't smell bad."

The two men agreed to sit with the boys. As Ben hurried out, he stopped to ask a waiter to bring some hot tea for them. He headed out the front door and sprinted along Front Street in the direction of Number Four station on Wilton Avenue. As he crossed Bay Street, he noticed a young policeman making his rounds. Ben stopped him and repeated what his boys said. The constable blew his whistle and a few minutes later, a heavy set constable came huffing around the corner from Wellington Street and joined them. They spoke for a moment, then 'Tubby' headed east towards the station. The first constable introduced himself as Henry Barnes and asked Ben to take him to the boys.

When they arrived back at the Queens, Michael and Danny told Barnes where they found the body. Barnes pulled a pencil out of one pocket, a receipt out of another, and then made a few notes on the back.

3

"Probably drunk and fell off the pier." He put the paper back into his pocket. "Can you show me exactly where this alleged body is?" Ben and Constable Barnes followed the boys down Lorne Street, their overshoes sloshing in the melted snow. As soon as they spotted the body, Ben sent Danny and Michael home.

It was just as the boys had described. The man was face down, half on the beach, half in the water. His arms were covered in sand and snow. The bottom edge of a long dark overcoat fanned out around the body's legs. Several seagulls pecked at his head, pulling off small bits of skin and hair. Most of the birds flew off when the men ran towards the shoreline, but a few lingered a couple of feet away, as though waiting for the intruders to leave.

"Bloody birds. You'd think they were vultures instead of gulls. Don't suppose the poor sot cares though, eh Constable?" Ben grabbed a handful of snow, formed a ball and threw it at the birds. It exploded when it hit the ground and the remaining gulls flew off.

Ben turned around when he received no answer. Barnes was standing a few feet back, staring at the dead man. All the colour had drained from his face.

"We can't just leave him there," Ben said. "Help me drag him the rest of the way out of the water. Constable! Pull yourself together. Grab his arm. He can't harm you."

Ben moved behind Barnes and gave him a little shove. Barnes stumbled towards the body and stopped.

"Looks like the waves and ice have partially buried him. We'll have to free him up from the sand first." Ben used his hands to move the cold, heavy sand off the dead man's arms so they could get a good grip. He reached under the stiff's right armpit and told the constable to grab the left. Barnes obediently did as he was told, and together they dragged the corpse a few feet up the frozen shore. The head had turned. Barnes looked down at his face, let go of the arm, ran under the pier and threw up.

Ben looked down the shoreline and spotted the Yacht Club in the distance. "Wait here," he said, and sprinted to the club. He returned ten minutes later with a tarp and a well-worn blanket. He dropped the tarp on the ground and placed the blanket over the corpse. He noticed Barnes had not moved from the edge of the pier and was staring at the lifeless form. Ben walked over to him and placed his hand on the constable's shoulder.

"How long have you been on the force?"

"Three months, Sir."

"Shouldn't you get someone with a little more experience to help with this?"

With the body covered and out of sight, the constable started to regain his composure. "I sent Constable Snider to get a senior office and the coroner. They should be here any time."

The sound of voices drifted down from the street above. "There they are now. Looks like one of the detectives with the coroner," Barnes said, waving his arms at the two men approaching in a buggy. They stopped the buggy at the end of Lorne Street and tied the horses to a post. The two men crossed Esplanade, then the train tracks and walked down to the edge of the pier. The shorter man carried a doctor's bag, so Ben figured the tall one must be the detective. The contrast between the two men was almost comical. The coroner was short and heavy set; his coat fit so tight it looked like it would burst open. His flaming orange sideburns stood out dramatically against his pale skin, even from a distance. The detective was at least twenty years younger, tall and lanky. His overcoat was open, revealing a suit that looked tailor made. He took long strides, and walked with an air of confidence; the doctor had to trot to keep up.

Hodgins looked at the covered body, nodded, then said, "Guess that's him then. He's all yours Doctor."

Dr. McKenzie was sweating, even though the temperature had steadily dropped over the past few hours. He took a hanky out of his coat pocket, and wiped his brow before kneeling down beside the corpse.

Hodgins buttoned his overcoat as he looked around. "I was told a couple of boys found the body. Where are they?"

"Yes, my sons. I didn't want them here any longer than necessary."

Hodgins glared at Barnes. "I hope you at least spoke to them."

"Yes, Sir," Barnes stammered. "I interviewed them at the hotel before they showed me the body. They don't know much. Just found him when they were playing."

"Right." Hodgins turned to Ben. "And who are you?"

"Ben Grove. Manager at the Queen's Hotel."

"Do you recognize the dead man?"

"Don't think so, but it's hard to tell."

"Hard to tell? Why? Either you know him or you don't."

"Take a look at him Detective. You'll see."

"The man's right," Dr. McKenzie said. "Even his mother would have trouble identifying him."

McKenzie lifted the blanket. "The whole left side is scraped down to the bone. What's left of the skin is barely hanging on."

"I figure it's from the ice in the harbour," Ben said. "Don't think he's been in there long though. I've seen people pulled from the water before. He's not all bloated

7

like you'd expect."

"This where you found him?"

"Not exactly," Ben said. "Didn't seem right to leave him there, what with the gulls pecking at him and all. I got the constable to help me pull him out of the water. The blanket's from the Yacht Club. It's always left open in case of emergencies."

"You shouldn't have moved the body. You've disturbed any evidence that might have been around." Hodgins scowled at Barnes. "You should have known better."

The constable opened his mouth to say something but the glare from Hodgins stopped him.

Hodgins continued, "I can see from the drag marks just how far you moved him. Wouldn't be surprised if it was a simple case of drowning."

"I'm not so sure," Dr. McKenzie said. "He has a lot of bruising. Might be from the ice, but I can't say positively. Bad cut on his side too. Edges are so straight it makes me wonder. Won't know until an autopsy is done."

"You saying it was murder?" the constable asked.

"No, I'm just saying it's not obvious if he drowned or was dead before he went in the water." He turned to the detective. "How are we going to get him up to the road and onto the wagon?"

"Why not just roll him onto the blanket and carry him in it?" Barnes asked.

"Your skills at observation leave much to be desired," Hodgins replied. "The only thing holding that blanket together is the dirt and dust. Pick him up in it and he'd remain on the beach. What's that?" Hodgins pointed at the tarp that Ben had dropped beside the body.

"I grabbed the tarp when I got the blanket from the Yacht Club. Found it first, but I saw the blanket and figured it would be more respectful covering him with it rather than the tarp. Brought both back."

"It looks strong enough to hold the body," Hodgins said. We can each take a corner and carry him up to the buggy."

CHAPTER TWO

Detective Albert Hodgins looked up as Dr. McKenzie approached his desk. "Well, Hamish, what can you tell me? Constable Barnes didn't take many notes at the scene yesterday." He held up the wrinkled receipt with a few lines of writing on the back. "I hope you have some information that will be of use." He let go of the receipt and watched it flutter down to the desk top, then gestured to the chair on the opposite side of his desk.

Dr. McKenzie sat down and placed a folder on the desk. "I'll write you out a copy of my notes in a few days, but I thought you'd want to hear what I found first."

McKenzie opened the folder, picked up the first sheet of paper, glanced at his notes, and relayed the information.

"I went through the pockets of the overcoat he was wearing. It had the name Lowe or Lorne stitched inside the collar. Not sure exactly as some of the stitches were gone. Didn't find much. He had sixty five cents and a train ticket, but the water has obliterated most of the printing. He also had this key." He reached into his breast pocket, pulled out a tiny flat key, and handed it to Hodgins.

Hodgins had a quick look before placing it on his desk. "Looks like a trunk key."

McKenzie looked at his notes again. "He had on blue overalls, a smock, and felt lumberman boots." He looked up at Hodgins. "I thought he might be a farmer, but he doesn't have the weathered skin I'd expect of someone who works outside. Hands have calluses, and he is rather muscular, so I'd guess he does some sort of manual work, just not out in the sun all day."

He turned the page over and continued. "I'd estimate his age to be about twenty-five. Clean-shaven, about five foot eight and 160 pounds. Nothing wrong with his heart, liver or kidneys. He was in excellent health."

"I'll have someone check to see if we have a missing persons report matching that description. What about cause of death?"

"Well," Dr. McKenzie hesitated. "I didn't find any water in his lungs, and there was no foam around his mouth. I'd say he was dead before he hit the water."

"Are you suggesting foul play?"

McKenzie smiled. "That's for you to determine Detective. It's my job to tell you what I find, nothing more. There were a lot of marks on his body though."

"What type of marks?"

McKenzie put the page back in the folder and picked up another sheet. "Let's see. He had contusions everywhere. The one on the back of his head, just at the hair line, had the most peculiar shape. Something about it was familiar, but I just can't put my finger on it. I'm sure it will come to me though. He was also missing a lot of hair on the left side of his head, and the left side of his face, as you saw, was scraped clear down to the bone. That damage probably came from the ice, but some came from the gulls. He did have another interesting wound; I took a good look at that cut I pointed out to you at the scene - the one on his left side, just above his waist. It didn't look natural. Too straight and even to come from a fall or being pushed around in the water. It definitely came from a sharp, thin object. Probably a knife. The autopsy also showed that his skull was fractured. Split right through. No way the ice would have done that either. Had to have been something heavy and solid. Foul play or accident - well, you'll have to figure that out."

The coroner put the papers back in order and stood up. "I'll write up a copy for you as soon as I can." He picked up his folder and headed for the door whistling what Hodgins assumed was another of his old Scottish songs. It amazed him how the coroner always managed to be in such a jolly mood.

Hodgins had made notes while McKenzie spoke. He tore a clean sheet from his notebook and jotted down the physical description of the body. He looked around the station to see who was available.

"Barnes," he yelled. "Check this out." He held the paper and waited while Barnes made his way across the room, bumping into almost every desk along the way. "Description of the body from the harbour. Check missing persons."

Hodgins pushed Barnes' wrinkled receipt around the desk, then ran his hand over it in an attempt to flatten it. He opened his notebook and copied the few words written on the reverse. He cursed Barnes under his breath, and then started adding his own comments and questions.

Half an hour later Barnes was back. "I think I found him."

Hodgins raised one eyebrow.

Barnes, grinning from ear to ear, handed a missing persons report to the detective. "The description is almost an exact match, Sir."

Hodgins looked skeptical, but took the report and started to read it aloud. "Fred Walker, age twenty six, 162 pounds, five foot seven. Age, weight and height seem to fit, but the name on the coat was Lorne or Lowe, not Walker."

"Keep reading, Sir."

Hodgins glared at Barnes, and the grin quickly disappeared from the young constable's face. "Sir," he stammered. "Look at the name of the person who filed the report."

Hodgins looked down at the report. "Well, Barnes. I do believe you have redeemed yourself - somewhat." Without looking up, he waved a hand at Barnes, indicating he was dismissed.

Barnes backed away and stumbled over a chair. "Thank you, Sir." He turned and raced back to his desk.

Hodgins looked up, shook his head and mumbled, "Clumsy git." He looked back at the missing persons report and re-read the name. George Lowe, Stouffville, cousin of Fred Walker. "Barnes," he bellowed. "Fetch me a train schedule."

* * *

Hodgins hopped off the trolley at the end of his road, and walked to the house he shared with his wife's family. He enjoyed living in the upscale neighbourhood, but wished he could afford a little house of his own. He opened the front door and his eight year old daughter, Sara, ran into his arms. He was astounded how she could greet him with such gusto day after day, as though he'd been away for months, not hours.

She helped him off with his coat and hung it on the lower hook of the coat tree. "Can we go skating tonight Daddy? Please?"

Sara had received a new pair of skates for Christmas and wanted to use them every day.

He took her hand and followed the aroma of the meal down the hall and into the kitchen. "Not tonight. You'll have to wait until Saturday."

Sara pouted, her lower lip quivering. "Just for a little while?"

He looked down at her sad face and smiled. "The skating rink won't be open after supper, and the ice on the pond isn't thick enough. We'll make a day of it on Saturday. Skating in the morning, then we'll have lunch somewhere – you pick. Then we can go to the display at the Crystal Palace. Just you, me and Mother. How does that sound?"

Sara's face lit up. "Skating and the Crystal Palace? Really Daddy? Oh yes, please."

In the kitchen Hodgins' wife, Cordelia, and her mother, were putting the finishing touches on dinner. Physically, his wife was a younger version of Euphemia. Both had wavy orange-ish-red hair. Their completions were fair, but unlike her mother Cordelia had a smattering of freckles across her cheeks and nose. They had the same green eyes, but Hodgins could see Cordelia's held a sparkle that was missing from his mother-in-law's. He kissed his wife on the cheek, then nodded at Euphemia, but said nothing to her.

"Irish stew. Smells wonderful, as usual," he said.

"Have you found out who that unfortunate man from the harbour is?"

"Possibly. We have a lead that I'll be checking out tomorrow. Have to take the train to Stouffville first thing in the morning."

"Was he murdered?"

"Really Cordelia," her mother exclaimed. "Why would you want to know such a thing?"

Cordelia enjoyed listening to her husband talk about his cases. At first, Hodgins felt the same as his mother-in-law. Women, proper ladies, should find murder morbid, frightening, something not to be discussed. However, he quickly discovered that by talking to Cordelia she helped him sort out his thoughts with her sharp, logical mind. More than once she noticed some minor detail that he had dismissed as unimportant, and he was able to link it to one or more other clues that helped him solve a case. He soon realized that going over the details with her helped him put everything in order. Hodgins looked forward to their evening chats. He picked up a spoon and sampled the stew.

"Tastes even better than it smells." He dropped the

spoon in the sink and made his way to the front parlour to sit with his father-in-law Harold, and wait to be called to the table.

CHAPTER THREE

Hodgins exited the train and stood on the platform at the Stouffville station buttoning up his overcoat. The platform filled with people going about their business; several business men heading to Toronto, a few salesmen with their sample cases, ladies heading out for a day of shopping he figured, and families off somewhere on a trip. The hiss of the breaks startled him. He watched as steam billowed out the entire length of the train, causing one lady's dress to swirl around her legs when she walked too close. A gust of wind blew the steam back under the train and caused Hodgins to duck when a derby hat shot past his head. Looking around for the ticket booth, he spotted one a few feet away, just outside the station house.

He walked over and asked the ticket man, "Can you direct me to Second Street?"

"Of course, Sir. It's not far." He pointed towards the south end of the platform. "Just go to Main Street there and turn right. First street you come to is Edward. Turn right again and the next street is Second."

Hodgins was glad the house wasn't far. He nodded his thanks and began walking, raising his collar to try to block the stinging wind. There wasn't much snow on the ground, so he knew at least his feet would be reasonably warm, despite the thinning soles on his patent leather boots.

He stopped briefly along the way to admire an enormous brick house, complete with gingerbread and a turret. It was just the type of house Cordelia would love to own. He couldn't wait for the day he, Cordelia, and Sara could move into a place of their own. He imagined Cordelia in the springtime, standing on the second floor balcony watching ladies strolling with their baby carriages, enjoying the sounds of the returning robins, and the scents of the flowering crab apple trees. Too bad this house was so close to the noisy train station. He wouldn't want to listen to the steam whistle and hissing breaks every day. With one last wishful look, he continued along Second, looking for the Lowe home.

A few minutes later Hodgins climbed the steps of a covered, white-washed porch attached to a little brick house at the corner of Second and Williams. He took a quick peek in the window as he crossed to the door. Fortunately there was no one in the room to see him snoop. The little wrought iron bench at the far corner of the porch looked inviting, despite the weather. He could picture himself sitting there in the summer early in the morning, watching the neighbours and enjoying a warm breeze.

He reached for the door knocker and noticed it wasn't the usual type. Instead of a hoop or straight knocker, this one was shaped like a hand holding a ball. *Silly thing to waste money on*, he thought. Hodgins lifted the hand and rapped it against the door three times then turned around and took in the surroundings. Except for the noise coming from the train station, it was very quiet. The soft whinny of a horse touched his ears, but he wasn't able to tell where it came from. The street was a mixture of large and small homes; some yellow brick, others red, with baton homes scattered throughout. Both sides of the street were lined with Maple and Oak trees. *Probably cool in the summer under the canopy of all those trees*, he thought, unlike the street he lived on. This would be a nice place to raise a family. Too bad it wasn't close to his police station.

Hodgins heard someone moving inside and turned back just as the door opened. A pleasant looking woman, wearing a dark blue dress and a flour covered apron, greeted him. Hodgins guessed she was his wife's age - early-thirties. He held up his badge and introduced himself. "I'm looking for Mr. Lowe. Is he home?"

"Please, come in. I'm Mrs. Lowe." She turned and

called for her husband. A slightly balding man, closer to forty, came downstairs and stood beside his wife.

"I'm George Lowe. What can I do for you?"

"You filed a missing persons report on your cousin, Fred Walker. Is there someplace we can talk?"

"Oh, where are my manners," Mrs. Lowe said. "Come in to the drawing room." She moved down the hall and opened a door. "Would you like some tea to take the chill away?"

"That would be nice, thank you," Hodgins said. Mrs. Lowe went to prepare the tea and George gestured for Hodgins to enter the parlour. He walked in, and went straight over to the fire to warm himself. George followed, closing the door behind him.

"Detective, where's Fred? Have you located him?"

"I'm afraid the news is not good. A body was found on a beach in Toronto. He fits the general description of your cousin." Hodgins pulled his notebook and pencil out of his coat pocket.

"We're not positive that he is your cousin. I don't want to go into too much detail, but it is difficult to identify him. The coroner has called an inquest for Wednesday at the Queen's Hotel in Toronto. We'll need you to come in and identify the body beforehand. If it is Fred, you'll have to attend the inquest."

George stared at the detective for a moment. "What do you mean it's difficult to identify him?"

"He was in the water and his face was damaged, quite possibly by the ice in the harbour. We haven't determined what caused the other wounds. The overcoat he was wearing had your name stitched into the collar."

George grabbed the back of the nearest chair. "Yes, it's possible. Fred borrowed it from time to time."

"I'm sorry to bring you such bad news, and so early in the morning, but I wanted to catch you before you left for work." Without waiting for an invitation, Hodgins sat on the matching chair opposite George. He noticed that the padded tapestry on the arms was a little thin and faded. He crossed his right leg, the ankle resting on his left knee, and used his inner thigh as a table for his notebook. The sun shone through the side window, illuminating the pages and pulling some of the winter chill from his face.

"Are you aware of any problems Fred had lately? Any arguments? Someone who may have had a grudge against him for any reason?"

"No," George said. He thought for a moment, chewing his lower lip. "Well . . ."

Hodgins perched his pencil over the notebook, waiting.

George continued, "He was quite upset on Christmas

day. I'm sure it's not connected."

"I'll be the judge of that. Something you consider trivial could be very important. What was he upset about?"

"A woman."

"Ah," Hodgins said. "You'd better start at the beginning."

George sighed and slumped down onto the chair.

"It started years ago, back in England. We hail from Norfolk. Fred was very close to a girl named Emily. After Fred's mother died, his father remarried. His new wife didn't get along with his children, so they were sent here to live with their aunt, my mother. Fred spoke of Emily often."

George sat up straight and put one hand over his mouth, then dragged it down over his beard. "Dear Lord. His brother and sister. They'll have to be told. Neither lives in town. Henry is a farmhand a few miles north, and Anabelle just married this past summer before moving to Schomberg."

George paused while Hodgins wrote everything down. Hodgins look up and said, "Continue please."

"Two years ago, Emily's family moved here. Actually, they only live a few blocks away on Albert Street. They became friendly again. On Christmas morning, around 10:30 I believe, Fred walked to her house for a visit. I recall the time because my wife had just put the bird in the oven.

Said it needed exactly six hours, and we planned Christmas dinner for 4:30. He was back home before noon, and very agitated."

Hodgins wrote for a few moments. "Did he say why he was upset?"

George stood and walked to the fireplace. He picked up a pipe from the mantle, reached into his pocket for his tobacco pouch and filled the bowl. He lit it and turned back to the detective.

"He wouldn't talk about it at first, and we didn't want to pry. At dinner he just blurted it out. Apparently, when he arrived at the Smythe's he discovered Emily had married a few days earlier. We knew she had other gentlemen callers, but we all assumed she would eventually marry Fred. He was just promoted to foreman at the sawmill and was planning to propose after the new year. We were all shocked."

Hodgins thought for a moment, wrote in his book, and then said, "Interesting. Did Fred speak to Emily after that?"

George shrugged. "I don't know. Fred didn't mention her again. He kept to himself the next several days. Then, on the twenty-ninth, he was out of sorts all day. Distracted. After supper he went up to his room and we didn't see him again. Neither of us heard anything from him; didn't notice him go out. We just assumed he was in his room all night.

My wife called him for breakfast but he didn't come down. She went up to his room, and he wasn't there. He must have risen early. I suppose he could have snuck out any time really."

"I'll need the full name and address of Emily."

"Emily lived with her parents, the Smythe's, at number five Albert Street. Afraid I don't know who she married, or where they live. Fred never said."

The door opened and Mrs. Lowe came in carrying a tray with a pot of tea, milk, sugar, and cups. The aroma of baking bread wafted into the room and Hodgins took a deep, satisfying breath. It was one of his favourite scents. She placed the tray on a small table beside the sofa and started to pour. Hodgins noticed she brought three cups and was still wearing the flour covered apron.

"Grace, this conversation is not something you need to hear," Mr. Lowe said.

She ignored him and handed Hodgins the first cup of tea. "Milk and sugar?" she asked.

"Thank you, no, black is fine. We were just discussing Miss Smythe's marriage. Don't suppose you know who she married?"

Mrs. Lowe poured some tea for her husband and a cup for herself, then made herself comfortable on the sofa, despite the scowl from George. "No, and it's the strangest thing. There was no announcement in church. I wondered why the Smythes didn't attend the service Christmas Eve. I was just saying to Louise, our neighbour, how odd it was that Emily was married without a big wedding. Well, there's usually only one reason why someone gets wed quickly without any fuss."

"Grace," George said. "You know how I feel about gossip. You'll have to excuse my wife, Detective. She does like to talk."

Hodgins made more notes, then closed the notebook and slipped it into his coat pocket with the pencil stub. "Quite all right." He turned to Mrs. Lowe and smiled. "I completely understand what you mean, Madame." He blew on his hot tea, took a sip, then turned his attention back to Mr. Lowe.

"I have a few more calls to make, but I need to ask one more thing. Did Fred have a trunk?"

"Yes. He brought one with him when he moved in with us last year after my mother passed," George said. "Why?"

"We found a key in his pocket. I'd like to see if it fits his trunk." He took one large gulp of his tea then reached over and put his cup on the tray.

George pointed up. "It's in his room, upstairs."

Hodgins stood and waited for Mr. Lowe to show him

the way. "Sir?"

George looked up at the detective, not sure what to do.

"The trunk?"

"Sorry, I was just thinking about poor Fred. It's this way."

"Poor Fred?" Mrs. Lowe asked. "George, what is going on?"

"They may have found him. I'll tell you later." He got up, put his cup and saucer on the tray.

Grace turned to Hodgins. "What happened to Fred? What aren't you telling me?"

"I said I'd tell you later," George said. "Just wait here until the detective leaves."

He led Hodgins to Fred's room at the end of the hall on the second floor.

Hodgins asked George where the trunk was kept. George shrugged. "Never really noticed."

Hodgins stood just inside the door and looked around the small bedroom; bed by the window, wash stand beside the bed, dresser against the wall beside the door, small table and chair against the far wall. There was no trunk in sight. There was a door in the wall opposite the table that Hodgins assumed was a closet. He walked over and opened the door. The trunk was against the back wall. He dragged it out, and then took the key out of his shirt pocket.

George came closer to watch as Hodgins opened the trunk. There was a barely audible click as he turned the key. Hodgins lifted the lid and both men looked in. Hodgins pulled out a couple of old grey work shirts, just like the one that the dead man wore, and a photo.

"Blast. I thought there would be something in here," Hodgins said. He dropped the shirts back into the trunk and turned the picture so George could look at it.

"That's Fred," George said.

Hodgins looked up. "I'll need to take this photo with me." Are you able to come to the coroner's office Monday? We have to find out if the body really is your cousin." George nodded.

They went back downstairs and Hodgins thanked the Lowe's for their time. Hodgins put his collar up as he went out into the cold again. Following the directions George had given him, he was at the Smythe home in no time. Another red brick house. Hodgins was amazed at both the differences and similarities between this small town and Toronto. In the city, there were rows of houses all the same, making it easy to go to the wrong door if you weren't paying attention. Here, the houses were of a different design, but again, many were almost identical. In the dark it would be very easy to walk into someone else's home by mistake.

Hodgins knocked on the front door three times before

anyone answered. The door jerked open, and a stout, annoyed, older gentleman stared at Hodgins.

"Yes, what do you want?" he barked.

Once again, Hodgins showed his badge. "I have some questions about Mr. Walker." The man introduced himself as Mr. Smythe and lead Hodgins into the front room.

"Yes, Fred Walker was here Christmas day. Came to call on my daughter. Why are the police interested in that?"

"Mr. Walker is missing. I need to speak with everyone who was here that day. I understand your daughter is recently married. Where might I find her?"

Mr. Smythe hesitated for a moment, then revealed that Emily and her new husband were living with the Smythes temporarily and went to fetch them. Hodgins walked over to the fireplace to warm himself. He looked around the room, noticing the difference between this home and the Lowe's. A large painting of Queen Victoria hung over the mantle with a small British flag sitting on either side. The floral wallpaper looked new, the colours still vibrant. He walked around the room examining the carvings on the furniture's walnut arms, running his hand along the grain, and admiring the high quality of the workmanship. While not rich, the Smythes seemed quite comfortable in their circumstances. He turned when he heard the door open.

A young woman in her early twenties, who he assumed

to be Emily, entered followed by her father and a rather plain but well dressed man. He could see why more than one man would be interested in Emily. Though not what most people would consider beautiful, she was one of the most striking women he had ever seen. Despite the bustle protruding at the back, and the numerous layers of fabric, he could tell she had an excellent figure, and there was something about those large, green eyes. Hodgins realized he was staring, and turned his attention back to Mr. Smythe.

Mr. Smythe introduced his daughter and her husband, Patrick Flanagan, who looked like he wasn't that much younger than Emily's father. She certainly had not married the better looking of her two suitors, judging by the picture of Fred he had in his breast pocket.

"My father-in-law said you wished to speak to us about the disappearance of Mr. Walker," Mr. Flanagan said.

Emily perched on the edge of the chair closest to the fire, and Patrick joined Hodgins in front of the fireplace. Hodgins took the notebook and stubby pencil out of his coat pocket and flipped through the pages, careful not to tear them.

"Most disagreeable chap, Walker," Patrick said. "Works at my mill. A common labourer."

Hodgins looked over at Emily and could see the deep concern on her face. He'd seen that look dozens of times over his career with the police. She was still in love with Walker.

"I believe Mr. Walker came here on Christmas Day?"

"Yes, that's correct," Patrick said. "Took the wind out of his sails when I told him Emily had married me only days earlier." A nasty little grin crept across Patrick's face. "He said some rather unpleasant things, and I practically had to throw him out the door. I may have shoved him off the porch to hurry him along. Haven't seen him since. Gone off to lick his wounds, I suppose."

Hodgins wrote a few words in his notebook, and then addressed Emily. "Have you seen Mr. Walker since Christmas, Mrs. Flanagan?"

Emily shook her head. "No," she said quietly. "Do you have any idea where he is?"

Hodgins hesitated, trying to decide how much he should reveal. "We found a man that fits his general description. George Lowe will be coming to Toronto to positively identify the body on Monday."

Emily's mouth formed a perfect tiny 'O', but no sound came out. She looked at her husband, then fell back in the chair. Her eyelids fluttered, and Hodgins thought she was about to faint. Rather than being alarmed, Patrick seemed put out by his wife's reaction. Sighing, he walked to the door, opened it, and called for Emily's mother to bring the salts.

Hodgins heard footsteps running down the hall and a plump, cheery looking woman hurried through the doorway carrying two small bottles: one containing crystals, the other was labeled ammonia. She placed the bottles on a small end table and opened them. She was just about to pour the ammonia over the crystals when Emily spoke.

"Put those away, Mother. I'm perfectly fine. I just had a bad shock. The detective told us that Freddie is dead." She pulled a lacy handkerchief out of her dress sleeve and dabbed her eyes. "It's dreadful." She raised the kerchief and covered her face.

"Freddie? You mean Fred Walker?" Mrs. Smythe asked her daughter. She stood beside the chair and cradled Emily's head against her chest.

"You'll have to leave now," Patrick said. "This has all been too much for my wife."

"Too much?" Emily got up from the chair. "Fred was a childhood friend. How do you expect me to react?"

Mrs. Smythe took her daughter's hand and led her out of the room. Hodgins could hear Emily sobbing as her mother took her upstairs.

Hodgins made a few more notes, checked his pocket watch, and then left. It wasn't quite noon yet, but he decided to have an early meal and a nice, hot cup of tea at the tavern beside the train station. It would be a more pleasant meal than whatever they had available on the train, and he could sit and enjoy it without rocking back and forth. *Might actually get to finish the tea this time*, he thought.

Despite it only being 11:30 a.m., the tavern had a lot of patrons, and he enjoyed listening to the sounds of murmuring voices, and the clinking of glasses and cutlery. The large windows at the front and side of the tavern allowed in sufficient light so none of the lanterns were currently lit. The pub near his station house had tiny windows and the lanterns were lit at all times. While he loved his wife's Irish cooking, he longed for some traditional English food. His mouth watered at the thought of Cottage Pie, a standard at most pubs. He loved the minced meat, mixed with peas and carrots, topped with mashed potatoes smothered in gravy. Hodgins hoped they served it in this little town.

He sat at a table near the oak bar and asked the bartender what was good. As soon as he heard Cottage Pie he knew what he was ordering. When it came, he took his time eating, savouring every bite. Just as he finished his Darjeeling tea, the tall clock in the corner chimed, reminding him he had to return to Toronto. He bundled up, and made his way back to the station.

* * *

33

The train started to move as soon as he sat down. When the conductor came by to punch his ticket, it reminded him of the washed out one that had been found in Fred's overcoat. He pulled the picture of Fred out of his pocket.

"Ever seen this guy?" he asked the conductor.

"Yes, Sir. That's young Fred. Works at the mill with my boy. Hasn't been around for a while though."

"When did you see him last?"

"Hmm, let me think." The conductor scratched the side of his neck a few times and looked up at the roof of the train car. "I believe it was on the train. Yes, I'm sure of it. I remember the argument."

"When? Who was he arguing with?"

"Just after Christmas. Not more than three or four days later, I'm sure of that."

"The argument, who was it with? Did you hear what they fought about?"

"Well, wasn't really a proper argument. Fred was very agitated. Funny thing. Mr. Flanagan was laughing. Couldn't hear what it was about. Not my place to listen in on private conversations anyway."

"Flanagan? Patrick Flanagan?"

The conductor wrinkled his nose. "Yes, that's him. I think that's the first time I ever heard him laugh. Can't tell you no more. That's all I saw."

"Thank you. You've been most helpful."

The conductor nodded and moved to the next seat to continue punching tickets, leaving Hodgins to wonder what had transpired between the two men. Mr. Walker was apparently angry, yet Flanagan laughed. *Could he have been taunting Fred? Why were they on the train together?*

CHAPTER FOUR

All through breakfast Sara chatted to her grandparents about her plans for the day; ice skating uppermost in her mind.

"It will be so much fun," Sara said. "I haven't been skating for such a long time."

"You know that's not true," Cordelia said. "Just a few days ago you were skating with your friend Laura."

"But that was just a tiny ice surface her father made in the back yard."

Hodgins laughed and turned to his wife. "My dear, skating on a ice surface someone's father made just doesn't count. It's not really skating unless you are on a pond or creek, or even the city rink."

"Oh how silly of me to forget." Cordelia looked across the table at Sara and smiled. "I do apologize. You were correct. You haven't skated in weeks."

Everyone burst out laughing, even the normally dour Euphemia. Sara just sat looking puzzled.

Once breakfast was over, Cordelia, her mother, and Sara, started clearing the table and doing the washing up. Harold disappeared to the back of the house, and Hodgins went into the front room to read the early edition of the Daily Globe. He pulled a chair near the fireplace and sat with his legs stretched towards the crackling fire.

He could hear Sara asking about the Crystal Palace and had a quick look the at paper to see if there was any mention of the current exhibit. There was nothing. He hoped it would be something of interest to a little girl. On page three he noticed an advertisement for houses and building lots for sale. The house on Elm Street was of interest; brick, ten rooms and bathroom, gas, and grates. He carefully tore it out and placed it in his vest pocket.

The sounds of clinking china and cutlery died down, so Hodgins got up and went back into the kitchen. Sara was sweeping the floor and Cordelia was cleaning the counter while Euphemia wiped the table. Since the cleanup was done, Hodgins announced it was time to go. Cordelia went upstairs to change her clothes and Sara raced to the front door. She removed her bright green cape with the rabbit fur collar from the hook and wrapped herself up. Picking up the skate blades that were waiting by the door, she was ready to go before Hodgins finished speaking.

"Sara, don't run through the house like that," her

grandmother scolded. "You're a lady, not a ruffian."

"Leave her be," Hodgins said. "She's excited. I don't often have a free Saturday, and she's been looking forward to spending time with her mother and me for days." He turned and smiled at his daughter. "She'll be lady-like."

Sara nodded her head eagerly. "Oh, yes, Daddy. I'll be good. Can we go now?"

Euphemia said, "You spoil that child." She made a face and went upstairs, passing Cordelia on her way down.

"Why does your mother always look like she's just eaten a lemon?"

"Oh, Bertie. Why can't you just get along with Mother?"

"I've tried. Lord knows I've tried. She never got over the fact I didn't complete my schooling. She'd rather her daughter married a respectable lawyer, and not," he winked, "a lowly man of the law."

"Albert Hodgins, are you trying to flirt with me?" Cordelia laughed softly and touched his cheek. "You don't do that often enough."

Cordelia's father came down the hallway carrying two sets of skate blades so Hodgins and Cordelia could skate with Sara and not just watch. "Found them. I knew I'd seen them on the back porch. Someone had thrown an old towel over them." He handed Hodgins the skate blades and said,

"You're right. She does look like she's eaten a lemon."

"Daddy," Sara whined from the front door.

"Off with you now. I don't think that child will last a moment longer," Harold said.

Hodgins, Cordelia, and Sara walked to the corner to catch the trolley down to Gerrard Street, where they changed to another that took them to the skating rink on Sherbourne. Sara sat at the back, waving to everyone she saw.

The trolley stopped in front of the rink. They couldn't see the ice through the high wooden fence that surrounded it, but could hear voices and laughter as they walked to the entrance. Hodgins was surprised at the large number of people already there. It was a nice day and it looked like half the city was enjoying it.

While he was strapping the skate blades to Sara's boots, one of her friends came over. She couldn't wait to tell Sara all about the new puppy she got. Sara squealed with delight. "A puppy!" She turned to her parents. "May I go over and see it today?"

Cordelia nodded, "I'll take you over before supper."

Sara grabbed her friend's hand and skated off.

Hodgins knelt in front of the bench and fastened a pair of blades to his wife's boots, then sat beside her and put on his own. "I wish we could do this more often. We don't spend nearly enough time together. Maybe this summer I can get some time off and we can rent a cottage somewhere."

Cordelia looked at him, surprised. "Do you mean that Bertie? We haven't been on a proper holiday since before Sara was born."

"Can't promise anything, but I'll try. I'll ask the criminals to take a few weeks off." He waved at Sara as she skated past with her friend.

"It would be nice to have a dog," he said. "We could take it on long walks, and it would teach Sara responsibility too."

"You know mother can't abide animals in the house."

He stood and held his hand out to Cordelia. "I know," he said with a grin.

* * *

Hodgins stomped his feet, removing most of the slush from his boots before entering the house. He dropped the skate blades just inside the door, hung his overcoat on the coat tree and walked into the front room. His father-in-law, Harold Campbell, was snoozing in the overstuffed chair that Harold had declared to be 'his' chair. He woke at the sound of Hodgins pouring a glass of whiskey.

"Don't mind if I do," he said.

Hodgins poured a second glass and handed it to

Harold on his way to the settee. He downed his drink in one gulp, set the glass on the carpet, then stretched out - feet hanging over the far arm of the settee.

"Oh, my poor feet. I could walk all day, but skating for an hour is too much. My ankles weren't made for balancing on thin blades."

"I remember days skating with Euphemia and Cordelia," Harold said. "They both enjoyed it so much. Didn't really care for it myself, but it was pleasant to sit and watch them. I wish I could have gone with you, but my leg won't let me." He rubbed his right leg for a moment. "Damn weather. Cold makes it ache more. A sport best left for the young. Speaking of which, what did you do with my grand-daughter? I don't hear her or Cordelia."

"They went to Sara's friend's house - that girl with the fizzy brown hair. Never could remember her name. She was at the rink and told Sara about her new puppy, so Sara had to see it." Hodgins got up, scooped his empty glass off the carpet, and went over to the tantalus on the sideboard to pour another whiskey.

"Can't picture Euphemia skating. Can't image her doing anything fun, no offense."

"None taken," Harold laughed. "She was different when she was younger. After my accident, we didn't get out much."

A sharp knock on the door interrupted their conversation. Hodgins got up. "Now what?" He looked out the front window. "It's Barnes, one of my constables. Guess my day off is over."

Hodgins answered the door and let the young constable in.

"Sorry to disturb you, Sir, but I was told to fetch you right away. Something about the bloke they found in the harbour."

Hodgins sighed, and put on his coat. "Let's go."

They walked to the corner and waited for the trolley. Barnes stared at his feet, avoiding eye contact. Hodgins noticed the man's discomfort.

"Don't fret lad. It's not the first time I've been called from my day off. It certainly won't be the last."

Hodgins tried to have a conversation with the constable, but only received one or two word answers, so he gave up and they rode to the station in silence.

Hodgins walked through the station house to his desk, and saw a man and boy seated in front of it. He recognized the gentleman immediately - Ben Grove. "What can I do for you, Mr. Grove?"

"This is my youngest lad, Danny. He has something that may be of interest to you."

Hodgins extended his hand. "Nice to meet you Danny.

What do you have?"

Danny shook the detective's hand briefly, then snatched it back as though afraid. Hodgins walked around his desk and sat down. He looked from Danny to Mr. Grove.

"Well?"

Mr. Grove tapped Danny lightly on the knee. "Show him."

Danny stood up, reached into his pants pocket and pulled something out. He kept his hand clenched and looked at his father. Ben nodded toward Hodgins. Danny extended his arm and opened his fist.

Hodgins reached out and took the round, white object. "Looks like a pearl cufflink."

"Says it was lying beside the body." Ben said. "Grabbed it before his bother pulled him away. My wife found it in their room this morning. Soon as he told where he got it, I knew we had to turn it over."

"Thank you for bring it in," Hodgins said to Danny. "It was the right thing to do."

As Ben and Danny left the station, Danny glanced back at the detective and smiled.

Hodgins turned the cufflink over in his hands, wondering what connection it had with the body, if any. *Expensive looking.* He got up and walked over to a window.

It glistened in the sunlight. He was certain it was a real pearl and just as sure that Mr. Walker could not afford such luxury.

CHAPTER FIVE

Monday morning George Lowe arrived in Toronto to view the body that had been pulled out of Toronto Harbour five days earlier. Hodgins led him to the morgue. Dr. McKenzie had the body laid out on a steel table, with a clean, white sheet covering him. George slowly moved beside the table and looked down at the shape. He took two deep breaths and nodded once. Dr. McKenzie lifted the sheet so only the right side of his face was visible. George gasped and took a step back. "It's Fred."

Hodgins waited several minutes as George composed himself. "I'm sorry for your loss. I realize this has been hard and you need to go home and start making arrangements, but I have to ask you a few more questions.

George nodded. "When can I bring him home for burial? We need to set up the front parlour and prepare his body for visitations."

"Probably in a few days," Hodgins said. "Do you recall if your cousin mentioned a fight with Emily's husband?"

"No, not that I can recall. Now that you mention it though, his trousers were rather dirty and wet when he came home Christmas day. His clothes were spotless when he went out. My wife commented on it, but I didn't give it a second thought. And he was rubbing his leg a bit. Was there an altercation at the Smythe's?"

"Mr. Flanagan said he threw Fred out."

"Flanagan? Patrick Flanagan? That's who she wed? I can't believe Emily married that bully. No wonder Fred was in such a state. Her parents probably had a hand in that. That would explain why it was kept quiet. I can't think of anyone who would have attended. Patrick Flanagan is not a popular man."

"Why is that? Because of his business dealings? Or maybe his personality? What would stop the neighbours from attending a rich man's wedding?"

Lowe twisted his wedding ring. I don't like to speak ill of people."

"Your cousin is dead. Don't you want to find out what happened? It's your duty to tell me everything you know."

Lowe let out a soft sigh. "It's a bit of both, but mostly business. Flanagan was feared by anyone who had dealings with him. But he does have money. The Smythe's would probably overlook everything else if they could marry Emily to someone well off."

Hodgins raised an eyebrow. "Was he violent or just hard and unfeeling?"

"He certainly was unfeeling, but he was never physically violent. Not as far as I know. He would on occasion be overheard threatening someone. A day or two later that person would have cuts or bruises. Sometimes worse. Flanagan was always someplace public when it happened. I've heard rumours that he pays someone to rough up anyone who doesn't cooperate, but it's only rumour."

"How does he make his money?"

"He's a businessman," Lowe replied. "He owns the mill where Fred worked. Also owns several properties that he rents out. Business as well as a few small homes. Even has some low rent properties in Toronto. I believe he travels there regularly to collect the rent personally."

Hodgins mulled that over. "If he's so well off, why is he living with the Smythe's? Doesn't he have his own house?"

"Yes, he has a large home on Victoria Street. I've noticed workmen there a lot lately. Probably staying with the Smythe's until the work is done. Oh, I remembered something after you left. In November, Fred was promoted to foreman at the mill. One of the other workers was expecting to get the position and accused Fred of buying the job. There was a fight. Fred was beat up pretty bad."

Hodgins picked up his pencil and flipped open his notebook. "I'll need this man's name."

"Fred never said who it was."

Hodgins closed his notebook. "Appreciate your help Mr. Lowe. I'll see what I can find out. Someone will contact you when you can come to collect your cousin's body."

George Lowe stood up and reached across the desk to shake the detective's hand.

Mr. Lowe left, and Hodgins picked up the folder containing the coroner's report. He had lost count of how many times he read, and re-read the contents. He opened his notebook again and studied the notes he took while at the Lowe's home. Everything seemed to revolve around Emily and her marriage to a wealthy, and apparently nasty, man. Where were these low rent properties in Toronto? Were they even relevant?

Hodgins grabbed his coat and hat and went outside to wait for the horse-drawn trolley to take him up to the Records Office to find the properties that Flanagan owned. Over the next few hours Hodgins sat hunched over a small table making pages of notes. He was completely unaware of the time until one of the clerks tapped him on the shoulder and pointed to his pocket watch.

Hodgins gathered up his papers and decided to walk

back to the station. Along the way he stopped at a street vendor and purchased a pork pie. When he got back to the station house, he went around to the side, looking for the stray mutt. He spotted it curled up in the crate that had been put out by one of the men. He dropped a few pieces of pie in the crate, and went in the side door.

CHAPTER SIX

Hodgins paced around the station waiting for Barnes, his head whipping around every time the door opened. The young constable finally entered the station house and Hodgins raced to his side. He whisked Barnes back out giving him a little nudge to hurry him along, causing the constable to stumble on the steps. Hodgins grabbed his arm and mumbled an apology, but didn't slow down.

"Where we off to Sir, if you don't mind me asking?"

"Train," Hodgins said as he rushed ahead. The street was filling with vendors and storekeepers, anxious to start the day. Barnes trotted along dodging the newsboys, trying to keep up with the detective's long strides.

By the time they arrived at Union Station Barnes was out of breath. Hodgins shook his head.

"You need to exercise more lad. Only a few blocks and you can hardly breathe. You should join the YMCA. They opened up one a few blocks from the station. Do you a world of good."

Before Barnes could think of a reply Hodgins was halfway to the ticket booth, leaving the constable standing by the door. He was back a few minutes later with two return tickets to Stouffville and a schedule.

"Train leaves in twenty-five minutes. There's an empty bench over there."

They sat in silence for about five minutes before Barnes worked up the courage to ask, "Who are we going to see?"

"I need to talk to the men at the mill. Find out who started the fight."

"Fight, Sir?"

"Seems one of the men was less than pleased that Mr. Walker was promoted. Have to find out who it was." Hodgins pulled his notebook out of his pocket, turned to the last page of writing and read the notes he made after Lowe had identified the body. "Back in November. Maybe the fight was about more than a lost promotion." He closed the small book and slipped it back into his pocket. He turned to face Barnes. "You need to ask around about Mrs. Flanagan. See if anyone knows why she married that arrogant man. Find out who her friends are. They may know something. You're about the same age - might be more apt to tell you things."

Barnes nodded in agreement as a conductor called for passengers to board. Hurrying to the train, Hodgins patted his overcoat pocket.

"Barnes, don't suppose you have a notebook?"

The constable smiled and reached into his pocket. He proudly pulled out a small, shiny leather-bound notebook.

"Got one last evening. Sir. I noticed you carry yours all the time and I figured I should have one too." He put his hand back into his pocket and drew out not one, but two pencils, freshly sharpened. He held them out for the detective's inspection.

Hodgins glanced at Barnes' purchases. "You're a quick learner Barnes. You just might make Sergeant some day."

* * *

The ride to Stouffville was uneventful and quiet. Hodgins read his note over and over. He jotted down questions, and underlined or circled items to follow up on.

Barnes chatted to a salesman who boarded at Riverdale and exited at Milliken. He watched Hodgins work away at his notes until they arrived at Unionville. An elderly lady who was travelling alone boarded. She reminded Barnes of his grandmother. He got up and sat with her for the rest of his ride.

By the time the train pulled into the Stouffville station, the sun was shining. It was still a bit nippy, but there was little wind and the sky was almost void of clouds. Hodgins commented how different it was from the previous Saturday.

"Hardly a soul around. Suppose Tuesday is not a busy day. Guess most people are already at work, like that gent over there." He pointed at a rail employee who was sweeping the last of the snow off the platform.

As they left the train station in Stouffville Hodgins pointed west. "The Smythes and Lowes live over there." Stopping at the end of the platform Hodgins turned east.

"There's the top of the mill. I believe there are a few shops a little further along. I'll see what I can find out from the mill workers and you talk to everyone you can. There must be plenty of folks in the shops who know Mrs. Flanagan. Find out if there's any gossip. It's a small town and people tend to talk. We'll meet up at the tavern beside the station for lunch."

They crossed a side rail and passed a large building on the opposite side of the road. Barnes pinched his nose. "Don't need to read the sign to know that's a tannery. How do those poor buggers stand it day after day?"

"Don't suppose they have much choice," Hodgins replied. Barnes stepped off the plank sidewalk to cross a narrow lane. Hodgins reached out and pulled him back. A wagon loaded with logs came thundering down. The pair of black draft horses stopped at the cross-road. The wheels of the wagon sent a spray of slush up onto the plank walkway, just missing Hodgins and Barnes. The horses snorted and stomped their large, hair-covered feet.

A farmer was coming across the main road at the same time. His horse reared up. They met the draft horses at the corner. The farmer flicked his reins and the chestnut nag settled down and trotted along. The man with the load of logs seemed to be looking for something in his pocket, paying little or no attention to his surroundings.

Barnes drew in a breath. "That was close. Good thing you yanked me out of the way. I could have been trampled. And I though for sure the logging wagon was going to plow right into that farmer."

Hodgins shrugged. "Imagine the beasts have been up and down that road so many times, they know what to do. Smart creatures, horses are. Smarter than a lot of folk I know."

The horses started moving again, crossing the road to the mill. "I'll follow this chap, and you see if you can find someone to open up about the Flanagans. And try to remember we are investigating a possible murder. This is not a social call."

"Sir?"

"I noticed you chatting it up with the salesman and lady

on the train. You can be very talkative. Let the people here have a chance to speak."

Barnes' ears turned red, and he stood looking like a scolded puppy.

"I'm not saying it's bad to be social, just keep in mind why we're here. You're good with people. Use it."

Barnes smiled. "Thank you, Sir. I'll try to talk less."

Hodgins nodded and crossed the muddy road heading towards the mill. The sounds of saws and rattling chains increased with each step. The pair of draft horses stood by a set of large doors waiting while the logs were unstrapped.

"Who's in charge here?" Hodgins asked.

"Don't need no more help. Try yer luck at the tannery."

Hodgins opened his coat briefly to show his badge. "Already have a job. Where's the boss?"

The driver looked at the badge, and then spit a large wad of chewing tobacco into a pile of snow beside Hodgins. Most of it landed in the snow, sinking in a few inches, a trail of slim hanging down the side. Some of the spittle hit Hodgins' left boot. The driver watched as Hodgins casually shoved his boot into some clean snow to remove the mess.

"Office is on the second floor." He pointed to a staircase leading up to a door, then turned back to his wagon.

Hodgins stopped at the foot of the stairs. It looked like they'd used the worst pieces of lumber available to build them. He put one foot on the first step and grabbed the railing. The step bowed under his weight and the railing shifted. He took a deep breath and quickly ascended, trying not to think about the wobbling under his feet. There was a sign nailed to the door that read *Office*. Hodgins lifted the latch and opened the door.

"State yer business." It took a moment for Hodgins to find the source of the voice. He closed the door, shutting out the bright sunlight, allowing his eyes to adjust to the dimness that remained. The room had no windows, just a few lanterns hanging on nails driven into the walls. They provided little illumination. "I said, state yer business. I'm busy and can't wait all day."

A scrawny man sat behind a table that was being used as a desk. There was a lantern and ledger-book in the middle, with an inkwell on one side and a cup of tea on the other.

"I'm Detective Hodgins. I need to speak with you about an incident involving Fred Walker. Are you in charge?"

The man pushed the ledger away and motioned to a chair near the desk. It looked like it had been made from the same wood as the stairs. Hodgins remained standing.

"Name's Horace Harmon. I run the place. Haven't seen Walker in weeks. That's gratitude for you. Promote the man, he gets into a fight, and then up and disappears. If you see him, tell him he's fired."

"Tell me about this fight."

"Why don't you ask him yourself?" Harmon asked.

"Can't. He's dead. Now, about the fight?"

"What? Oh, yes. Dead you say? How?"

"That's what I'm *trying* to find out. Who did he fight with?"

Harmon got up and walked over to a door at the back that Hodgins hadn't noticed. He opened it and the smell of freshly cut wood filled the room. Harmon stepped out onto a walkway. Hodgins followed.

Harmon looked around then pointed. "There," he yelled over the noise of the saws. "John Richardson."

"I'll need to speak with him. Can I use your office?"

Harmon mumbled something Hodgins couldn't make out, but agreed. He went down a staircase that led to the mill, and came back with a tall, muscular man, who appeared to be in his mid-twenties.

"This here detective needs a word with you."

"A detective you say? I'm honoured." Richardson bowed slightly.

Hodgins took an instant dislike to Richardson, with his

cocky, smug smile. He could tell from the young man's tone he thought quite well of himself. They all went into the office and Harmon closed the door, muffling the sounds from below.

Hodgins turned to Harmon. "I prefer to conduct my interviews in private, if you don't mind."

"Begging your pardon, but I feel I owe it to my employee to stay. I've heard how members of the constabulary bully confessions out of innocent people. This is my business and my office. Either I stay, or you leave."

The two men stared at each other for a minute before Hodgins spoke. "I understand it's actually Mr. Flanagan's business. You are just his employee."

"Well, yes, but . . ." Harmon blustered.

Hodgins reached out with his right arm. His hand pressed against Harmon's chest, pinning him against the wall. His face so close to Harmon's their noses almost touched. "Stay if you must, but don't interrupt." Hodgins released Harmon, turned and walked behind the desk straightening his jacket and then sat in Harmon's chair.

Richardson started to laugh. "I like you Detective. Now what can I do to assist you?"

Hodgins took the small black notebook out of his pocket, placed it on the desk and flipped it open to a blank page. He glanced over at Harmon, who stood by the door.

He scowled at Hodgins, but didn't move. His arms hung down at his side, his balding scalp shimmered in the light from the lantern hanging on the wall over his head. The few stringy hairs he had dangled over his eyes. Hodgins picked up the quill pen and dipped it in the ink well. He could feel Harmon's glare from across the room.

Hodgins wrote the date on the top of the page, then looked up at Richardson. "Fred Walker. I hear you didn't like him much."

The smile was instantly replaced by a scowl. "Cocky little git."

Hodgins made a few scribbles in his book. "Tell me about the fight a few months ago."

Richardson waved his hand as though dismissing the comment. "He was promoted to foreman and was bragging to everyone how he was so much better than me. I should've been promoted, not Fred." He turned to Harmon. "And I was right. Fred stopped coming to work weeks ago." Turning back to Hodgins he said, "I'm foreman now." The cocky smile returned. "Can't wait to rub that bit of news in his face."

Hodgins made a few more notes, and while writing said, "I'm afraid you won't get the chance." He stopped writing and looked directly at Richardson. "He's dead."

"Hmm, shame. I was rather looking forward to telling

him I was given his job."

Hodgins dipped the quill and wrote a few more things in his book. He helped himself to a piece of Harmon's blotting paper before closing the notebook. "I guess that's all for now." He got up and walked over to Harmon.

"Thank you for the use of your office. Might I impose a bit longer? I'd like to talk to some of your other employees. I'll just walk around the mill and chat with a few. Won't take them away from their work long."

Harmon said nothing, but opened the back door, allowing the detective to exit into the mill.

Hodgins walked around the saw mill, chatting with several of the workers. It was the same with each man; they listened to his questions, and then looked up at the walkway. Harmon and Richardson were standing side by side, watching Hodgins. One by one, each man shook his head and went back to work without answering one question.

Hodgins' frustration built. No one would talk to him. They were too scared to speak. *Is it Harmon, or Richardson, they are all afraid of? Or both?* A shrill whistle interrupted his thoughts. The machinery slowed to a stop and most of the men started to exit the mill. Hodgins pulled out his pocket watch and checked the time. Lunch break. He looked up at the walkway and nodded at Harmon and Richardson, then followed the men out of the mill and continued down to the tavern to meet Barnes.

CHAPTER SEVEN

Hodgins was a block from the tavern when he spotted Barnes crossing the road from the opposite direction. Hodgins called to him, and Barnes waited at the entrance. The constable opened the tavern door and held it for the detective. Hodgins pointed to an empty table in the far corner and they weaved their way over. One of the servers hustled to the table.

"Nice to see you again, Sir," the server said. Hodgins smiled at the pretty brunette. "What can I get you today?"

"The Cottage Pie was quite delicious. I think I'll have that again. And bring us a pot of Darjeeling tea. It was quite nice as well."

"I'll have the Cottage Pie too," Barnes said.

The server hurried off while the men removed their coats and settled in. Just as they got comfortable, she was back with the tea. She balanced the tray in her left hand, and dragged a damp towel across the table with her right. She put the tea pot in the centre of the table, placed a cup in front of each man and then hurried off again.

"Hope you had better luck than I did," Hodgins said.

Barnes opened his new notebook to the first page. Hodgins noticed how far through the book the pages changed from worn to fresh. He was impressed at the copious notes taken.

"After you went to the mill I walked a bit farther and came across the post office. I figured everybody in town goes in there."

"Good thinking," Hodgins said.

"There were several young ladies there. Turns out they were friends of Miss Smythe, er, Mrs. Flanagan. They all said pretty much the same thing. They met Emily through the church shortly after the family moved here from England. Seems they were all sweet on Fred, and couldn't believe she married Flanagan instead. I didn't tell them what happened to Mr. Walker. Was that wrong of me Sir?

Hodgins thought it over and said, "No, probably just as well. If they were that fond of him they may have become hysterical or something. Is that all they told you?"

"I got the impression that one of them may know something more, but didn't want to say in front of her friends. A Miss Penelope Cooke. I think I should try to talk to her alone. Maybe after lunch?"

"Maybe," Hodgins said. "What else?"

"After the post office, I walked a bit farther before coming back this way. Figured I might try my luck with the minister who married them. Found him in the Presbyterian church." He flipped the pages. "A Reverend Baker. Said it was most peculiar. Just the two families. The Reverend said he normally didn't perform weddings like that, but both Mr. Smythe and Mr. Flanagan were large contributors."

Barnes looked up at Hodgins. "Guess even the clergy recognize class distinction, eh Sir?" he said with a grin, but Hodgins wasn't listening.

Barnes turned around trying to see what had the detective's attention.

A young man stood just inside the doorway. Pulling a wool cap off his head, he glanced around the room, twisting it in his hands. When he looked in Hodgins direction, the detective stood and waved the man over.

"It's Will Greene, isn't it?" Hodgins asked.

Will nodded, but said nothing. He just stood beside the table looking around.

Barnes reached across to the next table and pulled over an empty chair. Greene slid onto the seat and slouched down. Hodgins and Barnes waited.

"I can't let them see me here," Greene finally said. He looked around again. "I saw you come in and followed. He hesitated, then spoke quickly. "He beat him real bad,

Richardson did. Thought he was going to kill him. Fred Walker, I mean. Couple of the guys had to pull him off Fred. You don't cross John Richardson."

The door to the tavern opened and Green's head snapped around, looking to see who came in. It was no one he knew, so he turned back to Hodgins. "He thought it was Fred's fault he didn't get promoted. When he found out it was Fred what was made foreman, well he just blew up. John harassed Fred every day. Messed things up and blamed Fred. Richardson's done everything he could think of to get on Mr. Harman's good side and make Fred look bad. Haven't seen Fred since the Christmas dance."

Greene stood, pushing the chair into the man sitting at the next table. He looked around nervously, twisting the wool cap again. "Gotta go. Mr. Harman sometimes comes in for a beer at lunch. He can't see me with you." He took one final look around, and darted out the door.

"That was odd," Barnes said.

"Not really." Hodgins flipped through his notebook until he found the few comments he made when he spoke to Greene in the mill. He made a little star and printed a tiny comment between the lines.

"I had the impression he wanted to tell me something earlier, but was afraid to say anything. The man he mentioned, Richardson, that's the bloke who fought with

Walker. A real blow-hard." He paused. "So, who do I believe? Greene and Richardson told totally opposite stories. Richardson said that Walker bragged about getting promoted. Just because I don't like Richardson doesn't make him a liar."

"True, Sir." Barnes paused to collect his thoughts. "The people I spoke to today, they all liked Fred Walker. If he was a braggart, I don't believe so many people would be all that fond of him."

Hodgins tapped his pencil on the tabletop. "Maybe. Maybe not. People have been known to fool others. That's how con-men work. Charm you out of your life savings. I'm not saying Walker was like that. Greene was convincing though."

"So how do we find out who's telling the truth?"

"Keep talking to people. There must be other folk who like or dislike the two men."

The server came back with their food, and Hodgins and Barnes dug in. It didn't take long for Barnes to devour his Cottage Pie.

"Good, isn't it?" Hodgins said. "I think it's even better than last time."

Barnes nodded and mumbled as he scooped the last few bits onto his fork and shovelled it into his mouth. Hodgins watched as the constable took a swig of tea, swished it around in his mouth, and then swallowed with a contented sigh.

"That was perfect," Barnes said. "Fills you up and takes the chill right out of your bones. Is your wife a good cook, if you don't mind me asking?"

Hodgins smiled. "She's a very good cook. It's a wonder I can still fit into my clothes. A very good cook indeed."

Hodgins glanced at the table behind Barnes and swore. "When did he come in?"

"Who?"

"Horace Harmon. The man running Flanagan's mill. Good thing that lad left when he did."

Hodgins signaled for the server, who was standing at the bar. They settled their bill and went outside.

"There, Sir. That's one of the young ladies I spoke to at the post office, Miss Cooke." Barnes pointed at an attractive lady across the road.

"I'm certain she wanted to tell me something about Mrs. Flanagan."

Hodgins looked at the woman, then at Barnes, who was staring at her - a big, silly grin on his face.

The corner of Hodgins' mouth curled up. "Pretty, isn't she?"

"What?" Barnes stammered and blushed. "Oh, yes. I hadn't noticed."

Hodgins laughed loud enough that the young lady turned. She saw Barnes and waved. Barnes waved back.

"Go, see what she knows. Be back here by three. There's a train at 3:15." Barnes was half way across the street by the time Hodgins finished speaking.

Hodgins wandered through the town stopping at some of the shops and businesses asking about Walker and Richardson. Most were too busy to talk, and the rest didn't tell him anything he didn't already know.

CHAPTER EIGHT

Wednesday evening Hodgins sat in the front room with his wife and father-in-law, going over the outcome of the inquest. The proceedings took less than an hour, and there really wasn't anything new to tell Cordelia.

"The two boys who found the body, Michael and Danny, were asked to repeat how they happened to find Walker." He laughed when he told her about Barnes' testimony.

"He had his notebook, the one he bought afterwards, and flipped through the pages as though reminding himself what happened. The judge had no idea that Barnes hadn't taken any notes at the time."

"How could he not have taken notes?"

"Oh, I guess I didn't tell you about that. He had a receipt stuffed in one of his pockets, and scribbled a few things on the back. That was his report."

Cordelia couldn't hold back her giggles, despite her husband's frown.

"I'm sorry, Dear. I know how particular you are about police reports. You must have been furious."

Hodgins nodded, and then smiled. "He did seem quite professional on the stand. The lad learns quick. Have to give him that."

He walked over to the fireplace and gave the logs a few pokes. "After Dr. McKenzie gave his report and explained the wounds, it was obvious to everyone it was foul play. I didn't need an inquest to tell me that."

"So what's next?" Harold asked. "Does anything change with your investigation?"

"No. I've been going on the assumption of murder all along. Now that the inquest is over, it's officially murder and not speculation. By not waiting I've gained a week. Got to people while things were fresh in their minds. If they knew it was a murder investigation, they may not have been so forthcoming with information."

"Do you have to make many more trips to Stouffville?" Cordelia asked.

"Probably a few more. Going tomorrow as it happens. Walker's body was released after the hearing and his cousin mentioned they'll be having the funeral tomorrow afternoon. I thought I'd attend, observe the mourners. See if anyone seems suspicious or out of place.

Cordelia's mother joined them and talk instantly

changed from murder to the social set; something Euphemia found acceptable for mixed company. She nattered on for over an hour before Hodgins excused himself and went upstairs for the night.

* * *

The next day Hodgins found himself in the little village of Stouffville once more. The St. James Presbyterian Church was overflowing with mourners. Standing just inside the door, he took in all the faces. He recognized several of the mill workers gathered together in the back corner. Up at the front of the church he spotted the Lowes. George seemed to be comforting a young man and women. He turned his head and saw Hodgins standing at the back. He touched his wife's arm and nodded towards Hodgins. The Flanagans and Smythes were also at the front. The large turnout seemed to validate what Will Greene had told him at the tavern. Fred Walker appeared to be quite popular. It was becoming more evident that Richardson's story was a complete fabrication. If Walker was as petty and mean as Richardson indicated, Hodgins doubted the church would be so full.

"Detective?"

Hodgins turned to find Will standing behind him. He reached out and shook Greene's hand.

"I see there are a lot of mill workers here," Hodgins

said.

"Yes. Mr. Flanagan shut the mill for the service."

Hodgins raised one eyebrow. "Really? He doesn't strike me as the sort to let a funeral stop business."

Greene snorted. "Don't think it was out of compassion or respect. Makes him look good. We can't go to the cemetery for the burial. It's straight back to the mill." He looked down as his old, dirty clothing. "I'd never come into a church looking like this, but I can't wear my good suit at the mill, and we don't have time to go home and change. Harmon will make sure we all head back soon as the service is over."

Greene started to move towards his friends, then stepped back. "Fred was real nice. I hope you find the bastard and hang him." Satisfied he'd said his piece, Green joined the other mill workers in the corner.

The look of hate that showed in Greene's eyes was brief, but it convinced Hodgins that it was probably Richardson who'd been kicking up a fuss at the mill. He reached into his pocket for his notebook and hesitated. He decided it wouldn't be right to make notes inside the church, so he slipped outside and stood at the bottom of the steps, out of the way of the people coming in. He jotted a note to check on Richardson's character and background, then went back inside.

The service lasted about thirty minutes; several young women cried throughout. When it was over, everyone filed out and either got into buggies and wagons, or went on foot, to the cemetery. Hodgins saw Harmon herding the mill workers like cattle in the opposite direction, back to the mill. Waiting for everyone to leave the church, Hodgins then followed to the cemetery, keeping a little distance between himself and the mourners. A black buggy went past, pulled by a large chestnut horse. He recognized the driver as Reverend Baker.

The mourners assembled around an open grave. Hodgins wormed his way through the crowd until he was close enough to the Flanagans to hear their conversation. Both were watching as the plain pine coffin was lowered into the ground.

"Stop your sniffling, Emily," Flanagan whispered. "You're making a spectacle of yourself. A married woman carrying on like that. What will people think?"

"He was my friend, Patrick. An old and dear friend. We grew up together. I don't care what people think."

"Do you think he ever suspected your little secret?"

Emily gasped and turned to say something to her husband when she spotted Hodgins. She touched Flanagan's arm. "Hush."

Hodgins smiled at Emily and removed his hat.

Flanagan turned around to see what Emily was concerned about. "What the hell are you doing here?" he bellowed. All heads turned.

Flanagan's face turned red and his eyes narrowed. "Can't you give us one day of peace?"

Hodgins shrugged. "Just paying my respects."

A soft murmur filled the air as people whispered among themselves, trying to figure out who the stranger was and why Flanagan was upset at his presence.

Reverend Baker moved to the head of the grave and everyone quieted down. Hodgins looked around and noticed several people staring at him. Most looked away, embarrassed, but one man kept eye contact for several seconds.

After Fred Walker was laid to rest, Hodgins watched as Emily walked over to the Lowes and spoke to the young man and woman he saw at the church. He was too far away to hear what was said, but Emily gave them both a long hug before leaving with her husband. George and Grace Lowe noticed Hodgins and walked over to speak to him, leaving the two young people at the graveside.

"Do you have news?" George asked.

Hodgins shook his head. "We're still following up leads. Nothing definite yet."

Someone watched them. He recognized the man as the

one who kept eye contact with him earlier.

"Who's that man there?" he asked.

Both Lowes turned to see. "Oh, that's Mr. Carter. He's not quite right in the head."

"Grace," George exclaimed.

Ignoring her husband's annoyance she continued. "He's really harmless. Kicked in the head a few years ago by a horse. Hasn't been the same since. Doesn't say much, just stares mostly."

She stopped talking long enough to call to the young man and woman to join them and then turned back to Hodgins.

"Fred's brother and sister. George telegraphed them yesterday. Sent one to their father too. He's still in England.

Grace moved between the two newcomers, placing one arm around each. "This is Anabelle and Henry. And this nice man is Detective Hodgins. He's going to find out who did this terrible thing to Fred."

"We're doing our best. I'm very sorry for your loss."

Anabelle gave Hodgins a weak smile. Her eyes were red from crying. Henry appeared angry.

"This is your best?" Henry waved his arms in frustration. "Why aren't you trying to find the fiend who murdered my brother?"

George placed a hand on Henry's shoulder. "That's

not fair, Henry. The detective has been here several times trying to get to the bottom of this."

Henry's face turned red. "I'm sorry. It's just hard to understand why anyone would kill Fred. Everyone liked him. I can't believe he's really gone."

Anabelle started to weep. Henry put his arm around her shoulder and led her a few steps away.

"You'll join us at the house Detective Hodgins?" Grace inquired.

"No, but thank you. I still have plenty of work to do." He tipped his hat and headed back to the train station.

CHAPTER NINE

Hodgins spent the next morning at the waterfront. He quickly scanned the area around the train tracks and road before wiggling the loose boards on one of the deserted buildings near Connors Wharf. Two of the buildings west of the wharf were deserted and he wondered if they played a part in the mystery surrounding Walker's murder.

He almost had the board removed when he heard voices. Hodgins released the plank and stepped around the corner out of view. He heard enough of their conversation to figure out one was an estate agent, and the other a client.

The men stopped at the corner of the building when they noticed Hodgins. "Wouldn't waste my time looking at that pile of scrap," the estate agent said. "Better buildings than that available down here." He handed a business card to Hodgins and continued up to the road.

Hodgins read the card before stuffing it into his pocket. Alexander Robertson, Estate Agent, 489 Church

Street, Toronto. *Might come in handy later*, he thought.

The wind had picked up and was blowing the snow around. Hodgins tightened his scarf and decided to retreat to the warmth of the records office again. He recalled reading something on his last visit, but couldn't remember what it was. He was sure it was relevant and needed to find it.

He found what he was looking for and returned to the station. Hodgins copied the list of properties he gathered from his two visits to the records office from his notebook to the blackboard. He sat on the edge of his desk and faced the board. He was still slightly irritated that he hadn't been able to get that loose board off the window to peek in. Hodgins was more frustrated after his new discovery at the records office.

"Damn, damn, damn," he muttered as he slammed his notebook closed and dropped it on the desk.

Hodgins stood and started pacing, stopping periodically to read what he had printed on the blackboard, cursing under his breath. Flanagan owned one factory and several homes in a seamy part of the city.

"Working late, Sir?"

Hodgins looked up to see Barnes standing behind him, overcoat buttoned, scarf tightly wrapped around his neck.

"Late? Is it?" Hodgins pulled out his pocket watch.

"Hmm, 7:13. Guess it is late." He tucked the watch back into his vest pocket, picked his notebook off his desk and grabbed his coat from the back of his chair. He breezed past Barnes without further comment, buttoning his coat as he went.

Staring out the windows of the trolley all the way home, Hodgins mulled over the day's discoveries. When he arrived, he hung up his coat, went straight to the front room, and dragged one of the chairs closer to the fireplace. He slouched down and stretched his lanky legs towards the flames. Heat slowly crept through his soles and up his legs, gradually warming him up.

Sara came running in. "Daddy, you're home." She tried to climb into his lap, but he pushed her off.

"Daddy's tired."

She stood beside the chair quietly, but Hodgins barely acknowledged her. Pouting, she ran back to the kitchen where Cordelia and Euphemia prepared dinner. Hodgins didn't hear his wife. He jumped when she touched his shoulder.

"Where is your mind Bertie? I've called you three times.

"Sorry dear, my mind was elsewhere."

"That's obvious. Even Sara noticed."

Hodgins rose from the chair and followed Cordelia

down the hall and into the dining room. All through dinner he mumbled and grunted. He yelped when Cordelia kicked his ankle.

"Mother asked you a question."

He looked from his wife to Euphemia, who sat glaring at him. A quick look around the table told him just how poorly he had been behaving. Sara fought back tears, and his father-in-law's usual jovial look was replaced with a furrowed brow and concern.

"I do apologize. This case is so puzzling. I just can't stop thinking about it."

He picked up his napkin and jotted his mouth.

"The meal was delicious, but I'm not terribly hungry. Please excuse me."

He dropped the napkin on his plate, covering the remains of his barely touched meal, and got up from the table. He went down the hall and retrieved his notebook from his coat pocket, then went upstairs to his room.

He removed his suit jacket and vest, taking care to hang them in the wardrobe. He crossed to the washstand in the corner and splashed water on his face. Feeling a little rejuvenated, he went to the davenport that was nestled beside the bedroom window. Hodgins rolled the chair out and sat down. He opened the book and re-read his notes, starting with the comments he copied off Barnes' receipt.

The bedroom door opened as Hodgins rolled out more wick on the oil lamp.

"You've not been yourself all evening, Bertie. Mother's been grumbling about your lack of manners." Cordelia stood behind Hodgins trying to see what he was reading. "Is it the young man those two boys found?"

Hodgins covered his mouth as he yawned. "It's become very frustrating." He pushed the notebook aside. "I have a couple of possible suspects, but I can't find anything to point directly at either." He got up and started pacing around the room.

Cordelia moved over to her vanity, out of his way. She removed the pins from her hair and started to undo the plaiting, running her fingers though to smooth out any snarls. She then picked up the tortoiseshell comb and slowly ran it through her wavy hair. Satisfied it was tangle-free, Cordelia picked up the matching boar-hair brush and started her daily routine; one hundred strokes every evening and every morning.

"Tell me what you know. Maybe if you say it aloud something will fall into place. Who do you think may have killed him? What was his name? Fred something?"

"Walker. His name is Fred Walker. He was only twenty six." Hodgins went back to the davenport to retrieve his notebook.

"Quite often it turns out to be someone the victim knew. Patrick Flanagan is still at the top of my list."

Cordelia stopped brushing and looked at her husband's reflection in the mirror. "Who is Patrick Flanagan?"

Hodgins sat at the end of their bed and placed the notebook beside him. "He's Emily's husband."

He held up his hand in anticipation of Cordelia's questions. "Emily is the woman Fred wanted to marry."

Cordelia smiled. "A love triangle? How interesting. Tell me more."

"Fred and Emily were friends when they lived in England. Sweethearts more like. Fred's mother died and when his father re-married, Fred and his siblings were sent here to live with a relative. Emily's family moved here too, but only a few years ago. Don't know why, yet."

"I assume Emily and Fred started courting after she moved?" Cordelia forgot all about her evening routine and moved over to the bed beside her husband. "Why did she marry this Flanagan fellow?"

Hodgins shrugged. "Don't know that either. Do know it was sudden. Secret too."

"A rushed wedding? You know what that usually means?"

Hodgins laughed. "Yes. Fred's cousin suggested as

much. Correction. His cousin's wife. You'd like her. She loves to gossip."

Cordelia stood up, placing her hands on her hips. "Bertie, are you saying I gossip?"

"Uh, no," he stammered. "I'd never . . ."

Cordelia laughed. "I'm only teasing. Go on."

"Flanagan practically threw Fred out of the house Christmas day. That's when Fred found out Emily was married. Flanagan was also seen arguing with Fred on the train. Far as I can tell, that's the last anyone saw of Fred. And Flanagan lied about not seeing Fred after Christmas."

Hodgins paced again. "Fred worked at the local mill. He was promoted to foreman in November. Guess who owns the mill."

"Patrick Flanagan?"

Hodgins nodded. Cordelia moved back to her vanity and resumed brushing her hair. "But if this Flanagan person had already married Emily, why kill him?"

"Because Emily was still in love with Fred. It was evident from her reaction when she found out. Flanagan is much older. Maybe he thought Emily would eventually leave him and run off with Walker."

Cordelia finished brushing her hair and started removing the layers of clothing so she could slip into her night dress. "You said you have a couple of suspects."

"Yes, a man about Walker's age. John Richardson. He was quite angry that Fred was promoted instead of him. Actually beat Fred pretty bad."

Hodgins picked up the notebook and flipped through the pages until he found the notes he'd made while talking with Dr. McKenzie. Cordelia came over and unbuttoned his shirt.

"It's late. Maybe if you sleep on it, it will fall together." She took the notebook from him and glanced at the sketch of the peculiar bruise. "Why did you draw a bird?"

Hodgins draped his shirt over the back of the chair and turned to face her. "Bird? What are you talking about?"

She pointed at the sketch. "Here."

Hodgins noticed she was holding the book upside down. He took it from her and turned it around a few times, looking at the sketch from all angles. "A bird. The bruise looks like a bloody bird. What the devil would have left a mark like that?"

He looked at Cordelia. "Instead of helping, you've just thrown another mystery into the jumble."

CHAPTER TEN

Next morning at the station house, Hodgins found an envelope on his desk. His name and rank were written in fancy script. *Detective Albert Hodgins*. No address – no stamp – no post mark. He turned it over and slipped his thumb under the flap to open it. A loud crash across the room startled him. Swearing under his breath he stuck his thumb in his mouth, sucking at the fresh paper cut. He looked up and saw Barnes bent down picking up the items he'd knocked to the floor.

Hodgins dropped the bloodied envelope back on the desk and yelled, "Barnes."

The constable looked up. Hodgins waved him over. Barnes placed the metal tray and papers back on the desk he shared with another constable, then hurried over to the detective.

"Sir?"

"Go fetch the evidence box with Walker's belongings."

Barnes scurried to the back room and appeared at the

doorway five minutes later, carrying a large cardboard box with 'FRED WALKER 07 JAN 1874' printed in large letters across the side. He winced as his knuckles scrapped the door frame when he tried to squeeze through. Barnes turned sideways and slid past without any further injuries. Huffing, he dropped the box onto Hodgins' desk. Removing the lid, Hodgins leaned it against the box and started pulling out the contents.

"Oh, that's rank." Barnes waved his hand in front of his face and took a step back.

Hodgins wrinkled his nose. "I guess the box was packed before the things were dry. Clothing does tend to hold onto smells when put away wet. Add the fishy lake water and... well, you just experienced it. Puts me in mind of the first time I went fishing with my older brother. I was so proud of my fish that I wanted to keep it as long as possible. Hid it under my bed. That smell lingered all summer." He gestured towards the chair in front of his desk. "Sit down, Constable. We need to go over everything and try to figure out what we've missed."

"Me, Sir?"

Hodgins nodded. "Yes, you. You were first on the scene. It was a sloppy job, but you've done some excellent investigating since."

"Thank you, Sir. I've tried my best."

Hodgins moved his tray, inkwell, and pen into his drawer, put the few other items from his desk on his chair in order to clear the top, and then slipped the unopened letter into his jacket pocket. He spread out Walker's belongings; a long overcoat, overalls, smock, felt lumberman boots, small key, coins, train ticket, and shirt. He placed a pearl cufflink on top of the grey work shirt and slid it in front of Barnes.

Barnes whistled. "Expensive looking cufflink. Must have cost a small fortune." He looked puzzled. "Where did it come from? I don't remember seeing it before."

"Guess I didn't mention it. Remember last Saturday when you came to fetch me? Ben Grove and his youngest boy brought it in. Seems the lad picked it up from beside the body. Don't even know if it has anything to do with Walker." Hodgins tapped the shirt with one finger. "What do you see? Do these two things go together?"

Barnes picked up the cufflink and examined it. He turned it over a few times and held it up into the ray of light that drifted across the room through the frosted window. He shook his head.

"No, they belong to different people. He picked up the shirt. "The fabric is rough. Belongs to a working man. The cufflink was bought by someone with money. Some labourers might have one set of cufflinks for their Sunday best, but he wouldn't of had it when working."

He put it back on the desk and placed the cufflink beside it. "A working man's cufflink would be plain. Probably silver, not gold like this one. Besides," he lifted the sleeve. "This one has button cuffs. Why would there be a cufflink on him?"

"Very good." Hodgins picked up the cufflink let it roll to the centre of his palm. "If this was just lying beside Walker's body by chance, it would most likely have been dropped recently. What are the odds someone who could afford such an expensive piece of jewellery would be strolling around the docks in his finery?"

"I've never seen a toff on the docks anytime I was walking my beat, Sir."

"Exactly. So for now, let's work on the assumption it was dropped by the murderer. Who is on our suspect list that can afford this?"

Barnes smiled. "Mr. Flanagan." He paused to think about it. "Oh." The smile vanished. "How do we prove it? I didn't see any initials on it."

Hodgins shrugged and started putting the items back in the box. "I think we need to go for a walk."

"Sir?"

"I was down at the wharf yesterday and saw a couple of vacant buildings. Turns out one belongs to Flanagan, and it wasn't locked. I feel it's our duty to check on it. Make sure no one's been using it and causing damage."

Barnes looked at the ceiling for a moment, nose crinkled, left eye closed. His mouth dropped and his eye opened as it dawned on him. "Yes, we'll have to thoroughly examine inside the building. Might just turn up something interesting," he said.

* * *

Hodgins pointed at the last building beside the side rail. It was deserted and even from a distance you could see the boards over the windows were loose, some starting to split.

"That one there belongs to Flanagan. Missed it the first time I went through the records. It's registered under his wife's name. According to the city records, he rented it to an import company for a few years, but it's been sitting empty since this summer past. From the looks of the building, I'd say whatever Flanagan was charging for rent was too much. I wouldn't pay one cent for a building this run down."

Hodgins and Barnes stepped over the tracks carefully, trying not to slip in the fresh snow. It had been snowing most of the morning, and it was undisturbed around that section of track. None of the trains had gone down the side rail that morning and the snow had accumulated a fair bit, resulting in the bottoms of their trousers becoming wet and heavy.

"Look, Sir." Barnes pointed at the large sliding door at the front of the building. "Footprints."

Hodgins stopped beside Barnes and looked at the trail of prints coming down from the road, across the tracks, into the building, and back again.

"Interesting." Hodgins smiled. "I'm sure Mr. Flanagan would want us to check it out. Make sure everything is in order."

The sliding door was slightly ajar, so Barnes walked over and peeked in. "Too dark to see anything. All the windows have been shuttered."

Hodgins had already gone over to the closest window, removed the board he had previously loosened, and worked at prying the shutters open. The wood was cheap and well weathered, giving way with little effort and allowing light to shine in.

Barnes slid the door open, making the building brighter inside. "There's another door at the back. I'll open it, then it we should be able to see well enough to have a good look 'round. Seems pretty empty though, so it shouldn't take too long."

By the time Barnes had the back door open Hodgins was already looking through a pile of blankets in the corner.

"Probably just some vagrant come in to sleep last

night," Barnes said.

Hodgins turned. "How long has it been snowing?"

"Two or three hours."

"Right. So if someone came in last night, before it started to snow, would there be tracks going in both directions?"

Barnes wrinkled his nose and brow while he thought. "No. There would only be one set going out."

"So?"

"Someone was here right before us." Barnes looked puzzled. "But wouldn't we have seen him?"

Hodgins walked to the sliding door, indicating for Barnes to follow.

"The snow was heavy earlier, and now it's eased off. Look at the footprints."

Barnes knelt down beside the prints. "The tracks are half filled in. Whoever it was must have been here 'bout a half hour or more ago." He stood and brushed the snow from his trousers.

"Correct. You're looking, but you haven't been seeing. You need to observe and absorb everything. You should have realized right off that the tracks were fresh, but not immediately left." Hodgins put his hand on Barnes' shoulder. "Stop rushing. The smallest thing could be crucial."

They went back inside and looked around the empty room. There was nothing in the pile of blankets, and the lone desk by the front window didn't even have one piece of paper left in it. They started to follow the tracks, wondering who was in the building that morning and why. Was it just a vagrant looking for a place to rest, or did someone come in and remove a piece of evidence? Was the building even tied to the murder? Hodgins wondered if they were wasting their time pursing this particular avenue.

CHAPTER ELEVEN

Hodgins was continually jostled on the busy streetcar Saturday morning, his thoughts about Richardson disrupted every time his foot was trod on. He was finding it difficult to piece everything together. Was Richardson the one who ended the life of Fred Walker? Was a promotion at work enough of a motive? *People have killed for less, and he was certainly petty enough.*

Hodgins's disdain for Richardson grew every time his name came up. Everyone seemed to confirm his initial opinion; the man was too arrogant, too cocky. *Doesn't make him a murderer though.* By the time Hodgins arrived at the front of the station, he'd made up his mind to find out all he could about Mr. John Richardson.

It was still early and very quiet in the station house. The lads on the night shift were doing the last of their paperwork, and not many of the day shift had arrived. He could hear mumbling in the tiny kitchen towards the back. Some would be having a final cup of tea before heading out into the cool winter air, while others would be trying to warm up before starting for the day.

Hodgins could see someone in the Inspector's office. *Must be important to get the Inspector up so early.* From the cut of the coat, the visitor had money. Hodgins walked to his desk to see if there had been any messages left for him. Since there was nothing, he told the desk Sergeant he was going back to Stouffville to poke around, and would be back mid-afternoon.

He walked down to Union Station and was pleased to find a train almost ready. He had just enough time to purchase his ticket and then buy the morning edition from a newsboy working the platform. The train was half empty, so he settled by a window, away from other passengers and opened the paper.

"Ticket, Sir."

Hodgins put down the paper and took his train ticket from his pocket. He recognized the conductor immediately.

"Good morning, Detective. Ticket please."

Hodgins smiled at the conductor's memory, and decided to press for some more information. "Good morning. I remember you said your son worked at the mill with Mr. Walker. I assume he is also acquainted with Mr. Richardson?"

"Yes, he knows him. It's a small town. Everyone

knows everybody, even if only in passing."

"So, you know him too?"

The conductor smiled. "In passing."

"Do you recall if he was on the train when you saw Mr. Walker and Mr. Flanagan arguing?"

"No, Sir. I didn't see him that day. I don't believe I've ever seen him on the train. But I don't work every train."

He punched the ticket, handed it back to Hodgins, and continued down the aisle.

Hodgins sighed and went back to the newspaper, hoping the distraction would clear his mind. He'd discovered a long time ago that the harder he tried to think about something the more frustrated he got. Once he relaxed and put his mind to something trivial, he would have some sort of revelation. Didn't seem to be working today.

Having finished the paper by the time the train pulled into Stouffville station, Hodgins left it on the seat for someone else to read. He stepped onto the platform, took a few steps, and stopped. He really didn't know where he wanted to go first. It was unlike him to head out without some sort of plan.

"Can I be of assistance, Detective?"

Hodgins turned and found himself looking at the train conductor again.

"No, I'm all right, Mister—?"

"Jones, Sir."

"Mr. Jones. Just trying to gather my thoughts."

"If it's Richardson you're wanting, he's probably at the mill. Saturday's their busiest day."

"Thank you Mr. Jones. I'll keep that in mind." Hodgins nodded and walked towards the main road. He automatically turned right without giving any thought as to where he was going, then realized he was headed to the Lowe's. George Lowe was clearing the snow off the front walk, and waved when he saw Hodgins.

"Do you have news, Detective?"

"No, we're still investigating."

"Oh, I see." The look of disappointment was heartbreaking. Lowe cleared the last bit of snow and invited Hodgins inside. They settled in front of the fire in the sitting room. Hodgins pulled out his notebook, flipped through a few pages skimming his notes, then looked up at Lowe.

"What can you tell me about John Richardson? Was the fight with your cousin unusual?"

"John? Is he the one who fought with Fred? Well, he was always a bit of a bully. Hardly a week went by when someone wasn't talking about him. During grade school most of the boys around here got at least one black eye from him. When he starting working he never stayed at one job very long. Always thought he knew more than the boss.

Seemed to settle a bit when he went to the mill though."

Hodgins added the information to his notes, and thanked Lowe for his time. He was putting his notebook away when Mrs. Lowe scurried into the room.

"I thought I heard voices. George, why didn't you tell me we had company?"

Before he could respond, she turned to Hodgins.

"Detective, sit back down and let me fetch tea and biscuits." She turned and headed towards the kitchen.

"Thank you Mrs. Lowe, but I really must be going. It's very kind of you but there are other people I need to speak to this morning."

She stopped and turned back to Hodgins and her husband. "It won't take but a minute."

"Thank you, but it's imperative that I gather as much information as I can so we can find out who killed Mr. Walker. If either of you think of anything further, please send a note to me at the police station."

After leaving the Lowe residence, he headed towards the mill. As he crossed the road to go inside, he could hear yelling. It was loud enough that Hodgins was almost able to make out the words over the sound of the saws. He walked through the large sliding doors at the front and spotted Richardson lambasting one of the workers. His face was inches from the young man, and he was poking the worker in the chest to emphasize his point. The young man cringed each time that finger jabbed him.

Hodgins stormed over and tapped Richardson hard on the shoulder. "Excuse me. Might I have a word?"

Richardson flew around, fist in the air ready to strike. The young man gasped. Hodgins didn't flinch.

Richardson stopped as soon as he saw who it was. He flexed his hand and dropped his arm. The smile that crossed his face was more like a grimace.

"Detective. To what do I owe this pleasure?"

Hodgins reminded himself to be civil. "A word please. Can we step outside"

"Of course. Anything to help the police." As Hodgins turned to follow Richardson outside, he noticed the look of relief on the young man's face.

"What can I do for you, Detective?"

"Just tying up a few loose ends. Can you tell me where you were January fifth and sixth?"

"I was in Peterborough. My sister got married on the third. Had a family gathering of sorts. I was there until last Thursday."

Hodgins wrote in his notebook and flipped back through the pages. *Drat*, he thought. *That's the day after the body was found.* When he looked up at Richardson, he noticed a knowing smirk on the man's face. Hodgins slammed his notebook closed and shoved it in his overcoat pocket. "That's all I need for now."

Hodgins turned his back on Richardson and started back to the train station. He thought he heard Richardson laughing, but wasn't going to turn around to check. He cursed most of the way along the street. He wasn't paying any attention to where he was going and collided with someone coming out of the post office.

"Oaf. Watch where you're going."

Hodgins mumble an apology and picked up the package the man dropped. He froze when he saw it was Flanagan.

"Oh, it's you again," Flanagan said. "I hope you aren't here to harass me or my family."

"No, Mr. Flanagan. Just checking a few things. Sorry to have disturbed you." Hodgins handed the package to Flanagan then realized he'd turned the wrong way when he left the sawmill. He backtracked, hurrying to get to the train station. Richardson was not likely the killer. If he left Peterborough to go to Toronto, he would definitely have been missed. Much as Hodgins wanted to arrest the man, he didn't have cause. And now he'd ruffled Flanagan's feathers. Hodgins had found out a few new minor details; nothing particularly helpful. The frustration made him more determined then ever to find out who killed Fred Walker.

CHAPTER TWELVE

Hodgins knew he was late for church, but he took his time brushing the lint from his suit jacket. He want to look his best. He gave the front of the jacket one final stroke. Something crinkled. He put the brush on the dressing table, and reached into the pocket.

"Oh, forgot all about you," he said. The letter that had been delivered to the station on Friday remained unopened.

"Hurry up Bertie," Cordelia called from the bottom of the staircase. "I don't care to be late again. Mother is already quite upset."

Hodgins placed the envelope beside the clothes brush and put his jacket on while rushing down the stairs.

His father-in-law had hired a carriage for the day as the temperature had dropped well below freezing. His mother-in-law glared at him all the way to the church. Bertie had been thinking of moving more and more the past several weeks. He leaned over Sara and whispered to Cordelia.

"We need to talk later today." She started to say

something, but he shook his head. "Later."

They arrived at the Church of the Holy Trinity on Yonge Street about five minutes before the service started and slid into an empty pew. Hodgins barely had time to sit when he felt a tap on his shoulder. He turned and faced the man who ran the haberdashery.

"Bin reading about that lad what was killed by the lake. Saw your name in the paper. Know who dun it?"

"Still investigating. We'll have the man responsible soon."

Several people hushed them and Hodgins turned back as the minister approached the pulpit. Hodgins didn't hear any of the service. He couldn't stop thinking about Flanagan and Richardson and was startled when Cordelia nudged him and told him to hush. He had a habit of mumbling when trying to sort out details, but had never done it in church before.

He tried listening to the end of the service, but was distracted by someone two rows up snoring. Sara clasped both hands over her mouth to hide her giggles; Hodgins put his arm around her shoulder. She looked up at him and he put one finger over his mouth and winked. Fortunately the choir started singing Holy, Holy, Holy, and drowned out her soft laugh.

Cordelia's father insisted on treating everyone for

lunch after church, so it was late afternoon before Hodgins had a chance to speak with his wife alone. She sat on the bed waiting patiently while Hodgins paced across the room. "What is it Bertie? You've been acting strange all day. You're starting to scare me."

He stopped pacing and blurted it out. "I think it's time for us to move."

Cordelia was stunned. "Move? But why Bertie? I don't understand." She got up and walked to the window. "I love this house. I grew up here. I can't imagine living anywhere else." She turned to face him. "It's mother, isn't it? I'll speak to her."

"No. Well, maybe partly." He walked to Cordelia and took her hands in his.

"I'm grateful to your parents. They took me in when my folks died. I don't know what I would have done without them. Moved out west to live with my brother and his wife most likely. Everything had to be sold to pay the bills. I was left with nothing. No money for the rest of law school. No home. Nothing, except you. We couldn't have afforded to get married without their generosity. Then Sara came along. I've lived off their charity for over ten years."

He dropped her hands and turned away from her. "I feel like I've failed you. It's time for me to support my wife and child."

Cordelia slipped her arms around his waist and laid her head against his shoulder.

"Oh Bertie. You haven't failed us. I had no idea you felt this way. If you want to move, we'll move. I suppose it's time for me to change too. Time to stop being a daughter and become more of a wife and mother. I don't care if we live in a tiny flat. As long as we're together."

He patted her hands. "Don't worry. I've been saving all these years. We can afford a house. Not quite this extravagant, but big enough."

Hodgins freed himself from Cordelia's grip and pulled her around to face him. "We won't struggle. You'll see."

Cordelia knew her mother would be devastated to learn Sara would be leaving. She was very attached to her grand-daughter. Cordelia reached for the chair at the dressing table and sat down. "What will I tell mother?"

Hodgins shrugged as he spotted the envelope sitting on the table. He walked over and picked it up.

"What's that?" she asked. "Is that blood?"

"Mine. Sliced my finger when I started to open it. It was delivered to the station on Friday. I get interrupted every time I try to read it."

"Well, there's no interruptions now."

Hodgins flipped open the envelope and pulled out a single sheet of paper. The message was short.

"Well? What does it say?"

"Hmm? What? Oh, nothing." Hodgins didn't look up from the letter.

"Nothing my Aunt Fanny." Cordelia reached out and grabbed it from his hand. "Oh dear heaven. Bertie, please tell me this is a joke."

"I don't think it is. I must be getting close. Wish I knew which direction to go." He took the letter back and read it one more time. Letters had been cut from a newspaper and pasted to the page.

DROP THE WALKER CASE
OR PAY THE PRICE.

CHAPTER THIRTEEN

Hodgins rose the next morning, a little groggy. He dragged himself out of bed and got dressed for another day of work. He walked over to the dressing table, picked up the envelope, and stuffed it back into his jacket pocket. *Is it a real threat, or is someone just trying to scare me?*

He cursed himself for allowing Cordelia to read it. He wasn't worried, but his wife had been jumpy all last evening, and her parents noticed. When she broke a dish after dinner, she told them she was just tired. Hodgins knew lying to her parents added to Cordelia's unease, and that infuriated him more than the letter. This morning they were both tired due to her tossing and turning all night. He was even more motivated to solve the case and put it behind him.

His mood lifted slightly as he caught a whiff of breakfast. He hurried down the stairs and into kitchen where Cordelia was preparing eggs, toast and sausages. He could already taste her homemade preserves. Early morning was his favourite time to relax alone with his wife. It was the only time the house was quiet as no one else was up.

Hodgins pulled one of the chairs from the table and guided his wife into it. "Don't fret so. It's just a hollow threat. Stop fussing and sit down." Feeling guilty for worrying her, he served his wife breakfast before sitting down with a plate of his own. Cordelia always had one hardboiled egg, one piece of toast, and a little jelly. Occasionally she had a sausage as a bit of a treat. Hodgins had a plate full of scrambled eggs, three or four sausages, and two pieces of toast drowning in Cordelia's peach jelly.

Cordelia pushed her plate away. "Bertie, what if it's real? Can't someone else take over?"

Hodgins put his hand over hers and smiled. "It doesn't work that way Delia. Believe me, there's nothing to worry about. Now eat something." He put her plate back in front of her, picked up her fork and placed it in her hand. "Eat. You'll need your strength when Sara wakes. You'll be running around trying to get her ready for school."

Cordelia nodded. "I supposed you're right. She does take it out of me in the mornings."

She ate a few bites of toast while Hodgins quickly cleared his plate.

"I do love your peach jelly," he said, and popped the last bite of toast into his mouth.

She poured him a cup of tea.

"No time. You take it. Sit, enjoy the quiet while you can." He kissed her and hurried out to catch the trolley.

Even though the sun had been up for a few hours, it was gloomy and cold. The dark clouds filling the sky indicated a storm was on its way. Hodgins was glad the trolley was crowded and wedged himself into the centre to hide from the wind. By the time he arrived at the station house his protective human wall had thinned, and he was wishing he'd had that cup of steaming hot tea before leaving.

As he stepped off the trolley he heard something. Looking around, he caught a glimpse of movement at the corner of the building. He supposed it was the stray dog. The crate one of the men had turned into a bed for it had been placed at the end of the alley, out of the way of the wind. The crate was also near the side door making it easy to sneak food out. The dog must be looking for handouts again. He walked into the alley to check on the mutt. Two men waited in the shadows.

"Is there a problem men?" Hodgins inquired.

One of the men stepped out of the darkness, holding something in front of his face so Hodgins couldn't tell who it was. Before Hodgins could say anything a burlap sack covered his head. Someone grabbed his arms and held them behind his back.

"Guess ya thought the note was a joke." Hodgins didn't recognize the gruff voice. "Maybe ya'll listen to this."

The blow to Hodgins stomach was unexpected and hard. He started to double over but the man behind him jerked him upright.

"This is fer sticking yer nose where it don't got no business bein'."

The next blow landed on his jaw. Hodgins could taste blood. Blow after blow followed. First the right side, then the left. Over and over. Blood ran into his mouth, mixed with bits of burlap. He tried to call for help, but only a gurgle came out. Hodgins managed to kick the man punching him, but it didn't slow him down. He became lightheaded.

"Who -" Hodgins started to ask.

The assault to his face stopped, but the relief was only temporary. One hard punch into his kidneys had him doubling over again. The man behind him let go. Hodgins hit the ground. Both men kicked him repeatedly. Hodgins felt a sharp pain in his side, then passed out.

Hodgins woke to the sound of barking. He was groggy and shook his head to try to clear it. The wave of nausea almost made him pass out again. He managed to sit upright and tried to look around. Everything was dark. The barking stopped. He felt something wet on his face. Reaching out he felt fur. The smell told him it was probably the station's stray. He moved his hands across his face, wincing at the pain. His eyes felt huge. They were swollen shut. The dog barked again. Louder and louder.

"Quiet down boy," a voice called from the far end of the alley. The dog howled and whimpered, and then barked continually.

Hodgins heard footsteps hurrying towards him.

"Move along," the voice said. Go sober up somewhere else or I'll have ta lock ya up."

Hodgins recognized the voice. "Harrington," he whispered. He felt a hand on his shoulder.

"Lord Jesus," Harrington said. "Detective Hodgins."

Hodgins felt an arm slip under his. "I'll help you inside. Can you stand?"

With the help of the constable, Hodgins got to his feet and slowly made his way down the alley and in through the back door. The next few hours were hazy as he slipped in and out of consciousness. He could hear voices and someone in the distance called for a nurse. He figured he was at the hospital, but his eyes were still swollen shut. There was a tightness around his head. He touched his head and felt gauze. A bandage was wrapped around, covering his eyes.

"How do you feel, Sir?"

"Barnes, is that you?"

"Yes, Sir. We were all worried. Who knows how long you'dve been laying there if it weren't for the dog."

"The dog? I remember the barking and the dirty thing licking me."

"If he hadn't been making such a fuss we wouldn't have known you were there. He may have saved your life." Barnes hesitated before continuing in a lowered voice. "Few of us chipped in and got the mutt a nice piece of beef, sort of reward."

Hodgins chuckled. "Might just do that myself." He licked his lips. "Is there any water?"

He heard footstep, the sound of water pouring, then more footsteps.

"Here. The nurse brought in a jug while you were sleeping." Barnes touched the glass against one of Hodgins' hands. He clasped it tight. His hands were shaking as he raised it to his mouth. Empting it in one long gulp, he held it out for Barnes to take.

"Thank you. Don't supposed they'd let me have a cup of tea?"

"Probably not," Barnes replied as he took the glass.

Hodgins listened as the constable walked back to the table to return the empty class.

"What time is it?"

"A little past two, Sir."

"Two? I've been out half the day. Does my wife know?"

"Not yet. I was waiting for you to come to. They gave you something to help you sleep. What happened? Who did this?"

Hodgins shrugged. "Didn't see. They were in the shadows and put a burlap bag over my head. Think one of them had an Irish brogue. Can you go fetch my father-in-law? I don't want Cordelia to see me like this. We'll talk tomorrow."

"Yes, Sir." Barnes turned to leave.

"Barnes, my suit jacket. Is it here?"

Barnes looked around. "Yes, it's on the chair."

"There's a letter in the pocket. Take it back to the station."

Barnes went over to the coat, found the letter and read it. He whistled. "Sir? - "

"Tomorrow Barnes. Now go."

CHAPTER FOURTEEN

Hodgins spent the next three days in the Toronto General Hospital. The doctor had to wait for the swelling in Hodgins' eyes to go down enough to allow him to check for damage. His examination showed the impression of what appeared to be a ring beside Hodgins' right eye. Fortunately the only damage to his left eye was a slight scratch to the iris, possibly from the burlap.

The doctor was concerned with the blood in Hodgins' urine, and wouldn't release him until the colour changed from red to light pink and there was no more pain when he pressed on Hodgins' kidney.

Cordelia came to the hospital each day after Sara went to school fussing and fretting over Hodgins' bedside. After the first day, he started feigning sleep, and even asked the nurse for a sleeping tablet.

Friday morning Cordelia and her father arrived at the hospital in a rented carriage to take Hodgins home. He was glad to finally be leaving the hospital, but was not looking forward to being fussed over all day by his overly concerned wife.

When the carriage stopped in front of the house, Hodgins struggled to get out. The bumpy ride had been more then he could endure and he desperately wanted some of the pain tablets the doctor has prescribed. With the help of Harold, he was able to get up the stairs and into bed. Sara ran into the room and was about to leap onto the bed when her mother grabbed her.

"Your father needs rest. Come down to the kitchen. We'll make something special for him. Would you like that?"

"Oh yes. We'll make Daddy some of grandmother's special chicken soup. That will make him all better." Sara ran past Cordelia and down the stairs.

"Is there anything I can do for you?" she asked.

"My tablets. Where are they?"

Cordelia took a small packet out her beaded reticule and handed him one tablet. He swallowed it without waiting for a glass of water. She tucked the quilt around him and went downstairs with her father.

"He'll be fine Cordelia. Try not to worry."

* * *

Over the next few days Cordelia was constantly hovering over him. She was staring at him every time he woke. With help, Hodgins was able to come down and sit in the front room where he chatted with his father-in-law, read the paper, or dozed by the fire.

The mixture of sympathy and fear was too much for him to take. He felt vulnerable and helpless. The inspector had told him to take as much time as he needed, but Hodgins was restless and frustrated sitting around doing nothing. He also was getting very tired of those looks from Cordelia's mother. He never realized just how annoying a simple 'titch' could be. Once he had the Walker case solved, he was going to start looking for a house.

Three days in the hospital and five days at home was all he could take. Sara was the only person who seemed unaffected. "You look funny, Daddy. Does it hurt?" He was glad she was too young to understand.

Nine days after the beating he was finally back at work. The young, new constables seemed afraid to talk for fear of saying something wrong. Some were shocked seeing a seasoned officer so badly beaten, and right outside the police station. The older officers made jokes. At least no one was fussing over him.

Hodgins sat at his desk and called Barnes over. He'd given Barnes a list of things to check and people to speak to earlier in the week when he came over to check on Hodgins' progress. Barnes sat in the chair opposite Hodgins and put his notebook on the table.

"Shall I get us both a cup of tea?" Before Hodgins could reply, Barnes scurried to the back room and returned with two cups, then settled down with his notebook. Hodgins was glad to see the lad beginning to show some confidence.

"I sent a wire to the police in Peterborough. They spoke to Richardson's sister and she confirmed he was there the entire time. He was never away for any lengthy period, except to pick up supplies at the store and someone went with him. I believe we can scratch him off the list."

Hodgins slammed his fist on the desk, rattling the tea cups. "Damn. I was hoping you could find a hole in his story." He took a gulp of tea and waved his hand at Barnes, indicating he should continue.

"I went back to the wharf and spoke to anyone working near Flanagan's deserted building. One person recalls seeing someone go into the building, but he was too far away to see him good, and he only caught a glimpse."

"No," Hodgins said. "It would be too convenient for someone to have seen him. Wouldn't want our job made easy, would we?"

The puzzled look on Barnes' face let Hodgins know his sarcasm was wasted. "Go on."

"I went back to the empty building and walked up to

the road. You know, where the footprints led."

Hodgins nodded.

"Spoke to some of the merchants again. A couple of them remembered seeing a man in his forties or fifties. Well dressed. He didn't stop at any of the businesses, so they didn't pay much attention."

Hodgins yawned, closed his eyes and leaned back in his chair. After a few moments he realized Barnes had stopped talking. He opened his eyes and saw Barnes drinking his tea, waiting.

"Sorry. Guess I'm still a little groggy from the tablets the doctors gave me."

He sat up, and pushed away from his desk. "Maybe another cup of tea will help."

Barnes jumped up and reached for Hodgins cup. "I'll get it."

Hodgins slapped Barnes' hand. "Sit down. The walk will help clear my head." He leaned over and looked at Barnes' cup. "I'll top up yours, too."

Hodgins came back with two steaming cups, each with a scone on the saucer. "The sergeant's wife did some baking for us again." He placed one cup in front of Barnes and sat down with his. "So, basically you're telling me we have nothing?"

It was Barnes' turn to nod.

"We've been over this time and again," Hodgins said. "There must be something we've overlooked. Someone must have said something that just wasn't right." He drummed his fingers on the desk. "Maybe we're looking at this all wrong. I've assumed it had something to do with Emily Flanagan. We never looked any further into Walker's background.

Hodgins flipped open his notebook and found a fresh page. He jotted down points as he talked. "We knew he was close to Emily Flanagan back in England, he had a fight with John Richardson, and an altercation with Patrick Flanagan." He looked up at Barnes.

"We don't know anything about him after he came to Canada. Could something have happened in those few years that lead to his death?" He sighed, "Another train ride to Stouffville. I wish there was another way to talk to him. Wouldn't it be nice if we could just push a button and talk to someone in another location? Guess that will never happen." He chuckled at the thought.

"I need to have another talk with his cousin and I don't want to wait until the weekend when he's at home. Send him a telegram and tell him I'll be taking the early evening train tomorrow."

* * *

Hodgins stomped his feet, and shook his overcoat to

remove the snow before stepping inside. "Thank you for seeing me tonight, Mr. Lowe."

"Anything to speed this up," Lowe replied. "Not to be rude, but what happened to your face?"

"Little altercation a week or so ago. Believe it or not it looks much better now. Hazard of the job I'm afraid."

"Yes, I suppose it is. Do you have news? I'm anxious to find out who killed my cousin." He took Hodgins' coat and hung it on a peg by the door, then led him into the drawing room. Two chairs had been moved close to the fireplace. Hodgins welcomed the warmth as a storm had started while he was on the train. Before Lowe closed the door, Hodgins could hear the sounds of happy chattering and clinking dishes coming from the back of the house. He guessed Mr. Lowe had not informed his wife of the telegram or visit, or she would be sitting with them.

Lowe sat in the chair opposite Hodgins and fidgeted with the sleeve of his jacket. "What can I do for you, Detective?"

Hodgins thought for a moment. He didn't want to make his questions sound like he though Fred had done something to deserve being murdered.

"Tell me about Mr. Walker's arrival in Canada."

Mr. Lowe relaxed a little. "Fred was twenty-two. Didn't know a soul. My father brought us over years earlier so I hadn't seen Fred since he was a toddler. We were practically strangers."

Lowe got a far-away look in his eyes. "Fred was rather shy at first, but we soon became close. He told me about Emily. Got the impression they were inseparable. I think he missed her more than he missed his father. He settled in quick enough though. My family had a farm just outside town. He shared a room with his little brother and me. His sister bunked in with my sister. I had just become engaged and married less than a year later. Fred came over to visit often, and I helped him get the job at the mill."

"So, nothing of consequence happened in the past, what, four years? No problems, no sweethearts?"

Lowe smiled. "Fred was young, good looking, single, and new. He was popular with the young ladies and in demand at the dances. He got over his shyness right quick."

"And he came to live here after your parents died?"

"Yes. Father passed away shortly after Fred arrived, and my sister married last year and moved to New York. Mother died shortly after. We sold the farm and took in Fred.

"I see. Fred had no problems? Not even minor ones?"

"No, nothing until that altercation with John Richardson last fall."

"Right." Hodgins slapped the cover of his notebook

closed. The flames in the fireplace flickered as a gust of wind whistled down the chimney.

"I have a few more people to talk to before heading back to the train station. It sounds like it's getting worse outside. If you remember anything, no matter how trivial, please contact me right away."

Hodgins bundled up and headed into the snow storm. He wanted to speak with Miss. Cooke. Barnes was so enamoured with her Hodgins was not entirely confident the interview was complete. Unfortunately she wasn't able to provide any further information, so he headed back to the train station to wait for the last train out. He cursed in frustration the entire way, and barely noticed how cold it was.

CHAPTER FIFTEEN

Hodgins was distracted all through supper. He normally enjoyed Cordelia's mutton; it was a rare treat. She always took care to make the entire meal extra special whenever they ate it. But Hodgins could have been eating boiled socks that evening and he wouldn't have noticed the difference. There was something about the Walker case he couldn't put his finger on. Something was telling him he had the proof, but he didn't know what it was.

When the meal was over he mumbled an apology and went straight up to his room. He paced back and forth for awhile, then stood looking out the window. An hour later the bedroom door slammed, breaking his concentration and causing him to jump.

"How could you be so rude?" Cordelia asked. "Mother is in a state and Sara is extremely upset. She thinks she did something wrong and is nearly in tears."

"Rude? Was I?" Hodgins hurried across the room and put his arms around his wife. "I'm sorry. I'm just so distracted with this case. I'll go talk to Sara soon."

Cordelia pulled away from him. "I'm frightened. In all the years you've been a police officer this is the first time you've been so badly hurt. When I first saw you at the hospital I thought I was going to lose you." Her lower lip quivered. "I didn't know what to tell Sara."

"I didn't realize it was affecting you so." Hodgins reach towards Cordelia.

She stomped her foot. "No. You can't make it go away with an embrace. I'm frightened and angry, and nothing you do or say will change that. All those trips to Stouffville, and now this." She lightly touched his bruised face and took a deep breath. The tension left her body. "When we married, I always thought the day might come when another officer came to the door. I accepted that. Now I have to deal with it. At least you came home – this time."

She forced a tiny smile. "Now, tell me what you've discovered and get this murder solved once and for all."

Hodgins kissed Cordelia on the forehead, then retrieved his notebook from his desk and sat down.

"I've only had two good suspects. Patrick Flanagan and John Richardson. Barnes confirmed Richardson's alibi, so that leaves Flanagan. Problem is, I don't have anything to tie him to the murder."

Cordelia walked over to the desk and stood beside him.

"What about the cufflink?"

Hodgins sighed. "Ah yes. The pearl cufflink. I haven't the foggiest notion whose it is. It may not even have anything to do with Walker."

He banged his fist on the desktop. "Blast. This is so frustrating." The pages of his notebook fluttered from the breeze his fist caused. They settled at the spot where he had copied the sketch of the bruise on the back of Walker's head.

Cordelia giggled and pointed. "What about your little birdie?"

Hodgins laughed. "That is the most peculiar bruise I've ever seen. Haven't figured that out either. What in tarnation would leave a mark like that?"

Cordelia patted his shoulder. "I'm sure I don't know, Dear. Can't the local police in Stouffville help?"

"No local police. It's a small town and there isn't much crime.

Hodgins closed the notebook and got up. "I'd better speak to Sara before she goes to bed."

* * *

His previous evening's chat with Cordelia left Hodgins with a strong feeling he was on the right track. Something about that darn bruise. He spent a restless night trying to piece it all together, rising early to allow his wife the luxury of sleeping late. He grabbed a couple of thick slices of bread and piled some peach preserves on them. The trolley was practically empty so he had no trouble finding a seat to eat his breakfast without making a mess.

He stepped off the trolley and strode towards the station. He hesitated when he reached the alley. Hodgins watched the shadows, ensuring no-one was lurking. Satisfied, he continued to the front steps. He took one quick look around before entering the building.

Hodgins walked past the desk sergeant, mumbled a 'Good Morning' and went straight to the back for a cup of tea. The stationhouse was quiet and he could hear the gentle snoring of one of the senior constables. A sure sign of an evening free of trouble.

Hodgins put the tea cup on his desk and removed his notebook as he walked to the coat tree to hang his overcoat. He opened the book to look for the first notes on the Walker case as he ambled back to his desk. Pulling a pad of long paper from the top drawer he copied what he figured were the key points, along with his thoughts about them. He had three pages filled by the time Barnes came in.

"Do you have new information?" Barnes asked. Without waiting to be asked he sat in the chair opposite Hodgins' desk. His eyes were wide, eagerly awaiting good news.

The reply was curt. "No." Hodgins put his pencil down and started drumming his fingers. "It's here. I know it is." He fanned the pages of foolscap. "The answer is in here – somewhere."

"What's that there?" Barnes pointed to a few words that Hodgins had circled.

Hodgins picked up his notebook and found the page with the notes from the autopsy and pointed to the sketch. "It's this damn bruise. My wife noticed that it's shaped like a bird." He turned the book around. "See?"

Barnes leaned in for a closer look. "Well, look at that. Is it important?"

Hodgins shrugged. "Not sure. I think so, but I can't for the life of me figure out what made it. If we can determine that, we'll probably have the killer. Whatever it was that made that mark, there can't be too many of them."

He tapped the circled notes on the pad of paper. "These two things are crucial, I just know it." He turned the pad so Barnes could read it.

"The bruise and the pearl cufflink." Barnes looked up at Hodgins. "Did you find out who owns the cufflink?"

Hodgins sighed, "No."

"Another train ride to Stouffville?" Barnes asked.

Hodgins nodded. "Yes, but not today. I need to have a plan. The only way to solve this will be to catch them off guard. If they think I know something one of them may slip up."

"Makes sense. I've used that trick on my younger brother lots of times." Barnes said. "He was so gullible." He smiled. "Still is."

"Somehow I doubt Flanagan is easily fooled. I'll need you to come with me. Might be more believable if it appears as though I brought help, anticipating an arrest." He glanced over at the calendar on the wall. "January thirtieth. It's been just over three weeks since those boys found Mr. Walker's body. Tomorrow is Saturday. Month end. If I'm any judge of character, Flanagan will be out early collecting rent from those properties he lets out. We'll take the first train after lunch tomorrow. He should be home by then."

CHAPTER SIXTEEN

Hodgins and Barnes purchased return tickets and boarded the one o'clock train Saturday afternoon, hoping to surprise Flanagan at home.

There were a large number of people scattered throughout the coach cars, most laden with parcels, returning from an early morning shopping trip. Hodgins made his way to an empty window seat and Barnes slid in beside him. Hodgins was still trying to figure out the key piece that continued to elude him, ignoring Barnes' attempts to engage him in conversation.

As the train travelled through the countryside, Hodgins stared out the window. The length of track between Toronto and Stouffville was thick with pine and spruce trees covered in snow. He didn't pay any attention as people departed and boarded at each stop along the way. Blue Jays called and screeched from the woods beside the tracks, and when Barnes pointed them out Hodgins slapped his arm down. Jackrabbits hopped out from under the trees and Red Tailed Hawks circled about, but Hodgins ignored it all.

Barnes frequently looked up from the newspaper he'd purchased at Union Station and tried unsuccessfully to draw Hodgins' attention to the picturesque scene outside. By the time the train pulled into Stouffville, Hodgins was still no wiser than when he had boarded.

As they walked to the Smythe's house, Hodgins fiddled with the collar of his overcoat. The wind had died down and he no longer needed it up around his neck. Barnes loosened the brightly coloured scarf he had wound around his throat and tucked inside his coat.

"Where did you get that thing?" Hodgins asked.

"My mother knit it for me for Christmas. It's quite warm."

"Oh, it's very... colourful."

They reached the Smythe house and approached the front door. Hodgins looked at Barnes, crossed his fingers, and knocked.

Mr. Smythe answered the door. He recognized the detective immediately. "Yes, what it is now?"

"I'd like to speak with Mr. Flanagan if he's home."

Smythe stepped back and gestured for Hodgins and Barnes to come in. "It's not about that business with young Fred, is it? Patrick told you everything before."

They stepped into the house and closed the door. "There have been some new developments. Won't take long. Is he in?"

Mr. Smythe looked past Hodgins at Barnes. "This is one of my constables. I thought it prudent to bring him along," Hodgins said.

Smythe glared at the detective, then snorted lightly. "Make it quick. My wife will be home soon and I'd rather you weren't here when she returns. Wait in the drawing room and I'll fetch Patrick."

Smythe ushered Hodgins and Barnes into the drawing room. Barnes remained by the door, acting like a guard, making it appear as though they knew more than they actually did. Hodgins walked over to the fireplace to admire the new family portrait that now hung over the mantle when a commotion in the hall caught his attention. The door opened and Flanagan entered, his wife, Emily was right on his heels followed by her father. Barnes reached over and closed the door.

Flanagan turned to his wife. "Emily, this is a not a discussion you need to be concerned with."

"Fred was my friend, a long time friend. I have every right to know what's going on." She crossed her arms and turned away from her husband. "I'm staying, and that's that."

Emily marched across the drawing room, sat on the edge of one of the chairs near the fire and looked anxiously at Hodgins. "Detective, Daddy said there was some new information. Do you know who killed Fred?"

"I just need to clear up a few details. He turned to Flanagan and pulled the pearl cufflink from his pocket.

Hodgins held his hand out towards Flanagan. "Do you recognize this?

Flanagan looked at the cufflink in Hodgins' hand. "I have a pair like that. Why?"

"When was the last time you wore them?"

"I don't know. Last fall possibly. I believe I wore them to the local businessmen's banquet in November."

"You didn't wear them around Christmas?"

Flanagan's face turned red. "I just said I haven't worn them for months. What are you getting at?"

Emily rose to get a better look at the cufflinks. "That does look like the pair you have." she said. "Daddy borrowed them for a meeting in Toronto just a few weeks ago." She turned her head towards her father. "Isn't that right Daddy?"

"What?" Smythe said. "Well, yes. I suppose I did."

Hodgins flipped the cufflink in his hand. He looked from Smythe to Flanagan and back to Smythe. "You wore the cufflinks last? Where are they now?"

Smythe shook his head. "I guess I gave them back to Emily."

Hodgins turned his attention to Emily.

"Yes, that's correct. I remember Daddy giving the box back and putting it on the dressing table. It was just last week I believe."

Hodgins caught a slight movement out of the corner of his eye. He turned his head just enough to get a better look without being noticed.

Smythe was looking at Emily and shaking his head, but she was looking at Hodgins.

"Just last week?" Hodgins asked. "He didn't return them right away?"

Emily shrugged. "I guess he forgot."

"And you're sure this is not one of your husband's cufflinks?"

"How could it be? It is very similar to his though. Patrick's very proud of them. Genuine pearls and 24k gold. He was livid when Harry, my little brother, damaged one of them. Left a mark on one of the bars. The gold is rather soft."

"Would you mind fetching them?" Hodgins asked.

"Of course." Emily hurried upstairs and returned shortly with a small red velvet box. "Here they are," she said as she entered the room. She opened the box. "That's odd."

Emily took one cufflink from the box and dropped it in Hodgins' hand next to the other one.

"These aren't Patrick's."

"What do you mean?" Hodgins asked.

"The one you brought is very good quality. You can see the color of the gold doesn't match this one. The pair I have are probably only 10k, not 24k."

Emily took the cufflink back from Hodgins and turned it over several times, then did the same with its mate. "There's no mark on them either. Someone must have replaced Patrick's with these cheap copies."

Hodgins examined the cufflink that was found by the body. "Hmm." He ran his fingers across the bar then showed it to Emily. "Is this the mark that your brother made?"

"It looks like it. That's the same place it was damaged." She looked up at Hodgins. "How did you get it?"

Hodgins looked behind Emily at Patrick. "It was found beside Mr. Walker's body."

Everyone turned toward Flanagan. Barnes took a few steps into the room.

"I don't know how my cufflink ended up with Walker's body." Sweat broke out across his forehead. "I didn't kill him. You've got to believe me." He took a hanky from his trousers pocket and swiped at his brow. "Why would I? I already had Emily. He was no threat to me, and my father-in-law had them last." He paused for a moment. "When exactly was he killed?"

"The coroner couldn't say, but it was the first week of January, maybe the fourth or fifth," Hodgins said.

"Well," Flanagan said. "That proves it. I haven't been to Toronto since the end of December. I was planning on making the trip this coming Monday to conduct some business."

"Can anyone vouch for you?" Hodgins asked.

"I'm sure my wife would be more than happy to." Flanagan turned to his wife.

"Emily, tell the detective I haven't left town all month." He waited. "Emily?"

Everyone's attention was directed at her, but she was examining the cufflinks she'd brought downstairs.

Flanagan reached out and placed a hand on her shoulder, causing her to jump.

"Tell him I've been in town all month."

Emily looked at her husband as though he was a stranger. "But how . . ."

Flanagan's neck turned red. "Emily! Tell the detective I have not left town for weeks."

Slowly she turned her head towards Hodgins, her eyes still on her husband. Finally, she looked at the detective.

"Patrick has not been gone for more than two hours at any one time. He's been keeping an eye on the men working on the house."

"That's right," Mr. Smythe said. "I was with him on some of the visits to his house. I'm an architect. He hired me to draw up the plans."

This was not going the way Hodgins had hoped. He walked towards the fireplace, glanced up at it and turned. He got half way across the room and stopped. He looked at Smythe and turned back to the portrait hanging over the fireplace.

"Nice portrait. It wasn't here at my last visit. That's an interesting walking stick you're holding in the painting."

Smythe puffed out his chest and smiled. "It was a gift from my employees when we left Norfolk."

"They must have though highly of you to give you such an expensive looking thing."

"Yes," Smythe replied. "My business was small, and my staff was like a second family. They knew I would be giving up my hobby when I moved, so they got it as a reminder. I had a good sized piece of land and was able to keep a few falcons. I'm afraid I'm unable to keep the birds here. Shame. Falconry is such a thrilling sport. Such beautiful creatures."

Hodgins remember the odd shaped bruise the coroner

mentioned. He walked over to Barnes and whispered to him. Barnes nodded. Hodgins turned back to Mr. Smythe. "Why did you do it Sir?"

"Pardon me? Do what?"

"Why did you murder him? At first I thought it was your son-in-law, but the walking stick was the final piece I was missing. What harm did Walker ever do to you?"

"You're mad. Daddy would never do such a thing." Emily rushed to her father's side and wrapped her arms around his waist. Smythe put his arm over her shoulder.

"This is absurd. Why would you think I did it?" Smythe turned to Emily. "Don't worry. It's all a mistake." He walked her to the chair by the fireplace and made her sit.

"You're just clutching at straws, Detective. I liked Fred. Why would I do such a horrible thing?"

Hodgins gestured towards Emily. "Your daughter just said you borrowed the cufflinks and went to Toronto a few weeks ago. When exactly was that?"

"It was the fifth. Monday afternoon. I was meeting with a new client. I can give you his name."

That won't be necessary. What time —"

Hodgins was interrupted by the slamming of the front door, followed by the giggling of a child. The drawing room door opened and a boy ran in, still wearing his snow-covered coat and boots.

"Harry!" Emily shouted.

The boy froze, and looked at everyone in the room. Mrs. Smythe hurried in after him.

"I'm sorry," she said. "Harry, you know better than that. Come here at once."

She noticed Hodgins. "You're that policeman, aren't you?"

Hodgins nodded.

Harry's mouth opened and his eyes grew large. "A real policeman?"

Hodgins smiled. "Yes, a real policeman. A detective."

Harry turned around and spotted Barnes. He walked over to Barnes and reached for one of the shiny brass buttons on his uniform.

"Harry, come here at once." Mrs. Smythe said.

The boy pouted and slowly followed her out into the front hall.

Hodgins watched closely as the boy walked past him and into the hall.

"Nice looking lad," he said. "I'd guess he'd be about four." He turned and looked at the boy again. "Hmm . . ." He took his notebook out of his pocket, flipped through the pages and pulled out the picture of Fred Walker. He looked at the picture again, then walked out into the hall and held the it beside the little boy's face. "Interesting."

Hodgins went back into the drawing room and showed Emily the picture of Fred.

"Can't help but notice how much Harry looks like Fred Walker."

Emily gasped and put her hand over her mouth.

Hodgins asked Barnes to close the door that Harry had left open.

"No," Emily said. She turned to her father. "Daddy, it's all for nothing. I married Patrick but everyone will still know."

"So, it's not a coincidence that the boy resembles Fred? Why marry that man and not the boy's father?" Hodgins asked, pointing at Flanagan.

"Blackmail," Smythe answered. "Fred had already moved when Emily found herself in a delicate condition. Once we knew, her mother took her on a tour of Europe. At least that's what we told folks. When they returned with the baby, we said it was ours. No one knew any difference." He glared at Emily. "Silly, stupid girl."

Emily covered her face with both hands and wept.

"Where does the blackmail come in?"

"When we moved here and Emily renewed her relationship with Fred, she started thinking about telling him. The boy is starting to look like his father, which you already discovered. If word got out, it would ruin her reputation, and the family name."

Hodgins looked at Emily. Her husband stood beside her chair, totally uninterested in her discomfort and distress. Puzzled, Hodgins turned his attention back to Smythe.

"But what does that have to do with Flanagan?" Hodgins asked Smythe.

"He showed up here one day with suggestions for some alterations to the drawings I did for his renovations." Smythe's eyes narrowed and he turned his head slightly towards Flanagan. "Quite rude if you ask me. I had gone upstairs to fetch the drawings and he overhead my wife and Emily talking about the boy. He had made several comments before so I knew he had an interest in Emily, but she wanted nothing to do with him. When I came back down he said if Emily didn't marry him, he would tell everyone about her indiscretion five years earlier."

"Buy why kill Mr. Walker," Hodgins asked.

Smythe stood tall. "I really don't know why you insist I did it."

"You had the cufflinks last, and one was found with the body. You noticed it was missing at some point. I'm sure it won't take long to find the jeweller who made the cheap copy. That's why you returned them to your daughter so late."

Smythe stood with his mouth open, the realization that

he had been caught crept across his face. His shoulders dropped.

"I didn't plan to. Emily was still in love with Fred; I couldn't risk her leaving Patrick for him. It would all come out, and we would be ruined. This is a small, close knit community, and very religious. My wife and daughter would be shunned, and the men would stop doing business with me." Smythe glanced over at Emily. The look of horror on her face was more than he could bear.

"I bumped into Fred on the way to Union Station after my meeting. He suspected something and was hounding me to tell him why Emily married Patrick. We got into an argument. People were looking, so we moved off the road down near the wharf. He turned away from me and I hit him with the walking stick. I didn't mean to kill him, I just wanted him to stop asking questions."

"Where is it?" Hodgins asked. "The walking stick. I assume you still have it."

Smythe nodded. "Couldn't bear the thought of getting rid of it. It's in the stand by the front door."

Hodgins gestured to Barnes, who quickly went to the front door. He returned with the walking stick and handed it to Hodgins.

"There was a deep cut on his side," Hodgins said. He ran his fingers around the decorative carving on the top of the stick. It moved. Curious, Hodgins gently twisted and pulled. Attached to the carving was an eight inch blade.

"I was frantic." Smyth said. "I panicked and stabbed him after he fell."

Mr. Smythe held his arms out toward Barnes and said, "I won't cause any trouble." Barnes reached for his handcuffs.

"Put your arms down. I don't believe handcuffs will be necessary," Hodgins said.

"Thank you for that, Detective. If I plead guilty, there won't be a lengthy trial, will there? Could we keep the reason a secret? I don't want my family to suffer any more than they already will."

"Detective," Flanagan said. "You said it was the walking stick. I don't understand. What made you change your mind about me and suspect Emily's father?"

"It was the falcon on the top of the stick. Walker had a bruise on his head that looked like a bird. The shape resembles the one on the walking stick." He opened his notebook to the sketch of the bruise and showed Flanagan.

Hodgins turned back to Mr. Smythe. "If we leave now we can catch the next train back to Toronto."

Emily started to cry. "Be brave Emily," her father said. "You must be strong for Mother and young Harry."

Hodgins opened the drawing room door and gestured

for Barnes to escort Smythe.

"Just let me get my overcoat," Smythe said.

CHAPTER SEVENTEEN

Hodgins and Smythe walked towards the train station, Barnes followed close behind. Hodgins stopped on the platform to read the schedule printed on the chalkboard outside the waiting area. He checked his pocket watch. It would be twenty minutes before their train departed for Toronto, so they went inside to wait.

There was a bench near the pot belly stove; Hodgins indicated for Smythe to sit, then sent Barnes to purchase a ticket for Smythe. They rested in silence listening to the sounds outside of the station: cattle mooing in the nearby pen waiting to be ushered to the slaughterhouse, the hissing of the engine that sat idling on the side rail, murmuring from travellers waiting for their train or for someone to arrive.

Hodgins looked over at the large round clock on the opposite wall. "May as well go outside and wait. Our train should be pulling in shortly." They got up and stood on the platform, near the doorway.

A stray dog was sniffing around looking for handouts.

"Looks just like the mutt that hangs around the station house, except ours is much fatter. Everyone sneaks the poor bugger food. Last month one of the men made a shelter for it out of an old crate and tattered blanket." Hodgins smiled. "Even feed it myself, sometimes."

"Got no use for them myself," Smythe said. "Useless creatures. Always begging for food. They don't serve much purpose, if you ask me."

Hodgins thought back to the morning in the alley when he was attacked. "If you treat them right they know it. Might even save your life some day." He pointed down the platform at Hodgins. "See, my constable understands."

Barnes had a few crumbs of beef pie in his coat pocket, left over from a hasty lunch. He'd walked to the end of the platform towards the dog, crumbs held out in his hand. The dog's tail wagging as it cautiously approached. It sniffed at Barnes hands, then gently took the scraps of crust and beef. It gave a quiet bark, and wandered off searching for more food.

Smythe watched Barnes and snorted. "Disgusting, filthy mongrel. Your constable probably has fleas now. He'll spread them all over the train."

Hodgins held up his hand. "Hush. What's that sound?"

"Sound? What? That whistle? The train over there I expect."

"Doesn't sound right. I've never heard a train make that sound."

There was a loud boom, then yelling. A woman screamed; Hodgins blacked out.

* * *

When Hodgins opened his eyes, he was no longer at the train station.

"Nurse, he's awake," Barnes yelled.

"Barnes, is that you? Where am I?"

"In the hospital. You need to rest, Sir. So you can heal."

"Where's Smythe?"

"That's not important now. The doctor said you need lots of rest."

Hodgins started to sit up, wincing as the pain raged through his head. "Blast man, tell me what happened. Something happened at the station in Stouffville."

"Everyone's talking about it, Sir. The boiler of the Fairlie engine Shedden exploded. Seems the safety valves failed. Three of the enginemen were killed. The force sent you flying back against the wall. Knocked you out cold. Where is the nurse?"

Barnes hurried to the doorway and hollered, "Nurse, doctor, someone. He's awake."

"That explains this headache," Hodgins said. "What

about Smythe? Is he here too?"

Barnes turned back to Hodgins.

"Uh, no, Sir," Barnes said as he walked back to Hodgins bedside.

"Good Lord. Don't tell me he got away?"

"No. A piece of metal went straight though his heart. Was killed instantly."

Hodgins lay back in his hospital bed. "Well, I guess that saves Her Majesty the expense of a trial and hanging. Case closed."

Barnes stood at the foot of the bed, twirling his helmet in his hands. "Uh, Sir?"

Hodgins noticed Barnes fidgeting. "Yes?"

"What about the two men who attacked you? It was because of Walker's murder. Don't we still have to apprehend them before we can close the case?"

Hodgins closed his eyes, and waited for the pain to subside. "If we continue to investigate, we'll eventually have to reveal why Smythe did it, right?"

"Of course, Sir. We have to tell the truth. If we don't tell why, it's the same as a lie."

"What purpose will it serve to let everyone know that Emily Flanagan had a child out of wedlock when she was eighteen?"

"Well..." Barnes started.

"Do you want to ruin her life and that of the little boy?"

"No, of course not. But isn't it our duty to continue?"

Hodgins sighed. "I don't care who beat me up in the alley. Obviously Smythe hired them, so they have no reason to harm me again. It's our duty to solve crimes and capture the criminals. We've solved this murder, and the guilty party has paid with his life. No need to drag innocent people's names through the mud. It'll be difficult enough for them. Wouldn't be surprised if they moved away."

"Since you put it that way, then I guess we've done all we can." Barnes noticed Hodgins yawning. "I'll leave you to get some rest now, Sir."

Barnes turned to leave and bumped into the doctor.

"Terribly sorry, Doctor. Do excuse me."

The doctor said something under his breath and walked around Barnes.

Hodgins called out to Barnes. "Wait, I have something I need you to do."

EPILOGUE

After spending a few days in Toronto General, Hodgins was sent home to finish recuperating. He was glad to be home, where he wasn't being poked and examined constantly. Early Saturday morning everyone sat at the kitchen table finishing up breakfast when someone knocked at the front door.

"Who could be calling at such an early hour?" Cordelia asked as she rose from the table. "It's only just past 8:00. Early callers usually mean bad news."

Hodgins smiled. "Not necessarily. Answer it and you'll find out. Take Sara with you."

Cordelia put her hands on her hips. "Just what are you up to Bertie?"

He shrugged. "Why do you think I'm up to something? It's cold outside. Hurry, go answer the door before he freezes."

"Before who freezes?"

Cordelia's mother rose. "For goodness sake. I'll get it."

Hodgins held out his hand. "No, sit. Let Cordelia and Sara get it."

Cordelia looked suspiciously at her husband. "Very well. Come on Sara. Let's go see what your father is up to."

Cordelia opened the front door and found Barnes standing on the porch. "Why hello, Constable. Come in and I'll call Bertie." She noticed a rope in his hand and followed it with her eyes. "What...?" She was confused. The constable was at their door, out of uniform, and with a dog.

"What's his name?" Sara asked. "Can I pat him?"

"Scraps." Barnes held out the rope for Sara to take. "He's right friendly, Miss, and loves to be petted." He stepped inside and closed the door behind him.

Hodgins came out of the kitchen with his in-laws, an agonized look clung to his face. His steps were guarded; he reached for the wall to steady himself. He was still rather wobbly from the explosion.

"Take your coat and boots off and come into the front room," Hodgins said. He popped one of his pain tablets into his mouth.

Cordelia glanced past her husband at her father, who shrugged. They hadn't been on social terms with the young constable, yet her husband was treating him like an old friend.

Sara led the dog into the front room and sat on the rug

in front of the fire. Scraps curled up beside her, tail thumping against the floor.

Hodgins looked at the dog. Its coat was shiny and free of tangles. "Are you sure that's the same dog?"

"Yes, Sir. Cleaned up quite nice. Dr. McKenzie treated it for fleas and gave it a bath. Beautiful, ain't he?"

"Do you like him Sara?" Hodgins asked.

"Oh yes. He's very nice, and so soft." She turned to Barnes. "Why do you call him Scraps? Funny name for a dog."

Barnes smiled. "He was always hanging around the police station, and me and some of the boys fed him scraps of food. Seemed like an appropriate name for him, don't you think?"

Sara nodded and stroked the dog's fur. Scraps stood up, licked Sara's face, and lay down with his head in her lap.

"Is this the dog that found Bertie in the alley?" Cordelia asked.

"Yes, he's the one," Barnes answered.

Hodgins walked over to Barnes and shook his hand. "Thank you, Barnes."

"My pleasure, Sir. Least I could do."

Hodgins started to walk to the front door with Barnes.

"The dog. Don't forget the dog," Hodgins' mother-in-law called out.

The front door opened, then closed and Hodgins came back into the front room alone. "That's what this room was missing." He walked to the fireplace and knelt beside Sara and stroked the dog.

"Bertie?"

"I asked Barnes to catch and clean up the dog. I'm sure Sara will take good care of him. He did save my life after all."

Death On Duchess Street

A Detective Hodgins Victorian Mystery

Book Two

CHAPTER ONE

"**D**on't you worry Mr. Nolan. I'll take good care of Olivia." Flossie looked across the street at the auburn-haired girl standing on the porch of the two-storey clap-board dwelling, three houses down. "Such a pretty thing, and so polite. Won't be any bother at all."

Kendall Nolan followed Flossie's gaze and smiled. "She's growing up so fast. Won't be long now before she's married with a family of her own. I wish her mother was alive to see how Olivia turned out. Ruth would be so proud of her."

His smile faded slightly as he thought of his wife, her death still fresh in his mind even though it had been over a year since she succumbed to the consumption.

Flossie reached out to touch his arm, but caught herself in time. Even though he was far from wealthy, Kendall Nolan was a respected businessman. *She* ran a boarding house. It would be highly improper for someone of her standing to make such an intimate gesture.

Kendall turned back to Flossie as she quickly brushed a

1

few small strands of hair back in place, in an attempt to disguise her near error in judgement.

A gust of wind kicked up and dragged a small branch part-way across the road. Kendall grabbed his hat just as the wind caught it. Flossie fought with her dress as it wrapped around her legs.

"My goodness," Flossie said. "I thought the storm was over. I don't think these old trees can stand up against another one so soon."

"I see one of the shutters has come loose on the McGregor home," Kendall said as he pointed to the house across the road. "There it goes."

The shutter came off in the wind and crashed to the ground, crushing the Hydrangea bush.

"I hope my home is still standing when I get back. As I told you yesterday, I'll only be gone for the night. I'll be back late tomorrow morning. I'm sure Olivia will be fine, but I feel much better making this trip knowing there's someone in the house with her overnight. I didn't realize how much I relied on my sister since Ruth's death. She was such a big help."

"Why isn't she isn't able to come this time, if you don't mind me asking?" Flossie said.

"She passed early in June."

"Oh, I'm sorry for your loss."

"The past eighteen months have been dreadful for me and Olivia. First Ruth, then Penelope." Kendall got a far-away look in his eyes. "Dreadful year."

They stood silently for a moment. The air felt heavy after the storm despite the lingering wind. He could hear drops of water falling from the trees onto the rooftop as the wind moved through the branches. Kendall pulled a hanky from his pocket and wiped the sweat from his brow. He shook his head, clearing his thoughts.

"There's been so much going on in the neighbourhood lately I'm rather uncomfortable leaving Olivia alone."

Flossie nodded in agreement. "I can't believe how the area has changed in the last little while. I was shocked to hear Miss Gurney was arrested for stealing. Her father's out of work; it must be difficult feeding all those children. Still, that's no reason to break into a neighbour's home."

"That's not what's disturbing me. It's that missing woman around the corner on George Street, and that man, a painter I believe, murdered in his home only one block south, on Duke. I've been seriously thinking about moving, but you've seen how long the house beside me has sat vacant. No one wants to live here anymore." Kendall turned to Flossie. "Forgive me, Miss O'Hara. I did not intend to bring up such dreadful things. I do appreciate your help with my daughter."

Flossie blushed at his comment. Even though she was not upper class, he still treated her as a lady.

He tipped his hat, turned, and crossed the muddy road. Kendall looked at his daughter, not paying any attention to where he stepped. Halfway across the road his left foot hit the edge of a puddle, a remnant from the storm the day before.

Olivia moved off the porch and waited for him beside the hired cab. She laughed as her father approached.

"What's so funny young lady?"

Olivia pointed at his pant leg and continued giggling. The bottom edge of Kendall's white linen trousers had turned dark from the muddy water.

"Oh well," Kendall said. "It's too late to change now. It won't stay wet long in this heat. I'll brush off the dried mud before the train reaches Coboconk." He opened his arms and Olivia stepped closer to give him a hug.

"I'll miss you Papa. Have a safe trip and don't worry a bit about me. I'll be fine. I am sixteen you know. A grown woman. Well, almost." She rose up on her toes and gave her father a kiss on the cheek.

"Now you mind Miss O'Hara tonight. I don't want to come home and find you've been too much work for her," he joked. His mind drifted back to his conversation with Flossie about the problems in the neighbourhood lately; his mood turned serious. "Make sure you keep the doors locked."

He kissed her on the top of her head and gently tugged on one of the ringlets that rested on her shoulder before climbing into the hansom cab and settling beside the carpet bag that Olivia had already placed on the seat. The driver gave a sharp snap on the reins, and the matching pair of reddish-brown Bay's picked up their hooves, pulling the cab away from the curb.

Olivia watched as her father travelled across Duchess Street, turned south on George, and disappeared from sight. She raised her skirts, and ran up the road to the boarding house, dodging the small rain puddles and deposits left by the horses.

Olivia was fond of her deceased aunt, but was looking forward to spending time with Miss O'Hara. Aunt Ruth always smelled of ointment and liniments. Miss O'Hara smelled of lavender and roses, just as her mother once did.

"What time will you be over, Miss O'Hara? I can make dinner for you. Father says I'm a very good cook."

"I'd love to join you for dinner Olivia, but I have two boarders and need to prepare their meal. Do you remember Mr. Webster? He stays with me quite often. Last time he mentioned that he spoke to you several times. He's here on business again. Would you like to come across and join us for dinner? I'm sure he would be happy to see you."

Olivia frowned slightly at the mention of Mr. Webster. She remembered the first time she met him and all the attention the young man lavished on her.

"Yes, I remember him."

"My other guest is an older lady. She speaks of her grand-daughter all the time and how much she enjoys visiting her. I believe her grand-daughter is just about your age. I'm positive a visit from you would be most welcome, and she always has sweets in her purse. She mentioned not being able to see her family tonight so she will quite likely be a little sad this evening. It will be just like a little party. Wouldn't that be more fun than eating alone? We can walk over to your house afterwards."

"Yes, that would be nice. I baked apple pies first thing this morning. I can bring one over, if that would be all right."

Flossie brushed Olivia's wind-blown hair away from the girl's face and laughed. "Yes, that would be delightful. What about lunch? Your father didn't mention what you would be doing during the day. You won't be alone, will you?"

"No Miss. I'm going over to Sally's. Her mother is packing a basket and we're having a picnic in the park with Lucy and Betsy - if it doesn't rain again and spoil things."

"Come over around five o'clock then, and you can help

set the table. I have lots of work to do, so you run along. I'm sure you and your friends will have lots of fun now that school is over."

Olivia said goodbye and ran back across the street.

Flossie stood on her lawn for a minute looking around the neighbourhood. It had changed so much since she took over the boarding house. She grew up in the area and remembered how everyone had taken pride in their homes.

The Nolan house was well maintained and had been repainted the previous summer. It was still a lovely shade of light blue, and made the surrounding homes look dingy.

The vacant house beside it looked tired and lonely. The overgrown lawn was almost a foot high, and the flower garden around the porch had more weeds than flowers.

She turned and looked at her boarding house. From a distance it appeared well maintained, but the white paint around the windows peeled, and the railing on the porch steps leaned outward, as though trying to get away.

Flossie sighed. "At least the lace curtains look nice," she said to the squirrel busy burying an acorn in the lawn. It scampered away as she bustled towards the front door.

CHAPTER TWO

Kendall paid the driver, picked up his bag, and made his way up the short walk to the porch.

"Olivia, I'm home. Olivia?"

He noticed the inside door ajar. Seeing his next door neighbour sweeping her porch, he called over, "Mrs. Green, have you seen Olivia this morning? I thought for sure she'd be here to meet me when I arrived."

"No, Mr. Nolan. I haven't seen her since yesterday. She went across to Miss O'Hara's at dinner time, and I haven't seen her since. Maybe she stayed overnight."

"Thank you. I'll go over shortly and check."

As he reached for the handle on the screen door he turned and looked toward the boarding house. Someone watched him from behind the front curtain. He waved, but the drape quickly closed.

Opening the door, he took a few steps in and dropped his bag on the floor beside the umbrella stand. Kendall removed his suit jacket as he went into the drawing room.

He stopped. The jacket dropped to the floor.

"Oh dear God. Olivia? Olivia?"

The sofa lay on its side, and some of Ruth's delicate figurines were scattered in pieces across the floor. He remembered the local girl who had been arrested for theft *I've been burgled.*

He backed out and hurried to the dining room to check if the silver was still there. Again, his eyes were drawn to the overturned chairs, then to the walls splattered with red spots and streaks. One small, bare foot stuck out from beneath a chair.

"Olivia!"

He ran to where she lay on the floor, throwing the chair off her limp body.

"No! Not my little angel."

He dropped to his knees beside her. Cradling her head in his lap, he called her name over and over.

His white linen suit soaked up his daughter's blood. The deep crimson formed a halo around his 'little angel's' head.

"Olivia. My dear God. Olivia."

Kendall gently touched her cheek. She was no longer warm and soft. He jerked his hand away in shock, her beautiful porcelain skin now cold and sallow.

"Mr. Nolan? Is everything all right?"

Kendall's voice had carried through the house. Alice Green could hear his frantic calls as she hurried across the

9

lawn to his porch.

"Mr. Nolan?"

She opened the screen door and stepped in, following his voice. When she reached the dining room, she stopped.

Backing away from the entry, she turned and ran.

"Help, help. Oh Lord. Someone please help."

Several neighbours came out to the street to see what the commotion was. Alice's husband, Sam, turned the corner from George Street, heading home for lunch as he did every work day.

"Sam! Find the constable," she yelled. "Quick. Something bad has happened to Olivia."

Her body shook as she wrung her hands, trying to comprehend the horrific scene in the Nolan house. Without waiting to find out what exactly was wrong, Sam ran back the way he'd come.

Constable Barnes was making his rounds. Sam ran up to him and grabbed his arm.

"Constable, quickly. Something terrible has happened. Hurry, please. On Duchess Street."

Mrs. McGregor had come out of her house and ran over to Mrs. Green to try and calm her.

"Whatever is the matter Alice?" she asked. "Why did you send for the constable?"

Alice looked over at the Nolan house. "Oh Catharine,"

she sobbed. "Olivia... blood everywhere... Mr. Nolan... horrible, so horrible." Catharine put her arm around Alice, and guided her to the shade of the old oak that stood between the Green and Nolan properties.

Constable Barnes came running down the street, with Sam several feet behind. Barnes stopped beside the oak as Sam collapsed on the ground by Alice and Catherine, his face red, and his breathing laboured.

Alice pointed to the Nolan home. Barnes ran across the lawn, up the porch, and inside.

In less than a minute he came back out, blowing his whistle to alert the other policemen in the area. Barnes dashed around the side of the house, placed one hand on the wall for support, bent over and threw up. He pulled a hanky from his pocket, wiped his mouth and took a deep breath.

"Oh Lord, what monster did that?" he muttered. "Keep your head Henry," he told himself. "Look at the scene, not that poor innocent child."

He turned around to see if anyone noticed him vomiting and talking to himself. He straightened his uniform jacket and pushed his helmet into place before going back inside to the dining room.

"Mr. Nolan. There's nothing you can do for her. Please, you have to leave the house. We need to investigate so we

11

can figure out what happened."

"Miss O'Hara," Kendall whispered. "Miss O'Hara."

"What's that, Sir?" Barnes asked. "Who's Miss O'Hara?"

"Runs the boarding house... up the street," Kendall sputtered. "Supposed to stay... with Olivia... last night. Where is she?" He looked up at Constable Barnes. "Where is she?" he whispered. Kendall clutched his daughter tighter. "You don't think...?"

The constable glanced at Olivia's body. Barnes could taste the bile rising and burning in his throat. He turned away, pretending to look around the room.

The coppery smell was overpowering as his hyperosmia increased his sense of smell. He was glad of it around food, but it was not a condition that benefitted a police officer. His stomach settled and he turned back to Nolan.

"We have to leave now, Sir. Please. We'll check the rest of the house."

Barnes put his hand on Kendall's shoulder and Kendall reluctantly released his hold on Olivia. He gently laid her head on the hard wooden floor. Blood seeped into the crevices. A few drops fell from his shirt cuff when he grabbed the table to steady himself as he stood.

Barnes swallowed hard and took another deep breath as he led Kendall out to the porch. When Alice saw Kendall's blood-stained suit, she fainted. Sam barely had time to grab her before her oversized frame hit the ground. Catharine removed her apron and fanned her friend's face.

Two officers finally arrived in response to Barnes' earlier whistle blows. He waved them over.

"Smith, hurry up to the station and fetch Detective Hodgins." Barnes turned to the other constable and pointed to the crowd that was gathering. "Keep those people away from the house. Stand guard at the porch. I don't want anyone going in and disturbing things."

Once Barnes was satisfied the house was secure he went over to Mrs. McGregor.

"Could you take Mr. Nolan over to your house? He's in shock and shouldn't be left alone. I'll send for a doctor to check on him as soon as I can."

Catharine bellowed at her husband, "Put the kettle on Franklin! Make yourself useful. Poor man needs a cuppa tea."

She led Kendall to a chair on her front porch, then hurried into the house. She returned a moment later with an old blanket and a cup of hot tea. "Added a wee dram to it. For medicinal purposes," she told Kendall as she placed the blanket around his shoulders. Satisfied he was comfortable, she sat in the chair beside him to watch the goings on. Reaching into her apron pocket, she pulled out a small bottle, took a swig, and leaned forward, straining to hear what the constable was asking Alice Green.

Barnes pulled his notebook out of his pocket and leaned against the old oak tree.

"Could I have your name please?"

"Mrs. Green. Alice," she whispered as she leaned against her husband.

"Mrs. Green, can you tell me what happened?"

She stared at the Nolan house. "Yelling."

"Who was yelling, ma'am?"

"Horrible. Blood everywhere."

"Who was yelling Mrs. Green? Was it the girl?"

Mrs. Green continued to stare at the house, now wringing her skirts.

"Mrs. Green?" Barnes reached out and touched her arm. She jumped.

"Mrs. Green, you said you heard yelling. Was it the girl?

"No. Him. *Olivia, Olivia*. Said her name over and over."

Alice's husband Sam had heard enough

"No more questions Constable. Can't you see my wife is in no condition to continue?" He helped her up off the grass and took her into the house.

Barnes turned the page of his notebook and started to interview the residents who had come out of their homes.

Until they had heard Alice screaming, no one knew

anything was wrong. Barnes turned towards the boarding house to inquire about Miss O'Hara when he saw Detective Hodgins run around the corner.

"Detective, thank God you're here." Barnes told Hodgins what had happened and led him into the house. The constable hesitated just inside the front door and pointed down the hall to the dining room.

"She's in there, Sir. It's pretty gruesome."

Hodgins took in the surroundings as Barnes spoke.

"Bloody walls? Must have been quite the fight. Amazing how much blood we have inside our bodies. Often looks like more than it actually is."

He turned and noticed how pale Barnes had become.

"Unfortunately you'll get use to it. Well, maybe not used to it, but you'll learn to cope. Only way to get things done."

He pulled out his weathered notebook, identical to the one the Constable had started using, and made a few notes.

"It looks like it may have started in the drawing room," Hodgins said. He walked down the hall, with Barnes following close behind. "Nothing is disturbed here by the door, but things have been broken in there. She must have run down that side of the hall. See there? The portrait on the wall is crooked, yet nothing on the opposite side of the hall is out of place." Barnes walked past the Detective and Hodgins reached out and grabbed Barnes by the arm.

"Watch where you step Constable. There's bloody footprints leading out the door. Could belong to the killer."

"No, Sir," Barnes said. "The hall was clean when I came in. I believe they belong to Mr. Nolan. He was cradling his daughter's body and soaked up a considerable amount of her blood."

"Just where is Nolan?"

"I asked one of the neighbours to watch him. They're on the front porch two over. He's pretty shaken up, as you can well imagine."

"Afternoon gentlemen," a voice said behind them.

They turned as Dr. McKenzie entered through the front door. "I've been told there's a body here."

"In here." Barnes took a calming breath and lead McKenzie inside the dining room.

McKenzie knelt beside Olivia and reached to start his examination.

"One moment Doctor," Hodgins said. "Constable, is this how you found the room? Has anything been touched or moved?"

"Mr. Nolan moved his daughter when he took her in his arms. I don't know if he moved anything else. Nothing has been disturbed since I arrived."

Hodgins made a quick sketch of the room, then allowed McKenzie to proceed.

"Such a pretty little thing," McKenzie said. "Why would anyone want to harm this wee lassie?"

"That's what I plan on finding out," Hodgins replied.

CHAPTER THREE

Hodgins waved his hand, motioning Barnes to follow him into the front hall.

"There's muddy footprints everywhere. I suppose they're courtesy of you as well?"

"No, Sir." Barnes placed his foot beside one of the muddy prints. "Bit smaller small than mine. And I do believe everyone else who came in is bigger than me, 'cept Mrs. Green, but I don't believe she tracked any mud in with her." He looked sheepish and half smiled. "Guess I was thinkin' about the girl and didn't notice them."

"What else do you see?"

Barnes looked around. "Well, as you said, there's mud everywhere."

"Mud and dirt. It's partly dried up so it was left awhile ago."

"Maybe by the guy what killed that poor child," Barnes exclaimed. He looked around again. "The stairs. There's more on the stairs." He walked to the foot of the staircase and pointed up. "They go all the way to the top."

Hodgins started up the staircase, keeping close to the wall, careful not to disturb the crime scene. Barnes followed, mimicking Hodgins' actions. Some of the steps had a print, others just globs of semi-dry mud. About half way up Hodgins stopped and knelt down.

"Look here. The prints only go down. They're far too large to belong to the child. Besides, how would her feet get muddy?" Hodgins cocked his head. "How did someone get upstairs during a rain storm without leaving prints?"

He stood and continued to the top. The prints were spaced farther apart than normal. "Looks like he was running. Probably chasing the girl."

"Olivia," Barnes whispered.

"What was that?"

"Olivia. The girl's name is Olivia."

Hodgins turned to face Barnes. The young constable still seemed pale despite the deep tan covering his face.

"You all right lad?"

"She's so young. Same age as my sister. Don't seem fair."

Hodgins sighed. "No, it's not fair. That's why we're here. To make sure someone pays for what they did to the girl. To *Olivia*."

They followed the mud down the narrow hall and into one of the bedrooms.

"Olivia's room," Barnes said peeking around Hodgins.

Hodgins nodded in agreement.

A single shelf on the far wall was lined with dolls of various sizes, with a ratty looking stuffed cat sitting in the centre. None were the same quality as the ones his mother-in-law had purchased for his daughter Sara, but most were well cared for.

One of the dolls had a crack running from the corner of her eye all the way down to her chin, and her once rosy-red cheeks were barely noticeable. Another was missing a shoe. A picture of Olivia's bare foot splattered with blood crossed through his mind. He concentrated on the task at hand and pushed the image to the side.

He focused on the room. The bed sheets and matching curtains were a faded pink. The dressing table had one bottle of lilac toilet-water, a couple of small silver hair combs, a hand mirror, and matching brush, all arranged neatly on a piece of frosted glass. A fan was spread open on one side of it, ribbons of all colours sat on the other side. The room was part child, part young woman.

Barnes tapped Hodgins' shoulder and said, "The window."

Hodgins turned his head and noticed the curtains fluttering. "It's open." He glanced down at the floor below the window. "More mud. He must have come in through this window. Did anyone check out back?"

"Don't know. No one said, so I guess not." Barnes paused a moment. "I'll go 'round back."

Hodgins listened to Barnes' boots echo off the wooden floor as he went down the empty hall and staircase, followed by a door slam.

The detective walked to the window, drew back the curtains and stuck his head out, watching for Barnes to come around the corner of the house. A ladder rested on the ground not far from the back wall of the house.

"Down there," Hodgins yelled, pointing to the ground below the window. "Anything?

Barnes walked back and forth, stepping over the ladder. The grass went right up to the back wall. There were a few depressions where someone might have stood, but no foot prints.

"Looks like the ladder was up against the house," Barnes hollered up. "There are two holes where it was set." He looked at the ladder. "Holes are about the right distance apart. It probably fell when he climbed inside."

"Stay put. I'm coming down."

Hodgins pulled his head in and took another look around the room. The crumpled sheets, half on the floor, spoke to him. She must have fled down the stairs and tried to hid in the drawing room, killer running after her. There was no blood in the room, so she probably heard him when the ladder hit the sill or when he opened the window. Going back down, he took another look at the crooked pictures on the wall, half way down the hall. The remaining pictures were still straight. *Probably caught up with her here.*

Hodgins hesitated at the bottom of the stairs. Dr. McKenzie and one of the constables were preparing Olivia's body for transport to the morgue. The young girl's body had been placed on a stretcher. Hodgins watched as Dr. McKenzie unfolded a clean white sheet. The constable took one end and they laid it over her still frame. The sheet flapped out like the wings of an angel, preparing to take Olivia to Heaven.

Hodgins wanted to speak with McKenzie, but decided it could wait. Instead he went out the front door, around the house, and joined Barnes in the back yard.

"Whoever did this came prepared," Hodgins surmised. "Either he brought the ladder with him or knew where to find one. Maybe one of the neighbours knows if the ladder belongs to Nolan. Can't imagine the bloke carried a ladder that size around un-noticed. It's not likely anyone was out in that storm, and it was extra dark with the thick cloud cover. I doubt anyone would have seen much. A herd of elephants could have stood in the yard and no one would have seen them."

"The killer could have come over from that empty house there, or up the laneway," Barnes said.

Hodgins smiled. "You're getting to be quite observant, lad. Might as well check the laneway. Who knows, we may get lucky and find something useful."

They walked over to the gap in the fence that separated the lane from Nolan's yard.

"Wonder how long that's been there?" Barnes asked.

Hodgins opened his notebook and jotted a few words. "Another question for Nolan."

He squeezed through the fence, and leaned against it to give Barnes some room.

"Watch out --"

"Ewwww."

". . . for the mud," Hodgins finished.

The dirt laneway had become a river of brown sludge. It sloped slightly so much of the rain ran down from the road. It was anything but dry.

"Don't know about you, but I don't think I want to check the lane today," Hodgins said.

"Won't get no argument from me, Sir." Barnes tried to retreat, but the four inch thick mud had a stranglehold on the constable's boots.

Hodgins laughed and held out his arm. "Grab hold and I'll pull."

Barnes twisted his body and reached back. They grabbed each other just below the elbow and Hodgins tugged. On the fourth pull one foot was released with a loud squelch.

Once Barnes had one foot on solid ground by the fence, his other foot followed with only a little resistance. He went through the fence back into the yard, Hodgins close behind, still chuckling.

"Can't have one of our constables looking like that," Hodgins said. "Better trot off home and put on a clean pair of trousers. And clean the muck off your boots. I'll see if McKenzie has finished up. Meet me back at the station. Get going now. Sharpish."

CHAPTER FOUR

Friday morning Detective Hodgins sat re-reading the notes Barnes had given him. He tossed them down on the desk and walked to his office door. Looking around the station house he spotted the constable coming from the back room, chatting with one of the men.

"Barnes!" he hollered.

Constable Barnes didn't need to turn around to know who wanted him. The officer he was with snickered.

"Whatcha mess up now, Henry?" he asked. Barnes shrugged and hustled over to the waiting detective.

"Yes, Sir?"

Hodgins motioned to the chair in front of his desk. "Don't look so worried. I just want to go over your notes."

Barnes sat down and a sigh of relief escaped his mouth.

Hodgins smiled and sat on the edge of his desk. He reached back and picked up the notes on Olivia Nolan.

"Your note taking is impressive. Much improved since the Walker case.

Barnes' face turned a deep crimson. "I've been trying

real hard, Sir. And it's never happened again," he stammered.

"Relax, Constable. You're not in trouble. I'm just saying you've come a long way, and in such a short time." He shook his head; the smile quickly fell from his face. "It's unbelievable someone could do that to an innocent child. I feel for her father. My Sara is several years younger, and I can't image finding her like that. It's too horrible to even think about."

He picked up a small silver frame that held a cabinet-card photograph of his wife and daughter. Hodgins moved around his desk and put the frame back in place before dropping into his chair. "I've got the coroner's report. McKenzie was his usual thorough self." He opened a folder and picked up a sheet of paper. "Seems the girl was beaten about the head. There were bits of wood in her hair and skin. That bastard even cut her throat." His voice wavered.

Hodgins hesitated for a moment. "She had bruises on her arms. Legs too. I suspect he tried to have his way with her. Fortunately McKenzie says the girl was not interfered with." He put the paper back inside the folder and slammed it down on his desk.

Neither man spoke for several minutes.

"We'll find him, Sir," Barnes said. "Someone must've heard something. With all the overturned furniture and broken figurines, he must've made quite some noise."

Hodgins nodded. "Yes, I'm sure she likely screamed too. It's summer, and it's been hotter than blazes. People may have had their windows open even a tiny bit during the rain, just for the breeze. I find it hard to believe none of the neighbours heard a sound. The thunder wasn't constant. We'll have to talk to them again. See if they've remembered anything now they've had time to mull the events of the evening over. Grab your notebook."

* * *

The men stood in front of the Nolan home. "Where is Mr. Nolan staying?" Hodgins asked.

"Two doors over, with the McGregor's," Barnes said.

Hodgins looked at the puddles scattered around the road. "Sure has been a lot of rain these past few days. Looks like we caught a break with the weather today. Maybe the sun will put these people in a better mood."

He took in the layout of the neighbouring houses. "She was killed on the thirteenth, Monday night, or possibly very early Tuesday morning. The houses aren't that far apart. Why didn't someone hear her?" He shook his head in disbelief. "Has the lady who stayed with Miss Nolan said anything yet?"

Barnes flipped through his notebook. "Miss O'Hara. She was supposed to have stayed with Olivia while Mr.

Nolan was away. Constable Smith went over to her boarding house yesterday, but she wouldn't tell him anything. She won't give a statement. Won't talk about it to anyone."

"We'll see about that. I'll pay her a visit while you see if the neighbours have any more information."

Hodgins crossed the road and walked toward the boarding house. He spotted a woman out back as he approached. He reached over the gate in the picket fence, lifted the latch and stopped short.

The gate wouldn't budge.

He rattled it a few times then gave it a good swift kick. It swung open, but didn't hang straight. The bottom hinge had come off. Hodgins looked around to see if anyone witnessed him damage it.

The street was empty.

Feeling guilty, he made a mental note to have one of the lads repair it. He left it open and went around the house to the back garden. "Miss O'Hara?"

The woman dropped her basket of vegetables and turned. "Gracious, you gave me a start."

Hodgins smiled when she turned. She bore a slight resemblance to his wife. Same Irish complexion and red hair. Miss O'Hara was several years younger though. "Sorry ma'am. I'm Detective Hodgins. I need to speak with you about Miss Nolan."

"Miss Nolan? Olivia? I didn't see a thing. I'm afraid there's nothing I can tell you. Now if you'll excuse me, I'm terribly busy." Flossie reached down, righted the basket and picked up the beets and carrots that had tumbled out.

"I must insist Miss O'Hara. We speak now or down at the station."

Flossie's shoulders dropped and she let out a tiny sigh. She pointed at a wooden bench under a thirty foot Maple.

"We can sit over there. I don't want my guests disturbed."

Hodgins nodded and moved towards the bench. Flossie left the basket on the ground and followed. Hodgins waited until she was settled before he sat. He removed his hat, placed it on the bench between them, and pulled his notebook and pencil out of his pocket.

"According to Mr. Nolan, you stayed overnight in the house with his daughter. Several things had been broken, the furniture was overturned, and an obvious struggle had taken place. I find it difficult to believe you heard nothing."

Flossie reached down beside the bench and pinched a dead flower from a Cleome.

"Miss O'Hara? Why didn't you get help?"

She mumbled something that Hodgins couldn't quite hear. "You'll have to speak up."

"I said I wasn't there." She dropped her head to her hands and cried. "Lord forgive me, I wasn't there." She pulled a lace handkerchief from her sleeve and patted her eyes.

Hodgins made a few notes, then asked, "Why weren't you there? Start from the beginning. Take your time." He sat with his pencil poised, waiting.

CHAPTER FIVE

Barnes watched Hodgins disappear behind the boarding house, then looked around at the surrounding houses, trying to decide where to go first. Empty house to the west of Nolan's, the Green's house to the east beside the mud-filled lane. Mrs. Green had found Kendall cradling Olivia's body, and had become hysterical when he tried to interview her that day. Mr. Green was none too pleased with him. They could wait.

Next was the McGregor home. Kendall Nolan was staying there until the police permitted him return to his own home. *Nope, don't want to disturb him just yet.* He turned back to the empty house. *Good place to hide.* Decision made, he cut across the grass and circled the house, looking for a way in.

The ground was wet and muddy from the intermittent storms and rain over the previous three days. The tall grass and weeds slapped against Barnes' trousers, quickly soaking him to the skin. He reached down and tried to pull the wet cloth away from his legs. As he twisted to reach the back of his pants leg, he noticed several muddy footprints leading to and from the Nolan yard.

Pulling his notebook out he tried to sketch the prints just the way Hodgins always did. Barnes didn't understand why the detective insisted on sketching out everything. They made copious notes on every case, but that was never enough for Hodgins. Knowing that Hodgins would want to check this himself, he ran up the street to the boarding house. He paused at the broken gate then continued around back, stopping at the edge of the garden.

"Pardon, Sir. Sorry to interrupt, but I've found something you'll want to see."

Hodgins closed his notebook. "That's all right Barnes. I'm done here, for now." He reached for his hat as he stood. "I'll have more questions later," he said to Flossie. He tipped his hat and left with Barnes. As they passed though the gate, Hodgins asked Barnes to find someone to repair it.

"Don't ask," was the only reply to Barnes' puzzled look.

"Over there, Sir. Footprints. Could be from the killer."

Hodgins followed him through the path Barnes had made in the wet, trampled grass. As they made their way around to the back, Hodgins surveyed the grounds. He didn't notice when the young constable stopped.

"Yee-ouch," Barnes screamed as the detective's foot connected with his heel.

"What the blazes?"

"Sorry, Sir. The prints are right here. Didn't want to wreck them."

"Hmm. Right. Good thinking."

Hodgins looked at the Nolan house, then at the vacant one. He motioned towards the empty house. "May as well see where the prints came from."

He walked parallel to the footprints, with Barnes close behind, and stopped at the back porch steps, where the prints seemed to vanish.

"What now, Sir?" Barnes asked. "There aren't any more prints. Bugger could have come from any direction."

Hodgins shook his head. "Look closer, Constable." He pointed to the top of the steps. "The porch."

Barnes took a few steps forward and examined the area around the top of the steps. Shrugging his shoulders he said, "Nothing but a few swirls of mud."

Hodgins sighed. "Haven't you learned anything man? Notice the porch has sunk a little on the west side. You can see where the rain has been flowing across and off the west end of the porch. The swirls of mud are quite likely muddy footprints that were partially washed away by the running water. The rain would have cleaned any marks off the steps. I think he was hiding inside."

"Very smart, Sir. I see what you mean. I guess we need

to obtain a search warrant then."

"Possibly. Find the owner. If he gives consent, then we don't need one." Barnes stood beside Hodgins, looking around. "Well, get on it, Constable. Haven't got all day."

Barnes nodded once, then headed off to search the records for the owner, while Hodgins walked up the steps of the house. He spotted a window at the east end of the porch and made his way down to it, stepping over a small branch that had come off a nearby tree. Some of the nails from the bottom board had come out and the window was partially exposed. He bent over to peer in, but with all the windows boarded up, no light was getting in except for a tiny sliver where the board had shifted. He could make out vague shapes, and thought it might be the kitchen, but wasn't really sure.

"Blast." He slammed his fist on the window sill, causing the un-nailed end of the board to slip a little more. He was tempted to pull the board the rest of the way off, but thought better of it. Didn't want anyone in the neighbourhood seeing him try to break in. He stormed off the porch, slipping on the bottom step.

"Damn."

He landed in the mud, and slipped again when he tried to stand.

"Damn, damn, damn."

He managed to get back on his feet, and looked around to see if anyone witnessed his undignified descent.

Hodgins tried brushing off the thick, smelly mud, but just made it worse. He knew he couldn't examine the Nolan house or interview the neighbours looking as he did. With as much dignity as he could muster, he hurried home to change.

* * *

Hodgins went in the back door to avoid tracking mud through the house He was glad he had saved enough money to purchase a house of his own, he just wished it wasn't so close to his in-laws. A house in the country would have been ideal. *Maybe when I retire.* He could almost hear his mother-in-law scolding him for tracking mud into the house. His wife, Cordelia, was so much more easy going than her mother.

The door barely had time to close when he heard the clicking of nails on the hardwood floor. A dog raced across the kitchen and jumped up, placing two hairy brown paws on Hodgins' chest, it's weight causing him to take a step back.

The dog had grown considerably since bringing it home six months earlier as a present for his daughter's ninth birthday. It had transformed from a dirty, scrawny, timid mutt into a healthy, sturdy, extremely affectionate dog.

Hardly looks like the same creature that hung around the station house. His hands automatically reached out and scratched behind Scraps' ears for a moment.

One of the sergeants had named the dog Scraps since that was what it had been eating for most of the first two years of its life. A lot of those scraps were courtesy of the men of the Toronto Constabulary, himself included.

Hodgins smiled as he remembered his stay in the hospital after the train explosion earlier in the year. Barnes had been speechless at his request to catch the dog, clean it up, and have Dr. McKenzie give it check up. His daughter and the dog had become inseparable ever since.

"Why are you home so early Papa?"

Startled by his daughter's sudden appearance, Hodgins pushed the dog away. Sara giggled when she saw his mud-covered suit. He glared at her, then smiled. He looked down at his clothing and started laughing too.

"I guess I do look quite the sight."

He removed his shoes and socks, placed them on the bumper of the pot belly stove, and walked across the kitchen. As he passed Sara, he ran a finger across his jacket and gently placed a drop of mud on the tip of her nose.

"Are you feeling better? Your colour seems much improved. How's your throat?"

"Yes, Papa. Much better. Mama called the doctor this

morning. He gave me some medicine. It tasted just awful, but it made my throat all better. Mama said I can go swimming in a few days."

He ruffled her hair. "As long as the doctor agrees."

Hodgins went up to his room, walked over to the dry sink, and poured water from the pitcher into the bowl. He removed his jacket, shirt and trousers then draped them over the arm of a small wooden chair. Cordelia came in while he was wetting the face cloth. She watched while he cleaned up, put on a fresh shirt and suit and ran a brush through his hair.

Cordelia looked from the dirty suit to her husband. "What have you been up to now?" she asked.

"Had a disagreement with a muddy step." He looked over at his soiled suit. "I don't think there was any damage, but maybe you can check it over. Might have caught it on something."

Cordelia walked over to the suit for a closer look. "I think I'll wait for it to dry before cleaning it. I'll examine it when I brush off the dried dirt. Do you have to go back to the station? It is rather late in the afternoon."

"Yes, I'm afraid so. I've sent Barnes out for information and I'd like to know what he finds. I'm sure I won't be long. I'll tell you all about it over supper."

He applied a small amount of wax to reshape his

moustache, then went back downstairs with Cordelia. They found Sara sitting cross-legged on the kitchen floor, wiping the last of the mud from his shoes, Scraps lay curled up beside her.

He knelt down, kissed her cheek, put his shoes on, kissed his wife and then headed back to Station Number Four.

CHAPTER SIX

Hodgins entered the station and immediately wished he could go back out. All the windows were open, but the stench of sweat hung in the air. He fought back the urge to leave and looked around for his constable.

"Barnes not around?" he asked no one in particular.

"Ain't seem 'im," replied someone behind him.

Recognizing the gruff voice of the desk Sergeant, Hodgins turned and addressed him. "Has he come in at all?"

The Sergeant shook his head. "Ain't seen him since he left with you earlier."

"Must still be looking for the owner of the vacant house," he mumbled. Turning, he walked into his office. As he sat down the station door closed with a bang.

All heads turned.

Barnes rushed across the room. Beads of sweat spotted his forehead. He stopped at Hodgins' office and leaned on the door frame, huffing and puffing from rushing in the heat.

Hodgins motioned to the chair in front of his desk and

Barnes dropped into the seat.

"Might I be so bold as to remove my helmet, Sir?" Barnes asked.

Hodgins waved his hand, dismissing protocol. "By all means. What's got you all worked up? It's too blasted hot to be rushing around."

Barnes unfastened the chin strap, removed the helmet and placed it at the edge of Hodgins' desk. He removed a hanky from his pocket and wiped his face before speaking. The clean white hanky was quickly covered in dirt and grit from the roads, a few streaks still remaining on the constables' slightly sun-burned face.

"Sir, I discovered who owns the vacant house. You won't believe it." Barnes took a few deep breaths. "William Howland."

Hodgins tilted his head slightly. "Howland? That name sounds familiar."

"He's the new President of the Board of Trade, Sir. Purchased the house..." Barnes pulled his notebook out and flipped the pages. "Here it is. He bought it just a few months ago." He looked up at Hodgins. "Shall I make inquires with him?"

Hodgins shook his head. "No, I think I'll take care of that personally."

Barnes looked relieved. "Very good, Sir. To tell the

truth, I'm not very comfortable talking to officials."

Hodgins smiled. "You'll get used to it eventually. Give it time. You've only been an officer for a short while. Board of Trade, eh? Wonder what he wants with a house in St. David's Ward? Not a district filled with the wealthy and connected."

"Maybe he plans to rent it. An investment like."

"Possibly. I seem to recall reading an article about him. I believe he wants to clean up the slums in the city. Could be he plans to take that challenge personally and purchased a house in a neighbourhood that's starting to get run down. Stop it in its tracks, so to speak."

Hodgins pulled out his pocket watch. "I think it best to leave the inquires until tomorrow, it's getting late and I don't want to interrupt his dinner. Write up a report on what you found and leave it on my desk. Speaking of dinner, I believe I'll head home and see what's waiting for me."

Both men rose from their chairs; Barnes headed towards his small table, Hodgins towards the front door.

"Oh Barnes," Hodgins said without stopping or turning around, "You might want to wipe the rest of the city off your face."

* * *

Hodgins stepped off the trolley car a few blocks from his house. The short walk before having his evening meal helped erase all thoughts of the day's crime.

Most of the houses he passed had beautiful gardens under the front windows. The fragrances along the way relaxed him and put him in a good mood by the time he walked through his front door.

His front door.

He enjoyed saying that after living with his in-laws for ten long years, but it had allowed him to put most of his paycheques into his savings account nonetheless.

Unfortunately they still weren't completely free of her parents. Even though he gave Cordelia an allowance for clothing and other women's things, her mother doted on her as though she was still a young, unmarried girl. She was twice as bad with Sara. While it was nice that his wife and daughter were dressed in the most fashionable clothing, it still put a dent in his pride.

He stopped on the sidewalk outside his house and smiled. They had only been there for a few weeks, but it felt like home. His smile faded as he looked at the property. The house had been vacant only a few months, but it was long enough that the lawn and gardens had suffered. He had a Saturday off soon, and planned on helping Cordelia as much as he could.

She had been busy buying up fabrics and sewing curtains, but most of the rooms remained sparsely furnished. Her parents insisted they take the bedroom sets with them, and he really didn't mind. They were quite nice and very well crafted.

They got a second hand table set for the kitchen, another for the dining room, along with a few other bits of furnishings from an acquaintance who was clearing out the house of his recently deceased, widowed mother. All very good quality and kept in immaculate condition.

All thoughts of his current case completely vanished and he let out a sigh of satisfaction before going inside. His movements echoed in the empty hallway, alerting the dog. Scraps came racing down the hall, nails clicking on the wooden floor. The dog tried to stop, but slid into Hodgins, knocking him off balance. He hit the floor with a thud, and Scraps pounced on top, trying to lick Hodgins' face.

He was used to Sara running to greet him, but he hadn't managed to figure out how to get inside without being bowled over by the new addition to the family. Both Cordelia and Sara came out of the kitchen to see what had happened. Sara started to giggle, then Delia. Hodgins stopped trying to push the dog away and scratched behind Scraps' ears instead.

"I hope a hall runner is on your list of purchases. The *top* of the list," he said to his wife. The dog had settled down enough for Hodgins to push him off and get up. "Just look at the scratches on the floor. Guess I'll have to add that to *my* list."

CHAPTER SEVEN

The next morning Hodgins walked past Nolan's house and paused at the laneway running past the east side of the house. He took a few steps in and stopped. The lane was still muddy from the storm.

Not wanting to soil his trousers or get stuck like Barnes had, he stepped back and continued to the McGregor house. A shutter stuck out from under a hydrangea bush and a pile of twigs and small branches lay beside the front porch. He stopped to survey the neighbourhood.

There was more damage then he remembered. He figured the distraction of the murder was to blame for his lack of attention; he normally took in everything surrounding a crime scene. Several of the houses had debris on their front lawns. A large branch leaned against the porch roof a few house over.

He started up the walk to the McGregor's front porch when a gust of wind raced through the branches of the Oak. A branch that had been broken during the storm came free and bounced off Hodgins' shoulder, landing on the walk in front of him. Without missing a step, he scooped it up and deposited it on the debris pile McGregor had started, then climbed the porch steps.

As he raised his hand to knock, the front door opened. Mr. Nolan rushed out and plowed into him.

Hodgins grabbed the railing to avoid falling.

Nolan dropped the satchel he was carrying. It popped open and a few shirts tumbled out. Nolan's hair stuck out in all directions and his suit was covered in wrinkles. Hodgins guessed he had slept in it.

Taking a closer look at Nolan's face, he noticed his eyes were red and puffy. *Maybe he hadn't really slept at all.*

"You can't go back to your home. Not just yet." Hodgins said.

Nolan shook his head. "Not going home. I'm leaving town for a few days. Need to clear my head." He knelt down to stuff the shirts back into the satchel.

"Relatives?"

"Friend."

"I still have several questions for you that need to be answered."

Nolan pointed up the street. "My carriage is here. Have to catch the train."

"Where will you be staying? What's your friend's name?"

"You can send a message care of the post office in Woodbridge." He stood and rushed to the curb, leaving Hodgins standing on the porch.

"Wot ya be wanting now?"

Hodgins jumped at the sound of the brusque voice behind him. Mr. McGregor stood in the doorway of his house. His thick accent suggesting he hadn't left Scotland that many years ago.

"Isnae a goot time ta be botherin' folk."

"I just needed to speak with Mr. Nolan, but it seems I'm too late. I may need to speak with you later." Hodgins tipped his hat and walked down the steps. The door slammed shut behind him.

He cut across the lawn and went next door to the Green's. Their property seemed untouched by the storm. *Maybe they just cleaned up quicker than McGregor.* It wasn't the best neighbourhood, but it wasn't the poorest either. Hodgins couldn't image leaving a shutter off his house. Lazy sot couldn't even be bothered to remove it from the front garden.

Hodgins knocked on the Green's front door. The scent of freshly baked peach pies wafted through the open windows. He didn't have long to wait before Mrs. Green appeared.

"Yes? What can I do for you?" She spoke softly and it

looked as though she had been crying.

"I'm Detective Hodgins. I have a few questions regarding the death of Miss Nolan."

Mrs. Green reached into her apron pocket and removed a lacy hanky. She waved in front of her face a few times then started sobbing before burying her face in it.

"Oh, that poor child. Never seen such a thing in all my days." She wiped her eyes then began to wail.

Hodgins recalled reading about her in Barnes' report. He had thought Barnes was exaggerating, but clearly this was a very emotional and highly strung woman. Mr. Green came barrelling down the hall.

"What have you done to my wife? Be off with you." He put his arm around her shoulder and started to close the door.

"Wait," Hodgins said. He put his hand out to stop the door. "I have a few questions about the murder next door."

Mrs. Green wailed even louder, which Hodgins had thought impossible. He showed his badge.

"Might I have a word with you? Only take a few minutes."

"Well, I guess I can spare a few minutes. Let me take care of my wife first." He shut the door, leaving Hodgins to wait on the porch.

He was glad the rain was over. The past few weeks were

the wettest Hodgins had seen for quite some time. A couple of days of heavy rain and strong winds followed by a few beautiful sunny days. The most recent rainfall had washed away the humidity. The sun was out and the air was fresh.

While he waited he looked over the garden running along the front of the house. It was immaculate. The steps were in the centre of the porch and the gardens on each side matched perfectly.

On either side of the steps was a well manicured deep red rose bush. Two more were at each corner of the house. Rows of gladiolus in all colours stood at the back of the garden against the house. When he first arrived he hadn't noticed that several of them were broken from the storm. Deep purple and yellow pansies filled the space between the front of the garden and the glads. He was curious to see the back garden, certain it was magnificent.

Mr. Green eventually opened the front door and stepped onto the porch, closing the door behind him.

"Forgive my rudeness. My wife has been quite upset. We all have. I've given her one of the tablets the doctor left. She should be asleep shortly."

"As I said, I just need a bit of information. There was a ladder laying in Nolan's back yard. Do you know if it belonged to him?"

"One ladder looks pretty much the same as another. I

know he had one. New last year. Number of the rungs on the old one were broken and rotting, so he replaced it."

Hodgins pictured the ladder as he made notes. The one in the yard wasn't very weathered, so it might be the new one.

"Don't suppose you know where he kept it?"

"I've seen him drag it out of the cellar once or twice. Now that you mention it, he did have it out the other day. Fixing some shutters before the storm. I remember looking out the window and laughing. He was still up on the ladder when the first bit of rain hit. He dang near fell off trying to hurry down. Left it up against the house."

Green blanched. "Is that how that monster got in? That's the first time I recall seeing Kendall be so careless. He must be beside himself."

Hodgins didn't answer. "Did you see anyone around the house Wednesday night?"

"No. The wife closed the drapes and I lit the lanterns. She did some knitting and I read the paper. The only sound was the rain pounding down on the roof and the wind howling. Didn't see or hear anything else. Lucky for me the storm didn't cause any damage here."

"Yes, I can see that. Only a few broken flowers." Hodgins pointed out the broken glads.

Green moved closer to the flower garden. "Oh, my

poor flowers. I didn't see them. Oh well, they'll do fine in a vase for a few days."

"One last question. Did Nolan leave his daughter at home often?"

"Yes. He travelled a fair bit — salesman. She wasn't alone though. His sister stayed with her after his wife, Ruth, passed."

"Sister? First I've heard about any sister. Do you know why she didn't stay this time?"

"She died about a month or so ago."

Hodgins made a few more notes before shoving his notebook into his jacket pocket. "Thank you for your time. I'll return in a few days when your wife has recovered from the shock."

As he left, he could hear Green muttering to himself as he tended his broken gladiolas.

CHAPTER EIGHT

Hodgins sat at his desk glancing at the clock every few minutes waiting for the Board of Trade to open. He knew from years of experience that interviewing businessmen and politicians was quite often unpleasant, unproductive, and frequently landed him in the Inspector's office. It had to be done though, unfortunately more often than he liked.

The hands of the clock finally approached nine. He'd heard Howland went to the Board office most days, so he was sure of a meeting as long as Hodgins was there when the office opened.

He walked to his office door and looked around the station house for Barnes. Several young constables were gathered together exchanging stories about the previous days arrests. They had some sort of competition going to see who had the strangest case.

"Barnes," Hodgins called. "Over here."

Barnes raced across the room, tripping over a chair along the way. "Sir?"

"How'd you like to accompany me to the Trade office to interview Howland? If we leave now we'll arrive as they're opening up."

Barnes' mouth opened and closed twice, but no words came out. He slowly shook his head.

"That wasn't a question, lad."

"Y-y-y-yes, Sir. I'll just grab my notebook."

"Don't look so scared. You were fine when you accompanied me to speak with Smythe and Flanagan last January. Both were businessmen."

"But Sir, that was just a small town. Mr. Howland is on the Board of Trade in Toronto. The president! He's much more important."

"Balderdash. He's just a man like you and me. I've heard he's quite pleasant. Nothing to be worried about. We're just going to ask him about the house, not arrest him."

The two men headed off to the Exchange Buildings at thirty-four Wellington Street East. Hodgins enjoyed the sunshine and walked briskly while whistling a snappy tune. Barnes lagged behind and frequently had to trot to catch up.

They headed down Parliament Street, taking several twists and turns down to King Street and towards St. James Cathedral.

"Magnificent building," Hodgins said to Barnes as he slowed to a stop opposite the main entrance. He pointed up at the tall tower.

"It's over three hundred feet tall you know."

"Yes, Sir. I've passed it often and spoken with the vicar several times. I know all about it. For example, did you know it's made from Ohio sandstone? Supposed to be the tallest in all Canada. Imagine that."

"Wouldn't surprise me," Hodgins replied. "Come along now. I want to speak with Howland before he gets too busy."

The Cathedral was only a few blocks from the Exchange Building on Wellington Street and they were at their destination in no time. The directory on the wall indicated Howland was on the second floor.

They went up the staircase and Hodgins admired the carving on the thick oak railing. He ran his fingers over it as he made his way up. Mr. Howland was getting ready to go to an appointment. Howland's office door was open and he'd overheard Hodgins speaking with his secretary.

"Let them in," he called out. "I can spare a few minutes."

Hodgins turned away from the secretary and walked into Howland's office. Barnes hesitated, but the glare from the pinch-nosed man sitting behind the small desk in the outer office made him scurry after the detective.

"A few questions Mr. Howland. Won't take long. I just

need to know about the house you purchased on Duchess Street."

"It's an investment. A rental property. Why are the police interested in it?"

"Did you read about the young girl who was murdered earlier in the week?"

Howland shook his head and shrugged. "Too busy to read the papers lately."

"Next door to your house. Footprints in the mud indicate the person responsible may have hidden inside the house. We'd like your permission to enter and have a look around."

"Certainly. By all means. The estate agent is still trying to rent it out." He scribbled a quick note on a piece of his personalized stationery. "Here, give this to him and he'll hand over a key. His name and address are included in the note." He gave the paper to Hodgins who passed it over to Barnes.

"You know, I've never even seen the house. I hope you don't believe I was involved?" He laughed nervously. "You don't need to mention my name, do you? Wouldn't look good, you know?" As an afterthought he added, "I must give the family my condolences. Can't image what they're going through."

Hodgins thanked him for his time and they made their

way back outside.

"I don't think he was involved, Sir."

"Why do you say that Barnes?"

Barnes scrunched his mouth and thought for a moment. "Well, he's a respectable business man, with a very important job." Barnes held up his hand. "I know what you're going to say. Respectable men have been known to commit crimes. It just don't feel right. Thinking of him as a murderer I mean. Nothing specific. I just believed it when he said he bought the house and was trying to rent it through an estate agent."

Hodgins nodded. "So you don't believe he ever set foot inside the vacant house?"

"No, Sir. I mean yes. I believe he never went inside. I don't think he's ever seen the house. Bought it sight-unseen. I'd like to speak with the estate agent though. His office is practically around the corner."

Hodgins put his hand on Barnes' shoulder and stopped walking. Barnes took one more step, then stopped.

"Sir?"

Hodgins smiled. "You're thinking it through. I believe Howland too, but I'd like to find out what the estate agent has to say. I'll let you take care of that while I check on a few other things. I'd like to find the lodgers that were at the boarding house that night. Also want to speak with Olivia's friends. See if they know anything. Maybe she mentioned someone she was afraid of. So far everything points to this not being random."

They walked up Church Street and parted company when they reached number twenty. Barnes went inside and Hodgins made his way back to forty-one Duchess Street to speak with Flossie again. A small sign nailed beside the door said *walk in*. He knocked and went inside.

"Hello? Miss O'Hara?"

"Just one minute."

Hodgins peeked into the room to his right. There were several chairs near the fireplace and a small table and two chairs in front of the window. A checkerboard sat on the table, the pieces set up, ready for a new game. The room was not filled with expensive furnishings, but everything looked clean and tidy. Miss O'Hara wasn't as nervous as she was when he interviewed her earlier.

She seemed to be a very pleasant woman, and rather attractive as well. Hodgins imagined she got quite a few repeat gentlemen boarders.

"Are you looking for a room?"

Hodgins turned around.

"Oh, Detective. What can I do for you? I told you everything the other day. I'm terribly upset that I shirked my responsibility and left Miss Nolan alone. Mr. Nolan trusted me. I let him down and Olivia paid for it. I can't even dare to show my face. Everyone must think me a terrible person." She sniffled and her eyes became moist.

"Perhaps you can be of assistance and help us find her killer. I'm hoping you can fill in a few blanks for me." He pulled out his notebook and searched for the pages he filled during their earlier interview.

He stopped and tapped his finger on one of the pages in his notebook. "Here it is. You said Olivia was spending that day with friends. Do you know their names?"

"I believe she mentioned Lucy and Betsy. Lucy Armstrong and Betsy Scott. I'm afraid I don't know where they live. She mentioned another girl but I don't remember her name."

"What about the people who were staying here that night? Are they still here?"

"No. Mr. Webster left Tuesday, but Mrs. Phillips is still here. She stays whenever she visits her daughter and grand-daughter. They have a tiny one-room flat so there's no room for her. They live only a few blocks away."

"Do you have an address for Mr. Webster? Where he lives? What he does?"

"I have his address in my files. He lives somewhere in Kingston. Sells musical instruments. Please, sit down and I'll fetch it." Flossie hurried down the hall and Hodgins walked over to the table in front of the window to enjoy the breeze.

She came back carrying a tray with two glasses of lemonade. "I thought you might enjoy something cool." She placed the tray on top of the checkerboard and took a piece of paper from her pocket.

"I've written down his address for you. He comes here every other Friday and goes back home the following Tuesday."

Hodgins took the paper, copied the address in his notebook, then folded it and tucked it between the pages. He put the book on the table and picked up one of the glasses. The lemonade wasn't too sweet, but it wasn't too tart either. He hadn't realized how hot and thirsty he was until he put the empty glass on the tray.

Flossie smiled. "I'm glad you enjoyed it. Would you like another?"

Embarrassed that he guzzled it down in one go, he quickly got up.

"No, thank you. It was delicious." He picked up his notebook and headed back to the station house.

CHAPTER NINE

Hodgins waited impatiently while one of the constables searched the City Directory. He drummed his fingers on his desk top and flipped through his notes without really reading them. He hoped that Olivia's friends knew something, anything, that would help locate the killer.

An hour later he had a list on his desk. There were only a handful of Scott's listed, but he had to turn the page over to see the full list of Armstrong's.

He counted – thirty four.

At least the constable had the sense to list the address and occupation of each one. He skimmed the short list first – something stood out.

The second name on the list had a familiar connection. Mr. J.G. Scott, barrister, and clerk on the Executive Council under Howland. Hodgins circled it. He wasn't sure if Olivia would have friends in such circles, considering where she lived. But did they always live there? *Another question for Nolan.*

If he didn't come back to Toronto soon, Hodgins knew he'd have to make use of the train schedule and go up to Woodbridge. He looked over the other Scotts. None lived in St. David's Ward, so he continued on to the Armstrong's.

About half way down the list he found James Armstrong, 162 Duchess St. He circled it. He had two possibilities, but he was hesitant about Mr. Scott. He decided to hold off checking on Scott and headed down to Duchess Street to find Lucy Armstrong. She would lead him to Betsy and confirm if it was the same Scott family. Hodgins hoped it wasn't the lawyer.

He glanced at the clock. Half past twelve. He decided to grab a quick bite from one of the street vendors down on Queen Street, then continue down to Duchess Street. The Armstrong's should be through with their meal by the time he arrived.

* * *

Hodgins walked across Queen while munching on a beef pie. He turned down George, then walked along Duchess looking for the Armstrong house and cursed himself when he realized he was at the wrong end. Olivia lived at number forty-one and Lucy was at one hundred sixty-two. He could have saved time if he had just stayed on Parliament. At least it gave him time to eat his pie.

He walked almost the entire length of Duchess before

finding the house, a single storey clap-board just before Parliament. Hopefully Lucy was at home and not out with friends. If she was anything like his daughter, she'd be at the pond cooling off.

He knocked and waited. He could hear raised voices, then someone came clomping towards the door. He was surprised when a woman appeared. He was certain it had been a large man walking down the hall. She was quite tall and somewhat overweight. There were bags under her eyes and he could hear children's screams coming from somewhere inside. She tucked some stray hairs into the loose bun on the back of her head and shifted the baby she held against her ample hip.

"Yes?" The word dragged out, revealing how tired she must be.

He showed his badge. "Do you have a daughter named Lucy?"

"Lord, what's that girl done now?"

"She's not in any trouble. I'd like to speak to her about Olivia."

She turned her head and yelled, "Lucy, there's a copper out here what wants to talk to ya 'bout Olivia." She closed the door and went back inside, leaving Hodgins standing on the step.

He could hear muffled yelling, followed by the sound

of a hand hitting flesh. A young girl opened the door. Her eyes were red and she was rubbing her cheek.

"Mama said you want to speak to me about Olivia?" she asked softly.

"Can you think of anyone who would've wanted to hurt Olivia?"

"No." Lucy sniffled and wiped her sleeve under her nose.

"Did she have a beau? Did any of the boys from school pester her?"

Lucy hesitated. "No. Nobody from school. Can I go now?" She turned and looked at the door. "Mama needs me to help."

Hodgins felt she was hiding something, but didn't want to push her. Not just yet. Clearly she was afraid. *Afraid of her mother, or someone else?* He needed to speak with her when she felt free to answer his questions.

"Just one more question, then you can go. Can you tell me where Betsy lives?"

"Somewhere on Shuter Street. Never bin there. Gotta go."

Lucy turned and ran back inside. He could hear more shouting as he walked away. Hodgins removed the folded list from his notebook and searched through the long list of Scotts, looking for an address on Shuter. He stumbled as he walked off the curb at Berkeley.

"Blast. John G. Scott. The man on Howland's council. And a barrister."

Hodgins didn't want to get on the wrong side of a barrister. At least he wouldn't likely be home this early. He turned on Sherbourne and walked up to Shuter, looking for number eighty-one as he made his way west.

He wondered how someone in Lucy's situation could have met and become friends with the daughter of a barrister. They lived in different wards and wouldn't have attended the same schools or social events. He doubted Lucy had ever attended a social event.

Hodgins watched the numbers decrease and saw eighty-seven as he approached Jarvis. *Not much farther.* Unlike Duchess Street, most of the homes along this section of Shuter were brick. *Definitely a higher class neighbourhood.*

He stopped in front of a yellow brick two-storey house. The house seemed rather plain. The front was completely flat. No porch or even a crown over the doorway. It's only feature was the tiny peak and window at the roofline. The house beside it on the corner was much grander. The extra floor on top gave it a finished look.

He glanced down the street and noticed the tall tower of St. Michael's Cathedral. *All in all a very nice neighbourhood.*

Not wanting to risk being there when Mr. Scott arrived,

Hodgins stopped putting off the visit to the lawyer's home and walked up to the door. His knock was answered by a middle-aged housekeeper.

Hodgins always kept a few cards in his pocket for just this sort of occasion and handed one to the housekeeper as an introduction. "I'd like to speak with Miss Betsy Scott."

She read the card and looked Hodgins up and down. Hodgins figured she was deciding whether or not to admit him.

"Wait here please."

Hodgins stepped inside before she could close the door in his face. She gave him a dirty look then slowly walked down the hall and into a room off to the right. It was much nicer inside.

The floor was polished to a shine, and the vase sitting on the side table looked quite expensive. There was a doorway on the other side of the table. He took a few steps in so he could get a look inside.

The fireplace looked like it might be marble. A large portrait of a man hung over the mantle. He suspected it was Mr. Scott as the gentleman was holding a law book. He heard the rustling of skirts and turned his attention down the hall. A very elegant, but stern looking woman approached. She stood straight and tall, yet seemed to float. Her shoes made no sound on the bare wooden floor. He guessed the jewels around her neck were genuine emeralds.

"I understand you wish to speak with my daughter. She's only a child. What could you want with her?"

Hodgins quickly removed his hat. "I'm investigating the death of her friend, Olivia Nolan. Is she home? It's very important."

Her face softened. "Olivia. Tragic. Betsy is too upset to see anyone."

"It's crucial that I speak with her as soon as possible. Every day wasted puts us farther away from finding the man who did it."

Mrs. Scott paused to consider the request. "Very well, but I insist I stay with her."

"Yes, of course. Thank you."

Mrs. Scott gestured to the room Hodgins had been looking at. "Wait in here."

Hodgins stepped in to wait for her to return with Betsy. He was immediately drawn to the large bookcase that practically covered the south wall. The shelves were filled with law books. He ran his fingers over the spines, remembering his year at Osgood Hall. If circumstances had been different, he might be living in a house like this. He heard voices in the hall and moved away from the books.

Mrs. Scott returned with her daughter. Betsy was very much like her mother. The same chestnut hair, perfect posture and skin like porcelain. No doubt there would be a long line of suitors soon.

Mrs. Scott and Betsy sat on the sofa. Betsy reached over and took her mother's hand for support.

"Please be seated," Mrs. Scott said.

"Hello Miss Scott. My name is Detective Hodgins. I'm trying to find out who harmed your friend. Would you mind answering a few questions?"

Betsy looked at her mother. Mrs. Scott nodded.

"How long have you been friends with Miss Nolan?"

"Only since last summer. Mother was shopping for fabric and I went with her. It was hot so I went up the street to the druggist. They have a soda fountain. Olivia was in there with her father. He was speaking with the chemist so we chatted while we were waiting. We've been friends ever since."

So that explains how the girls met. Happenstance, nothing more. Hodgins remembered how Lucy faltered when he asked her about boys bothering Olivia and decided to try a different tactic.

"Lucy told me about the boy that was bothering Olivia."

Betsy gasped. "She did? But he wasn't a boy, exactly."

Interesting.

"Lucy couldn't remember his name. Do you? Did you

ever meet him?"

"Olivia called him Johnny. I only saw him once. He was quite handsome. He kept asking Olivia to marry him, but she wasn't interested."

"What did you mean when you said he wasn't exactly a boy? How old is he?"

Betsy bit her bottom lip while she thought about it. "Well, he was older, maybe twenty." Her eyes grew wide. "Do you think he did it? He's seen me with Olivia. Do you think he'll come after me?" Betsy started to cry.

"I'm sure you have nothing to worry about." Seeing how distressed she had become, he decided to end the interview before Mrs. Scott did. He stood up.

"I won't keep you any longer. Thank you for your time. I'll see myself out."

CHAPTER TEN

Barnes was waiting when Hodgins arrived back at the station. He hurried over to update Hodgins about the estate agent.

"Quite a chatty fellow is Mr. Lake. Almost talked me into renting a house. Anyway, he confirmed that Mr. Howland purchased the house on his recommendation. Finally had someone interested in renting it, until the murder."

Barnes stood at Hodgins' desk waiting for him to say something. Hodgins nodded but didn't respond to his report. Instead, he grumbled something about Mr. Nolan leaving town last Saturday. Three days had passed and he still had not returned.

"I just don't understand it," Hodgins said. "How can the man just up and leave when his daughter's been murdered? I know I'd constantly be asking questions, wondering what the police were doing, and when I could bury her. I don't think he's made any arrangements. When would he have had the time?"

Hodgins slammed his fist on the desk.

"What is wrong with that man? I need to talk to him *now*." He scribbled on a piece of paper and thrust it at Barnes.

"Send this telegram at once. He said he can be contacted through the Post Office in Woodbridge. If he doesn't reply by the end of the day, I'm taking a trip up there myself. In the meanwhile I guess I'll try to track down John Webster."

Barnes read the note before leaving, just in case he couldn't read the hurried writing. Satisfied, he hurried off to the telegraph office.

Frustration gnawed at Hodgins. Needing to do something other than grumble, he went home to pack a bag then headed to the train station for the next train to Kingston to look for Webster.

He arrived late in the evening. After chatting with a railway employee to get directions to a hotel and the police station, Hodgins got a carriage at the Grand Trunk station and headed down Montreal Street into the heart of Kingston. He went straight to the Grand Hotel, glad that the expense would be covered. For the first time in a quite a while, he slept in.

Between working the murder case and moving into a

new home, he was worn out. Hodgins was surprised to see it was after eight when he woke up. Normally the aromas coming from the kitchen were enough to rouse him, no matter how tired. Unfortunately he couldn't smell Cordelia's cooking from Kingston.

After a leisurely breakfast, he walked to the police station, hoping they would be willing to help with his inquiries. He filled them in and said he was trying to find a person of interest. Someone who had been staying across the street from the scene of the crime at the time.

They were more than happy to oblige, and with the assistance of one of their constables, Hodgins had a list of establishments handling musical instruments. Fortunately it was not long; two dealers and three manufacturers. He started with the dealers – they weren't very far.

G. Adams was at the top of the list, so he headed there. Hodgins thought it funny that Adams also dealt in sewing machines and agricultural implements. *How the devil do they connect?*

The conversation with Adams was short. Yes, John Webster had worked there, but he fired him about a year earlier.

"Do you have any daughters Detective?"

"Yes. Sara. She just turned nine."

"Few more years and you'll understand better. Just wait

'till the lads start hanging around." Adams tugged at his shirt collar and lowered his voice. "Had a spot of trouble two years ago. My girl's got a wild streak. Some blighter seduced her." His hands balled into fists and he started to bang them against the arms of the chair. "Had to send her away for a bit. Couldn't have that happen again."

He wouldn't go into further detail. Adams told him Webster was currently employed with James Purdy, right across the road.

Before he made his way to Purdy's he thought about what Betsy had told him. Someone named Johnny had been bothering Olivia. *Could John Webster be that Johnny?* Hodgins pulled out his pocket watch to check the time. Eleven thirty. He'd speak with Purdy, then find something to eat.

As this was his first visit to Kingston, his thoughts wandered, thinking about everything that had happened over here in recent years. Uppermost in his mind were the Prime Ministers. John MacDonald, Canada's first appointed Prime Minister was from Kingston, as was the current Prime Minister, Alexander McKenzie. *Seems the Scots are taking over the country.*

He found Purdy's establishment easily but had to wait before he could speak with the owner. Hodgins enjoyed the company of a rather attractive young woman who was trying to concentrate on some paperwork.

The door to the inner office finally opened and two men came out. They shook hands and the younger one left, waving to the young woman and ignoring Hodgins. The elder one turned to Hodgins.

"I'm James Purdy. What can I help you with? Sewing machines? Musical instruments? How about some modern farming equipment? We sell only the highest quality."

Hodgins showed his badge. "I need to speak to you about one of your salesmen. John Webster."

Purdy rolled his eyes. "Come into my office and tell me what he's been up to this time."

Purdy sat in a rather plush looking, broken-in brown leather chair behind a large oak desk. Hodgins sat in a rigid wooden one opposite him.

"What's this all about then?"

"I'm only making inquires. A young girl was murdered last week and Webster was staying in a boarding house just up the street. He might have seen or heard something that could help with my investigation. I have reason to believe he was acquainted with her. He stayed at the boarding house on a regular basis. Is he about?"

Purdy steepled his hands and tapped his fingertips.

"Young girl you say?"

"Yes. Fifteen or sixteen."

"Hmm, mighty young for Webster," Purdy said. "I'm

afraid he's on the road. I like to keep him travelling."

"Good salesman?"

"Better than most. The only reason I keep him really."

Hodgins detected something in Purdy's face. Something he wasn't saying.

"I understand from Abrams he had a spot of trouble with Webster and let him go. Are you having the same bother?"

"Did you see that young lady in the outer office?"

Hodgins smiled. "Hard to miss. Very attractive."

"My daughter. I keep Webster on the road to minimize any contact he might have with her, if you get my meaning."

"If he's only a fair salesman, why not just let him go?"

"As I said, he's not great, but he's actually my top seller. Relies a lot on his looks and charm. He should be spending more time selling the product, not himself. He definitely has a way with the ladies. Doesn't matter the age. A lot of the music teachers are women and he's managed to sell some of my more expensive instruments to places we've previously never been able to get orders from."

Hodgins laughed. "So you're taking advantage of *him* before he takes advantage of your daughter."

Purdy tapped the side of his nose and winked. "Spot on. Might even get him selling the sewing machines to the seamstresses. Don't think he'd be any good selling my farm implements though." Purdy started laughing. "He'd probably get run through with a pitch fork."

Hodgins was getting more and more curious to meet this Webster character. "When do you expect him back? Can I have his address?"

"Won't be back for a few days yet. When he's in town, he stays with his folks. They live on Pine Street." Purdy gave Hodgins directions.

"You married Detective?"

The question caught him off guard. "Yes, he said slowly. "Why do you ask?"

"Got a lovely sewing machine just in. Latest model." Purdy wrote on the back of a business card and held it out towards Hodgins. "Give this to one of the dealers I've listed in Toronto and you'll get a good discount."

Hodgins smiled and took the card. "Have to check with my wife."

They shook hands and Hodgins went in search of a meal. The Grand Hotel had good food so he decided to eat there. Easier to submit one bill for the hotel and his meals when he got back.

As he walked, he read the card before putting it in his pocket. Cordelia just might like her own sewing machine so she didn't have to keep going to her mother's.

After his slightly pricey meal at the hotel Hodgins

walked down to Routley's and bought a doll for Sara and some earrings for Cordelia. He knew he shouldn't be spending his money on items they didn't need, but he couldn't resist.

Hodgins went back to the hotel and collected his satchel before hailing a passing hansom cab to go see Webster's parents. When he arrived, he asked the driver to wait as he wouldn't be long.

He left his card and asked them to have their son get in touch as soon as he was back in Toronto next week. Hodgins climbed back into the buggy and told the driver to take him to the Grand Trunk Railway Station. He wanted to catch the evening train so he could be back in Toronto by morning.

CHAPTER ELEVEN

Hodgins arrived home in the wee hours Wednesday morning and had only managed a few house sleep on the train. He didn't want to disturb Cordelia, so he didn't bother going to bed. He made himself as comfortable as possible in the drawing room and tried to catch a bit more sleep before she woke.

He was up before Cordelia so he made his own breakfast. Lingering in the kitchen, he waited for his wife and daughter to rise. He was in no rush to get to the station and poured himself a second cup of tea.

Cordelia came down an hour later. She could tell he had something he wanted to talk about, but Hodgins refused to speak until Sara was at the table. He was smiling, so she knew it wasn't anything bad, and he had a small, oddly shaped package sitting on the table in front of him.

"Can you give me a little hint?" she asked.

"No, wait for Sara." He leaned back in the chair, crossed his arms over his chest, and smiled.

Cordelia went upstairs to hurry Sara along.

Sara skipped into the kitchen ahead of her mother and kissed her father before sitting at the table.

"Good morning, Daddy." She eyed the package. "Is that for me?"

Cordelia stood behind Sara, waiting to find out what was going on. Hodgins slowly loosened the knot in the string. Sara squirmed in her chair.

"What is it Daddy?

Hodgins slid the package over to Sara. She pulled the paper back and squealed in delight. Sara got off the chair and threw her arms around him.

"Thank you Daddy. She's beautiful." She sat back down, picked up the doll, and wrapped its long blond curls around her fingers.

"Bertie, you spoil that child sometimes. With this new house we can't afford to be so frivolous."

Since Cordelia seemed so concerned about their finances, he figured it was time to fill her in. Hodgins had never told her just how much money he had been able to save while they stayed at her parents all those years. They had no mortgage to worry about and there was still a fair bit of money in the bank. It wouldn't last forever, but they could occasionally afford a few indulgences. He decided they'd discuss their finances once he solved Olivia's murder and he could give Delia all his attention.

He reached into the inside pocket of his jacket and pulled out a small box.

"Then I suppose I should return this?"

He handed it to Cordelia. She took the lid off and gasped.

"Really, you shouldn't have bought them."

Cordelia held up the earrings. Two thin silver chains about one inch long, with a pearl dangling on each end. "They are quite breathtaking though."

She kissed him, then showed them to Sara. She held them up against the doll's head and they both giggled.

"What will you be busying yourself with today?" he asked.

Cordelia sighed. "Over to Mother's again. I need to finish sewing the draperies. I'll be glad once everything is finally finished."

Hodgins smiled as he thought about the card Mr. Purdy had given him. He was certain Delia was forgive him one final surprise. "I'm sure it will get easier soon."

Cordelia put the earrings back in their box and moved Sara's doll off the table. Once breakfast was over, He reluctantly headed to the station house.

* * *

Hodgins went directly to Barnes' desk to inquire about Nolan.

"Have you received a reply to the telegram yet?"

"Yes, Sir. Said he won't be back for several more days."

"Blast that man. What's wrong with him? He doesn't seem to care that someone murdered his daughter. How can he be so callous?"

Hodgins banged his fist on the desk.

"I need to speak with him *now*. Do we even know who he works for? What he sells? All I know is he's a salesman. Travels a lot."

Barnes flipped through his notebook. "According to neighbours he sells one of those patent medicines. An elixir if you will."

Hodgins groaned. "Don't tell me he's one of those charlatans selling cure-alls that cure nothing?"

"Not at all. I haven't had time to confirm it, but one of his neighbours mentioned he works for Lyman's. Very respectable firm. Office in the St. Lawrence Building over on Front."

"Lyman's you say? I think I'll stroll over and see what they can tell me about him. While I'm gone, why don't you go down to the vacant house beside Nolan's and see if you can find anything inside that could help with the case."

* * *

Hodgins entered the office of Lyman Brothers & Co., introduced himself to the elderly clerk, and asked to speak with one of the owners. The clerk explained that the owners were in the main office in Quebec, but one of the sons was available.

The clerk rose from his chair and hobbled over to the inner office. He knocked and entered. Hodgins could hear murmuring through the closed door. A few moments later the clerk came out.

"Mr. Lyman will see you now."

Hodgins smiled at the clerk and went into the office.

"Detective Hodgins, what can I do for you? I'm Henry Lyman. I assume it has something to do with the murder of Nolan's daughter? Terrible tragedy. I know my father and uncle would like to attend the funeral. Do you know when it will be?"

Hodgins shrugged his shoulders. "Unfortunately she's still with the coroner. Nolan left town and there's no one else to release the body to. He should be back soon. What can you tell me about Kendall Nolan? What kind of man is he?"

"I'm afraid I don't know him personally. I work at the Montreal office. Only in Toronto a short while. Making the rounds, checking in to make sure everything is running smoothly. I'll be going up to Ottawa tomorrow, then back home."

"I see. Is there someone here I could talk to that knows

him? I understand he travels quite a bit. Does he have a set route? Regular customers he visits?"

"My clerk should be able to help you there. He's been here since the company started and knows everyone. I do know Nolan is our best salesman in the region. Number three overall. His name comes up quite often."

Lyman got up and went to the office door to speak to his clerk. "The detective has some questions about Nolan. Please assist him all you can." He turned back to Hodgins.

"I have several reports to write before the end of the day. I'll leave you in the capable hands of Mr. Fuller."

Hodgins knew a dismissal when he heard one. He thanked Mr. Lyman and went back to the outer office.

"Do you know Mr. Nolan's customers and routes?"

"Yes, Sir." Fuller rummaged through a cabinet drawer and pulled out a file. He brought it back to his desk and spread out the papers.

"Our experienced salesmen don't have any set route or schedule. They just go by past orders and know when to pay a visit to their customers. The new ones start out on a set schedule, but once they know their customers, they figure out what route and times work best. Nolan is quite experienced and has had the same stops for several years."

Hodgins looked over the reports. Nolan had quite a large territory to cover. No wonder he was away from home so much.

"Might I trouble you for a copy of his customers, addresses and how often they place orders?"

"Certainly."

While the clerk wrote out the list, Hodgins asked him about Nolan.

"What can you tell me about Kendall Nolan? Is he a hard worker? Sociable?"

"He comes in fairly often to get more supplies. Works really hard to stay on top. Pleasant chap. Speaks of his daughter often." Fuller stopped writing and looked up at Hodgins.

"Can't imagine what he's going through. He was quite distressed when Mrs. Nolan passed. Then his sister, now his daughter. She came in with him a few times. Very polite and pretty. Such a shame."

He finished writing the list and handed it to Hodgins. "Is there anything else?"

"No, not at the moment. If I need anything I'll send one of the constables over."

"Do you know who did it?"

"Still making inquiries. Thank you for your time."

Hodgins was still annoyed that Nolan was staying in Woodbridge for so long. As he left Lyman Brothers & Co. he grumbled and mumbled to himself. Hodgins found it impossible to get inside Nolan's head. He hadn't realized how loudly he was grumbling until he passed a lady who reprimanded him for his foul language.

He needed to find that man and soon. Remembering the schedule he recalled seeing a late morning train and hurried to Union Station. A train was leaving in thirty minutes.

While waiting for the train to pull in he read over the list Fuller had given him, looking for clients around Woodbridge. He found two: a druggist, S.J. Snell, and a Dr. J. Wilkinson.

Hodgins sat on a nearby bench and opened his notebook to add to his notes. Observations and Questions. Not many observation, but a lot of questions.

The more he thought about how Nolan was acting, the angrier he got. Slamming his notebook closed he jammed it in his jacket pocket. He heard a small rip and swore. Hodgins took a deep breath and held it for a few seconds, then slowly let it out. He felt a little better. A few more deep breaths and he felt more like himself. Examining his pocket revealed only minor damage. *Just a few broken threads.* He wondered if he could repair it himself so Cordelia didn't find out. She had enough to do without having extra sewing on account of his temper.

He walked over to the schedule board and noted the

time of the last train back. He hoped he could make it as it would be very expensive to hire a buggy to return home. He had to be careful with his spending and he wasn't certain a long buggy ride was an expense he would be reimbursed for.

The thirty minute wait went fairly fast and Hodgins was soon on his way to Woodbridge. He checked his pocket watch. It would take about an hour to get there. That didn't leave him much time to find Nolan.

As soon as he arrived he inquired as to the location of the post office and was happy to discover it was not far from the station. Hopefully someone there knew exactly where Nolan could be located.

It was a scorching, hot, sunny day, and unfortunately there were no clouds. The shade from the trees and buildings along Pine Street did nothing to help combat the heat of summer.

When he arrived at the post office he found the door propped open and a number of people inside. The ladies fanned themselves and the clerk wiped his brow continually. He never seemed to get every drop of sweat.

Hodgins waited his turn impatiently, tapping his foot and looking at the cuckoo clock on the wall behind the counter every few minutes. When he was finally served, his frustration grew. He showed the clerk his badge.

"Do you know Mr. Kendall Nolan?"

"Yes, I know Mr. Nolan. Not well mind you. Comes in every week or two to pick up mail."

Hodgins made a note in his trusty notebook. "Every week or two you say? What about his address? Where does he live?"

The clerk shrugged. "Sorry. Don't know. He wasn't one for passing the time of day, ya know? Just picked up his mail and left."

Hodgins slapped his notebook on the counter. "Blast and damnation!"

"Such language. Should be ashamed of yourself."

Hodgins turned and discovered a lady standing behind him. He guessed she was in her sixties at the very least.

"I'm terribly sorry. Please excuse me." Hodgins turned red from both the heat and his embarrassment. He turned back to the counter and picked up his book.

"I wish these small towns had some sort of law enforcement. Make my job that much easier." He nodded at the clerk and avoided looking at the lady waiting her turn as he hurried out of the post office and off to his next stop.

Neither the druggist nor the doctor had seen Nolan for weeks. Didn't expect him until next month, and neither knew where he lived. The only good thing for Hodgins was he wouldn't have to worry about missing the train home.

He trudged back along Pine and veered off towards the

tavern. He noticed there seemed to be a tavern near every train station. He figured if he had to wait for the train, he may as well have a beer or two to help him cool down. Something gnawed at the back of his mind and he couldn't quite put his finger on it.

Rather than dwell on it, he took out the list of customers and tried to figure out where Nolan might have gone. He read over the dates. Most of the customers placed large enough orders that Nolan didn't have to visit any one of them too frequently.

Something twigged.

He looked at the order dates for Snell and Wilkinson. Nolan only came to Woodbridge every six or seven weeks yet the clerk at the post office said he picked up mail every week or two. *Why would Nolan pick up mail here frequently? He doesn't even live here.*

CHAPTER TWELVE

When Hodgins arrived back in Toronto, he made a quick stop at the station to see if Barnes had any news. It appeared that he too was getting frustrated.

"So many leads that all seem to go nowhere," Barnes said. "I checked both the front and back door on the vacant house. No sign of anyone breaking in. The locks weren't forced and all the windows are boarded up. Few loose boards, but none missing.

"Since the estate agent provided the key, I figured I may as well go in. Went upstairs and checked those windows. Nothing out of place. There's a thin layer of dust everywhere. No footprints. No hand marks. Doesn't appear as any furniture was moved or disturbed in any way."

Barnes flipped the page of his notebook and kept talking.

"I circled around the outside again and it does appear as though someone else had done so, probably looking for an easy way in. More prints the same size as the ones we saw earlier."

He turned his book to show Hodgins his sketch.

"See here?" Barnes pointed to an 'x'. "I made a mark where there were prints around the windows. There, and here too."

"What about the laneway?"

"Still full of mud."

Hodgins nodded. "Good work. At least we were right to think someone wanted to hide in the empty house."

Since nothing new had turned up, Hodgins decided to head home after one final stop. He took the card from Purdy out of his pocket and read the back. Mr. Purdy had written the name and address of two places in Toronto that sold his sewing machines.

Even though he knew they still had money in the bank, he would have to watch is spending. A sewing machine was something his wife would use for years, so it was worth the small extravagance.

He went to the closest shop and showed the card. The clerk fetched the owner and Hodgins was treated like upper-class. He didn't bother to tell them he was just a copper.

The store had received a delivery that morning, and the shipment contained two of the new models. Hodgins gave the owner his address and arranged for delivery Saturday. It was his day off and he wanted to be there when it arrived.

* * *

When he opened his front door, the house was unusually quiet. No aromas drifted down from the kitchen, even though he could hear faint sounds as Cordelia prepared their evening meal. Only the dog had taken the time to greet him at the door, and that was with less gusto than usual. Seemed the heat was affecting everyone.

When he walked into the kitchen he saw Sara sitting at the table peeling and cutting carrots. Cordelia turned to greet him. She brushed some loose strands of hair from her face with the back of her hand. Several stuck in place.

"Oh dear. I can tell by the look on your face you've had a bad day."

A weak 'harrumph' was all Hodgins could manage as he sat down. His usual walk from the trolley had not cleared his mind this time.

"I made lemonade Daddy. I'll pour you some."

Sara hopped off the chair and walked to the ice box, plucking a glass from the cupboard shelf along the way. The ice box wasn't very big, but it was quite handy. Something his mother-in-law didn't even have. It had a compartment on the top for the ice and a spigot so you could pour out the cold water as it melted. The double doors on the front opened to reveal two shelves. A glass pitcher sat on the top shelf.

Sara poured out the lemonade and took it to her father.

He downed it in one go. *Not quite as good as Miss O'Hara's.* He had sense enough not to say that out loud.

"Thank you Sara. It was just what I needed."

Scraps had stretched out on the floor near the ice box, tongue hanging out. Hodgins got up and filled the dog's water bowl with some of the melted ice water. Scraps drank it down, then licked Hodgins' hand before stretching out across the floor.

During dinner there was little conversation. Sara chatted a bit about her new doll. One of her friends had come over and they played with it in the morning, then Cordelia took them down to the beach in the afternoon.

"How are the draperies coming along?" Hodgins asked. He wanted to tell Cordelia about his latest purchase but decided to keep it a surprise.

"Slow. I just couldn't bear the thought of being enveloped in all that cloth on such a hot day. And you know how mother's Irish temper flares up in this heat. Best to stay away. Hopefully it cools down soon. I would like to get them finished. They'll help keep the house cool."

Cordelia didn't inquire about his current case as they both had decided not to talk about it in front of Sara. She was used to hearing them talk about the various thefts and even some murders, but this was different. They felt it best not to discuss the murder of a child when she was around.

After Sara went to bed, Cordelia sat down in the drawing room to talk with her husband.

"What is bothering you so? Is it because a young girl was killed?"

"No. Well yes, but that's not all. It's her father. I just don't understand him. He asked no questions. Hasn't yelled because we haven't arrested anyone. Hasn't even asked about burying her. McKenzie wants to release her body, but Nolan has disappeared."

He paced around the room, unfastening the top two buttons on his shirt and loosening his collar. "I just can't fathom what's going through his head. He said I could contact him through the Woodbridge post office, but they have no idea where he lives. No one I spoke to does either. Even more puzzling, the post office clerk said Nolan picks up mail regularly, but his order schedule has him going up only every two months."

"That *is* puzzling. But why is he having correspondence sent there instead of his home?"

"Exactly. That's what I want, no *need*, to find out."

"I've been reading another of those delicious crime books. The gentleman was having certain correspondence sent to his office instead of home."

"Understandable Delia. He wouldn't have business matters sent to his house. But Nolan's house is his office in a manner of speaking. Course he could have business letters sent to Lyman's."

She waved her hand, dismissing his comment. "No, you don't understand. Those letters were personal. Something he was keeping from his wife. I can't wait to find out what. Maybe Nolan has a secret. Would you mind sitting down? You're making me dizzy."

Hodgins smiled and stopped pacing. "Interesting. But why all the way up in Woodbridge? Why not right here in Toronto?"

Cordelia shrugged and smiled. "That's why you're the detective Bertie, not me."

He walked over to where she was sitting and kissed the top of her head. "Sometimes I'm glad you don't read those silly romance stories like normal women. After I check in at the station tomorrow I'll go back up and ask more questions. If he spends so much time there someone has to know something.

CHAPTER THIRTEEN

Hodgins rose early and made his way to the station house. The heat had broken over night, so he walked over rather than wait for a trolley. The air was still, absent of a breeze, but the lower temperature was relief enough. Even the song of the robins seemed cheerier.

Not many people were about yet. The news boys had picked up their papers and were heading to their spots. Hodgins hailed one down, bought a paper, and tucked it under his arm.

The station house was unusually quiet. Hodgins went into the back room, made a cup of tea then went to his office. The copy of the train schedule he had picked up earlier was still laying open on his desk. He circled the time the first train headed north then checked his pocket watch. *Plenty of time yet.*

He drank his tea then went over to the maps that were piled on a table against the wall. He rummaged through them until he found one with Woodbridge on it. He figured if Nolan went to the post office often but no one knew where he lived, he must be staying out of town somewhere. *But where?*

He located a couple of possibilities. Just a little south of Woodbridge was the town of Brownsville, and another just north-east called Pine Grove. *If Nolan has a secret, is it possible he stays in one of those towns and uses the post office in Woodbridge to hide his whereabouts?*

He went back to his desk to wait for Barnes. While any of the constables would do, he preferred to use whoever was first on the scene. He seemed to be working with Barnes quite often, and that suited him fine.

The change of shift started and the door constantly opened as some of the men left and others arrived. The chattering got louder and louder. Hodgins looked up every time he heard the door. Ten minutes later Barnes arrived.

"Barnes." Hodgins waved him over. "Have you run a check on Nolan?"

Barnes came over and stood in the doorway, looking surprised. "No. I didn't think it necessary. You don't think he killed his own daughter, do you?"

"No, no. Nothing like that. But he's hiding something and I need to find out what. Use some of the boys. Check records here, and everywhere in a hundred mile radius if necessary. Pay particular attention to the Woodbridge area."

"That will take some time, Sir."

"Well you'd better get cracking then. I'm heading up there now to try and track him down. There has to be at least one person who knows where he's at." Hodgins stood and slipped the newspaper back under his arm.

"Right away, Sir." As Barnes stepped back out of Hodgins' office his heel hit the leg of a chair that had been pushed away from the desk right outside. He fell backwards, fortunately landing on the seat of the chair. Barnes turned a deep shade of red as the laugher made its way through the station.

Hodgins picked up the train schedule and slipped it in the inside pocket of his jacket. "I'm counting on you Barnes. I'm confident you'll find something right quick."

Hodgins spoke loud enough for everyone to hear, hoping it would ease some of the ribbing. He managed to hold in his laughter until he was well away.

The train ride went by fast as Hodgins became engrossed in the paper. Two young ladies out Woodford way had gone missing. Hodgins hoped they hadn't met the same fate as Olivia and would soon be found, safe and sound.

He flipped though the paper and turned to the sports. The baseball club from Brooklyn had visited Guelph and they somehow managed to beat the Guelph Maple Leafs by a whopping 15-1. He figured the Guelph team was simply worn out from winning the world championship last month in Waterdown, New York. Hodgins was just reading about the small pox breakout in Peterborough when the trained slowed for the station.

On his arrival in Woodbridge there were a surprising number of people in town. Probably trying to catch up on errands left undone due to the recent bad weather. Most were farmers or their wives.

He asked everyone if they knew Nolan and where he could find him. Person after person told him the same thing, either they didn't know him, or if they did, had no idea where he lived. For a man who was in town regularly, he didn't seem to have made any friends.

The morning dragged on until he finally had a bit of luck. One person gave him some hope. He didn't know where Nolan lived, but he had seen him in Pine Grove about a week ago, loading supplies onto a wagon.

Hodgins thanked him, then went to the livery stable to hire a buggy so he could get to the little village to the north-east. The town was larger than he expected. His first stop was the general store where Nolan had been spotted. He hoped Nolan was staying nearby.

The store had a generous wooden porch with a pair of rockers to the left of the door. A bicycle leaned against the wall off to the right. He could picture a couple of old men in the rockers passing the day, reminiscing.

He tied the horse to the post out front and went in. Only three ladies were inside. One was at the counter selling her fresh eggs to the owner. Two others were at the far side, bickering over a bolt of fabric.

Hodgins eyed the jars of candies and thought of Sara. She loved licorice and hard candies and the store had ample supply of both. He knew Cordelia would object and he really didn't want to carry it around so he continued walking around. He didn't do much shopping and was amazed at the multitude of canned goods, flour, grains, and fabric. It seemed everything a person could want was available in one spot.

As he passed the hanging weigh scale he gave it a quick poke. He looked around and was relieved to see no one had noticed his child-like behaviour. He made his way back to the front to wait for the ladies to finish their business and leave.

"Find what yer looking fer?"

"Actually, I came in search of information." Hodgins introduced himself, then continued. "Are you acquainted with Kendall Nolan? I'm told he was here recently."

"Oh my. Is something wrong? Is he in trouble? Seemed like such a nice chap."

"No, he's not in any trouble." *At least not yet.* "I'm trying to locate him. Do you know where I can find him?"

"Why yes. He has a small farm just outside town." He pointed towards the east. "Third one up the road."

Hodgins thanked the man and turned to leave.

"Won't find him here though."

Hodgins groaned. Did Nolan ever stay put? He turned back to face the grocer.

"Saw him head out 'bout an hour ago."

Hodgins wondered how a salesman could afford both a house in the city and a farm. Even a top-notch salesman wouldn't be that well off.

"Him and his wife moved in three, maybe four, years ago. She don't come in much. Nice enough looking woman."

Hodgins nodded and left. He untied the horse and got in the buggy. Frustrated, he went back to Woodbridge and sat in the tavern until the next train back to Toronto.

He re-read his notes and added a few more. Maybe Nolan's late wife had money. He'd have to see what Barnes had uncovered. *Strange. The store owner hadn't mentioned Nolan's daughter.* Maybe he didn't know she was dead. Nolan probably didn't want to talk about it.

CHAPTER FOURTEEN

Hodgins arrived back at the station tired, dusty, and without any answers. He dragged himself up the steps of the building. Several desks around Barnes were covered in books and newspapers. It looked like Barnes had recruited three of the constables to help him compile a background on Nolan. Hodgins went over to see what they had found out.

"Not a lot yet, Sir," Barnes said. "We did find the church record for his marriage. Also found a little write-up in the paper." Barnes picked up a newspaper from 1858. "They had a small service at her parents home – Mr. & Mrs. Fred Johnson. Fred worked in one of the mills. Doesn't appear to have bin anythin' fancy."

"So, they weren't particularly well off then?"

"I wouldn't think so."

"Puzzling. It seems our Mr. Nolan has a farm up Woodbridge way. Town called Pine Grove." Hodgins took the paper from Barnes and read the small write-up.

"He was only a salesman. I thought maybe her family

had money."

"That is puzzling," Barnes said.

"Well, keep digging. Concentrate farther north. See what you can find."

Hodgins walked to his desk and dropped his notebook on top. He opened the drawer and took out a pad of long paper and started copying some of the notes from his book, then pinned them up on his office wall.

Somewhere between Monday evening and Tuesday morning someone climbed through Olivia's bedroom window, chased her downstairs, then killed her.

The girl wasn't interfered with, and nothing seems to have been taken from the house. Just furniture and whatnot toppled over or broken. The man may have come in through the laneway.

The laneway!

He hadn't gone back to check it again. Figuring it should finally be dry enough, Hodgins left the newspaper on his desk, picked up his notebook, then hurried off to the lane.

Since there had been no rain for several days and the temperature remained high, the river of mud in the lane had practically dried up. It was hopeless to try and find footprints. They would have been washed away long since.

He examined the boards where they had been broken

off and allowed access to the back yard. He couldn't believe he missed doing that earlier. The murder of Olivia must have affected him more than he wanted to admit.

He had seen quite a number of dead children over the years, but this was the first time he had to deal with the murder of one. And it was such a brutal death. He needed to focus on his job. Try to forget the image of the young girl, all battered and bloody. Try to simply investigate. It wasn't going to be easy to put his personal feelings aside, but he had to.

Hodgins found a tiny scrap of fabric caught on the rough edges of one of the boards. It felt like flannel. Based on the height he found it snagged, it must be from someone's shirt. It wasn't much to go on and it could have been there for days, weeks even. Flannel shirts were quite common, owned by most labourers. Rather a warm fabric to be wearing in July though. Most men wore cotton.

This had to be one of the most frustrating cases he had worked on. There were next to no clues. The board cracked as he slammed his fist against it. A few flakes of whitewash floated to the ground.

"Blast and damnation." He shook his hand, then wiggled his fingers. Nothing broken, but his knuckles would be bruised for days.

So far he had only one good suspect. John Webster. He

had been giving Olivia unwanted attention and was just across the road the night she was killed. Hopefully he could track him down next week when he was back at Miss O'Hara's.

Hodgins took one last look around the outside of Nolan's house, then started back to the station. He walked east on Duchess and glanced south as he crossed Sherbourne. He could see Duke Street and remembered the painter. He had forgotten there was a man murdered nearby and they still hadn't found the person responsible. It wasn't his case, but maybe they were connected. *Carter's in charge of that one.* He decided to talk to him when he got back. See if he had any leads.

It was late in the afternoon by the time Hodgins arrived back at Station House Four. He had stopped on Queen to buy a pie from one of the street vendors and was finishing it when he entered the station. Carter was just getting ready to leave.

"Hold up a minute Carter. I'm working on a murder that might be connected to your case. That dead man from Duke Street. Mind if I look through your files?"

"That young girl? Terrible thing. Wouldn't want that one. If there's any chance you can find a connection, be my guest. Even if they ain't connected, you may notice something I've overlooked. Maybe a fresh set of eyes will help. If they are linked, we can close both in one go."

Hodgins thought about that missing woman who lived on George Street. She still hasn't been located. Could all three be connected? Hodgins wondered if it was simply a coincidence that so many things had happened in such a small radius. He hoped there wasn't a maniac running around the city.

Hodgins went to the cabinet and found the file on the painter. He took it over to his desk and laid the papers out.

McKenzie's autopsy report indicated the body had likely been in the house for a few days before he was found. Hodgins tried not to think how that would have smelled. The cause of death was stabbing. The knife was still in the body when they found him. It was assumed to be from the kitchen as it matched other knives found there.

Olivia had been bludgeoned to death with a piece of firewood, as well as having her throat slit. They hadn't found the knife. *Were they all weapons of convenience? Could it be possible the same person committed both crimes after all?*

Hodgins slid over the pad of paper he'd been writing on earlier. He added a few more things about his case, and added points from Carter's file. There were a few similarities.

Both places showed signs of a struggle, and the weapons seems to be found conveniently at the homes by the killer. Did someone break in intending only theft? Carter had no leads, except a vague description from a neighbour. She had heard yelling a few days earlier and saw a man running from the house. She couldn't provide much of a description, only that he was tall and bulky.

Hodgins realized he had no idea what Webster looked like. Only knew his age. He'd have to remedy that. Miss O'Hara could help. He pulled out his pocket watch and checked the time. Cordelia would be expecting him home soon, and he was too tired to go back to Duchess Street. He'd speak with Miss O'Hara tomorrow. Maybe he'd just send Barnes instead. Hodgins tore the sheet from the pad and pinned it up next to the other pages before heading home.

CHAPTER FIFTEEN

The high temperatures were back and Hodgins woke feeling sticky and uncomfortable. He turned towards the window. It was open but the curtains were still. He threw back the sheets and swung his legs over the side of the bed. Using the sleeve of his dressing gown, he wiped the beads of sweat from his brow, then pushed himself off the bed.

Cordelia stirred but did not wake. Hodgins tiptoed to the dressing table and splashed his face with the water from the basin. The water was tepid, but it felt good. He attended to his morning routine, dressed, and went down to the kitchen.

It was quite early, but he couldn't sleep. He tore a chunk of bread from yesterday's loaf, smeared some peach jelly on it and wrote a short note for Cordelia before heading to the station.

It was far too early for the trolley so he walked. He noticed how quiet it was outside – the birds were still in bed. His steps were slower than usual, partially due to the heat and partially because he was deep in thought. The quiet helped him mentally organize all he knew about the girl's death.

That salesman, Webster, might've had something to do with Olivia's death. He had been bothering her and she spurned his attentions. Webster stayed at the boarding house often enough to know the neighbourhood and the residents. He conveniently left town before her body was discovered. Coincidence? And Webster has a reputation with young women.

Hodgins had no proof and no other suspects. Damn inconvenient of the man to be on the road when Hodgins desperately needed to talk to him. He kicked a pebble and watched it bounce out into the road.

When he arrived at the station it was just as quiet as the rest of the neighbourhood. There was hardly anyone there, and those present were trying to stay cool. The only sounds were from paper being fanned and the occasional yawn. He noticed a few uniforms with the top button open, but he didn't say anything. He hadn't bothered to do up his top button either.

He went into the back and automatically made a cup of tea, then went into his office and wrote down some ideas he had.

As soon as Barnes came in Hodgins sent him off to get

Webster's description while he went in search of Dr. McKenzie. The whistling coming from inside the coroner's office let Hodgins know he was in.

"And what can I do for you this bonnie morning Detective?"

"Do you recall the details of the painter's autopsy? Any similarities between that and Olivia Nolan?"

McKenzie tugged at his bushy red whiskers. "Nothing I can recall. Let me check my records." McKenzie retrieved the two files and spread the papers across an empty autopsy table.

"One stabbed, one beaten. Neither body had any unusually markings on them. What makes you think they could be connected?"

"Nothing really. Just that both murders happened only a block apart and only a couple of weeks between them. Grasping at straws I suppose."

Hodgins looked over McKenzie's shoulder at the reports. "Nothing on the clothing?"

"Only blood and paint on the painter, and blood and bits of wood on the girl. I was going over her clothing again yesterday just before I left." He pointed towards an evidence box. "Had one of the constables bring that over late yesterday afternoon. Was going to see you today as a matter of fact. I found one black strand of hair on her clothing, and she has auburn hair. Don't know how I missed it."

"What about the painter? Any black hairs on him?"

"He had black hair himself, so yes, there were black hairs on him. No way to tell for certain if they were his or not. Took a look under the 'scope and they seemed similar, so I imagine the hairs on his clothing were his own. The strand I took off the wee lassie will be in the evidence box. I can show you the comparison between the girl's and the ones from the painter if you'd like. Don't know what good it'll do if they're different though. No way to tell where they would have come from."

"I'd be interested to see them. Even if I can't find out where the hair came from, it might just connect the two."

Hodgins watched as McKenzie took the hair from the evidence box with Olivia's belongings and placed it on a microscope slide. McKenzie had two microscopes sitting side by side on his table. He put the hair from the painter under the other. He looked at one, then the other, then back to the first one. He refocused the scopes and went back and forth between them several more times before turning to Hodgins.

"See for yourself. Don't believe they came from the same person. The hair found on the painter is thick and course. The one from Olivia's clothing is in much better condition. Left by someone who took care of his appearance I'd say. The strand off her clothing is longer and has a bit of a wave too."

"So nothing to connect the two then? Blast." Hodgins thanked McKenzie for his time before turning and heading back to the station.

Barnes arrived about fifteen minutes later.

"Well?" Hodgins asked.

"Got a right good description of Mr. Webster. He's got longish black hair, 'bout to his shoulders, beard and moustache, green eyes, slender and round about six foot tall."

Hodgins drummed his fingers on the desk top. "Could be."

"Could be what, Sir?"

"That painter that was killed over on Duke Street near the beginning of the month. A neighbour saw a tall man running away. Said he was bulky, but if it was dark and he was running I don't suppose she could really tell how heavy he was. Bulky could just mean he was muscular."

"But Miss O'Hara said Webster was slender."

"She just may have meant he wasn't fat. Blast. He won't be back in Toronto for days yet. It seems he comes here every two weeks. That would put him here when the painter was killed too. I wish there was a way to get in touch with people right away, no matter where they were."

"That would be nice, but I can't see that happening, Sir. Rather unrealistic don't you think?"

Hodgins sighed. "You're right. Silly idea really."

"But why kill a painter?"

Hodgins looked past Barnes. "Finally."

"Sir?"

Hodgins pointed towards the door and Barnes turned to look. Kendall Nolan had just come in and walked over to the sergeant's desk. The sergeant pointed to Hodgins. Nolan waved and walked over.

"Talk to the lads who worked with Carter. Find out if the painter had a wife or lady friend. Webster has a reputation," Hodgins said.

Barnes hesitated and watched as Nolan approached.

"Off with you. Now."

"Yes, Sir." Barnes nodded at Nolan as they passed, and went to talk with the other constables as Hodgins greeted Nolan.

"Mr. Nolan, you're a hard man to find." Hodgins wanted to yell at the man, but held his tongue. "Have a seat. I went up to Woodbridge twice but no one seemed to know where to find you. Finally tracked down someone who directed me to Pine Grove."

Nolan paled. "You... You were in Pine Grove?"

"Yes. Was even given directions to your farm."

"You went to the farm?" Nolan whispered.

"No. Man who gave me the directions said you'd just left town a bit earlier. Didn't see any point riding out, what with you not being there and all."

Nolan seemed relieved and his colour returned.

"Tell me, how does a man of your means afford two homes? I gather the one in Pine Grove is a fair size. The farms I passed all seemed quite large."

"Inheritance. Why were you looking for me? Have you found the man who killed Olivia?" Nolan moved forward in the chair and grasped the edge of the desk. "When can I bury her? She should be with her mother now."

"Dr. McKenzie has been ready to release her for several days. We were waiting for you to show up."

Hodgins thought he sounded a little sharp, but he just didn't like Nolan. It was nothing he could put his finger on, but ever since Nolan rushed out of the city he had a bad feeling about him.

"Is something the matter?" Nolan asked.

Hodgins realized that he was staring at Nolan's hair. Blonde. Hodgins figured the girl got her colouring from her mother. He didn't really believe he had killed his own daughter, but anything was possible.

"No, just thinking. If you leave me the details, I'll make

sure your daughter's body is sent wherever you'd like."

Nolan blanched when Hodgins mentioned his daughter's body. Hodgins felt sorry for the man, understanding how he must feel. He just couldn't comprehend Nolan's actions though.

Nolan wrote down the name of the church on a page that Hodgins had torn from his notebook.

"I suppose I'd better speak with the vicar over at St. James and make the arrangements." He slid the paper over to Hodgins. "My late wife Ruth loved the chapel there."

CHAPTER SIXTEEN

When Nolan left, Hodgins went over to Barnes' desk. "Don't suppose you came across anything about an inheritance? Nolan claims that's how he got the farm."

"No, nothing like that. Could be in a local rag though."

Hodgins sighed. "Nothing is coming together on this one. You keep looking here. I'll go back to Woodbridge and Pine Grove and ask around some more."

Hodgins went back to his office and looked through the desk drawers for the train schedule. It had been shoved to the back of a drawer and was stuck in a tiny crack in the wood. He wiggled it around, trying not to tear it. He only lost one small corner. He ran his finger down the page checking the times. *Too late for the morning train.* He'd have to wait until one. Wouldn't give him much time if he wanted to get the last train back as there weren't very many going back and forth.

With Barnes and a few of the lads checking on Nolan and time to kill before the train left, Hodgins decided to take a side trip to a bookstore after lunch. With all the plans his wife had for a garden, Hodgins realized they would need help.

Neither had gardened before as his mother-in-law wouldn't allow them near *her* precious garden. He figured there must be books on the subject.

There was a book seller on King Street which was on his way to Union Station.

Cordelia had packed up some of the remnants of last evenings meal so he had a good lunch before leaving. A bit of cold beef, a chunk of bread and one of her delicious strawberry tarts. She even thought to include a linen napkin. He spread it out on his desk and placed his food on top, then went to the back room and made another cup of tea.

As he stood by his desk munching away and reading over the sheets he had pinned to the wall, he made a list of suspects. It was very short. William Howland, President of the Board of Trade. *Already eliminated.* John Webster, salesman. *Undecided.* Kendall Nolan. *Is he really a suspect?* Hodgins put a question marked beside his name. And what about the missing woman and the dead painter? Were they connected? He circled the last two.

Hodgins had a few ideas running through his mind, but nothing concrete. He needed more information. Finishing his lunch, he left the station and walked down Parliament to King, turning west. He found the shop of Rowsell and

Hutching just past Church Street.

A little bell tinkled as Hodgins opened the door. There was no one in sight. *What's the point of the blasted bell when no one comes to help?* He wandered around looking at the books and stationery items, not really certain what he was after.

"May I be of assistance Sir?"

Hodgins looked up. *Where did he come from?* A middle aged man approached. He was undoubtedly the thinnest man Hodgins had come across. A strong gust of wind would probably blow him clear across Lake Ontario.

"I find myself in need of a book on flowers and such. We've just moved and the gardens have been frightfully neglected. I don't know where to start. I thought there might be a book?"

The man's eyes lit up and he clapped his hands. "Oh, I have just the thing. Imported from England. They have the most magnificent gardens there, don't you know. Follow me."

He scampered towards the back and behind a tall bookshelf. Hodgins followed. He walked behind the shelf and watched the clerk running his fingers along the spines of the books.

"Ah, here it is. *The Gardener – A Magazine of Horticulture and Floriculture.* It's by David Thomson." He spoke the author's name with reverence. Hodgins assumed he must be an expert. The clerk handed him the book.

Hodgins was surprised by the size and weight. He flipped to the end. Almost 600 pages.

"A magazine?"

"Yes, rather a misleading name, isn't it? It's a new publication, 1873. Quite modern." The clerk spoke about the book and the author, extolling his many qualities.

Hodgins thumbed through the book while the clerk nattered on, and came across a page with the heading *Hints for Amateurs*.

"I'll take it. Would you be good enough to hold it for me until the end of the day?"

The clerk looked doubtful. "Well, I don't know..."

"I'm Detective Albert Hodgins." He pulled out his badge. "I assure you I will return for it. I'll pay in advance."

The clerk smiled. "Detective you say? Of course. I'll be happy to put it aside for you."

Hodgins paid for the book and checked his pocket watch. He'd spent more time in the store than he thought, as the clerk had prattled on about the book. He had to hurry to the train station or he'd miss his chance to go to Woodbridge today.

Hodgins settled into a seat near the rear of the passenger car and dozed off. The windows were all down and the wind whistled though the car keeping him from a deep sleep.

He opened his eyes when he heard the conductor shouting, "Woodbridge, next stop Woodbridge" as he walked through the train.

As soon as he got into town he walked to the livery, hired a buggy again, and headed to Pine Grove. He stopped at the general store as that seemed to be the only place he was able to get information. He wanted to see if he could find out anything further about Nolan. The store owner recognized him.

"Good afternoon, Detective. Still looking for Mr. Nolan?

"No. I spoke to him this morning. He mentioned something that got me wondering. Do you know who previously owned his farm?"

"Matter of fact I do. Used to belong to my brother."

"Your brother?" Hodgins was puzzled. "You're related to Nolan?"

He shook his head. "Whatever gave you that idea? No, no. My brother decided to try his hand farming out west. Just got it into his head one day it was better farming out there."

"Must have misunderstood. I thought he got the farm from a relative." He took his notebook out of his jacket pocket and jotted down what he just learned. "Unfortunate about his daughter."

"Daughter? They have no children." The store owner laughed. "I do believe we're talking about two different people."

Hodgins nodded. "Could be. Nolan is in his forties, balding slightly, average height, stocky but not fat. Sells pharmaceuticals."

"Yes, that's Mr. Nolan, but he doesn't have a daughter."

"Strange. Won't keep you from your customers any longer." He tipped his hat and went back to the buggy.

He sat thinking for a moment. He noticed the store owner kept saying they, as though Nolan's wife was still alive. He decided to look for the farm even though Nolan was still in Toronto.

Hodgins remembered the directions he was given from the last visit. If he followed the road east, he should find it.

Hodgins cursed at the beast pulling the buggy. The horse was being quite temperamental. It didn't seem to matter if he was gentle or relied heavily on the whip. The horse went at a pace it was comfortable with, completely unconcerned with what Hodgins wanted.

He counted the farms as he passed them, and he was finally at a laneway heading to the third one. A small white house sat at the end of the long lane, with a barn farther back on the property. It didn't appear that Nolan was growing any crops, but he spotted a fair sized vegetable garden out front of the house.

He drove the buggy up and a woman in her early thirties came out to greet him. Hodgins thought she might be a housekeeper, but something told him otherwise. *Too well dressed.* He took a chance.

"Mrs. Nolan?"

"Ya, I'm Mrs. Nolan."

"Mrs. Kendall Nolan?"

"Ya. Do ya know my husband? 'Fraid he ain't here. Won't be back for several days."

Hodgins showed his badge. Mrs. Nolan took one look at it and fainted.

CHAPTER SEVENTEEN

Hodgins leapt off the buggy and ran to her side. He lifted her and placed her in the rocker on the porch, out of the sun. As the clerk in town had commented, she was pretty, but he noticed deep lines around her eyes, and she wore a lot of make-up. *Unusual for a farm wife.* She started to come around.

"Are you ill? I can take you into town to the doctor." Hodgins didn't even know if there was a doctor in Pine Grove.

She waved him away. "Must be this blasted heat."

"I only wanted to inquire about your husband. I have a few questions. But if you're not feeling well..."

She look relieved, as though she'd expected him to say something else. *Funny. Nolan had seemed relieved when I told him I hadn't gone out to the farm.* At least now he knew why.

"What did ya wanna know?" She leaned forward and spit out a small wad of chewing tobacco.

Hodgins raised an eyebrow as he pulled out his trusty notebook and thumbed through the pages.

"How long have you been married?"

"A little over four years."

"You bought the farm shortly after?"

"Ya. Ain't no law a'gin it. Why ya interested in my husband and our marriage?"

"Do you know where he stays when he's in Toronto?"

She shrugged her shoulders. "Boarding house or hotel I expect." She bit her bottom lip. She wasn't telling him everything, but he let it go, for now.

"There was a murder on the street where he stays. Did he mention it?"

She eyed him suspiciously. "If'n ya already know where he stays, why'd ya ask me?"

"Just checking, in case he stayed at more than one place."

She didn't seem all that upset or shocked. "He's bin rather upset the past few days. Didn't want to talk about it. That must be why."

"Hmmm. Must be." He turned to a clean page and made some notes. When he looked up at her again, she was tapping her fingers on the arms of the rocker, and she still seemed pale.

"Are you sure you don't want me to take you to town?"

"No, I'll just sit here in the shade. I'm fine."

Hodgins stood, thanked her for her time and went back

to Pine Grove. He had noticed a couple of churches earlier as he went through town. He stopped at the first one, looking for a record of the marriage. He wasn't even sure they were married there, or even married at all.

A quick chat with the vicar and he left without any information. He went to the next one and found what he was looking for.

The minister had a record of the marriage. Hodgins copied down the details from the registry and drove the horse hard in order to make the last train. When he got back to Toronto, he remembered to stop and pick up his gardening book before going home.

* * *

After dinner Sara went out into the back yard to play with Scraps, and Cordelia and Hodgins went out to the back porch to watch. The previous owners had left a large bench behind, too heavy to move. It needed a new coat of paint but was quite sturdy. Cordelia took the opportunity to ask about the murder.

"You won't believe it," he told her. "Never in your wildest dreams can you guess what I found out today." He leaned back grinning. "Go ahead. Guess."

"Since I haven't a clue what you're referring to I won't even try. What have you found out?"

"Nolan has another wife."

"So? Lots of people remarry."

He leaned forward. "No, you don't understand. His wife died a year or so ago. This wife has been around for over four years."

Cordelia's hand flew to her mouth. "No!"

"Yes. Bad enough the man's lost his daughter. Now I have to arrest him for bigamy. Interesting woman though. Rather rough, if you know what I mean. Even chews tobacco."

Cordelia tisked.

"Think I'll wait until after he buries Olivia. It's not like he knows that I found out. His wife, the second one, isn't expecting him for several days. He's making burial arrangements today, so his daughter will be laid to rest before he goes back up. I'll bet anything one of the neighbours will have something arranged for after the service and funeral. Can't imagine he'll be able to go back to Pine Grove until the next morning so I'll catch him first thing. The service is over at St. Andrew's. Maybe tomorrow afternoon I'll wander over and see what the arrangements are."

"You don't think it's possible he killed his daughter so he could live with his new wife, do you?" Cordelia asked, then thought for a moment. "Could he have killed his first wife?"

"Now that's interesting. He married the second one four years ago. His first wife just died last year. Maybe he got tired of juggling them."

It was getting dark so they called Sara in. Hodgins went down the hall and picked his jacket off the post at the end of the upstairs railing where he had draped it. Retrieving his notebook and pencil from the pocket, he went into the sitting room and sat on the edge of the chair. Resting the notebook on his knee, he mumbled as he wrote.

"Check out the first wife. How did she die? Was she ill long or was it sudden?" He glanced up as Cordelia came in.

"Good thinking Delia. Personally I don't believe the man has it in him to plan a murder, but one never knows."

He propped his elbow on the arm of the chair and tapped his lips with the pencil.

"Wonder if either of the women knew about the other?"

"Is it possible the second wife did in the first?"

Hodgins looked shocked for a moment, then laughed. "Really Delia. Where do you pick up such things? 'Did in' indeed. However..." He paused to mull it over. "Woman have been known to commit murder. Usually poison or some such thing. Can't imagine a woman chasing a girl and bashing her head in with a piece of firewood."

He noticed his wife pale slightly. "Sorry Dear. Guess

those stories you read aren't quite as gruesome as real life."

"It's not that. I was just thinking about Sara. How horrible it must have been to find his daughter like that."

Before Hodgins could respond, the back door slammed. He heard the hurried clicking of Scraps' claws on the floor. The dog turned into the room, sliding into the door frame as he went. He ran to Hodgins and put his big hairy front paws on his lap. Hodgins pushed him down and tried to wipe the mud off his trousers.

"Guess not everything has dried up yet." The dog sat in front of him, mouth open, tongue hanging off to the side. His tail thumped on the floor.

Sara came in holding a towel. "Sorry Daddy. He ran past me when I let him in. I tried to grab him to clean all the mud off his feet, but he was too fast."

"You just had to have a dog. Should've found a smaller one." Cordelia smiled and got up. "Guess I'd better clean the floor. Sara, give your father the towel so he can get some of the mud off, then grab that dog and come help me."

CHAPTER EIGHTEEN

S ince Hodgins had the day off, he slept in for the first time since his short trip to Kingston. *Could get used to this.*

When he finally went downstairs, Sara had already finished breakfast and gone to visit a friend for the day. Scraps picked himself up from his spot beside the icebox and went to greet Hodgins. He was rewarded with a good scratch behind the ears.

Cordelia, having heard him move about, was busy preparing their breakfast. He kissed her on the cheek then took the kettle off the stove. He made two cups of tea, one black, one sweet for his wife. Cordelia placed a jar of her peach jelly on the table, then served up the eggs and sausages. When she brought over the fresh-baked bread she finally sat down.

"What do you have planned for today?" he asked.

Cordelia took a sip of tea. "I think I'll go over to Mother's this morning and see if I can't finish up the draperies today."

"Can't that wait a bit? I haven't seen much of you this week. Thought we could spend the morning together. Maybe tackle the weeds in the garden? It'll be much too hot in the afternoon."

Cordelia took a bite of her eggs, considering what to do. "Well, I suppose the drapes can wait until next week. It would be nice to start on the garden. Give the poor flowers a chance to grow. Maybe we can clear a space for vegetables? If I plant some beets, broccoli and turnips, they'll be ready for fall."

Hodgins looked at his pocket watch and smiled.

"I bought quite a large book on gardening yesterday. It'll take all winter to read it."

"Yes, I saw it on the small table in the front room. I was looking through it and saw a chapter on vegetables for winter and spring."

"Need to buy some tools. I'll do that once we've finished breakfast. One of the hardware stores on King should have hoes, rakes, and the like. Paterson & Son maybe, or Rice Lewis."

They finished their breakfast, chatting about what they wanted or needed to do in their garden. Hodgins had grabbed a piece of paper and pencil and started making a list. He left Cordelia cleaning up the kitchen and rushed off to buy the necessary garden tools, wanting to get back and start working on the gardens before they got sidetracked. If he didn't keep busy, Cordelia would know something was up as he'd just be pacing around looking at his pocket watch all morning. He couldn't wait to see her reaction.

Hodgins found what he had on his list, plus a few other items the clerk suggested would be useful. He'd hired a buggy as he knew he would end up with far more than he could handle.

With the tools in the back yard and buggy returned, Cordelia set about restoring the gardens. After changing into the pair of denims the clerk had recommended, and an old shirt, Hodgins was ready to tackle the pathetic garden along the front porch. He left Cordelia in the backyard with Scraps, marking out an area for her vegetables. There was already a small patch, but it wasn't near large enough to suit her.

Hodgins went out front with his new trowel and wheelbarrow. Since he hadn't thought about buying one of those before he left, he was more than glad he rented the buggy. He positioned the wheelbarrow within easy reach, got down on his knees and went about digging up weeds.

He was pretty certain he could tell the different and not dig up any flowers. At least not enough that anyone would notice. He managed to get about half-way through the garden to the left of the porch steps when the delivery man arrived. Cordelia was still in the back. Hodgins helped the man put it in the room off the kitchen. Fortunately Cordelia was facing away from the house and couldn't see them struggling with it, and Scraps was sleeping under a tree. He would have raised a fuss if he saw Hodgins moving about.

The room was going to be a pantry, but it was big enough to double as a sewing room. At least for the time being. There were a few unpacked boxes in the corner, and a small table that Hodgins had snuck in the night before.

He made sure the machine was set up so Cordelia could look out the window. It would also provide her with more light than the lantern would. He hadn't thought about a chair, but she could use one from the kitchen.

As soon as the delivery man left, Hodgins went out to fetch Cordelia.

He kept his hand on the door so it wouldn't bang shut. Keeping one eye on the dog, he crept across the yard, ensuring neither his wife nor the dog heard him. Cordelia was standing, surveying the area she had marked off. Hodgins reached up and placed his hands over her eyes. Scraps woke up when she screamed.

"Hush, you'll have the neighbor's thinking I beat my wife."

"What are you up to Bertie?"

Scraps ran over, barking and jumping, trying to get in

on the game.

"Come with me." Hodgins turned her towards the house and stood behind her, making sure he kept his hands over her eyes. "Just walk straight. I'll tell you when we reach the porch."

She took a few steps and stumbled as Scraps jumped in front of her. Hodgins grabbed her, laughing. He allowed her to go as far as the porch before covering her eyes again.

He took one hand away to open the door and held it with his foot. The dog scampered in. With her eyes firmly covered, he guided her through the kitchen and into the side room. Scraps ran ahead to investigate what was behind the door that had always been closed. Hodgins removed his hands from her eyes.

"Oh my, it's beautiful." She went over and ran her hands across the machine. She traced the gold scrolling with her finger. The color sparkled against the jet black case of the machine. She turned the hand crank a few times before turning back to Hodgins.

"This looks brand new. How can we afford such a thing? Really, you shouldn't have... but I'm glad you did." She ran over and threw her arms around his neck. "No more trips to Mother's to use her old machine. She'll be so jealous."

"I'll have to get you a chair for it, and I can put up some

more shelves. Anything you need, let me know."

She took a step back. "Are you certain we can afford it? A used machine will do just as well."

"Don't worry. I got a good discount from the dealer."

There was a knock on the front door and Scraps went tearing down the hall, tail wagging, barking all the way.

"What else have you been spending our money on?" Cordelia stood with her hands on her hips.

Hodgins put his hands up in front of him. "I swear I haven't bought anything else."

Hodgins called the dog and Cordelia put Scraps in the backyard. Hodgins opened the front door to an embarrassed looking Barnes, holding a covered plate in his hands. Hodgins raised an eyebrow.

"What's this?"

"Um, my mother baked you something. Says a gift of fresh-baked bread to welcome someone to a new house is good luck or some such thing. She wanted to give you a few weeks to settle in." Barnes shrugged. "May your family never know hunger."

"That's very nice of her. It smells wonderful. Why didn't you bring her along?"

"Said she didn't want to impose."

"So she sent you to impose instead."

Barnes' eyes grew wide. "Sir, I didn't mean to intrude."

He thrust the plate into Hodgins chest and stepped back.

Hodgins laughed and took the plate. "I was only joking with you. You and your family are always welcome here." He looked over Barnes' shoulder and pointed. "You might want to find more excuses to drop in on your days off."

Barnes turned around and saw a middle-age couple walking up the path to the house next door, followed by a young woman in her twenties.

"Oh, she's the most beautiful girl I've ever seen." Barnes stood gaping, his lower jaw slowly dropping farther and farther down.

The man spotted them, waved, then cut across the lawn towards them. "Hello neighbour."

"Good day Mr. Halloway."

"Who's this fine young man?" he asked, thrusting his fleshy hand toward Barnes.

"Mr. Halloway, this is Henry Barnes. He's one of my constables."

Halloway shook Barnes' hand vigorously, pumping it up and down several times. "Constable, eh? So you have a steady job. Good. Good."

Barnes gave Hodgins a puzzled look and shrugged. "Hello Mr. Halloway. Nice to meet you."

"Oh, and manners too. Very good, very good."

"Barnes has ambitions to become a detective, and he's

quite good. Won't be long before he out ranks me," Hodgins remarked.

"Very good, very good. Are you married young man?"

"Um, no Sir."

"Good looking lad like you? Sweetheart?"

Barnes turned deeper shades of red with each question. "No Sir, no sweetheart."

Halloway reached out and straightened Barnes' tie. "Good looking, snappy dresser, well groomed, fit by the looks of you. Quite the catch."

Hodgins decided to rescue Barnes from further interrogation. "I'm afraid we have to go Halloway. My wife's been anxiously awaiting this bread. She'll have my hide if I stay and yabber on too long."

"Quite right, quite right. I know what you mean." Halloway winked. "My missus is the same. Nice to meet you young man. Hope to see you again." He turned and strolled back to his house and Hodgins ushered Barnes inside.

"He's trying to marry off his daughter. Seems he's taken a liking to you."

"That was very embarrassing, I don't mind saying. But his daughter is quite breathtaking."

"Come in and say hello to Cordelia. She'll want to thank you and your mother for the bread. Scraps will want to say hello too."

CHAPTER NINETEEN

Barnes only stayed long enough to say hello to Cordelia and have a little rough and tumble with Scraps in the backyard. While he was doing that, Cordelia wrote out a thank you note to his mother. Barnes took the note and hurried off home. Hodgins noticed Barnes looking over at the house next door, probably hoping for a glimpse of the daughter again.

Hodgins went into the backyard to see what Cordelia had been doing while he had worked out front. She had marked off an area at least ten foot square, right in the middle of the lawn. The old shabby looking garden was still there, but Cordelia had expanded it on all sides. She had roped off an area with sticks and twine, all ready for Hodgins to start to digging.

"Rather large, isn't it? For broccoli, beets, and turnip I mean."

"Come spring I want to plant all sorts of vegetables. If we dig it up now, there will be less to do in the spring. I'll only plant a few rows now."

"Good thinking. Probably be all muddy and wet in the spring. Don't relish the thought of digging then."

Hodgins looked around the yard, stopping at the large maple on the east side.

"You know what might be nice? A shelter for the dog. Already got a fence around the property so he can run around. Might be nice to have a small place for him to go if it starts to rain. Can't be too difficult to build. Just four walls and a roof. Right under that tree. He seems to like it there anyway." He took another look at the large dog.

"Well, reasonably small."

"Before you get too carried away, why don't we have some lunch? It's getting too hot to do much more anyway."

They both changed into clean clothes and Cordelia prepared a light meal. Once they finished, Hodgins helped clean up. She gathered up her fabric and dragged a kitchen chair into her new sewing room to work on the draperies. Hodgins went over to St. James Cathedral to speak with Reverend Mitchell.

"Sorry to disturb you, but I was just wondering what arrangements have been made for Olivia Nolan. I understand her father wished to have the service here."

"Yes, he came in yesterday. How sad to lose one's child. She was such a nice girl. Came in often with her mother. Mr. Nolan was not a regular church goer, but Mrs. Nolan was quite devoted. The service for Olivia will be tomorrow afternoon at two."

"Do you know where she will be buried?"

"Mrs. Nolan is buried in our cemetery up on Parliament. Olivia is to be laid to rest beside her."

Hodgins reached out to shake the Reverend's hand. "Thank you for your time."

Hodgins was thinking about the death of the first Mrs. Nolan, and without even realizing it, he headed off in the direction of the cemetery. A half hour later he entered through the large black wrought iron gates on the east side of Parliament Street. He had no idea where Mrs. Nolan was buried or why he even came to the cemetery, but it was a pleasant spot with a nice view.

Hodgins was immediately drawn to the chapel off to his left, up on a small hill. The spire at the front was noticeable from quite a distance and he had been curious about it before, but never had the time to check it out. He went part way up the walk then veered onto the grass and circled around.

The chapel was magnificent from every angle. The cemetery was nestled among the trees, making it feel much cooler than it was. Hodgins could hear the roar of the water from the Don River somewhere off to the east. He turned back and walked around the north side, and circled back towards the entrance. He wandered around looking at some of the headstones, wondering what had happened to the people, especially the young ones.

Hearing a sound up ahead, he followed it. Two men were digging a grave. He walked over. The men looked up, nodded and kept digging. Hodgins looked at the headstones by the grave being dug. The one on the right had Ruth Nolan's name on it. He had found Olivia's final resting place.

He was on duty Sunday, but the cemetery was only a twenty minute walk from the station on Wilton. He thought he would attend the service, and had a feeling Barnes might wish to join him.

Hodgins had already planned to wait until Monday to confront Nolan about his two wives and arrest him for bigamy, so he would keep his distance at the cemetery. Since he thought Nolan might move up to Pine Grove, Hodgins checked the train schedule to make sure he was at the house on Duchess well before Nolan could leave to catch the first train to Woodbridge.

Hodgins looked at a few more graves and found the marker for Reverend James Fielding, the fourth Bishop of Toronto. It was a large but simple stone, in the shape of a cross. Since there was nothing for him to do at the cemetery, he headed back home.

* * *

Scraps was still in the yard, but he had moved from under the maple as the sun had shifted the shade. He had wiggled under a bush in the back corner and fallen asleep. Hodgins called him and he came running into the kitchen and straight to his water bowl. *We'll have to put a bowl outside for him.* Scraps flopped down beside the ice box and Hodgins went into the sewing room to see how Cordelia was enjoying her new machine. She hummed as she sewed.

"Works ok then?"

"Oh yes. It sews so smoothly." She stopped at the end of the seam and reached down to her side.

"I've got one complete set done already." She held up some chintz curtains. "I'll have them all done by the end of next week I'm sure."

"Room's a little drab, don't you think?" He asked. "Maybe some wallpaper?"

"Plenty of time for that. I'm just happy I don't have to carry the fabric back and forth to Mother's all the time. I wouldn't mind a work table though. I'm certain we can find a second hand one somewhere."

Sara came home in time for dinner, her dress dirty around the bottom, with a blue stains down the front.

"What ever have you been in to?" Cordelia asked.

"We went picking berries. See?"

139

Sara held out a small cloth-covered basket. Cordelia lifted the cloth, revealing a basket full of blueberries.

"May I bake a blueberry pie tomorrow? Please?"

"Yes, after breakfast you can help me bake a pie. Now go upstairs, change into a clean dress, and bring that one down so I can try to get those stains out, then I'll show you what your father bought."

She took the basket from Sara and sent her upstairs.

CHAPTER TWENTY

Hodgins stood in front of Barnes' desk. "Have you found out anything about that woman in Pine Grove?"

"Yes, it seems she has a bit of a record. Nothin' big. Petty theft mostly. How could a man like Nolan get mixed up with someone like that?"

"Who knows? What else do we know about her?"

"Full name's Mary Elizabeth Cooper. Hails from Buffalo near as I can tell. I sent a telegram down Friday. Got a reply Saturday saying they were sending some information up on the train. Just waiting for it to arrive. Hopefully it comes today, or at least by Monday."

"Let me know the moment it arrives."

Hodgins went into his office, but found himself at loose ends. *Maybe if I take my mind off it for a bit.*

He pulled the pad of foolscap out and started sketching. Trying to assess the size of his dog, he added figures to the drawing. Scraps head was about waist high. The doghouse needed to be tall enough for the dog to stand. He was finishing up a very detailed drawing when the church bells rang, signalling the eleven o'clock service. He folded the paper, slipped it into his pocket, and went back to reviewing the case.

Hodgins had been so immersed in sorting out the details, he missed lunch. He unwrapped the leftovers that Cordelia had packed and ate hurriedly. Hunger satisfied, he stepped outside his office.

"Barnes."

Barnes came rushing out from the back, spilling his tea. "Yes, Sir?"

"How'd you like to attend a funeral?"

Barnes stared blankly

"Olivia Nolan is being buried today. Thought you'd want to tag along."

Barnes put the teacup down on Hodgins' desk "Yes, Sir. Very much."

"Come along then. The service at the church should be over. Expect they'll be taking her up to St. James Cemetery 'bout now."

They left the station and turned up Parliament. The procession was a few blocks ahead of them. Picking up their pace, they soon fell in step with the people at the back. Hodgins recognized the Green's and McGregor's. He though he spotted Miss O'Hara a little farther up.

"Quite a few older children," Barnes commented.

"Natural, I expect. She probably had a lot of friends. Everyone seemed to like the girl."

Once they arrived at the cemetery, Hodgins knew exactly where to go. He grabbed Barnes by the arm and pulled him off the roadway.

"Over here."

They cut across the grass and stood far enough from the open grave to be out of the way, but close enough they could easily observe everyone. Hodgins also did not want to intrude. A child's funeral was always more sombre.

The adults were quiet – no one seemed to want to speak. Several of Olivia's friends were crying. The sound carried through the quiet cemetery. They quieted down a bit once Reverend Mitchell started to speak.

"Sir," Barnes whispered. "Have you noticed Miss O'Hara? She's the only neighbour keeping her distance from Mr. Nolan. Before the preacher started, everyone approached him. Everyone except her."

"Yes, I did notice that. She actually looks a little guilty. Hasn't really spoken to many, and those she did speak with, she didn't look in the eye."

The grave-side service ended and Hodgins nudged Barnes. "Look. Miss O'Hara is scampering off."

They watched as she hurried out of the cemetery.

Everyone else lingered, paying their respects. A few went inside the chapel. Mrs. Green turned around and saw them standing off to the side. She spoke to her husband, then approached them.

"Nice of you to attend. You're welcome to come back to our house. I'm sure Mr. Nolan would appreciate that."

Hodgins noticed that she was much calmer now. A nice change from the hysterical women he met earlier.

"Thank you," Hodgins said, "but we have things to attend to."

She started to leave, then turned back. "Do you know who did it?

Both men shook their heads.

"Thought maybe if ya did, he might change his mind about moving." She turned and joined her husband by the grave.

"I knew it," Hodgins said. "He's going to go live with the second wife. First thing tomorrow you and I are going to his house to arrest him. Don't want him getting on the first train out. You can take him back to the station and I'll have another chat with Miss O'Hara. She knows something."

They made their way back to the station on Wilton Street and the desk sergeant called Hodgins over as soon as they stepped through the door.

"There's a copper from New York what came in a short while ago. He's in with Chief Draper now. A Captain Harrison."

"Hmm. Must be about Mary Cooper. Wonder why a captain was sent up?"

Hodgins was telling Barnes about their visitor when Draper came out of his office with the Captain. He called Hodgins over.

"This is Captain Thomas Harrison, New York Police. Got some interesting news about your Mary Cooper."

Draper turned to Harrison. "Detective Hodgins is handling this one. I'll leave you in his capable hands."

The Chief went back to his office and left Hodgins and Harrison to talk.

Hodgins took Harrison into his office and gestured towards the chair opposite his desk.

"What brings you up here? We were expecting information to be sent, not a Captain."

"We've been looking for Mary Cooper for five years. She's a person of interest if you will. Her husband died under mysterious circumstances. While the autopsy was being done, she scarpered. Turns out he was poisoned. We think she either done him in herself, or got some poor slob to do it for her."

Harrison leaned on the desk towards Hodgins. "Did she

murder another husband up here?"

"No. Maybe. I don't know. She's married, and her husband's child from his first marriage was just murdered. We're going to arrest him tomorrow for bigamy."

"Well I never. Murdered a child? Wouldn't have thought that of her. Didn't seem the sort. Ya just never can tell. Bigamist husband you say. Interesting case you got there."

"She's not at the top of my list of suspects, but she is on it. I don't even know if she knew about the first wife. After we arrest Mr. Nolan, the man she married, I plan on taking the first train up to where they're living. About an hour's ride. You're more than welcome to accompany me. We can both question her."

Hodgins thought for a moment. "I guess you have seniority, so to speak. If she is a suspect in the murder of her husband in New York, you'll have to take her back for trial. If we find her guilty, you can send her back up to us when you're through with her. If you don't hang her first." He pulled out his notebook.

"I'll fill you in on everything here. You may as well stay a few days, if that's agreeable with you. Toronto has many fine establishments."

Hodgins called Barnes over and the three of them spent the next few hours reviewing all the information they had, and tossing around ideas until the end of the day.

Harrison left to go back to his hotel. Hodgins and Barnes went home.

* * *

Once their evening meal was eaten, the kitchen cleaned up, and Sara put to bed, Hodgins and Cordelia settled into their chairs in the front room. They always sat in the same two chairs; his a simple arm chair, hers the settee. She frequently had sewing or needlework spread out, or Sara snuggled in close. Hodgins picked his gardening book off the end table and notice a few pieces of paper sticking out from between the pages.

"What's this?"

"I was looking through it earlier and found a few items of interest. There's a page on spring flowers, and some information on roses. Also a section on growing fruit trees. I thought we might try one or two that I could use for preserves. Now put the book down and tell me what's new with the young girl's murder."

Hodgins put the book in his lap. "Very well, but I do believe you are becoming a little gruesome my Dear. I went to her burial this afternoon. Took Barnes with me. He seems particularly affected as he has a sister the same age. Noticed one of the neighbours acting oddly. When we got back to the station, there was a Captain from the New York

147

Police speaking with Draper."

He leaned forward and smiled. "You're going to like this bit. That second wife I was telling you about? Seems she's wanted in New York regarding the death of her husband."

Cordelia's eyes grew wide. "Oh that is a delicious bit of information. This is by far the most interesting case you've had for certain. Do you think she killed that poor child?"

Hodgins settled back. "Don't know what to think. Harrison, that's the Captain from New York, he doesn't think she would harm a child, but it's been several years since he knew her. We're going up to Pine Grove in the morning to get her. Right after arresting Nolan for having two wives that is. Will have to find out if she knew her husband was already married. It's gotten quite complicated." He closed his eyes and rested his head on the back of the chair.

"I wonder," Cordelia said.

He opened his eyes.

"Could she have found out that her husband was married and hired someone else to kill his daughter? That way she'd have him all to herself. He would be able to move up to Pine Grove and she would see him more."

He sat up. "Hire someone? Hmmm. Doubt there's anyone in Pine Grove or the entire area that's a hired killer.

Mostly farmers and merchants. But she does have a history in New York. Might know some undesirables down there. What made you think of it?"

"Why, I'm a woman. The only logical thing would be to dispose of any obstacles between me and my husband. Quite simple really."

Hodgins laughed. "Of course, quite logical. For a woman."

"Now, why don't you invite the Captain to dinner tomorrow? I'd like to meet a policeman from New York. He must have some interesting stories to tell."

CHAPTER TWENTY-ONE

Hodgins arrived at the station to find Harrison already waiting.

"Early bird I see."

"Couldn't sleep. I'm anxious to finally catch up with Mary Cooper. Don't like to have cases left incomplete."

"As soon as Barnes arrives, we can go down to Nolan's. We'll have plenty of time to catch the first train afterwards. Shall we have a cup of tea? Barnes isn't due for a bit."

They chatted and reviewed their plans for the day. Barnes arrived about twenty minutes later and the three of them walked down to Duchess Street. There was a hired buggy out front and a trunk sitting on the porch. The front door was wide open. Hodgins knocked on the door frame and they walked in.

"Hello?"

"Be right down." The words floated from the second floor. Nolan came down the stairs carrying a satchel. He stopped mid-way when he saw Hodgins and Barnes.

"Do you have news?" He rushed the rest of the way

down.

Nolan looked at Harrison but didn't ask who he was.

"Going somewhere?" Hodgins asked.

"Can't stay in this house. You understand."

"Where are you heading?"

"The farm in Pine Grove. You already know about that. Going to move there permanently."

"Yes. Did I tell you? I went back up there the other day. Met a very nice lady. Attractive too. A Mary Cooper. Or should I say Mary Nolan?"

Nolan dropped the satchel by his feet.

"Oh."

"Indeed. I'm placing you under arrest for bigamy. You do realize that you can't have more than one wife at a time?"

Nolan said nothing. Hodgins gestured to Barnes, who stepped forward with a set of handcuffs. Nolan put up no resistance.

"Constable Barnes will escort you back to the station while Captain Harrison and myself pay a visit to Miss Cooper. Oh, Captain Harrison is with the New York Police. Seems your lovely wife is wanted for murder. Did you know that?"

"No," Nolan whispered. "It's not possible." He looked from Hodgins to Barnes. He started to sway. Barnes grabbed him.

"Olivia. Did she kill my daughter?"

"We don't know yet," Hodgins replied. "But we aim to find out."

* * *

Hodgins and Harrison got in the buggy Nolan had waiting and went to Union Station to take the first train to Woodbridge. They hired a buggy and went to Pine Grove to get Mary Cooper. They had decided that Harrison would stay in the buggy, hat pulled down, just in case she recognized him.

Hodgins knocked on the front door.

"Morning Detective. What brings ya up here a'gin?"

"I'm afraid there's been a bit of trouble. May I come in?"

She stepped back to let him enter and looked past him at Harrison. "What about yer friend?"

"We don't need him at the moment." He entered the house, closing the door behind him.

"We kin talk in here." She led him into the kitchen and plucked a cigar out of the jar sitting on the table. She lit it and leaned back in the chair. "So what's this all about?"

Hodgins was startled as he had never seen a woman smoke a cigar before. First the chewing tobacco and now this. *Interesting woman*. Ignoring his impulse to comment, he got on with the reason for his visit.

"I'm afraid your husband has been arrested."

"Arrested? Whatever for?"

Strange. She doesn't seem all that surprised.

"I don't know how to say this delicately, so I'll just say it in plain terms. When you married Kendall Nolan, he already had a wife."

He studied her face. There was no shock.

"Really?" She seemed calm.

She already knew.

"Had a daughter too. He's been arrested for bigamy."

"But if his wife is dead, then he's not a bigamist, is he?"

I never mentioned she was dead.

"She was quite alive when he married you."

"I see."

Hodgins watched as she processed the information.

"Oh, he wouldn't have..." Mary changed her mind and stopped. "What about the girl? I ain't taking care of his kin."

Hodgins thought she seemed to be rather cold and unfeeling.

"She was murdered."

The stunned look on her face revealed she hadn't known.

"Who wouldn't have done what, Mary? What were you going to say?"

"Nothing. When did she get herself killed?"

"Almost two weeks ago."

"So that's why he's bin so funny lately."

Hodgins continued with the script he and Harrison had worked out. He was certain that she had not killed the girl or hired someone else to do it.

"I'd like you to come back to Toronto with me. Confirm Mr. Nolan is the man you married."

"I'd like ta come to the city. Nothin' much to do out here."

He pulled out his pocket watch.

"We need to leave if we're to catch the next train back."

After she was settled in the buggy beside Harrison, he raised his head and pushed his hat back.

"Hello Mary. Been keeping well?"

It only took a minute for her to figure out who he was. She swore and tried to get off the buggy, but Hodgins was blocking her way. She was pinned in between them.

"What's the matter?" Hodgins asked. "Aren't you happy to see an old friend? Don't you want to see your husband?"

She crossed her arms over her chest and stared straight ahead. She didn't speak another word all the way to Toronto.

* * *

When they arrived back at the station, Mary was put in the

interrogation room, alone. Hodgins and Harrison sat at Hodgins' desk. Now that Mary was out of sight they could speak freely. Hodgins filled Harrison in on the conversation in Mary's kitchen.

"She already knew Nolan was married. I'm certain of that. But it was a surprise that his daughter was dead. She started to say something but stopped. I wonder if maybe she knows who might have done it."

"What exactly did she say?"

"Let me think. Something like *he wouldn't* or *couldn't*, then stopped. Wouldn't elaborate on that. Maybe now we've got her here she'll say more."

"Do you know if there's a hired hand at the farm?"

"Don't know. Why?"

"Saw a man out back while you were inside. When he saw me looking at him he ducked behind the house. Didn't get a good look, but he seemed familiar. I think he was maybe in his thirties, but he was too far away to be certain."

"If he worked there he'd have no reason to hide. Could be that's who she was referring to. When I glanced out the kitchen window I saw someone go into the barn." Hodgins stood.

"Shall we get started?" He asked.

Captain Harrison nodded and followed Hodgins into the interrogation room. Mary sat at the far end of a long table, hands folded and resting on her lap. She didn't acknowledge either man. Hodgins and Harrison sat on opposite sides, surrounding her as they had done on the trip into Toronto.

"Mary, you know you'll be taken back to New York with Captain Harrison and stand trial for the murder of your husband. It might be helpful if you told us what you know about the murder of Olivia Nolan. It will show you are cooperative. If the jurors find out you were involved with the death of a young girl, they won't show you any mercy."

Mary stared at the wall and continued her vigilance of silence.

Harrison stood up and shoved his face in front of her. "Damn it woman. Say something."

He grabbed her hands and slammed them on the table top. She winced.

"Hold on there Harrison. No need to be so rough." Hodgins grabbed Harrison by the wrist. "I don't go in for that sort of thing. Leastways not with a woman, cold as she might be."

Harrison released his grip but did not back away from her.

"Maybe if we let her sit in a cell she'll feel more like talking," Hodgins said. "We've got Nolan down there and he knows all about her. Even thinks she killed his daughter.

Might prove interesting to have them side by side. If Nolan doesn't get to her, maybe the rats will. They're quite large you know."

Hodgins took Mary's arm. She pulled away and stood up. They escorted her down to the cells and locked her in next to Nolan. He rushed over and reached through the bars.

"Come here you bitch. I'll get you for what you did to Olivia."

Mary backed away. "No, it weren't me."

"I hate you for what you've done."

Mary ran to the front of the cell, grabbing the bars with both hands. "You have to let me out. Lock me up if ya must, but not here."

Nolan was still reaching through the bars, trying to grab hold of her. "You murdering bitch. I'll kill you for what you've done."

Nolan sank to the floor sobbing. "My precious Olivia."

Hodgins turned to Harrison. "We don't get many woman in our cells, but they generally will do anything to get out. Nolan seems convinced she did it. Between the rats and Nolan, she's certain to break down. Guess she's surrounded by rats." Hodgins laughed at his joke.

Harrison grumbled about not having more time with her, but did as Hodgins wanted. They left her to the barrage of insults and threats coming from Nolan.

Since they had been in such a rush to get Mary Cooper into a jail cell, lunch had been forgotten until their stomachs rumbled. They went out and got a meat pie from one of the street vendors.

"Have you been to Toronto before, Captain?"

"No, first trip. Thought it might be much like New York, but it's not. Not so crowded. Seems a bit more peaceful. Rather enjoy the bustle of the city myself."

"I guess it's all what you're used to. It's not always quiet though. Especially down by the waterfront. Had our fair share of riots too, mostly courtesy of the Orangemen. Even had a circus riot back in '55 that involved the Orangemen. Clowns, if you can imagine. Because of a brothel."

Harrison looked skeptical. "Clowns and a brothel? You're pulling my leg."

"No, not at all. It really happened."

The both had a good laugh and shared a few off colour jokes over that.

"Any more thoughts about the man you saw at the farm? If he seemed familiar, maybe he's an old acquaintance of Mary's?"

"I'm sure I should know him, but it's been five years since I dealt with her," Harrison said. "Will have to remember who she associated with back then. It'll come to me eventually."

"Before I forget, my wife has insisted you join us for supper tonight."

CHAPTER TWENTY-TWO

Cordelia rushed around getting everything ready. She was able to find enough flowers between the weeds to make a nice centrepiece for the table. Sara had been given her supper early and was told to stay upstairs out of the grown-ups way. She whined enough that she was allowed to meet Captain Harrison *then* she had to go straight upstairs.

At six thirty a knock sounded on the door. Sara held onto Scraps while Hodgins answered it.

"Good of you to join us. Come in. Excuse the disarray but we've just moved in and are still putting the house in order."

Scraps barked.

"Nice dog ya got there," Harrison said.

The dog pulled away from Sara and bounded down the hall towards Harrison, tail wagging excitedly. Hodgins grabbed him before he could jump up.

"He gets rather excitable when new people come by."

Harrison stroked the top of the dog's head, and Scraps' tail thumped against the floor. Cordelia came out of the kitchen and stood with Sara.

"I'd like you to meet my family. My wife, Cordelia, and our daughter, Sara. You've already met Scraps."

Harrison walked over to Cordelia and handed her a box of chocolates. He reached into his pocket and pulled out a bag of sweets for Sara.

"Thank you for inviting me."

Sara was sent upstairs for the evening and Hodgins and Harrison went into the sitting room. Scraps followed. Cordelia went back to the kitchen to finish preparing their meal. She had picked up a nice piece of roasting beef, potatoes, carrots, and onions. The roast was sitting in it's drippings, soaking up the flavour.

Hodgins had purchased a bottle of wine for the occasion. That was one thing that was missing from the house as spirits were not at the top of the shopping list. Too many necessities to purchase first. His father-in-law always had whiskey on hand, but it wasn't something Hodgins had a great love for.

The wine was sat breathing on the dining room table. Hodgins wasn't really certain what that meant, but his wife said it was necessary.

Cordelia placed the beef on a platter and the vegetables in bowls. One by one she took them to the table. She frowned as she surveyed the settings. They didn't have anything they could consider their best dishes. Not yet anyway. At least it was a full set of dishes and there were no cracks or chips. Satisfied that everything was presentable, she called the men into the dining room and they made small talk over their meal.

When Cordelia served the cake she had made earlier in the day, she asked about Olivia's murder. Harrison looked at Hodgins and raised an eyebrow.

"Not to worry. My wife seems to enjoy discussing my cases. Very special woman, my Cordelia."

"Special indeed." Harrison wasn't sure what he should say. "Go into much detail?"

"Well, some. Depends on the circumstances. Didn't go into all the details about this one, what with it being so brutal, and a young girl."

"I'm a strong woman Captain Harrison, but I do have a daughter. I didn't want to hear exactly how she died. My husband generally knows when to stop. So, have you learned anything new?"

"Still mulling over your suggestion that Miss Cooper, the second wife, hired someone to kill the girl. So far there's nothing pointing in that direction. Not ruling it out though."

Harrison looked across the table at Cordelia. "You suggested that? Whatever made you come up with that conclusion?"

"Woman's logic," Hodgins said. He grinned.

"It's quite simple really." She explained it to Harrison much the same way she told her husband. "Women will often take drastic measures to get or keep a man."

Both men laughed. Cordelia stood up. "I really don't see why that is so funny." She picked up the empty plates and stormed into the kitchen.

"I think we've offended your good wife."

"She'll calm down quick enough. Delia really does come up with some very insightful thoughts. Don't mind admitting she's helped me more than once."

"Glad to hear you acknowledging it." Cordelia said, coming out of the kitchen with a fresh pot of tea. "Now, tell me about Mrs. Nolan, or Miss Cooper, or whatever you're calling her. What did you find out from her?"

"She's not sayin' much," Harrison said. "Knows she's going to be facing a murder trial back in New York. Should've seen her when we threw her in the cell beside Nolan. If there wasn't bars between them, your husband would have another murder on his hands."

"Goodness! Whatever happened?"

"Nolan's sure she killed his daughter," Hodgins said. "I won't repeat some of the things he called her."

Cordelia blushed slightly. "I think I can imagine."

"She knows something though," Hodgins said. "She

163

started to say something to me back at the farm but changed her mind. She seemed genuinely shocked when I mentioned the murder of the girl."

"Don't forget about that man I saw hiding behind the farm house," Harrison said. "Wish I got a better look at 'im. Still can't place him."

"Farm hand?" Cordelia asked. She turned to her husband. "Was it a working farm?"

Hodgins shrugged. "Why hide if he was a hired hand?"

Cordelia nodded in agreement. "So, maybe he was a hired hand, just not for the farm. Someone she knew from New York possibly?"

"Back to that again?" Hodgins smiled and turned to Harrison. "If she wasn't a woman she would make a good detective."

Harrison almost choked on his tea. "A woman detective?" he said when he finished coughing. "Never happen. Can you imagine? Suppose you also think woman will be running the country some day too. Preposterous."

Cordelia sat back and crossed her arms. "And why not? Not all women are mindless and feeble. Just like not all men are smart and strong."

"Bah," Harrison said. "Never happen."

"Let's not get into politics, please," Hodgins said. "Murder's much more interesting and less volatile, so to speak."

"So what are you going to do tomorrow? Beat a confession out of her?"

"Cordelia," Hodgins exclaimed. "I do not beat my prisoners, often. And never a woman."

She smiled.

"You're husband's a little too protective if you ask me. She's a murderer first, woman second. Maybe you should move her *into* Nolan's cell. Just for a few minutes."

"What you do with your prisoners in New York is your concern. Until you take her, she's my concern." Hodgins thought about what might happen if the two were put together, then smiled briefly.

"Might be interesting though. Putting them in the same cell I mean."

They talked a bit longer, then Cordelia cleared up while Hodgins and Harrison went back to the sitting room. They drank wine, argued good naturedly over the treatment of prisoners and laughed some more about women running the country before Harrison went back to his hotel for the night.

CHAPTER TWENTY-THREE

Harrison came up to the station mid-morning and sat with Hodgins in the interrogation room. Mary Cooper was brought in. She didn't seem quite as defiant after spending the night in the dank cell with the rats and an angry husband for a neighbour. Hodgins had been told that sometime during the night Nolan threw his full bedpan at the bars separating the two cells.

Mary was deflated, withdrawn. She sat in the chair at the end of the table, just as she had the day before. Again, she stared at the wall. This time she slumped a little. The hardness had left her face. Hodgins got up and went to the far side of the room, indicating for Harrison to follow.

Hodgins spoke quietly. "I think she may talk now. The night in the cell seems to have taken all the fight out of her. Nolan's reaction to her probably put her over the top."

Harrison looked over at Mary. "You're right. She seems much more placated. Maybe too much so. Looks to me like she's gone inside herself, if you know what I mean. Then again, it might all be an act."

"Guess we'll find out soon enough. I think gentle methods are required."

Harrison snorted. "Gentle methods. Not in my jail."

"It's not your jail."

They took their places at the table. Hodgins touched her arm.

"Mary."

She slowly turned her head and looked at him. He removed his hand.

"Mary, what do you know about Olivia's death?"

"Nothing." Her voice was barely audible.

"How did you know that Nolan was already married? When did you find out?"

"Few weeks ago." She sighed. "Might as well tell you." She looked over at Harrison. "I'm gonna hang anyway."

Harrison slammed his palm on the table. Mary jumped. "I knew she killed her husband five years ago. As good as just admitted it."

"I'm not concerned about that. Mary, how did you find out Nolan was married?"

Mary glanced sideways at Harrison. "Freddie Calhoon."

"Four Fingers Freddie? How the hell would he know that?" Harrison asked. "Wait a minute. Is that who was hiding out at the farm?"

"Four Fingers Freddie?" Hodgins said. "Should I even

ask?"

"Lost the thumb off his left hand in a knife fight. Made him even more ornery than he was to start with. Mary used to keep company with him. We thought he might've been the one who done in her husband, but he was playing cards and drinking when the man was poisoned. Not his style anyway. Quite handy with a knife, except that one time."

"So, this Four Fingers Freddie is in Toronto?" Hodgins asked Mary.

"Yes. I sent him a letter. Asked him to come up and follow Kendall. He was away so much, just didn't seem right. Sent Freddie the train fare and he came right away."

Mary stopped talking and stared blankly at the wall again.

"Mary," Hodgins said. He touched her arm again. "Mary." No response. He turned to Harrison. "I don't think she's going to say anything more right now."

Mary was put back in her cell and the men headed towards Hodgins' office. Harrison glanced out the window and stopped. "There."

"What?" Hodgins said.

"That man over there. I'm sure that's Calhoon."

Hodgins looked out the window as Harrison ran out the front door and across the street.

"Shit."

Hodgins ran after him. The man ran down Regent Street, Harrison close behind. Calhoon was getting away.

Should have called him Fast Freddie, Hodgins thought as he caught up to Harrison. They ran past St. David Street and saw Calhoon turn left on Sydenham, then left again at Sackville. Hodgins could see Freddie had stopped at Queen and was looking both ways repeatedly, trying to figure out where to go. He turned around. Hodgins and Harrison gained ground.

"We've got 'im now," Harrison said.

Calhoon turned left on Queen, then scurried down St. Paul's. Harrison stopped to catch his breath. "Damn. Bugger's getting' away."

"Maybe not. That's a dead end street he just turned down. Don't recall if there are any fences though. We might still catch him."

As they approached St. Paul's Street, Calhoon was just exiting back onto Queen. He quickly turned around and went back down. The street ended at the back of a large building. There appeared to be no exit. Calhoon turned and pulled a knife.

"Get back or I'll run ya clear through."

"There's one of him and two of us. We can rush him," Hodgins suggested.

"Last time I had him in my jail, it took five of my men

to subdue him. Two ended up in the hospital."

"Great. Any suggestions? Is he wanted?"

"Always have my eye on him, but he's not wanted right now."

Hodgins thought for a moment. "Maybe we can talk to him. If he's not wanted, he's got nothing to be afraid of."

"Ha. Not Freddie. He's not a talker. And he hates all cops."

Hodgins took a few steps toward Calhoon.

"I ain't kiddin'. Come any closer and them'll be yer last steps."

Calhoon made stabbing motions with the knife. Hodgins took a few more steps.

"Either yer mighty brave or awful foolish," Harrison said. He took a step forward.

Hodgins noticed movement at the end of the lane. He moved back with Harrison and spoke softly. "Look at the back of the road."

"Where the hell did he come from?"

At the very back, creeping around some crates, was Constable Barnes. His arm hit a crate and it toppled over.

Calhoon turned.

Hodgins ran forward. Barnes approached cautiously. Harrison swore and ran to help.

Calhoon turned back and forth between Hodgins and

Barnes, swinging the knife. Every time Calhoon turned towards Barnes, Hodgins took another step closer. Harrison circled around. Hodgins was just beyond the reach of the knife. Calhoon turned towards Barnes again, and Hodgins tackled him.

They hit the ground. Harrison tried to help, but they were rolling so much he couldn't get a grip on Calhoon. Barnes ran up, holding a piece of broken crate.

Calhoon and Hodgins stopped rolling, with Calhoon on the top. Barnes slammed the wood down on Calhoon's back. He fell to the side and Hodgins sat up. Calhoon staggered to his feet and Harrison leveled him with a punch to the jaw. Calhoon fell back, unconscious.

"Where did you come from Henry?" Hodgins asked Barnes.

"I noticed the Captain here rush out, then you, so I followed. When I saw the man run down St. Paul's I went down Sackville. There's several small alleyways, like that one over there." He pointed to the alley between Queen Street and where the scuffle had taken place. "There's another one right at the end of the lane, just before the last building."

"Calhoon must not have gone right to the end before turning back," Hodgins said. "Let's get him back to the station." He started to stand and fell back, gripping his side.

"Sir? Are you all right?" Barnes asked.

Hodgins pulled his hand away. His palm was red. "Seems I may have gotten in the way of his knife."

CHAPTER TWENTY-FOUR

Barnes and Harrison half carried, half dragged Calhoon up to the station house. Hodgins trailed behind holding his side. Harrison took Calhoon inside and got him locked up while Barnes assisted Hodgins up to the hospital on Gerrard.

The wound wasn't deep and Hodgins refused to stay in the hospital. He was stitched and bandaged and went back to the station house.

"Has our friend come to yet?" he asked Harrison.

"Yeah, a little while ago. Your jails getting' mighty full. He wants to know what he's being charged with. Told him we hadn't been planning to arrest him, least ways not until he assaulted a fellow officer. You're more than welcome to have him." Harrison laughed. "Keep him off my streets for awhile. Guess your cut ain't too bad or they wouldn't a let ya out."

"Doctor said I was lucky. If it hadda gone any deeper it would have cut into my kidney." Hodgins winced as he lowered himself into the chair behind his desk.

"I think you should go home," Barnes said. "Rest up a bit."

"Nonsense. As long as I don't get into another barney I'll be fine. I think we'll let Calhoon stew in the cell for a while before questioning him. Is there still an officer down by the cells? If Mary gets too close to Nolan, he'll probably strangle her through the bars."

"Yes, Riley's down there."

"Good. Have a word with him. Tell him to keep an ear out for any conversation between Calhoon and Mary."

Barnes nodded and went to talk to Riley.

Hodgins was getting hungry so he opened the lunch Cordelia had packed. Leftovers from last evenings meal. She had put in extra for Harrison. Hodgins went to the back for tea, then spread the beef, bread, and cake across his desk.

As Barnes walked past the office, he noticed the constable eyeing the cake and licking his lips. Cordelia had packed an overly generous slab, so Hodgins broke off a piece of the cake, waved Barnes in, and handed it to him.

"Thank you, Sir. I do so like your wife's chocolate cake." He stuffed it in his mouth as he continued to his desk. Hodgins could hear the sounds of pleasure as Barnes chewed.

"That boy certainly does enjoy his food," Hodgins said to Harrison. "Especially sweets."

Hodgins felt a little better after he filled his belly; almost made his side hurt less.

"Have to make sure that the dog is under control before entering the house tonight." He put his hand to his side. "Today's not a good day to have a large, over-friendly dog," he said to Harrison.

Hodgins grasped the arms of his chair and made to stand up. A sharp pain ripped through his side and he lowered himself back down. He took a deep breath and tried again, slowly this time.

"Shall we take a stab at getting Calhoon to talk?" He placed his hand on his side. "Bad choice of words."

"You're a stubborn man, Detective," Harrison said.

Hodgins ignored the comment and waved Barnes over.

"Bring Calhoon up to the interrogation room. Check with Riley to see if Cooper or Nolan said anything useful. They may have argued and forgot there was a copper listening. He waited with Harrison in the interrogation room for Calhoon to arrive. Barnes entered behind Calhoon and shook his head, indicating Riley heard nothing. He took out the key to the handcuffs, but Harrison stopped him.

"I don't think that's wise boy. Leave him cuffed."

Barnes looked over at Hodgins.

"Leave him."

Barnes left, but stayed outside the door.

"I guess you know Captain Harrison. Why did you run off?" Hodgins asked.

"He's a copper. Don't need no other reason."

"What brings you up to our fair city?"

"Holiday?" Calhoon suggested.

"That's not what Miss Cooper said."

Hodgins looked at Harrison and nodded. They had already agreed to let Harrison take the lead. Hodgins didn't have the strength to deal with someone like Calhoon and he didn't want him to find out he had been stabbed.

Harrison had Calhoon's knife. He got up and stood beside him.

"Nice blade." How'd ya like to find out how it feels?"

He held the blade against Calhoon's neck, just hard enough for his skin to indent. Calhoon didn't flinch.

"We know Mary had you come up to spy on her so-called husband. What else did you do?"

He moved the knife so the tip pressed into Calhoon's neck, then pushed until a thin trickle of blood appeared. Harrison looked over at Hodgins.

"Try not to mess up the floor. Blood's a bugger to clean up." Hodgins was torn between stopping Harrison and letting him continue but the pain in his side won, for now anyhow.

Calhoon remained still. He shifted his eyes to look at

Hodgins.

"It ain't a crime to watch somebody."

"No," Hodgins said, "but you did assault a police officer."

Calhoon moved and a bit more blood trickled out. "You started it. You jumped me. I should charge you."

Hodgins shrugged. "Who's the judge going to believe?"

"What do ya want to know?" Calhoon growled.

"Miss Cooper. What did she have you come up for?"

"Like Mary told ya. To follow that Nolan guy."

Harrison pressed harder on the knife.

Calhoon sat still, not wanting to draw more blood. His lips barely moved.

"I told ya what you wanted to know. She didn't ask me to do nothin' else."

Hodgins looked over at the window and waved Barnes into the room. "Take him back to his cell."

Barnes walked over to Calhoon but Harrison still had the knife to his throat.

"Captain," Hodgins said. "That's enough."

Harrison hesitated before removing the knife. After Barnes had taken Calhoon away Harrison turned to Hodgins.

"I coulda got him to talk. Just needed a bit more coaxing is all."

"Not today." Hodgins placed both hands on the table and rose slowly.

"I think I'll take Barnes' advice and go home after all. You're welcome to stay and go over everything with Barnes. Nothing more."

Harrison grumbled and nodded in agreement. Hodgins spoke to Barnes, leaving explicit instructions not to allow Harrison access to their three prisoners. He also asked him to go see Dr. McKenzie and find out everything he could about Mrs. Nolan's death last year. He then took a very rough, very bumpy, and very painful carriage ride home.

CHAPTER TWENTY-FIVE

After spending the previous evening being pampered by his family, Hodgins was ready to return to work. He hated lying around the house, and he didn't feel his injury was that bad. Cordelia tried to get him to stay home for a few more days, but he wouldn't listen.

"That Webster fellow should be in town today. I need to track him down before he disappears again."

"Surely Constable Barnes and Captain Harrison can speak to him."

"No. Don't want Harrison talking to him alone. Barnes is only a constable, and still new. Harrison will run roughshod over him. Don't want him scaring off Webster. He can be quite the bully." He hadn't told Cordelia about Harrison drawing blood from Calhoon.

He kissed Cordelia and headed out. The walk took twice as long as usual but he wasn't up for any more jostling on a buggy or trolley. Harrison had arrived before him and was with Barnes. It sounded as though he was taking over. Barnes looked relieved to see Hodgins.

Harrison turned to face the detective

"How much longer are you going to hold Mary Cooper? Seems to me the only thing she's done wrong was marrying Nolan. No law against being stupid, leastways not in New York. I'd like to take her back for trial."

"Once I'm certain whether or not she was involved in the girl's death, then you can have her. 'Course even if she was involved, I suppose you'll have to take her anyway. You were looking for her first. Send her back if you find she's innocent. If she's not, well, can't have a trial for a corpse, and can't hang her twice. End of the week suit you?"

"Bin waiting this long, another couple days won't make no never mind."

"Detective Hodgins," the desk sergeant called.

Hodgins turned and the sergeant waved him over. "Man here to see you. Got one of your cards."

He walked over and the young man held his hand out. "My name's John Webster. My folks said you wanted to see me. Something about Olivia Nolan? Tragic what happened. Not sure why you want to see me though."

"Come into to my office."

Hodgins perched on the front edge of the desk and Webster took the chair. He studied Webster's appearance. It was easy to see why women fell for him: Good looking young man; bit of a twinkle in his eyes; long dark wavy hair, just past his shoulders. *Dark and wavy? Just like the one found on Olivia.*

"Did you see or hear anything that night? Someone creeping around? Anyone around during the day who looked suspicious?"

"No, no one that I can recall. I've been here often enough to know all the neighbours. Didn't see anyone who didn't belong."

"What was your relationship with Miss Nolan? I understand you were," he paused. "Friendly?"

Webster looked down at the floor and whispered, "We were to be married." There was a slight tremble in his voice.

"That's not what I've heard. Didn't she turn you down? More than once?"

Webster's head snapped up. "Yes, but only because she thought it too soon, that she was too young. We would have married when she was a little older."

Hodgins looked through his notebook. "Understand you had a bit of bother with your former employer. A Mr. Adams? Something to do with his daughter."

Webster's ears turned red. "That was over a year ago."

"I see. And your current employer, Mr. Purdy, seems to think he needs to keep you away from his daughter. If you were planning to marry Miss Nolan, why carry on with another?"

Webster smiled. "I'm a young man. Not married *yet*."

"Miss Nolan's friends told me that she wanted nothing to do with you. That you were bothering her. Are you certain you didn't see her that night? Tried something on, and killed her when she said no?"

Webster stood, clenching his fists. "How dare you? I would never hurt Olivia. Never."

"Calm down. I need to eliminate people. You do want to find out who did it, don't you? Where were you that night?"

Webster remained standing for a moment, then slowly sunk back into the chair. "I suppose you're just doing your job. I was at the boarding house with Miss O'Hara."

"Until what time?"

Webster said nothing.

"You're not suggesting you were with her all night, are you?"

Webster smiled. "No, all's the pity. She's quite a handsome woman. I did convince her not to go across to the Nolan house, but alas that's *all* I could convince her of."

"Right. I'll confirm that with Miss O'Hara." Hodgins called Barnes over. He stood and whispered so Webster couldn't hear.

"Did you look into the death of that painter fellow? Was he married?"

"Yes, I mean no. Yes, I spoke to Constable Smith. No the painter wasn't married. Recluse actually."

"So there's no reason to believe the two murders were connected. No love triangle involving Webster?"

"No, doesn't seem so."

"Blast."

Hodgins dismissed Barnes and turned back to Webster.

"That's all for now. But you're not to leave town until I say so."

"But I have my calls to make. People are expecting me. I'll lose orders."

"Hang your orders. I'm trying to find out who killed your *fiancé*. Until I'm convinced you had nothing to do with it, you will stay put."

"But —"

"I suggest you send word to your customers."

Hodgins remained standing. Webster took the hint and left, then Hodgins went over to Barnes' desk to speak with Barnes and Harrison.

"What have you found out about Mrs. Nolan's death?"

"Nothin' useful,' Harrison said. "She was sick for some time. Nothin' suspicious according to your doctor."

"Sir," Barnes said. "I recalled you mentioned that woman what disappeared over on George Street. I asked around about that."

"And?"

"Turns out she'd run off with her boyfriend. Her friend received a postcard from her the other day. Seems they just got on the train and went to Alberta."

"So it's just a coincidence we have two murders and a disappearance in the same neighbourhood about the same time... Damn."

He sat on the desk beside Barnes. "Let's think this through. We have three suspects. Four maybe. Mr. Nolan, Miss Cooper, and Mr. Webster. Not really convinced about Cooper and Nolan. It's just a feeling. I have no evidence one way or the other. They're not at the top of the list, but I'm keeping an open mind about them. What about Calhoon?" He turned to Harrison.

"Could Calhoon harm a young girl?"

"Hmmm. He's quite ruthless, but a young girl? I've seen him slap around the boys who do jobs for him, but he actually seems to have a soft spot for the ladies."

"What about Olivia's father?" Hodgins asked. "He's genuinely grief-stricken. Then again, it could be guilt. With her out of the picture, he could move in with Miss Cooper and keep up the pretense of being legitimately married. He was in the process of doing just that when we arrested him. 'Course he's not too fond of her now."

Harrison joined in. "Mary Cooper is already under

suspicion for murdering her husband, and I truly believe she's got it in her. You may not think so, but I'm certain she'll be convicted for that one."

"What about Mr. Webster?" Barnes asked. "We know he's a rogue, but a murderer?"

"Crime of passion maybe?" Hodgins said. "We have four suspects. We need to narrow it down. Get me some paper, will you Henry?"

Barnes pulled a pad of long paper from his desk drawer and handed it to Hodgins.

The detective got off the desk and took a deep breath as a pain shot through his side. He put the pad down and spoke as he wrote.

"Nolan said he was out of town. The stationmaster or one of the porters can confirm that. I have the name of the customer he claims he had business with. Barnes, you take care of checking that. If he has two witnesses to say he was out of town, then we can cross him off.

Webster said he was with Miss O'Hara. I'll speak to her and find out what time that was. 'Course he could've snuck out afterwards, so he can't be completely eliminated.

Hodgins turned to Harrison. "Since you're familiar with Calhoon, would you like to have another go at him? *Without* the knife this time?"

Harrison made a fist and smacked it against his other

palm. "Let me at 'im. I'll find out anything ya need to know."

"Just make sure he's still breathing when I return."

CHAPTER TWENTY-SIX

Hodgins left to go down to Miss O'Hara's wondering what shape Calhoon would be in when he returned. What should have been a pleasant fifteen minute walk took painfully closer to thirty, but he wasn't going to let his wound stop him from doing his job.

He leaned heavily on the railing as he dragged his aching body up onto the large verandah of the boarding house. He paused to catch his breath before knocking on the front door.

"Good morning Miss O'Hara. I need to ask you a few more questions."

"Certainly Detective." Flossie joined him outside. "Shall we sit? It's nice and shady." She pointed to the white wicker chairs arranged around a small table at the east end of the porch.

Hodgins waited until she was seated before gingerly lowering himself onto the chair. He pulled out his notebook and pencil.

"Mr. Webster said that he was here with you the evening that Miss Nolan was killed. Is that true?"

"Oh, I'm so ashamed for what I did. If I hadn't let Mr. Webster talk me out of staying with Olivia she'd still be alive."

"Or you might very well be dead too," Hodgins mumbled. Unfortunately he spoke louder than he intended.

Flossie's mouth opened and she gasped. Hodgins thought she looked pale and feared she might faint.

"I do apologize. I should never have suggested such a thing." He waited until her colour returned.

"How late were you with him?"

"We played cards with my other lodger and my friend, Cecelia Groves, until about ten, then we sat and talked until close to midnight. They went up to their rooms, Cecelia went home, and I checked to make sure all the doors were locked before I retired."

"And he didn't leave after that?"

"No, I don't believe so. Leastways I didn't hear him. There's a squeaky step on the staircase and my room is closest to the top. The house remained quiet. I'm certain I would have heard if anyone went downstairs."

"Has anyone stayed in the room Mr. Webster rented?"

"No, since he's here regularly, I keep the room vacant for him. I'm rarely filled up, unfortunately."

Hodgins wrote down what she told him then put away his notebook. He stood slowly.

"Would you mind if I had a look in his room? He knew Miss Nolan and there might be something useful tucked away."

"Certainly. It's this way." She rose and Hodgins followed her up to the second floor. The third step from the top squeaked loudly as she stepped on it.

"See. I told you I would've heard if someone went out after retiring. It's quite loud now and seems so much louder at night."

She walked down the hall and stopped at the last door. Hodgins was experimenting, putting his weight down at different spots. The step squeaked each time.

"I suppose someone could hop over that one, but I guess he wouldn't land quietly." He went down to the door that Miss O'Hara had opened.

"I've cleaned the room and I assure you he left nothing behind."

Hodgins entered the room, quickly surveying it. He walked over to the dresser and opened the drawers, one by one. Each was empty. There was one shelf on the wall, and a small table sat beside the bed. Both were empty.

"If you do come across something of his, anything at all, please contact me right away. I won't keep you any longer. Thank you for your time."

Thirty minutes later he was back at the station house. Barnes was at his desk, but Harrison was no where to be seen.

"Where is he then?" he asked Barnes.

"Still with Calhoon." Barnes looked uncomfortable. "He told me to leave. There was a lot of noise, but it's been quiet for some time now."

"Damn. You should *never* have left him alone with Calhoon."

"But he's a Captain, Sir."

"A Captain *and* a bully. Not your fault. Come with me."

They hurried to the interrogation room. Hodgins grimaced and held his side. He glanced through the window as he passed.

"What the... "

"Hodgins opened the door. "Get out. Out of this room and out of my station."

"Oh dear Lord," Barnes said, peering around Hodgins.

Calhoon was sitting against the wall, Harrison kneeling in front, fist raised for another strike. Calhoon's face was a bloody, pulpy mess. Blood dripped from Harrison's knuckles.

"Get some of the boys," Hodgins said to Barnes. "We need to get him up to the hospital, if it's not already too late."

Barnes ran for help. Harrison had not moved. Hodgins stormed over, grabbed Harrison' raised arm and yanked him to his feet, ignoring the searing pain in his side.

"I said *get out*. I don't want to see your face in this station again. I'll have Miss Cooper brought over to your hotel when we're finished with her. Better yet, why don't you just go back to New York on the next train, and I'll have her escorted down."

Hodgins pushed Harrison out of the room as Barnes rushed down the hall with two other constables.

Harrison sneered, "You're all too soft. He was ready to talk. Just needed a bit more coaxing."

"A bit more of your coaxing and I'd be calling the coroner. For your sake he'd better recover. Go back to the hotel, now." Hodgins kept pushing Harrison until he stumbled out the front door.

The two constables came out carrying Calhoon, one on either side of him. It looked like they were supporting a drunk. Barnes followed. Hodgins reached for Barnes.

"Stay here, they can manage. It's only a couple of blocks."

"Sir, I think you should accompany them up to the hospital." He pointed to the front of Hodgins shirt. A small red spot had appeared and was slowly expanding.

Hodgins looked down. "Must have loosened a stitch. Nothing to worry about."

They stood on the steps; Hodgins glaring at Harrison's back while Barnes watched the constables carry Calhoon around the corner and out of sight.

"I told Smith to stay at the hospital and bring back word soon as the doctors are finished. Hope that's all right?"

"Good thinking. I don't trust Harrison. Wouldn't put it past him to double back and have a go at Calhoon in the hospital. Might put him off to see the police there. If Smith isn't back in a few hours, I'll go up and check on him. Have one of the lads stay overnight if need be."

They went back inside and over to Barnes' desk. Hodgins picked up the paper he had been writing on earlier and re-read the names.

"I'm sure Nolan didn't kill his daughter. Don't know if he would've hired someone. Who knows what type of characters he meets on his travels. Still need to confirm where he was."

"I've sent a telegram to his customer in Coboconk. I'll go to the train station and see if anyone remembers seeing him that day."

"I'm also certain Miss Cooper didn't do it. Unless she's a very good actress, I believe she was unaware the girl was killed. That leaves Webster and Calhoon. Unless it was totally random, then we're back to the beginning. I have a feeling it was deliberate though. Whoever did it must have known she was alone in the house. Don't know how Calhoon would know that, but Webster made certain Miss O'Hara stayed away from the Nolan house."

"But why would Webster kill her? He said he wanted to marry her."

"My wife probably has some logical theory on that," Hodgins mumbled.

"Sir?"

"Nothing. Miss O'Hara seems quite certain no one left the boarding house after she locked up though. The step has quite a distinctive and loud squeak. I suppose if someone wanted to, they could've avoided that particular step somehow. Don't forget to go to the station and see if anyone remembers seeing Nolan that day. I think I'll have another chat with Miss Cooper. I have a feeling there's something she's not telling me."

* * *

Since the interrogation room still had blood splattered about, and Chief Draper was out for the rest of the day, Hodgins had Miss Cooper brought to Draper's office as it was more private than his. She was even more withdrawn than before.

"Miss Cooper. Mary. Is there anything else you can tell

me? Did you ask Calhoon to come up for any reason other than to watch Nolan?"

She sat with her hands in her lap and seemed focused on the edge of the desk. She said nothing.

"What happened when Calhoon told you about Olivia?"

She raised her head and looked directly at him. "Happened?"

"Yes, when you found out that your husband had been married for years and had a daughter, what did you do? You must've been angry."

"I was shocked, but when Freddie told me Kendall's wife was dead, figured it didn't much matter now. Except for that girl. I wanted my husband home more, but he couldn't stay because of her."

"So you wished her harm? Wanted her out of the way?"

She looked shocked. "Freddie suggested the same thing, but it wasn't her fault. Damn girl was a hindrance. Not worth killing though."

"You never asked him to get rid of Olivia then?"

"No, only to follow Kendall and find out why he was away so much. I ain't all that educated, but I know salesmen don't spend that much time away from home. I knew somethin' was up."

"How did you meet Nolan?"

She smiled. "On the train. We got to chatting and he invited me to lunch. I had just moved up from New York and didn't know a soul. He spent money on me and I liked it. I think he was trying to re-live his youth. At first he was just someone to buy me things, but he kinda grew on me. When he proposed, I said yes." She shrugged

"Knowing what I do now, I guess his wife was sickly and he was in need of female companionship, if ya know what I mean. Never understood why he insisted we live in the country. Suppose he didn't want me bumping into any of his friends."

Hodgins watched her closely as she answered his questions.

When she was first brought up from the cell she kept her eyes down, refusing to acknowledge him. As soon as he suggested she had something to do with Olivia's murder, she changed. Her head snapped up. Was more alert, but not too defensive. She responded the way people generally do when accused of something they didn't do.

Over the years, Hodgins had developed a sense for when people were hiding something. He decided she was innocent. At least of this. She had never denied killing her husband five years earlier when it was mentioned, and he didn't feel the need to bring it up again.

"I'll be sending you back to New York with Harrison

tomorrow. I'd wish you luck, but I think we both know how that's going to turn out."

She smiled weakly. "I've had a good life so far. Well, maybe not good, but definitely fun."

He signalled the constable who had been standing guard, to come in.

"Take her back to her cell. First thing tomorrow take her to Harrison at his hotel. He'll be taking custody of her. Escort them both to the train and see them off."

Hodgins remained in Draper's office, thinking. Calhoon seemed more than agreeable to help Mary. She couldn't have much money to pay him to come up. She'd said she sent him train fare, but there hadn't been any mention of payment for his service.

Is it possible Calhoon is in love with Mary? She was fairly attractive and seemed nice enough for the most part. Women like her were often loud and bad tempered, but not Mary. He got up and went to Barnes' desk.

"Come with me. We're going to check on Calhoon. I want you to agree with whatever I say to him. I'll fill you in on the way."

* * *

When they arrived at the hospital they were directed to Calhoon's room. Constable Smith was sitting on a chair outside.

"How's he doing?" Hodgins asked. "When Riley returned he said the doctor was still examining him."

"Some busted ribs, cuts and bruises on his face. The doc wants to keep him for a bit, but said he'll live."

"Right. I'll need you to stay a bit longer, but I'll send someone to take over shortly."

Hodgins opened the door and entered, Barnes right behind him. A nurse stood beside the bed, checking on Calhoon's bandages. She started to leave but Hodgins asked her to stay.

Calhoon's face was completely wrapped giving him the appearance of a mummy. There were two small slits where his eyes were, and a small opening for his nostrils. The gauze went around his mouth allowing his two swollen lips to stick out. The sheet covered his body so Hodgins couldn't see if the rest of Calhoon was wrapped like his face.

"I'm gonna die, ain't I?" Calhoon asked. His speech was laboured and soft.

"Is there anything you want to get off your chest before that happens?" Hodgins asked.

Calhoon said nothing.

Hodgins looked over at Barnes, who stood on the opposite side of the bed. Barnes started to say something, but Hodgins shook his head. Barnes nodded that he understood, but the confused look on his face was one

Hodgins had seen many times.

Calhoon thinking he was dying changed Hodgins' plans slightly. Hodgins was certain Barnes would remember their earlier conversation and follow along without giving anything away. He turned his attention back to Calhoon.

"You're in love with Mary, aren't you?"

Calhoon turned his head slightly to look at Hodgins.

"That's why she didn't have to pay you to follow Nolan around."

"I'd do anything for her," Calhoon replied.

"But she's married to someone else. Why not kill him so you could have Mary all to yourself?"

"You don't understand."

"Why don't you explain it then?"

Calhoon turned to stare at the ceiling.

"She's my little sister."

"Your sister?" asked a shocked Barnes. "I don't see a family resemblance."

"*Half* sister."

"Well that explains why you didn't kill Nolan. I think I'm beginning to understand," Hodgins said. "You wanted your sister to be happy." He paused a moment. "You thought she'd be happy if Nolan's daughter was out of the way. That's why you killed her. An innocent girl."

"Mary's first husband was a lazy drunk. Violent too."

Calhoon said. He winced and put a hand to his ribs, but kept talking.

"Gonna die anyway, so may as well admit what I dun. Going to Hell anyhow. Yah, I kilt the girl, and ya can't hang me fir it 'cause I'll already be dead."

Hodgins looked over at the nurse. "You heard his confession?"

She nodded.

"That's all I needed." He signalled to Barnes. "May as well go back to the station and write up the report."

Barnes was grinning ear to ear as they left.

"Very clever of you, Sir. He's going to be surprised when he finds out he's not actually dying."

Hodgins put his hand on Barnes' shoulder. "We're all going to die lad, eventually. He'll just be going out at the end of a rope."

* * *

"I'm glad you found out who murdered that poor child," Cordelia said as she settled into the settee. "I suppose in his mind he thought he was doing a good thing for his sister. I don't have any siblings, but I can't imagine actually killing someone just to make a sister happy."

"I love my brother, but I would never kill for him. Unless he was in danger of course. I would do anything to protect my family. If anyone ever hurt you or Sara, I don't even want to think what I would do to them."

"Well, now that that's over, I was thinking we should have a party to meet our new neighbours." She held up a hand. "Before you say no, I thought maybe towards the end of August we could have an afternoon lawn party. Nothing fancy. I've been so busy getting the house together I haven't been able to meet anyone properly, just a quick hello or wave.

"They could drop in any time during the afternoon. We can serve cold drinks and sandwiches. And maybe you can invite Constable Barnes and his family. I've noticed how fond you've become of him, and I'd love to meet his parents."

"I think that's a wonderful idea. I haven't met any of our neighbours, except for Halloway. And it would be nice to invite Henry and his family. He has a younger sister, same age as poor Olivia. She's older than Sara, but they might become friends."

Hodgins thought about Mr. Halloway and the constable, and smiled. "You know, Barnes seemed quite taken with their daughter, and Halloway was most impressed with Barnes. I'm sure Henry would like the chance to meet her. Who knows what might become of it?"

Cordelia laughed. "I never imagined you as a matchmaker Bertie. I've spoken to her very briefly, and she seems quite nice. Now you definitely have to invite him."

Hodgins sighed. "I wish I could invite my brother over. I haven't seen him since we wed. He's never even met his niece. And you're right about Henry. I think maybe I've sort of adopted him as a substitute brother. Always wanted a younger one. I'll write to my own and invite him and his family to visit with us. We have plenty of room now that we have our own place."

"That's a wonderful idea. You do that tonight and I'll post it first thing in the morning. Tomorrow Sara can help me make invitations for the party and hand deliver them. Then I'll make a list of everything we need to have ready before the party."

Hodgins smiled at the thought of seeing his brother again and went in search of some stationery.

Corpses For Christmas

A Detective Hodgins Victorian Mystery

Book Three

CHAPTER ONE

Detective Albert Hodgins should have been surprised the Christmas reunion with his older brother would turn out to be less than pleasant, but he wasn't. Not really. Jonathan had arrived late Friday evening, December 4 after an exhausting three-day train ride from Boston. The heavy bags under his eyes gave evidence of how little rest he'd managed on the Pullman sleeping car. He'd gone straight to Hodgins' guest room, too tired to have a conversation, an occasional snore the only indication of his presence.

Jonathan stumbled downstairs and into the kitchen just as Albert , Cordelia, and Sara were finishing their breakfast. Cordelia rose to set a place for him, but he waved her off.

"Not now, thank you." He rubbed his belly. "Stomach's still a tad unsettled, what with all the jostling on the train and bad food. Just a cup of tea, if you don't mind."

"Mommy makes the most scrumptious breakfast," Sara said, neatly cutting her last piece of sausage and popping it into her mouth.

Jonathan sat beside his brother and looked at the young girl peeking around Albert, smiling. "Why, you must be Sara. I hadn't realized you were such a big girl. My Cora's very excited to meet you."

Not wanting to be left out, Scraps padded over to sniff the intruder. Satisfied he wasn't a threat, he licked Jonathan's hand then went to the back door.

"Sara, put your coat on and take the dog out back." Cordelia turned to Jonathan and Albert, full tea cup in hand. "Take this and the pair of you can go into the sitting room to get reacquainted."

Hodgins refilled his tea cup, grabbed a couple of scones, then ushered his brother down the hall. Jonathan settled back into one of the high-backed wing armchairs by the fire and closed his eyes.

"It's been too long. I should have come back to Toronto for a visit sooner."

"Fault's not all yours. We could have gone down to Boston to see you just as easily. Could have kept up with the correspondence too, I suppose."

"So, it's settled. We're both as bad as each other." Jonathan opened his eyes and nodded at the scones Hodgins had brought in. "Those as good as Sara said?"

"You tell me." He handed one to Jonathan. Half of it

disappeared in one bite.

"What was it she said? Scrumptious? I agree. Maybe I can manage a bit of breakfast after all."

Hodgins lifted the plate, extending it to Jonathan. "Here, have the other one. Now, tell me what this business deal you came early for is all about."

Jonathan stuffed the scone in his mouth and washed it down with some tea. "Oh, it's nothing, really. Possibility of a new shipping contract. Captain won't be back in Boston for a few months and I wanted to settle it before he sails back to the England." He hesitated, tearing a chunk out of the last scone. Jonathan popped it into his mouth, then washed it down with the rest of his tea. "Truth be told, I wanted a bit of time to myself. Elizabeth's been talking about this trip for weeks, and it's become somewhat tiresome. I also wanted to speak with you without the family around."

Hodgins sensed Jonathan wanted to discuss something other than old times. "What's troubling you brother?"

Jonathan stared at the fire and shrugged. "Just wanted to talk to my brother, that's all."

Hodgins wasn't convinced, but he remembered how difficult it'd been growing up to get Jonathan to say anything before he was ready. "Stubborn as ever."

Jonathan opened his mouth to reply, but a knock on the front door stopped him.

"Who the devil comes calling unannounced on a Saturday?" Hodgins grumbled. "Can't be good news."

Jonathan laughed. "When is an unexpected knock on a police officer's door ever good news?"

Hodgins set his teacup on the floor beside his chair before getting up. "In my experience, practically never."

Snow rode in on the back of a cold wind as he opened the front door. A constable he didn't recognize stood on the front porch, hopping up and down, trying to stay warm. He stopped when he saw Detective Hodgins.

"Sir, they've found a body and you've been requested."

"Haven't seen you before. Must be new. Step in out of the cold."

"Constable Perry, sir. Thank you, sir."

"Now what's this about me being asked for?"

"Asked for you special. Headmaster's request."

Hodgins was puzzled. "Headmaster? Whatever are you going on about, Constable?"

"Ketchum School, sir. Grounds-keeper found a body this morning. In the school yard. Headmaster said he knows you. Demanded no one should touch nothing 'til you've been fetched."

"Fine. Tell them I'll be along shortly." Hodgins shut the door behind the constable and turned to find his brother standing in the doorway of the sitting room. "Damn. Take one day off to visit with my brother and it lasts…" He glanced at the hall clock. "All of two hours.

"Who was that?"

"Harry, or was it Perry? Got a batch new of recruits last week." Hodgins shrugged. "Can't get their names straight. Most of them probably won't last the month. Someone found a body at Sara's school and sent for me. Why the devil would someone leave a body in the school yard?" He shook his head and sighed. "A day off is frequently never a complete day off."

The detective removed his overcoat from the peg and walked down the hall to the kitchen door. Cordelia stood at the window watching Sara playing with Scraps.

"Delia,"—he chuckled when she jumped, always amused at how easily she startled. "I've been called out. Jonathan's decided he's able to eat after all. I know the dishes have been washed and put away, but would you mind fixing him something?"

She put her hands on her hips, her Irish temper surfacing. "Albert Hodgins, are you suggesting I'd be put out to prepare a meal for your only brother?"

He took a step back, waving his hands. "No, not at

207

all. Won't be long."

As he passed his brother, Albert made him promise not to mention where the body had been found. "I'll tell her myself when I know more. You may as well use the time to get reacquainted with Cordelia."

Hodgins slipped into his overcoat, buttoning it as he made his way down the hall.

Last night's heavy snowfall made the trek to Ketchum School slow. At least it was only about four blocks away. A few people were out taking care of their Saturday errands, the wagons and buggies leaving ruts in the snow, along with a few deposits from the horses. Hodgins walked on the road, following the buggy tracks as much as possible, carefully avoiding the dung. By the time he reached the school, the dampness from the snow had crept almost to the knees of his trousers. The wet pants clung to his legs, causing him to shiver. Headmaster Gruger rushed over to greet him.

"Detective Hodgins, thank heavens you're here. This is terrible, just terrible. Can you imagine if the children were here? Oh, no, that would be utterly terrible. Why would someone leave a body here?"

Gruger wrung his hands and looked back towards the constable and grounds-keeper standing near the body. Hodgins surveyed the area while the headmaster blathered on. He jumped in as soon as Gruger stopped for a breath.

"Why did you ask for me?"

Gruger looked shocked. "Your daughter is a student here. I assumed you'd want to deal with this personally."

"Yes, of course. I understand. Don't some of the children normally play around here on the weekend? I'm surprised they aren't making snowmen or having a snowball fight. We'll work as quickly as we can. Wouldn't want a child coming across the body. Disturbing sight, even for an adult. Do you know the victim? Does he work here?"

Gruger shook his head. "Haven't seen him before. We'd never hire someone as rough looking as that chap. Please, can you move him now? With all this snow the children are sure to be here soon. As you said, the field makes for a splendid place to build forts and have a snowball fight."

The more Hodgins thought about the location of the corpse the more anxious he was to find out what happened. If there was a murderer hanging around the school, maybe he'd keep Sara home for a few days.

"Why don't you go inside Headmaster? Get out of the snow and cold." Hodgins turned to the constable that dragged him from his nice warm house. "Has the coroner been called?"

"Yes, sir. Another constable went right away. Should be here soon."

"Right," Hodgins said. "What have you found out so far?" He glanced at Gruger's back. The headmaster walked slowly, reluctant to leave. "Don't suppose you recognize the dead man?"

The constable indicated he didn't as they walked over to the body. The area was covered in about a foot of freshly fallen snow, obliterating any indication of the direction the victim and murderer came from. The body sat propped up against the brick wall of the school, a bloody handkerchief tied around his head. It had slipped and the right eye peeked over the top, staring but not seeing. The snow around the body was tinted pink from blood, and one woolen sock stuck out from under the corpse. Hodgins crouched down beside the dead body and surveyed the school yard.

"Look from this angle, Harry." He motioned for the constable to kneel. "The snow is laying smooth and undisturbed everywhere except there." Hodgins pointed toward the treed area to the south. "It looks rough, as though the new snow covered a path where someone trod."

"It's Perry, sir." He crouched down beside Hodgins and nodded. "Suppose so, sir."

As Hodgins started to respond to the new recruit, the sound of bells caught his attention. He turned his head and watched a wagon approach, silver bells glistening along the harness. "Looks like the coroner is here and ready for the holidays. Why don't we get out of his way?"

McKenzie greeted Hodgins with a jolly hello and smile, then nodded towards the constable. Hodgins was on friendly terms with both Dr. Hamish McKenzie and his wife. McKenzie groaned as he knelt down beside the body, both knees cracking; first the left, then the right. The sound carried in the stillness of the morning.

"Getting too old and too fat to do this," he muttered. He looked up at Hodgins. "Want to talk to you later. Will you be in your office this afternoon?"

"Hope not. It's my day off. I'd like to get back home, if at all possible. What can you tell us about this poor chap?"

"I assume you've noticed he has a handkerchief tied around his head, covering his eyes? Well, almost covering his eyes. Looks like it used to be white."

"Stop stating the obvious, Doctor," Hodgins said as he smiled.

McKenzie lifted the lower edge of the hanky but didn't try to remove it. "There's a bullet lodged over his left eye. Just the tip is poking through the skin. No wounds anywhere else that I can see." He lifted the flat cap perched on the man's head. "Correction. Blood here, on top of his head." He dropped the hat back down, and lifted the hands one at a time, examining them carefully. "No signs of a struggle or attempt to fight off whoever did this."

McKenzie put one hand on the school wall and grunted again as he slowly got to his feet. "If you don't need me for anything else, I'll take him back and examine him and his clothing inside where it's warm. If someone wouldn't mind helping carry him to my wagon, I'll get started."

Perry and the grounds-keeper carried the corpse over, dropping him in the back hard enough to bounce the wagon and startle the horse.

"Little more care if you please. He may be dead, but he deserves to be treated with some respect. Is that how you'd want your body handled after you pass?"

"No, Doctor," Perry mumbled.

The grounds-keeper just turned and walked back towards the school, totally ignoring the doctor's question.

"There's not much more I can do until we hear back from the coroner. Snow's pretty much covered any possible evidence," Hodgins told the constable. "Ask the grounds-keeper if he has a shovel you can use. Clear away some of the snow. See if anything dropped in it. I'll be at home if you find something significant."

"Shovel snow?" the recruit asked. "Doesn't seem like something a copper should do."

Hodgins glared at him. "If you plan on staying employed with the Toronto Constabulary, you'll bloody well do what you're told, without moaning. There's a lot more unpleasant things you'll be doing, so think yourself lucky it's only snow."

The young man stared at Hodgins for a moment, mouth open. After mumbling an apology, he scurried after the grounds-keeper.

Hodgins took one last look around before heading down the laneway to Scollard and back to his home on Lowther.

As he passed McKenzie's wagon, the coroner reminded him he wanted to have a chat. "Why don't you and your wife join us for your evening meal? Say seven o'clock?" Hodgins asked. "You can meet my brother."

"Splendid idea. Looking forward to it. Seven it is."

* * *

Scraps came racing down the hall as soon as the front door opened. Even though the dog had been given to Sara as a birthday gift, it was quite attached to Hodgins. Leaning against the door, Hodgins braced for the impact. The scrawny stray had turned into a large, affectionate, but fiercely protective dog. His head banged back on the door when the dog jumped. Scraps' front paws planted firmly on Hodgins' chest, pinning him to the door.

"Down boy. Let me get my coat off." He gently pushed the dog away and brushed the snow from his overcoat before hanging it on the peg.

"I see you've got that beast well trained," Jonathan joked. "I hope you can teach him some manners before Elizabeth arrives with the children. Much as she like dogs, I don't think she'd appreciate being knocked over by him."

"Don't worry. Your wife will be quite safe. He only does that to me. Don't know if I should be pleased or insulted." He caught a whiff of the aroma wafting down the hall from the kitchen. Cabbage soup. "Smells like I've arrived in time for lunch."

Hodgins and his brother went into the kitchen, Scraps trotting ahead, leading the way.

"Soup will be ready in about twenty minutes," Cordelia said. She looked her husband up and down. "Why don't you get out of those wet things before you catch your death."

"Yes, dear. Oh, we're having company tonight. Dr. McKenzie wants to talk to me about something. It sounded important so I invited him and his wife to dine with us. Hope you don't mind."

Cordelia wiped her hands on a towel, draping it over the back of a chair as she moved to her husband. She took Hodgins' suit jacket, hanging it on the back of a chair near the wood stove. "Not at all. You know I love any excuse to have a party, even a small one. And I haven't seen Morag in quite some time. It's short notice, but I've plenty of time to prepare. Now go put something dry on."

He snatched two of the cooling scones and tossed one at his brother on his way out of the kitchen.

* * *

"That was a splendid meal, Cordelia." Dr. McKenzie smacked his lips and rubbed his belly. "You're a wonderful cook."

"Thank you, Hamish. I'm so glad you and Morag could join us. We don't see you near often enough."

"Afraid it won't be any more often in the future. That's what I want to talk to you about Albert."

Morag rose and joined Cordelia at the sink. "I'll help you and Sara clear while the men have their little chat, and I'll tell you all about it."

Hodgins, Jonathan and Hamish retired to the sitting room and Hodgins poured them each a whisky.

"OK, you've got my full attention, Hamish. What's on your mind?"

"If you wish to speak in private, I can take the dog for a walk," Jonathan said.

McKenzie shook his head. "No, nothing confidential. Stay in where it's warm." The doctor turned back to Albert. "Wanted to tell you personally, before you hear it from someone else. On Monday I'll be handing in my notice. These old bones just can't take it much longer."

"Then we'll be seeing more of you, not less."

"Afraid not. We're moving back to Scotland. My sister isn't well and I'd like to spend some time with her before … well, you understand."

Hodgins glanced over at his brother. "Yes, I understand what it's like to be separated from family. At least my brother is only a train ride away. A rather long ride, but fortunately we're on the same continent. I'll be sorry to see you go. We'll have to throw you one heck of a wing-ding. Send you off proper."

"How long has it been since you've seen your sister?" Jonathan asked.

"Ach, longer than I'd care to admit. I've only been back home once since moving to Canada. Our children are grown with families of their own. My eldest boy is in Australia, of all places. Professor at the University of Sydney, teaching chemistry. Me and the missus are too old to travel much. Figure if the children are going to be travelling to visit us, they can come over to Scotland to do it just as easily as coming here.

* * *

Despite Cordelia's protests, Morag took the towel from Sara and dried the dishes as Cordelia washed them.

"We can chat easier this way," Morag said.

Cordelia smiled and asked Sara to finish clearing the table.

"Such a lovely child," Morag commented, as Sara placed the dirty dishes by her mother, then put away the dried ones.

Sara blushed, then moved across the room. She knelt down by the wood stove to scratch Scrap's head, listening as her mother and Mrs. McKenzie chatted while finishing up the dishes.

"We've been away from Scotland far too long. I miss everyone. My younger brother and his family don't live too far from Hamish's sister, so I'll be able to visit both often. They've found us a small cottage right around the corner. I just wish we were going under better circumstances."

"Does your husband have any other family?" Cordelia asked.

"No, just the one sister. She stood with me at the wedding all those decades ago. We became fast friends the moment Hamish introduced us. She never married. When we found out she was ill, I wrote my brother. His whole family has been helping out when they can, and my nieces have been doing a lot of the cleaning and cooking this last month or so. She's gotten so much worse recently and may not be able to live on her own much longer. I'm so afraid we may not arrive in time." Mrs. McKenzie wiped her eyes with the corner of the towel. "Gracious, I don't know what came over me."

Cordelia put down her wash rag and took the towel from Morag, replacing it with her own lace handkerchief. "Sit. You must be terribly upset. I can only imagine how you're feeling."

"It's all so overwhelming. We have to pack or sell everything, and Hamish will have to find a replacement coroner. All I can think about is poor Elspeth. She was such a free spirit. Full of life. The last letter from my sister-in-law painted a bleak picture of a total stranger. So frail and completely dependent on them.

"Ahem."

They turned to find Albert and Hamish standing in the doorway. The doctor held his wife's lamb-wool coat and muff.

"It's time we were heading home, my dear. We've lots to do still and it's getting late. Beside, the good detective has to start planning our bon voyage party." He winked at

Hodgins. "You can save the tears for then."

His voice softened as he went over and helped her on with her coat. "Everything will be fine. We'll have plenty of time with her. You'll see."

CHAPTER TWO

After church the next day, Hodgins kissed Cordelia and Sara, then hailed a hansom cab to take him to the station house. It was much too cold to walk across the city. A wool blanket sat neatly folded on the seat so he draped it over his legs for warmth. It matched the larger one over the back of the horse.

When he arrived at the station house he was relieved to discover no new major crimes needing his attention. He just settled behind his desk when Constable Barnes popped in.

"Sir, I'm glad you're here. The Inspector has been asking for you. He's quite agitated."

"What now? It's been pretty quiet lately. We've no high-profile cases at the moment, just one unidentified corpse. Don't suppose the inspector told you anything?"

"No, but the desk sergeant did. Seems someone came in late yesterday afternoon." Barnes flipped open his notebook and checked the last entry. "Man by the name of Gruger."

Hodgins groaned. "He's the headmaster at Sara's school."

"Is Sara in some sort of trouble?"

"No, some fool went and got himself murdered. That corpse I mentioned. Surprised you haven't heard about it. I'll check in with the inspector then fill you in. Don't go far. I have a feeling we're going to be busy."

* * *

An hour later Hodgins returned from the inspector's office. As he passed an empty desk, he shoved the chair out of the way, with considerably more force than necessary.

"Barnes, my office." Hodgins slammed the door after he entered. A moment later Barnes eased the door open and slipped in, closing it gently behind him.

"Sir?"

Hodgins paced behind his desk.

"You know how much I dislike politics? Well, Gruger, the headmaster at Sara's school, has gone to the Chief Inspector and insisted not only that I personally handle this, but to keep him informed of our progress. The Chief gave our Inspector a right earful, which he passed on to me. He blathered on and on. I thought I'd never get out of there."

Barnes cocked his head to the side, a puzzled look on

his face. "Sir? Progress on what?"

"What? Oh, sorry." Hodgins waved his hand towards the chair in front of his desk. "Sit. Got so worked up I forgot I hadn't filled you in." He stopped pacing long enough to let Barnes know what had happened on his so-called day off.

"It's that unidentified corpse. Someone left a body leaning up against Ketchum School. One of those new constables dragged me from my nice warm house to look into it. Wish they'd open up a station house in my neighbourhood. The city's growing and we have to keep up."

"Not much need for one up in St. Paul's Ward yet. Most of the north end is brick and tile yards or open space. East side's still sparsely populated. Your home is in the only area with a proper neighbourhood."

Hodgins finally sat. "True. Lots of homes on the west side, but it's still fairly quiet. A nice neighbourhood, as you well know."

He noticed Barnes colour slightly at the indirect mention of the pretty, young neighbour Barnes was sweet on.

"One good thing about this case – it's not far from home. I can check on the site and question the people who live around the school either on the way to work or the way home."

The faint smile disappeared as he thought about the location.

"Just wish it hadn't happened at Sara's school. Or any school for that matter. Not something I'd want any of the children to find, even though it wasn't too gruesome." A huge grin spread across his face. "I think you would've been able to handle that one."

Barnes turned bright red.

"Don't worry lad. I don't believe everyone knows you've puked at two murder scenes this year. New recruits haven't been told, yet." Hodgins couldn't hold back his laughter.

Barnes sat straight, pulling his shoulder back. "Seen my fair share since then, sir. I'm used to anything now."

Hodgins doubted someone so young could harden up after only a year, but he didn't say so.

"No need to be embarrassed because you have compassion. Just try to hide it better."

"Yes, sir."

"Get your coat and scarf. We need to get over to the school and have a good look around. Seems the headmaster didn't go inside out of the way after all. Just went around the corner of the building, then came back to watch after I left. Nosey old prat. Apparently, Gruger told the Chief Inspector that the constable cleared a large area of snow and only briefly looked through it. The Chief lectured our Inspector on procedure and the training of new recruits. Track down"—Hodgins flipped through his notes—"Perry. Find out why he hasn't submitted a report. I'll have a little talk with Sergeant Evans later and make sure he stresses the importance of speedy reporting to that new batch of nitwits we've got. No one enjoys the paperwork, but it needs to be done while it's fresh in the mind."

They were half-way to the front door when McKenzie limped in. Hodgins raised an eyebrow.

"Whatever happened to you, Doctor?"

"Arthritis is bothering me. Kneeling in the snow Saturday didn't help. Stiffened right up. Like I said, getting too old for this. Need to loosen up my knee, so I thought I'd save you a trip to my morgue. I have my preliminary findings and the man's belongings. Spent all morning examining him. Found something in his pocket you'd be interested in." He handed Hodgins a small card. "It's never easy with you, is it?" McKenzie chuckled.

"What the blazes? How…? I don't understand."

Barnes peered over Hodgins' shoulder. "Oh my. Why would the dead man have your brother's business card?"

"That's a very good question, Constable. I wish I

knew the answer. Jonathan hasn't been back to Toronto for over ten years. Came in Friday on the last train. Picked him up at the station myself."

"To continue," McKenzie said, "I can't give you a positive time of death. Difficult to say what with it being so cold, but my best guess is he was shot sometime Friday evening, probably early evening based on the partially digested meal in his stomach."

"I suppose I'll have to ask Jonathan to come down and look at the body. Maybe he can identify him. Could the dead man also have come in from Boston? What can you tell me about the wound?"

"Single shot through the back of the head. Bullet entered the right side about an inch from the ear and lodged over the left eye. Looks like a .45. There was blood and serum under the scalp on the top of the head. Bits of wood too. I'd say he was bashed on the head with a club of some sort. Can't tell which wound came first, but the bullet was the cause of death." He handed Barnes a small bag. "Contents of his pockets." He smiled and whistled as he exited the station.

"May as well see what's in the bag before we leave. Empty it on that desk and let's have a look." Hodgins took a couple of steps toward an empty desk, Barnes close behind.

Barnes unfolded the top of the bag and tipped it over. A few coins rolled across the desk, stopping at the edge. A red hanky with frayed edges followed the coins, and a folded envelope came halfway out. Barnes reached in and pulled it the rest of the way. The only other items were a pocket watch and a single woolen sock.

"There's something inside the envelope," Barnes said. He unfolded it and lifted the flap. "Sir, look at this." He handed the envelope to Hodgins.

"That's a fair bit of money. Couldn't have been a robbery. Even though the pocket watch isn't expensive, a robber could have got something for it from one of the City's less than upstanding pawnbrokers. Both the watch and money would have been quick enough to grab and run." Hodgins counted the money. "There's fifty dollars here. Why would a thief murder someone and leave so much money behind? And the sock. I saw it sticking out under his leg. How did a sock get under the body? He was wearing shoes, and I'm certain he had socks on both feet." He put everything back inside the bag, except the red hanky. "If this was in his pocket, whose hanky was tied around his eyes?"

Barnes pointed to the business card. "What about that?"

Hodgins thought about it for a few minutes, flipping

it through his fingers. "Did I tell you Gruger was an old school mate of Chief Inspector Paulson? I may have been ordered to keep Gruger informed, but I'm not about to tell him my brother may be involved. Not yet."

He stuffed the hanky inside the bag before pushing it across the desk. "Log this as evidence, then we'll go check the area around the school."

Barnes picked up the small bag, but didn't move.

"Something wrong constable?"

"Don't you want me to log that, too?" Barnes pointed to the card Hodgins still fidgeted with.

"Need to speak with my brother about this. Why don't you just enter it as a business card on the evidence list?"

"Yes sir," Barnes said softly. "Whatever you think is best." He avoided looking Hodgins in the eye.

Barnes turned to go back to his desk, but Hodgins stopped him. The look of disappointment on the constable's face was too much.

"Put down Jonathan's name. I'm sure it's all quite simple to explain. Can't be showing favouritism now, can we?"

Barnes smiled. "No sir. Law's the law."

* * *

"Looks like the children had one heck of a snowball fight."

Barnes placed his hands on his hips. "And they've destroyed the entire area."

Footprints riddled the park beside Ketchum School along with smashed snowballs, and the remnants of two snow walls. A few children had arrived to play after changing out of their Sunday best. Hodgins went over to the boy who looked to be the oldest.

"Were you here yesterday, young man?"

"Yes, sir. Is it true then? Heard tell a man was murdered right here in this very park." He was wide-eyed and full of excitement. Hodgins remembered being afraid of nothing at that age.

"Unfortunately. Do you think you can assist us?" The other children had crowded around Hodgins and Barnes, anxious to hear all the gruesome details. "I'm sorry, but I can't tell you very much. Ongoing investigation, but maybe you can help us solve it."

All the boys bobbed their heads in agreement, the few girls with them stood back a bit, except one. She looked to be about seven or eight. The girl spoke up.

"My uncle is with the North-West Mounted Police. He told us always to help whenever we can. Not even wait to be asked." She stood with her arms crossed as though waiting to be told to be quiet, with a look that suggested she was more than willing to fight anyone who tried to stop her.

"North-West Mounted Police? Impressive." Hodgins had heard about the new force established the previous year on the advice of Prime Minister MacDonald. "And what's your name?"

"Sally French." She uncrossed her arms and leaned forward. "Are you really going to let us help?"

"Yes, Sally. I'm really going to let you help. Were you all here yesterday?"

A chorus of *yeses* echoed around the circle of children.

"Can you help us search among the trees over there? You have to be careful and go very slow. And don't touch anything. If you find something, yell. Either Constable Barnes or myself will come to you."

The children ran across the park to the trees. "Slow and careful now! Hodgins hollered after them.

"Sir, they're children. Shouldn't they be sent home?"

"Do you want to spend all day in the cold, looking through the woods?"

Barnes grinned. "No."

"Right. You look over there and I'll start at this end."

Hodgins recalled the uneven trail that seemed to lead to the body and he followed in that general direction. Little Sally was looking in that area and yelled as Hodgins approached. A tree branch about two feet long and a couple of inches thick lay in the snow. It was near the edge of the woods, and there was a sticky patch of something coppery-red on it.

"Barnes, over here."

All the children came running, beating Barnes to the spot.

Barnes bent over, resting his hands on his knees, huffing and puffing.

"You're out of shape, Constable. We'll never win that hockey game against Station House One if all my officers are in such bad condition. We'll have to set up a training schedule."

"Yes… sir." Barnes took a few more deeps breaths.

"Is that wot killed him?" One of the boys asked. They had enclosed Hodgins in a circle, straining to see what was in the snow.

"Could be. Look around and see if you can spot anything else. And remember, if you find something, don't touch it."

"What is it? What did the little girl find?" Barnes asked.

"Remember McKenzie found wood chips in the wound on the victim's head? I think this may be what caused it." Hodgins picked it up and handed it to Barnes

After an hour of searching, nothing more was found,

so Hodgins dismissed the children. "Thank you all for your assistance. You can run along now."

"Aw, do we hafta?" one boy asked. A disappointed groan from all the children echoed through the trees before they slowly made their way back to the half-destroyed snow fort.

Hodgins noticed Sally hadn't joined the rest of the children in the park.

"What's your name?" she asked.

"Detective Hodgins."

"Oh, I've heard Grampa talk about you. Says you're very smart. Wait 'till tell him I helped you."

Barnes laughed as Sally ran off, presumably home to tell her grandpa. "You're famous, sir."

"Did she say her name was French? Isn't that the name of the Commissioner of the North-West Mounted Police? Couldn't be the same family, could it? She said her uncle was with the North-West, but French is a fairly common name."

Barnes shrugged.

Hodgins pointed to the branch the constable held. "You get that back to Dr. McKenzie. See if he has any way to determine if it's the same wood as the chips he found. Take a hansom cab. When you get back here, start talking to the neighbours along Berryman. I'll start on Davenport

Road."

Barnes went in search of a cab, holding the branch with both hands. Hodgins walked up the road and knocked on the door of the first house. A lady who looked to be in her forties answered the door.

"Who's there, Ma?" The voice sounded like it came from down the hall.

"I'm Detective Hodgins." He raised his voice so both the lady and her son could hear. "Need to ask a few questions."

A young man came out of one of the rooms in back and joined them. He smiled and extended his hand to the detective. His mother seemed nervous, looking from her son to the detective repeatedly.

"What brings the law out on such a cold day? And a detective at that?" the young man asked.

"Unfortunately, someone was murdered by the school. Did either of you see or hear anything Friday evening? A gun shot perhaps?"

"Oh my!" The lady exclaimed. She fanned herself with her hands.

"Didn't mean to upset you, Mrs.?"

"Perkins," the young man filled in. "I'm her son, Daniel." He turned to his mother. "Go sit down, Ma. I'll take care of this."

Daniel waited until his mother had gone towards the back of the house before answering Hodgins' question.

"No, Detective. We didn't hear anything like that. We were together, having a quiet night. My mother was making a list of things she needs to do to prepare for Christmas. My sister and her family will be arriving in a few weeks. I was reading the newspaper, catching up on the events. All in all, a rather dull evening."

"Thank you for your time. Here's my card, in case you remember something. Anything."

Daniel read the card. "Isn't this a little out of your territory? Station Four is clear across town."

"Sounds like you're familiar with us, Mr. Perkins."

Daniel laughed. "Not me personally. Some of my friends. Little to much too drink at times. Nothing serious."

Hodgins' thought it peculiar that Daniel would be aware of the location of the stations, but he let it pass. "Unusual circumstances, as I said. Contact me if you remember anything."

"Now that I think about it, there was one thing. Heard two men yelling. Didn't last long."

"What time was that?" Hodgins dug his notebook and pencil out of his overcoat pocket.

"Can't rightly say. A bit after we dined. I'd guess

maybe eight or nine o'clock. It was off in the distance so I didn't bother looking out the window."

Hodgins jotted it down, thanked Mr. Perkins, then continued on to the neighbour's. He'd only made it to five houses when Barnes arrived back.

"Doctor McKenzie said he'd try his best to identify the wood. Any luck, sir?"

"Man at number four said he heard some yelling but so far none of the other neighbours heard it. One man thought he might have heard a gunshot, though. Couldn't be positive what it was, as they were singing and playing music."

"I'll check with them people over there." Barnes pointed to Berryman Street. "Maybe they heard or seen something."

"Make sure your notes have proper grammar, Constable."

Barnes look confused, then realized what he'd said. "Yes sir. Sorry sir."

"You're one of the few constables with a proper education. Don't try to hide it. Off with you now."

Barnes nodded and ran up the street. Hodgins detoured to Bishop Street, but no one there admitted to hearing anything. The house on the corner was empty so he jotted a note to remind himself to come back another day before continuing up Davenport. The elderly couple at number sixteen invited him in for tea and biscuits. Hodgins was never one to turn down a hot beverage and food, especially on a day so cold. The elderly lady ushered him into a small room with a roaring fire and four over-stuffed and over-used chairs.

"Have a seat, young man. Let me take your coat." She had the coat off his back before Hodgins could protest, then she pushed him towards one of the chairs. "Sit, please. I insist."

Hodgins sank down and found the chair surprisingly comfortable. The elderly lady scurried off while her husband sat in the chair opposite him, smiling.

"I'm Harold Cotter, by the way. Mable will be back shortly with a little snack. Do you have children Detective?"

Before Hodgins could answer, Harold continued. "We have seven children, fifteen grandchildren, and two great-grandchildren."

Hodgins grinned as he pictured the short, stocky couple surrounded by a family of little chubby grandchildren. He was spared further details when Mable returned with a tray laden with a tea pot, a stack of cups, and biscuits. Before either had the opportunity to start talking again, Hodgins told them what he was there for.

Mrs. Cotter sat the tray on a small table, broke open a biscuit releasing a column of steam, then smothered it with jam and placed it on the saucer before handing Hodgins his tea. His mouth watered. He took a bite and listened as the couple started up again.

"Oh, I told you Harold. Those two were up to no good."

CHAPTER THREE

Hodgins quickly swallowed his biscuit as the Cotters argued about the men she'd mentioned.

"They looked shifty," Mable said.

"Nonsense. They were simply walking down the street."

"But they walked shifty."

"Oh, pshaw. No such thing as walking shifty."

Hodgins interrupted. "What two men?"

"Why those two beggars." She lowered her voice. "One was a negro."

"Martha, no need to whisper. It's not a crime to be a negro. You don't know anything about them. I've met a lot of beggars who were the nicest people you'd ever want to meet. Why just last year—"

Hodgins cut him off. "What can you tell me about the two men?" He took another bite of the biscuit before it cooled. It practically melted in his mouth. Distracted by the biscuit, he missed what Harold said. "Could you repeat that, please?"

"Like Martha said, two men. One like us, the other a

negro fellow. I'd say both were middle aged, but can't say for certain. Only saw them from the window, and it was quite dark out, what will the clouds and all."

Hodgins balanced the tea cup and saucer on his knee while writing in his notebook. Fearing he was about to spill the contents, he looked for a spot to place his cup. The small table Mable had placed the tray on sat in the centre of the grouping of chairs, but it was a stretch for him to reach. He decided to set his cup on the floor beside his chair.

"Did you hear any arguing or gunshots Friday evening? Say around eight or nine?"

"Gracious no. We were asleep by nine. Take more than a gunshot to rouse us before morning. Up before the birds, we are. Early to bed, and all that," Harold said.

Since nothing else could be learned from them, Hodgins helped himself to another biscuit with jam before leaving. None of the other residents on the street heard or saw anything. He met up with Barnes an hour after leaving the Cotter's and discovered a few of the people Barnes spoke to also mentioned the two beggars.

"Do you think it might have been them?" Barnes asked. "Several people saw them Friday evening about the time Dr. McKenzie thinks the man was shot."

"Could be. We need to find them and see what they

have to say. If it was them, why kill him? Nothing seems to have been taken. Why leave all that money behind?"

"Maybe they were looking for something specific. Not concerned about the money."

"I suppose anything's possible."

Hodgins and Barnes headed back to the station house. The wind whipped the heavy snow around, stinging their faces, so Hodgins flagged down the first hansom he saw. Unfortunately this one didn't have a lap blanket for the customers but at least they were protected. The wind ripped the folding cab door from Barnes' hand just before it shut. Hodgins laughed when Barnes almost fell out trying to grab the door. The trap door on top of the cab slid open and the driver called down.

"Where to, gentlemen?"

"Station House Four," Hodgins answered, and the door slid shut.

"I'll have the driver drop you off so you can fill out a report about the two beggars, then I'll continue to the morgue to see if McKenzie had any luck with that tree branch," Hodgins said.

The trip across Toronto was slow. At Carlton and Jarvis, two carriages blocked the road, right in front of St. Andrew's Church. Their wheels locked, apparently when one of the drivers passed too close to the other carriage.

Hodgins leaned back and closed his eyes, listening to the men yell and cuss. Eventually the two rigs were separated and everyone resumed their journeys. Another blast of wind assaulted them when they arrived at the station and Barnes opened the cab door. He fought to keep control of it as he exited, so Hodgins reached over to help. Snow blew in before they got the door shut. Hodgins brushed the flakes away and rapped on the roof of the cab. "Morgue, please."

The driver snapped the reins and continued on. When they arrived, Hodgins paid the fair, pulled up his collar, and ran into the morgue, almost slipping on the front steps. McKenzie sat at his desk, writing. He looked up when he heard the door open

"Just writing out my resignation. First order of business tomorrow. Suppose you're here about the branch young Barnes brought in."

He put the letter in a drawer and indicated for Hodgins to follow him to a table where a microscope sat.

"Take a look."

Hodgins leaned over and looked through the eye piece. "OK, what am I looking at?"

"Bits of wood found in the skull." He changed slides. "This is from the piece Barnes brought in. Notice any similarities?"

Hodgins shrugged. McKenzie put a third slide under the microscope lens. "Now do you see any difference?

"Yes. The spots are spaced farther apart."

"Pores. That one is maple. Now look at the other two again."

Hodgins carefully changed the slides, going back and forth between them. "The spots, er, pores, are a lot smaller and closer together on the sample from the branch and skull."

"Yes. I believe they're both from mountain ash. It's not an exact science, but I'm more than reasonably certain the wood bits in the scalp match the branch. Are the bits in the scalp from that specific branch? No way to be sure, but the blood on it would indicate a connection."

"Thank you, Doctor. I'll take this branch back and mark it as evidence. As you say, no way to be sure, but it was found near the body. At least I was correct about the coppery substance being blood."

"You've got a well-trained eye. And I have a little surprise you'll be happy about. There were some hairs caught under the bark. Same colour and texture as the dead man's. Again, no way to be certain, but I'm confident this was used to club him."

* * *

Hodgins dropped the branch on Barnes' desk as soon as

he returned from the morgue.

"Log this as evidence. It's not the murder weapon, but it was likely used to bash the poor chap on the head. Hopefully he was unconscious before being shot. Can you fetch me that envelope?"

Barnes took the branch then joined Hodgins in his office a few minutes later, envelope in hand. Barnes pointed to the printing in the corner of it. "Campbell, Hugh & Son, Ropemaker, Aurora. A pay envelope maybe?"

"Fifty dollars is a rather large wage, don't you think, Constable?"

Barnes nodded in agreement. "Would you like me to fetch the train schedule?"

Hodgins laughed. "You know me well, but no, not yet. Hopefully my brother can tell me who we have in the morgue." He hesitated. "Maybe you should have it handy in the morning, just in case."

* * *

Hodgins and his brother retired to the sitting room after supper, leaving Cordelia and Sara clearing up. "Sara's quite excited to meet your daughter. If she has her way, she'll be dragging Cora all over the city."

"Cora's excited too. Been asking all sorts of questions. For some reason she's expecting Toronto to be quite different from Boston. Thinks it's all wilderness up here," Jonathan said.

"Hmm, yes. I suppose it will be a little different, but I'm afraid she's going to be disappointed if she's expecting to see bears roaming the streets."

Hodgins pulled out his police notebook and Jonathan glanced at it.

"You were quiet all through supper, Albert. What's on your mind?"

"I have to ask you something. It's about the man found at the school."

"Me? What could I possibly know that would be of any help? I haven't been back in Toronto for over ten years."

Hodgins slipped the card out of his notebook and handed it to Jonathan.

"We found this in his pocket. He was shot sometime early Friday evening. You arrived late Friday night. How did he get your card?"

"I told you, I relocated my premises last year. The address here is the old one on Stillman. I may have done business with him some time prior to the move."

"Would you mind coming down to the morgue and have a look at the chap? See if you can tell me who he is."

Jonathan paled slightly and Hodgins grinned.

"Don't worry, big brother. He's not been all bashed about. Looks like he's sleeping. Won't take but a minute."

Jonathan got up and walked to the sideboard and poured a whisky, which he downed in one gulp.

"I'd forgotten how squeamish you are. Just like Barnes."

"Yes, you mentioned the lad in your last letter. You weren't all the impressed with him, as I recall.

"He's changed a lot over the year. Going to be a good detective one day. Nice lad. Been courting the young lady next door. Expect they'll be married soon."

"Sounds like you're fond of him. Have I been replaced?"

"Replaced?" Hodgins looked at his brother, surprised by the question.

"We've been apart for a long time. Our correspondence infrequent."

Hodgins thought a moment before speaking. "Yes, I have come to think of him as a brother, but not a replacement. We'll have to make an effort to keep in touch, though."

"You must find time to visit us in Boston. We can go fishing like we used to."

"Haven't gone fishing in years. I believe I still have our old poles up in the attic."

"Too cold to use them now, but I'm sure there's something else we can find to do. Maybe included that Barnes chap.

CHAPTER FOUR

Grey clouds blocked the sun making the morning eerily dank. Hodgins sensed the dread in his brother grow as they approached the city morgue. Jonathan stood at the foot of the stairs, his complexion pale despite the redness from the cold. Hodgins placed a hand on Jonathan's shoulder.

"Are you ready? Will only take a minute. I promise. Just try to think of him as though he's sleeping, like I mentioned yesterday.

Jonathan nodded and they entered the morgue, gagging as the rotting stench of the corpse hit his nose.

"Guess it is rather ripe in here," Hodgins said. "Good thing you didn't have breakfast. I'd say you'll get used to it, but you won't. Try not to think about it. Works for me. Quick look and we'll be on our way."

Hodgins motioned for the coroner to expose the victim. Dr. McKenzie lifted the white sheet that shrouded the corpse.

"Dear God!"

"You know him?" Hodgins asked.

Jonathan gagged again. "His face. It's swollen, but I recognize him. Brown. Anthony Brown. Worthless piece of trash."

"Not a friend then?" Hodgins grinned. "Your colour's coming back. Wasn't all that bad now, was it?" He turned to McKenzie. "May as well cover him back up."

Jonathan turned and hurried back out into the cold. When Hodgins joined him, Jonathan was leaning against the stone wall, eyes closed, breathing deeply. He jumped when his brother touched him.

"I didn't realize you'd be so shaken up. I'm sorry, but it was necessary."

Jonathan nodded. "I understand. It was the smell more than the dead body."

"Try going in there on a hot summer day." Hodgins' smile disappeared as Jonathan gagged and ran to the side of the steps. "Just like Barnes," he mumbled.

Jonathan pulled out a hanky and wiped his mouth, "Barnes? That constable of yours? What about him?"

Hodgins chuckled. "Reacts the same way. I need to get a statement from you, but what's say we have a drink, to steady the nerves?"

"Good idea."

They walked in silence for several blocks before

Hodgins hailed a passing hansom. "Yonge and Queen," he told the driver.

Hodgins tried talking to Jonathan, but he was still too disturbed by his visit to the morgue. Jonathan leaned against the side of the cab, eyes closed, so Hodgins settled back, listening to the soft clomp of the hooves as the horse made its way to their destination. He gently shook Jonathan when they arrived.

Hodgins paid the driver while Jonathan took in the surroundings. "The Bay Horse Hotel. It's still here? We spent a lot of our time here before the accident." Jonathan turned to his brother "I'd like to visit their graves before I go back to Boston."

"I'll ask Delia to help the children make a special wreath and we can all visit Mama and Papa's graves before Christmas. Now, let's get inside and find a spot near the fire."

The hotel had both a dining room and a lounge with a bar. They chose to sit in the lounge and found an empty table close to the brick fireplace. It was too early for lunch so they had the room almost to themselves.

The open shutters on the windows allowed sunlight to fill the room, making it seem somewhat cheery, despite the lack of decorations. The only staff was a familiar-looking barman, who came over as soon as they were seated.

"Jonathan Hodgins. Ain't seen you in here for…" He shrugged as he tried to remember.

"Over a decade," Jonathan said. "Can't say I've missed seeing your ugly mug."

The barman slapped him on the back, laughing. "You still chasing the ladies?"

"No. I'm married, with two wonderful children. Have a thriving business down in Boston."

"Jonathan came up for Christmas. His family will be joining us Friday. We just came in for a quiet chat and to get reacquainted. What better place then the Bay Horse?" Hodgins said.

"Well, I'll leave you to it then. What'll it be? First drink's on the house."

"I'll have a beer, and I think Jonathan could use a whisky."

"Make it a double."

Their drinks were in front of them minutes later. Jonathan downed his whisky while Hodgins twirled a glass of beer. "Tell me about Brown. You said he was a piece of trash. What did he do? How do you know him?"

"Used to work for me. When I started to relocate my shipping business closer to the docks I discovered he'd been stealing from me. I admit I hadn't checked him out before hiring him as I needed the help and he was strong and available. I was more interested in his muscles than his character. As my business grew, I needed more help and he recommended a couple of blokes."

Jonathan stopped and indicated for the barman to bring another shot.

"My bookkeeping skills aren't very good. You remember when I tried to help Father with the books at the store? Got a right ear-full and sent back to stocking the shelves. I didn't need help with the accounts at first, as I was just starting. Nothing complicated. As I gradually became established over the years I began making good money so I didn't care about how up-to-date anything was, both the accounts and the inventory. Elizabeth insisted I put everything in order before the move. Found out the bugger'd been stealing from me for years, along with his two friends. Fired all three on the spot."

The whisky came and disappeared as fast as the first. "God, will anything get rid of the taste that smell left in my mouth?"

"Slow down, Jonathan. I don't want to have to carry you home before lunchtime. And that taste will go away. So, you fired them. That's all?"

Jonathan couldn't look his brother in the eye. He slid the glass across the table, from hand to hand, staring at the tabletop.

"No." He stopped sliding the glass and rubbed his left arm. Jonathan's voice dropped to little more than a whisper. "I started asking around, telling some business acquaintances about them. Warning them. Word spread and Brown and his friends couldn't get work. They came after me, Bertie."

Hodgins sipped his beer, waiting, remembering when their father tried to pry anything out of Jonathan. Patience was something Albert hadn't inherited and he hoped it wouldn't take all day. By the time Hodgins finished his beer, Jonathan resumed his tale.

"The three of them jumped me one night after I closed up. Fortunately, a few of the dock workers were nearby and came to my aid. Always knew it would come in handy one day to stay on friendly terms with the men on the docks. They knocked all three unconscious. They were still out when I limped back with the police."

"Why didn't you tell me about that? Is that why you stopped writing me? Were you injured? Three against one. You've never been much of a fighter."

"Broken nose, fractured arm, and more bruises than I could count." Jonathan smiled. "I suppose it's high-time I learned to fight, now that I'm closer to the docks. Lot more men like Brown hanging around down there. Can't expect to find a friendly dock worker handy all the time."

"That's the smartest thing I've heard you say all morning. One of my men is a champion boxer. Champion among all the station houses that is. How about I ask him to give you a few lessons?

"Appreciate that, little brother."

Since there seemed to be nothing left to say and it was close to noon, Hodgins waved over the barman and ordered two steak and kidney pies and a pot of tea.

"I think we can forego a formal statement," Hodgins said. "I'll just add a few lines to the file. If we need any additional information, I can write it up at home."

When they finished lunch, Jonathan decided he felt well enough to do some Christmas shopping while Hodgins went to the station.

* * *

Hodgins walked over to Barnes' desk and handed him a piece of paper. "Here, put this in the file. Dead man's got a name now. Anthony Brown." He looked around. "Where's Baxter? Did he finish that sketch of Brown? I'd like to take I with me. Where's the train schedule? Time to go to Aurora and visit the ropemaker. Campbell, I believe? See what he has to say about the envelope containing that fifty dollars."

Barnes pulled a well-used schedule out of his desk

drawer. It'd been folded in haste multiple times and was full of creases, rips and even had a corner missing. Barnes smoothed it out best he could and turned it to face Hodgins.

After studying it for a minute, Hodgins placed his index finger part way down one of the columns. "Here. First train out tomorrow isn't too early. I can be at the Aurora depot shortly after ten." He peered up at Barnes. "Don't suppose we have a map of Aurora?"

Barnes shrugged. "Don't recall ever having need of one, but I'll check. We have maps of most of the towns. Have you ever been up there?"

"Never had the need. One of these days I'll have to plan some trips around the area with the family. Remember the trips we had to make to Stouffville last January? Your first murder investigation. Pretty little village. Maybe in the spring we can pick a spot and hop on the train. Wonder if they allow dogs on the train?"

"Sounds like quite an adventure."

"Maybe if you're still courting that pretty little neighbour of mine, you can both join us."

Barnes turned pink and stammered. "Well… maybe… you see…"

"Trouble?"

"No, sir." Barnes looked around and noticed several

of the constables listening and snickering.

Hodgins asked him to step into his office, closing the door behind them.

"What's wrong lad?"

Barnes looked at the floor and shuffled his feet.

"You know I'll help any way I can, but you need to tell me what's wrong."

Barnes mumbled, head still down.

"Speak up, Constable. And look at me. Please."

Barnes raised his head and looked directly at Hodgins and a lopsided grin slowly appeared on his face. "I was going to ask her to marry me."

Hodgins came around the desk and slapped Barnes on the back. "Congratulations, Henry. She's a lovely girl, and her folks seem quite taken with you."

"And my Ma likes her, and my little sister gets along with her like they're old friends. I was thinking of asking her after Christmas. Maybe New Year's Eve."

"That's wonderful news. I'm sure my wife will want to throw you a party."

Barnes' eyes went wide. "What if she says no? You can't tell anyone. Not even Mrs. Hodgins."

"You're secret's safe with me. Now why don't you send a wire to the Boston Police Department and see what they can tell us about Brown. I'll see if I can find anyone who saw the two tramps. They may have jumped on one of the trains."

Barnes went to send the telegraph and Hodgins bundled up in his overcoat and scarf and started out to Union Station. The biting wind had died off and it was turning into a nice day, so he decided to walk. It gave him time to think. So many changes were coming. Eighteen hundred and seventy five was going to be different. Hodgins couldn't believe Dr. McKenzie was handing in his resignation and moving back to Inverness. What type of person would be replacing him? Would the new coroner get along with him and the rest of the police? Barnes would likely be getting married in the spring. Hodgins had no doubt she'd say yes. He'd seen the couple together many times. They were mad about each other. Over the past year he had taken Barnes under his wing, grooming him to one day be a detective. They'd grown close; Barnes, a substitute for the brother that had moved out of the country a decade ago; and Hodgins, a replacement for the father Barnes had recently lost. Before he knew it, Hodgins had made it to Simcoe Street and Union Station.

He bypassed the main building and headed for the tracks. If the tramps had jumped the train, they wouldn't have been seen by the employees inside. Hodgins noticed the station agent had wrangled one of the railway constables into helping clear the snow off the platform. They'd moved down to the tracks to clear the plank walkways used by employees by the time Hodgins reached them. He identified himself and gave a description of the tramps.

"Have you seen them around here lately? Or maybe someone reported seeing them hanging about?"

"Yes," the constable said. "I recall them. Don't see too many white men travelling with a negro. Chased them off the train yesterday. Can't say for certain they didn't come back."

Hodgins wandered the surrounding area questioning the men working for the shipping companies loading freight cars, preparing them for hook-up and departure. No one actually saw the tramps leave the area so it was possible they'd doubled back, jumped onto a car farther along the tracks, and were long gone. He checked back with the station agent to see where the trains were headed around the time the tramps were seen, and had telegraphs sent to all the possible stops. If they got off somewhere they would've been seen.

Not anxious to make the trek back to the station, he lingered near the wood stove in the waiting area. Even if he took the trolley, he'd still have some walking to do. Frustration at not being able to track down the tramps built up and he swore. No one was waiting for a train, so he wasn't concerned about keeping his voice down. After circling the stove a few times, he made his way over to the station agent.

"Do you think it at all possible those two tramps hopped the train without being seen?"

The station master shrugged. "Anything's possible, Detective. Not enough employees to watch every inch of the track."

"Yes, I know about not having enough men. In your opinion, where's the most likely spot they could've managed it?"

"Oh, that's easy. Westbound, just past where Queen and King meet and the tracks bend off. Eastbound, maybe around the dry dock or anywhere north of Kingston Road. Only things east of De Grassi are farm lands. No one to see what you're up to 'cepting a bunch of cows."

Hodgins smiled. "Somehow I don't think I'd get much out of them, except maybe a bucket of milk." He extended his hand. "Thank you for all your assistance. I'll have one of my constables check in with you to see if anyone answers the telegrams."

Hodgins raised his collar and fastened the top button before heading out to catch a trolley. The wind had picked up while at Union Station and he didn't relish the forty-minute walk back to the station on Wilton Avenue.

He arrived to find Barnes at his desk, a map folded out across it. "Found a map of Aurora. It's not very big. The town that is. Couldn't find a business directory."

"I'll ask around when I arrive. Town that size, probably won't be difficult to find someone who knows where I can find the ropemaker."

CHAPTER FIVE

N ext morning Hodgins sat on the train headed north. Settling back, he opened the morning issue of the Globe and Mail, hoping the two-hour ride would pass quickly. He'd ridden enough trains to barely notice the constant rocking. The train slowed once shortly after leaving the station and he asked a porter what the problem was.

"Nothing to worry 'bout Mister. Lots of snow on the tracks. Jest taking it easy-like."

He nodded and the porter moved on to answer questions from other passengers and check tickets. Hodgins listened briefly to some of the conversations around him. Most were discussions of Christmas events, family gatherings, and gifts. It seemed quite a number of people would be receiving hand-knit sweaters, mittens, and scarves.

Trying to ignore the voices, he skimmed the front page, chuckling at the advertisement for Christmas Cattle. An image of cows wearing garlands, with a little silver star on their heads, passed through his mind. Farther in was another ad, this one more interesting. Comedian John Murray was appearing at the Royal Opera House in Rip Van Winkle. He tore it out and stuffed it in his pocket, thinking it might be a pleasant outing once Jonathan's family arrived.

Hodgins turned back to the news. Constable McClennan from Station One arrested two people for assaulting a street car driver. He clicked his tongue in disbelief at people's horrid behaviour. The city had become crime-ridden lately. Men being assaulted simply for doing their jobs, and more than the usual amount of shoplifting. He thought about the items he'd heard about. Small things: silver bracelets, lace handkerchiefs, even socks. The one person who'd been caught said it was a Christmas gift for his wife. Times were hard and people did what they had to. Unfortunately, more than one family would have someone in jail for the holidays.

As he started his third time through the paper, the train finally pulled into the station in Aurora. Once it came to a stop, Hodgins assisted a young mother off, taking her parcels so she could carry the baby. After handing the packages off to her waiting husband, Hodgins asked him if he knew where Campbell's was. The young man directed him to the ropemaker's place of business on Yonge Street.

Hodgins hadn't realized Yonge went so far north. He pictured the map of the rail line that ran this way and wondered if the road continued all the way up as well. As he stood at the corner of Yonge and Wellington he looked north at the long stretch of road. Campbell's business was just a short walk away. A long building, about fourteen feet wide, sat on the west side of Yonge, just north of Wellington. Hodgins guessed the building had to be several hundred feet long. He walked through the main door and saw only a few men working inside. A staircase led up to a door on the second floor, the word *Office* painted in black on the frosted glass. One of the workmen hollered at Hodgins without stopping his work.

"Help you, Mister?"

Hodgins pointed to the office. "Campbell in there?"

"Believe so."

Hodgins made his way to the stairs, weaving through piles of ropes. When he reached the door, he knocked and went in before Campbell could reply. He introduced himself and got straight to the point of his visit.

"Is this one of yours?"

Mr. Campbell took the envelope in his pudgy fingers. "Yes, I suppose so. It looks like my clerk's writing. Why are the police interested in it?

"It was found in the possession of a murder victim.

Just trying to track his whereabouts before he was killed."

"This was found on a dead man you say?"

"Man by the name of Anthony Brown. Do you know him?

Campbell shook his head. "Name doesn't sound familiar, but then again, I do business with folks from out of town and don't know them all by name. Not every one asks for paperwork."

"He's about five foot six, late thirties, black hair, bushy beard." Hodgins pulled a piece of paper from his jacket and unfolded it. "One of my men sketched him. Does he look familiar? It's a pretty good likeness."

Campbell studied the sketch for a moment. "Sorry, I can't help."

"Well then, can you tell me why he'd have one of your envelopes, containing fifty dollars?"

Campbell's attitude changed. He stood straight, pulling his shoulders back and his eyes narrowed, making them all but disappear among the folds of fat. "What are you implying, Detective? Why, anyone could have found that envelope and used it for their own purpose. Fifty dollars! That's quite a sum. You aren't suggesting something underhanded?"

"No, not at all. As you say, the envelope could have come from anyone. Somebody may have taken one from your office, or even removed it from the trash bin."

Suspicion deflected, Campbell relaxed a little, but remained guarded. "Don't keep the office door locked. People go in and out all the time."

"Would you mind if I spoke to your employees? Show them the sketch?"

"Certainly. Always willing to cooperate with the constabulary. Don't think you'll find any of them can help. Trust my employees completely."

Campbell escorted Hodgins through the factory down a walkway that ran the length of the building along the south wall. The main work area sat a few feet lower. Several strands of rope of varying lengths stretched from one end to the other, supported by trestles every ten feet or so.

A foreman paced along the walkway, watching the process and barking out orders. They stopped to show him the picture of Brown. He didn't recognize him, and handed the sketch back to Hodgins before resuming his yelling.

"Why are there men running back and forth?" Hodgins asked Campbell.

"They're guiding the rope, making sure it twists properly. Call them donkeys. The fibres are short, so they need to be twisted together properly or they won't hold.

As the rope twists it gets shorter. The drive mechanism at that end moves as the rope length changes." Campbell pointed at the other end. "Those ends are fixed in place. Once the rope is done, it's wound onto those wooden reels, over on the north side."

"Looks simple enough," Hodgins said.

"Like to give it a go?" Campbell asked.

Hodgins smiled. "Don't suppose I'll ever get another opportunity. Never know when a new skill could come in handy."

"Follow me. Making some rope for a freight ship at the far end." He led Hodgins to another set-up, much larger than the last. Instead of thin strands attached to several hooks, strands already twisted together forming ropes about two inches thick were being worked into one larger rope, with the aid of an exceptionally large crank.

"Wally, give this detective a go, will you?"

Hodgins grasped the crank and started to turn. "My word! It's harder than it looks." He grabbed the handle with both hands and turned it again. Exhausted after only a few turns, he relinquished the crank to Wally. "I think I'll stick to police work." He reached into his pocket and pulled out the sketch of Brown. "Ever seen this guy?"

When Wally took the sketch, his rough and calloused hands practically crushed the paper. Hodgins looked down at his own hands, surprised to see a redness to them after only turning the crank a few times.

"Sure, I know 'im. Why that's Tony. Can't say where's I've seen him for a bit. His wife probably knows where he's got to."

Hodgins raised an eyebrow at the familiar use of the nickname Tony and wondered why Jonathan hadn't mentioned Brown was married. "Don't suppose you'll be seeing him again. He was murdered Friday evening. You say he has a wife? Where might I find her?"

Wally dropped the sketch. "Murdered?" He took a step back. "You don't think I did it, do you? Ain't see him for ages."

"No, just trying to find out more about him. Who he's seen. Do you know where he lives?"

"Over on Seal Street, other side of the tracks. Number four."

Hodgins picked up the crumpled sketch, thanked the man, then went in search of Mrs. Brown. He never liked having to be the one to tell someone their loved one was dead. Every time he had to, he imagined how Cordelia would react if another officer came to his house to tell her he'd been killed. Twice this year he'd ended up in the hospital and Delia fussed so much he went back to work early. Hard as he tried, he'd never been able to find a nice way to break the news. Probably was no nice way. He ran the words through his mind repeatedly, until he found himself in front of number four.

A chill worked its way through his clothing and into his bones as he stood staring at the tiny house. A gust of wind spurred him up the walk to the door. He hesitated before knocking. After straightening his collar and brushing off some of the snow, he raised his hand. Flakes of faded green paint sprinkled to the porch each time his knuckles hit the door. A young woman wearing a torn apron, loose hairs sticking out of a once tight bun, opened the door. The bulge under her apron told Hodgins she was with child. This was going to be worse than expected. Loud wailing came from somewhere at the back of the house.

"I'm coming," she yelled over her shoulder. She turned back to Hodgins. "It's not a good time. Whatever you're selling, I'm not interested."

"I'm Detective Hodgins, Toronto Constabulary. I need to speak with you."

She glanced at the badge as he pulled back the label of his overcoat. Her shoulders dropped. "Come in." She pointed to a small room on his left.

"The twins just won't stop crying. Please, warm yourself by the fire while I try to quiet the babies."

Hodgins stomped the snow off his boots and finished unbuttoning his topcoat before going to the crackling fire. It wasn't large, but definitely welcome. His stomach rumbled when he caught a whiff of freshly baked bread. Trying to ignore it, he set his thoughts on how to tell Mrs. Brown her husband had been killed.

She wasn't at all what he'd expected based on Jonathan's description of Brown. He expected her to be stocky, like her husband, rather rough, and definitely older. Tired as she was, it wasn't at all difficult to tell she was an extremely handsome young woman. Could it be possible she didn't know what her husband was like? So many men kept their wives in the dark when it came to business dealings, not wanting to muddle their weak minds. Weak indeed. Cordelia was as intelligent as most men he knew, more even. He'd learned early in their marriage just how good a business women she would have been, given the chance. After all, who was it who ran the household and kept most of the household accounts? The wife. The so-called weak woman. He turned at the sound of rustling skirts.

Mrs. Brown joined him in the small sitting room, a sleeping baby in each arm. He estimated they weren't much more than a year old.

"Let me help you." Hodgins took one of the babies

so she could lower herself onto the settee with a semblance of grace.

"I can tell you've a way with babies, Detective... Sorry, what was your name again?

"Detective Hodgins, and yes, I have a daughter, almost grown now. Going on ten." He reached into his pocket and handed her the wrinkled sketch, then sat in a chair opposite her.

She placed the sleeping baby beside her and unfolded the paper. "Why, this is a drawing of my husband." She closed her eyes and took two slow breaths. "What's he done now?"

"Do you have family or friends who can stay with you, or you with them?"

"Please, Detective. I know my Tony isn't a saint. Just tell me what's he done."

"Well, he hasn't actually done anything that I'm aware of. I'm very sorry to tell you, but your husband has been murdered."

Mrs. Brown looked at him as though she didn't understand, cocking her head to one side, then the other. Something in her eyes changed. She seemed to age at least ten years. "D-d-dead? Wait, you said murdered. It wasn't an accident? You're certain of that?"

"Yes, ma'am. Of that I have no doubt. Is there

someone who can stay with you?" He glanced down at her belly as she put her hand on the large bump. "Soon?"

She nodded. "About two months." She picked up the baby and held it close. "Murdered," she mumbled. "But who?"

She looked at him, waiting for an answer. Her eyes grew red and moist, but no tears fell. Mrs. Brown remained remarkably composed. Hodgins wondered if she wasn't all that upset at the news, or simply refused to cry in front of a stranger.

"We don't know, but we're looking into several possibilities."

"Hodgins. I've heard that name before, not recently."

"My brother, Jonathan, knew your husband in Boston."

Her eyes narrowed slightly, her tone changed. "Yes, I recall now." The ice in her voice could have frozen the fire. "If there's nothing else, I have things to attend to. Where is his body? I'd like to send for it."

What else had Jonathan not told him? The look in her eyes now reflected pure hatred. Hodgins felt embarrassed and guilty, even though none of it was his fault. "We'll have him sent up. You won't have to do anything. I'll make the arrangements personally when I return. Shall I have him sent here, or is there another place you'd prefer?"

"Here is just fine, thank you." Her tone now clipped, he knew he'd outstayed his welcome.

"Day after tomorrow, then?"

She nodded, took the baby from him and escorted him to the door. It was too cold to wander around and check out the town, so he went to the Beresford's Railway Hotel on Mosley Street for a bite and beverage while waiting for the train back to Toronto. He showed the sketch to the staff, discovering that Brown had been in a few times, but no one had been on friendly terms with him.

CHAPTER SIX

The train ride back felt longer than the ride up. Hodgins chatted to a fellow passenger about the day's news and half-listened as the gentleman prattled on about his business. Hodgins wasn't particularly interested in learning all about the Provincial Insurance Company, but that didn't deter the man. The train finally arrived in Toronto and Hodgins hurried back to the police station. He almost walked into Barnes as the constable exited the station house.

"Evening, sir. Was your trip a success?" Barnes stood aside to allow Hodgins to get in from the cold.

"If by success you mean do I know who the killer is, then I'm afraid the answer is no." He shook off his coat and draped it over a chair by the wood stove. "Found Brown's widow."

"Breaking the news of a death is the worst part of being a copper."

"You're right about that. Young woman with two small babies, twins, and another on the way. I hope she has

271

family to help her now. Funny, her tone changed when I mentioned her husband knew my brother in Boston. Soon as she heard his name she became almost hostile. All but asked me to leave. Which reminds me, I need to let McKenzie know to ship the body to her. I think I'll head back on Saturday, if I can. I'd like to talk to more people, find out what Anthony Brown was like, and if anyone had any problems with him. So far, I've only got my brother's opinion of him. Brown spent time in jail, so he's no saint, and even his wife first thought I'd come because of trouble. I'd like to hear a few other opinions.

"Surely, you don't doubt your brother's word?"

"No, not at all. But people do tend to exaggerate somewhat. Done it myself on occasion. We need to treat this like any other investigation. Forget he's family and check his story is all I'm saying."

He wondered why Jonathan needed to come up a full week before his family. He'd barely mentioned the business meeting since he'd arrived. As far as Hodgins knew, Jonathan only had that one meeting scheduled. The more he thought about it, the more confused he became. Just when was Jonathan's meeting? There'd been no mention of it, and he never left the house on his own. Any time Jonathan ventured out alone, Scraps had been with him. Not too professional to take a dog to a business meeting. Had he lied about it? Hodgins shook the thoughts from his mind. "Any word from the Boston police on Brown?"

"No, nothing yet. I'm sure we'll hear soon."

"If there's no word in a few days, ask again. Now off home with you. I've held you up long enough."

Hodgins went into his office and spent the next half hour writing up his notes and adding his thoughts before going home, too.

* * *

Dinner was quieter than usual. Both brothers avoided talking of the deceased and anything related to the case, but the looks they exchanged gave away their thoughts. Hodgins wondered if there could be the slightest possibility Jonathan was involved in the death of Brown. Could Jonathan have changed so much over the past ten years? He dealt with a lot of rough people, and Hodgins' suspected not all of Jonathan's customers even remotely resembled upstanding citizens. Cordelia finally broke the silence.

"I'm so looking forward to seeing Elizabeth again, and finally meeting your children. We keep saying we're going to go down for a visit, but it just never happens."

"Oh, yes," Sara chimed in. "I've got so many things to show them. And we can make Christmas decorations."

"Their train will be here Friday afternoon. Elizabeth spoke of little else right up to my boarding. She hollered something as the train pulled out, but the hiss of steam drowned her out," Jonathan said. "And Cora's looking forward to meeting her cousin. Little Freddie's more excited about the train ride."

Hodgins pushed the case to the back of his mind and joined in. "Likes trains, does he? Well, I have a little pull around here. I'm certain I can arrange a tour of Union Station. Maybe even a short ride with the engineer. Think he'll enjoy that?"

"I'm sure he will. So will I, truth be told. Remember that train Father gave me for Christmas when I was six?"

"Don't tell me you still have it? Last time I saw it, most of the paint had peeled off."

"It's the only thing I have to remind me of him. Must have taken him days to carve it. The wheels still turn. Keep it on the top shelf of the bookcase in my office."

They chatted about the arrangements for Jonathan's family, then Sara helped clear up and wash dishes. Jonathan settled in front of the fire with a book while Hodgins took Scraps for a walk.

With the evening reasonably mild, the air crisp, wandering around the neighbourhood with the dog relaxed him. It gave him time to mull over the facts of the case. He wished he could find the time alone with Delia to go over this with her. Hodgins' and Scraps walked up and down several streets, enjoying the solitude. Few buggies were about and he only encountered one other person out for a constitutional. He recognized the man but couldn't recall his name.

As he approached home, he noticed Barnes entering the house next door, and smiled. Cordelia would be furious that Hodgins hadn't told her about Barnes intention to propose to their beautiful, young neighbour, but he'd promised the lad he'd keep his secret.

CHAPTER SEVEN

Hodgins woke several times during the night, pondering how much his brother had changed. He longed to go over everything with Delia as she had a way of making him pull the facts together. She looked so peaceful, not restless like him. Hodgins sat on the edge of the bed and cleared his throat. Delia murmured and rolled over. He rose and walked to her side of the bed, reaching down to gently shake her shoulder. He stopped inches away. The next few weeks would be hectic. He didn't have the heart to disturb her knowing how little sleep awaited her. Sighing, he crawled back into bed, his childhood memories of Jonathan pushing their way to the front of his mind.

They'd been close growing up and remained so even into adulthood, or so he'd thought. Why hadn't Jonathan told him about the attack by his former employees? Was there something he wasn't saying about Mrs. Brown? There was no mistaking the change in her demeanor and attitude once she realized he was Jonathan's brother. Had Jonathan fallen in with a bad lot in Boston? Was it even slightly possible he'd murdered someone? How could he possibly arrest his own brother, and at Christmas-time? If found guilty, he'd hang.

Hodgins stared at the ceiling, watching the shadows shift as the wind raced through the branches, rearranging them and pushing the clouds along. Unable to fall back asleep, he rose, went down to the sitting room and lit the fire. The tall clock in the hall showed 3:05. Scraps padded in and lay on the rag-rug in front of the fire, completely unconcerned as to why someone was up so early. Hodgins sat staring at the writing on the pages of his notebook. Nothing came together. He tapped his pencil on the book, and Scraps raised his head and barked softly, tail thumping on the floor. Hodgins leaned forward and scratched the dog's head.

"Maybe a walk, eh boy?"

Scraps sat up, tail thumping faster. Hodgins went over to the window to check the weather. It wasn't snowing and the wind had died down somewhat.

"You're in luck boy. Seems like a fine night for a quick stroll."

Hodgins slipped the notebook into the drawer of the side table before heading upstairs to dress. When he came

277

down, Scraps sat at the door, leash in mouth. He'd quickly learned by putting his big, hairy paws on the wall, he was tall enough to remove the leash from the hook. Hodgins put on his overcoat and leather gloves, then wound a scarf around his neck before removing the leash from Scrap's mouth and fastening it to the collar. With Scraps pulling him along, they ventured out into the darkness.

Hodgins found the stillness comforting. The silence of the early morning broke only with the occasional clump of snow falling from a branch or rooftop. The air was colder than expected, making both his and Scraps' breath visible. Hodgins cursed himself for not bringing a lantern. Clouds filled the already blackened sky, blocking what little light there was. They strolled along the road, not needing to be concerned about dodging horses, sleighs, or buggies. Scraps trotted ahead, tail up, enjoying the unexpected romp. Hodgins followed behind mindlessly, paying no attention to where the dog led him.

Usually, quiet walks helped sort out his thoughts, but it wasn't working. When they approached the next street, Hodgins looked up at the street sign, surprised to find they'd crossed Yonge Street and were already up at Mount Pleasant and St. Clair. It was after four-thirty when they returned home. He fed Scraps and headed back to bed, hoping to get a couple hours sleep.

* * *

The aroma of coffee roused Hodgins from a deep sleep. Muffled voices mixed with the sizzle of the sausages caught his attention. They had company. He dressed, glancing at his pocket watch before placing it in his jacket pocket. It was almost nine thirty—way past his time. He raced down the stairs and into the kitchen. Barnes sat at the table with Cordelia and Jonathan, enjoying breakfast.

"Why didn't you wake me?

"You had such a restless night I didn't think a few extra hours would hurt." Cordelia placed a plate in front of him, and kissed his cheek. "Did you have a nice walk this morning?"

Hodgins raised an eyebrow. "I didn't realize you were awake. It was all for naught, anyway. I just can't figure this one out." He looked over at Barnes. "Inspector angry?"

"No, sir." Barnes swallowed the last bite of his sausage. "He hasn't come in yet either. Finally received a reply from Boston, though. Thought you'd want to know." His eyes flicked towards Jonathan briefly. "Some interesting information."

"You can tell me all about it on the way in." Hodgins scarfed down his breakfast and hurried Barnes out the door.

"May as well take a cab. There's a small coupe there,

on the corner." The men hurried along the road, calling out for him to wait.

"Station House Four," Hodgins told the driver. Once seated, the detective rapped on the roof and the driver snapped his reins, jerking the coupe when the horses suddenly moved. Their hooves barely made a sound, the packed snow muffling their steps.

They settled back, blanket over their laps. "I assume there's something about my brother in the report from the Boston police? Something unpleasant?"

"Yes, sir." Barnes looked down, twisting the edge of the wool blanket.

"Out with it, lad. Forget he's my brother."

"It's nothing major, just a few drunken brawls. And one complaint from a lady."

Hodgins turned to face Barnes. "A lady? What type of complaint?"

"Lewd comments, unwanted attention, if you catch my drift."

Hodgins was shocked. Could his brother have been unfaithful? He'd have to have a long talk with him before his family arrived on the weekend.

"Who made the complaint?" Hodgins hoped it wasn't who he suspected.

"Mrs. Brown."

"Damn. Our Mr. Brown's wife? Well, she is quite attractive, and young. I'm beginning to think I don't know my brother as well as I thought. I hope it went no further."

Hodgins glanced out the tiny window, spotting a boy on the corner waving the morning edition at passers-by. He hoped it contained nothing about Brown's murder and the lack of information the police had. "What about Mr. Brown? Anything on him?"

"His last release was in July. Seems he was in and out of jail on a regular basis. They didn't know he'd left town. Got quite a lengthy record, going back to when he was a lad. Apparently, he's been out on the streets since he was six or seven. Stealing at first, then assault and extortion. Put more than one bloke in the hospital. Sounds like no one will miss him, except maybe his wife. She's been arrested a few times, too. Mainly petty theft. Nothing recent."

"I'm not completely certain his wife will miss him," Hodgins mumbled, more to himself than to Barnes.

As soon as they arrived at the station house, Hodgins paid the cab driver while Barnes went ahead to retrieve the report from his desk. He joined Hodgins in his office.

"Any word on those two tramps? They must be somewhere. Can't have vanished into thin air."

"Nothing yet. I'm planning on going down to Union

to chat with the station agent. See if they've any word from the other train stations."

"Off with you then. We need find those two."

* * *

An hour later Barnes returned. He raced into Hodgins' office, a huge grin plastered across his face. "Telegram came into Union Station while I was there." Barnes handed the paper to Hodgins before brushing the snow from his shoulders. "They've been spotted west of here, over in Berlin. Two tramps were thrown off the train just before it pulled out last night. One white man, one coloured. Must be the same ones. Might still be there."

"Good. I believe Berlin has a sheriff, so wire him and ask him to round up some men to find the tramps and hold them somewhere. Promise them food and shelter from the cold. Warm feet and a full belly should keep them content until I can arrive."

"Right away, sir."

Hodgins decided to take a break from the case and go through some old files. He still had a couple of unsolved deaths from earlier in the year. Suspicious, but indeterminate if they were murders or accidents. He needed the distraction. Hodgins stood and stretched out his back, then went out to the filing cabinets and rummaged through the drawers, not looking for anything in particular. His fingers stopped when he came to a file labelled *Willson, Unsolved.*

Several hours and many cups of tea later, he hadn't discovered anything new in the Willson shooting. When he returned the file to the cabinet, Hodgins noticed how dark it had become outside. He pulled out his pocket watch. Almost seven. He grabbed his coat, but as he passed Sergeant Evans' desk, the clicking of the telegraph machine stopped him. Hodgins waited while the sergeant wrote up the message and handed it to him. Finally, the reply from Berlin saying they had the two tramps. Hodgins wired back that he'd take the first train out in the morning.

CHAPTER EIGHT

That evening, Hodgins joined Cordelia and Sara in the kitchen, watching while they prepared the evening meal. Sara peeled and cut the potatoes then placed them in a pot of water, struggling to carry it to the wood stove. Hodgins got up to help, but Sara refused.

"I'm old enough to do it by myself." Both hands gripped the handle as she made her way across the kitchen. She managed the trip without spilling any water, but couldn't lift it high enough to set it on the stove.

Hodgins rushed over, relieving her of the load. "Don't want you to burn yourself. And don't ever be afraid to ask for help, no matter how old you get."

Sara pouted and crossed her arms.

"I know you're old enough, you're just not tall enough." He tugged her braid. "Maybe I can build you a step until you grow a little more."

Sara threw back her head and stomped to the sink to chop the carrots. Hodgins followed and reached over to steal one.

"Don't know if I'll return before Jonathan's family arrives on Friday. I hope to take the last train back tomorrow, but I'll plan on staying over for a day or two in case the weather turns."

"Don't rush the investigation," Delia said. "If you have to stay for a few day, I'll simply have Jonathan hire a carriage to pick his family up."

"Can we all go?" Sara pleaded. "Please?"

"I don't see why not," Hodgins said. "Better hire two carriages. Won't be enough room in one for everyone plus their luggage. Their train should be pulling in shortly after two. I'll ask Barnes to check for any delays, and I'll wire him if I'll be late getting back from Berlin. I'll try my best to get home in time. With luck, I'll be escorting two prisoners."

"I'll pack up some leftovers for the train ride. No sense spending good money on stale sandwiches."

"Where's Jonathan? I need to talk to him."

"He took Scraps for a walk."

"No wonder the house is so quiet. It's cold, so I don't imagine they'll be out long." He took out his pocket watch to check the time. "It's already after seven-thirty. They should have the sense to be home by now. When did they leave?"

"Oh, about thirty minutes ago, I guess." Cordelia

covered the pot of boiling potatoes, then added another log to the fire below before joining him at the table. "What's troubling you, Bertie? You've barely mentioned the case. That's not like you at all. Is your brother somehow involved?"

"Never could hide anything from you, Delia. I honestly don't know if he's involved. I do know there's secrets he's keeping. Just don't know if they're relevant. He's not the same man I grew up with. That much I do know for certain."

Before Cordelia could press him for more information, they heard barking from the back yard. The outer door to the small porch slammed and Cordelia hurried to the kitchen door, making sure it couldn't open, trapping the wet dog and Jonathan.

"Sara, rub him down with that old blanket. I don't want mud and snow tracked through my clean house."

Jonathan edged the door open an inch. "I assume you're referring to the dog and not me." He slipped off his overcoat and draped it on the back of a chair, while Sara rubbed down Scraps, giggling at her uncle's remark. He placed his overshoes beside the chair and stepped into the kitchen. "Why the serious face brother?"

"We need to talk." Hodgins walked down the hall and into the sitting room, Jonathan close behind. Hodgins faced the fire, hands clasped behind his back.

"Have I done something to anger you, little brother?"

"Why didn't you tell me what happened in Boston?"

"As I said earlier, I didn't want to worry you. The attack was brief, the men arrested and jailed."

"Not that." Albert turned to face Jonathan. "Why didn't you tell me about Mrs. Brown?"

"Oh." Jonathan dropped onto the closest chair and buried his face in his hands. "It's not something I'm proud of. I was drunk." He looked up, hands raised. "I know. That doesn't excuse my behaviour. Lizzie was away with the children, visiting her parents. We needed a break from each other. How could I possibly tell my younger brother that my marriage was a failure? I'm the eldest and should be setting an example. And you've always had such high morals. Everything was always right or wrong, nothing in between. I was drunk and missing my wife. Janel came in, looking for her husband. I tried to take advantage."

"Janel?" You're on familiar terms with her? How far did it go?"

Jonathan got up and stood beside Albert, placing his hand on his arm. "You have to believe me, Albert. Nothing happened. One of Brown's cohorts was in the bar and escorted Janel, Mrs. Brown, home, then told Tony.

Albert brushed Jonathan's hand away. "I've seen the

report from Boston. It happened shortly before your attack. Could it be he was less concerned with being fired and more concerned about his wife's honour?"

Jonathan shrugged. "Maybe a little of both."

"Does Elizabeth know?"

"Dear God, no. As soon as my bruises and broken arm healed I went to her parents' home and pleaded with her to return with me. Promised I'd spend less time at work and more time with my family. We're quite content now. Won't ever have what you have with Cordelia, but we're happy enough."

Albert tried to read Jonathan's expression while listening to the sorrow in his voice. *He's my brother. I have to believe him.*

"Then we won't speak of it again. Please, no more secrets. Drink before we eat?"

Sara burst into the room, half-dried dog at her side. "Mommy said supper's ready."

She grabbed her father's hand and practically dragged him down the hall and into the kitchen. Once they were seated and served, Sara did most of the talking while they ate, listing everything she planned on doing with her cousins. The list didn't change much from one meal to another, but she seemed to be including more decorations. Hodgins wondered where they'd find space for them all.

"I've waited ever so long to meet Cora." Sara rattled on, pausing occasionally to eat. "We write all the time. I've even made her a Christmas gift, but it's a secret."

Hodgins nodded and smiled, only half listening as he thought about his conversation with Jonathan. Sara would be meeting her two cousins for the first time and he was beginning to feel like he was meeting his brother for the first time as well.

Once the meal was over, dishes washed and put away, Sara got ready for bed. The two brothers headed to the sitting room; Jonathan chose to read, while Albert decided to get some sleep.

"I have an early train to catch, so I'll bid you goodnight. Keep an eye on everyone while I'm gone. Not certain when I'll be back. It all depends on how it goes with the two tramps. I'll wire if I'm delayed past Friday."

Jonathan glanced up from his book. "Don't worry about us. We'll be fine. I hope you find your murderer. Not that I'm sorry Brown's dead."

"Don't suppose you're alone with that sentiment," Hodgins remarked before heading upstairs. He was about to climb into bed when Cordelia came into the bedroom.

"There's a piece of beef and a couple of biscuits wrapped in a cloth in the tin by the window. Don't want the mice to get it before you do. Is everything sorted with

Jonathan?"

"Yes. Seems he and Elizabeth had a spot of trouble and separated briefly. He says they're fine now. Don't mention it when she arrives."

"She may want to talk about it, but I'll wait until she brings it up. If she doesn't I'll mention a friend who's having trouble. Maybe it'll encourage her to say something."

Hodgins walked over and kissed her forehead. "I've no doubt you'll find out and make her believe it was all her idea to tell you."

CHAPTER NINE

Hodgins rose before the sun the next morning. The birds hadn't even woke yet. Off in the distance horse bells jingled. "At least I'm not the only fool up this early," he mumbled while packing a few things in a carryall, before attending to his morning routine. After dressing, he started a fire in the fireplace so Cordelia would wake to a warm room, then made his way downstairs, avoiding the one step that always squeaked.

Once in the kitchen, he started a fire in the stove and put the kettle on to boil, then lit the fire in the sitting room. The downstairs would be comfortably warm by the time the household awoke. When he returned to the kitchen, Scraps had moved over by the heat and gone back to sleep. Hodgins retrieved his lunch from the tin, placed it in his carryall, then searched for the rest of the biscuits in the ice chest. He set two of them on the stove to warm while he poured his tea, and managed to grab the biscuits before they blackened, almost dropping them as they burned his fingers. He slathered them in some of

Cordelia's homemade apple jelly and watched as it melted into the crevices. Tea drank and biscuits devoured, he slipped on his overcoat, wrapped his scarf around his neck and headed out the door.

With no cabbies in sight he had to walk several blocks before finding a ride. Despite having his gloved hands buried in his pockets, his fingers were practically frozen by the time he hailed a cab and wrapped himself in the passenger blanket.

When he arrived at Union Station, the platform and waiting lounge were practically empty. The hour was too early for most travellers. The few individuals about were loading freight into wagons, probably brought in by White Star's *Atlantic*, sitting in the harbour since yesterday. Hodgins wondered if that's who Jonathan's meeting was with. A lucrative contact if won. He ambled to an empty bench beside the pot belly stove in the waiting area after purchasing his ticket. Fifteen minutes later, he was seated on the seven-thirty train. It was scheduled to arrive in Berlin at ten-thirty, so he placed his ticket on his lap and immediately fell asleep.

About two hours later he woke to find a young boy sitting across from him, staring. Hodgins smiled at him, but his expression never changed. A woman sat beside the boy, sleeping.

"What's your name?"

Nothing. The child didn't even blink. Hodgins shrugged and checked the time. The train was due at the Berlin station in another hour. He pulled out his notebook to find the Sheriff's name—Davidson. One of the porters walked through the car, so Hodgins asked if he knew where to find Davidson. Hodgins noticed the boys eyes widen when he mentioned the sheriff.

Hodgins continued to read and re-read his notes. He looked up when he noticed the train slow, followed by the shriek of the whistle. Hodgins peered out the window, and the town eventually came into view. He placed his carryall on the empty seat beside him, ready to exit as soon as the train pulled in. The squeal of the breaks finally woke the woman across from him. The boy sat up on his knees and whispered something in her ear. She turned her gaze towards Hodgins. He smiled and introduced himself.

"Good morning ma'am. Couldn't help but notice your boy's interest when I asked about the sheriff. I'm Detective Hodgins from the Toronto Constabulary.

The little boy's mouth dropped open. "A real detective?"

"Yes, a real, honest-to-goodness detective."

"Little Alfy's fascinated with lawmen. He was ever so excited when we took him to see The Scouts of the Prairie last year while we were in Norfolk. We even met Buffalo Bill and Ned Buntline afterwards."

Alfy's head bobbed up and down while his mother spoke. "They kilt real injuns. A whole bunch of 'em," he added.

Hodgins smiled and ruffled the boy's hair. "I'm sure they did. If you'd ever like a tour of a police station next time you're in Toronto, just come to Station Four. Tell them Detective Hodgins invited you. Enjoy your day."

The train finally came to a stop and Hodgins exited. The wind wasn't as strong now and the sun had warmed the air, but he still tightened his scarf as he hurried along the streets, trying to follow the directions given him. He located the sheriff easily. Unlike Hodgins' large brick station house, Berlin's station was a board and batten building. The main office was one room, not more than forty feet square. A bulletin board hung on the wall, half filled with posters, most of which Hodgins recognized. A single file cabinet stood beside it, with a pot belly stove a few feet away. The sheriff's desk was just off to the right of the door, with a rather large man sitting behind it. They chatted briefly before Hodgins asked to question the tramps.

"Did they give you any trouble, Sheriff?"

"No, not at all. They claim they haven't done

anything but were glad to be out of the cold. Your wire didn't say why you're looking for them. What is it they're suspected of?"

Hodgins sat in the chair in front of the Sheriff's desk, dropping his bag at his feet.

"There was a murder the other day and they were seen in the vicinity. I'm not saying they did it, but they may have seen something. They left town right after, which would normally be suspicious, but they're tramps so it's not unusual for them to be travelling."

"Rather odd to see a white man travelling with a coloured one, so I knew who you were looking for right off. They've been through here before and no one ever had any complaints about them. They're both skilled carpenters. Could make a good living if they chose to stay in one place."

A gust of cold wind burst through the room when the front door opened. A scrawny woman Hodgins guessed to be in her forties came in and sat a basket on the desk.

"Breakfast for your guests as ordered. Little late, but I've been busy." She drew back the cloth covering the contents, revealing two thick slices of bread and a couple of pieces of ham. Steam rose from the freshly baked bread, filling the air with a mouth-watering aroma.

"Thank you, Daisy. Don't suppose you could spare a

few more slices for two famished lawmen?"

Daisy put her hands where her hips would be if she had any substance to her. "Why the devil didn't ya ask for more in the first place? Person could catch their death going in and out of the cold." She wrapped her shawl around her head and continued to grumble as she stomped out the door, slamming it behind her.

"Woman's never happier than when she's got something to complain about." Sheriff Davidson picked up the basket and headed to the back. "Help yourself to the coffee. It's not the best tasting, but it's nice and hot."

Hodgins found a reasonably clean cup and filled it with the dark liquid. It was stronger than he was used to, but it warmed his insides. The fire was low, so he took it upon himself to add another log. It crackled and popped as it provided much needed warmth. Davidson returned, retrieved the empty cup that sat on his desk and joined Hodgins.

"I've not had occasion to come out this way before. Based on the name, I'm guessing there are a lot of German's in the area."

They moved over to the Sheriff's desk before continuing their conversation. Davidson leaned back, his bulk causing the chair to groan as he put his boots up on the desk. "The area was first settled by Mennonites. Didn't get the Germans until after the Napoleonic wars. We've quite the assortment of skilled tradesmen here. Food's not bad either. Still prefer my wife's steak, eggs, and bread through." He glanced down at Hodgins' carryall. "Planning on staying awhile?"

"Not sure. Feels like there's a storm brewing so I thought I'd come prepared."

"There's a clean boarding house down the street, run by our charming Miss Daisy."

Another rush of cold air brought a second basket from Daisy, still grumbling. They ate in silence, Hodgins hungrier then he'd realized, the food in his bag long forgotten. Once the ham and bread were consumed, Hodgins stood.

"Guess I'd better speak to the two men now."

Davidson showed Hodgins to the back where the tramps were, retrieved the now empty basket, then went back to his desk.

When Hodgins saw the two tramps, their appearance surprised him. Instead of a pair of weather old men as he'd expected, they were relatively young. The negro wore a straw hat, dirty brown pants and was probably about thirty-five, while the other was maybe still in his twenties. Both stood and politely greeted the detective. Hodgins noticed the negro was bow-legged and stood several inches shorter than his own six-foot two frame. If not for the bowed legs, Hodgins guessed he'd be his height. He tried not to laugh as he wondered if the negro's weight made his legs bow so much. The white tramp, however, towered over him. He had hair as red as Doctor McKenzie's and spoke with a thick Scottish accent.

"People call me Scotty. My friend here goes by Curly." Both tramps laughed at the joke as the negro didn't have a hair on his head. Hodgins thought it peculiar that the men would be so jovial after being arrested. Maybe they weren't guilty of anything and it was just a coincidence they'd been seen in the area Friday evening. He took an instant liking to them.

Curly spoke first. "Not that I'm complaining to have a roof over my head and a hot meal in my belly, but what's we locked up for?"

"I need to know where you were last Friday evening."

Scotty and Curley looked at each other, shoulders raised, heads shaking.

"We dinnae have much occasion to take notice of the day or time," Scotty answered.

"No, I don't suppose you do. Maybe it would help if I told you that you both were seen in Toronto and caught trying to hop a train."

"Toronto? Yes, we visited your fair city recently,"

Curly said.

"If you don't mind me saying, you both sound fairly well spoken for a pair of tramps."

"Ah, yes." Curly spoke up first. "I spent my younger days in the employ of a fine gentleman in the south. He insisted I had some learning and conduct myself appropriately. When I left after the old gent passed away, I found it to my advantage to continue so. Folks are less leery when you sound educated, especially when you don't look like them."

Hodgins turned to the young Scotsman. "And you?"

"Spent a few years at the University in Glasgow before I plucked up the courage to leave. Was nae interested in following in me father's footsteps. No interest in business, but I enjoy working with my hands." He nodded towards Curly. "We met by chance on a train from New York City a few years ago and have travelled together since."

Both men seemed to Hodgins to be quite content with their chosen path. He couldn't image either harming anyone. "Do you recall what you did while in Toronto? Anything at all?"

The stocky negro sat back on the cot and leaned against the wall. "Let me think. Spent some time on a farm. Helped build a lean-to on the back of the house.

Babe on the way and they needed more room. Scotty fixed the cradle the man tried to build." He slapped his knee and barked out a laugh. "Sorriest cradle I ever did see."

"Aye. I would nae put a dead dog in something so wobbly. The misses was so pleased she packed enough food for a couple of days when we left. We went through the city on the way to the station. If you say that was Friday, then I will nae disagree."

Hodgins made notes in his little book. "Don't suppose you know the name of the farmer?"

"Don't have much need for names," Curly replied.

"Suppose you also don't have much need to recall where they lived either?"

Both shook their heads. "North of the city is all I can tell you," Scotty said. "Took the better part of a day to reach the train."

"North, right." Hodgins wrote that down and wondered how long it would take to find the right farm.

The land north of the city was sparsely settled, small settlements dotted along the more highly travelled carriageways, numerous farms on the outskirts of each town. Maybe someone would know a family about to have a baby. Hodgins flipped through his notes. "Some people saw you near Ketchum School. What were you doing there? Said you were arguing."

The two tramps looked at each other and shrugged. "Don't know nothin' 'bout a school, but we did have a lively conversation or two," Curley said.

"Large brick building near the north end of Toronto, park and woods beside it," Hodgins prompted.

"Aye, I believe I know where you mean," Scotty said. He turned to Curly. "That'd be where we *discussed* which direction to go next."

"That's right. I remember now. Is that why we're locked up? Is it a crime to argue with a friend?"

"No," Hodgins said. "Man was found murdered on the school grounds."

Neither man seemed surprised. "We saw no one, Detective. The streets were empty when we went by," Curly said.

"And we killed no one," Scotty added. He held up his calloused hands "These hands bring wood to life, not take life from the living."

Hodgins had no reason to either believe or disbelieve the tramps, but his instinct said to believe them. He had no witnesses to the crime and no evidence pointing to anyone, except his brother.

He sighed and left the back room, not bothering to close the cell door.

"May as well release them, Sheriff. But ask them to

stay in town."

"You don't think they're responsible then? Good. I could use their carpentry skills myself. Wife's been at me to fix some things, and the weather does feel like it's going to take a bad turn. I can probably keep them busy for a few weeks. Meals and lodgings in exchange for work."

As Hodgins was reasonably satisfied the tramps weren't responsible, and the sheriff would be keeping an eye on them, he decided not to stay over in Berlin. The next train back was at 3:37. He checked his pocket watch. Plenty of time before it pulled out, so he stayed and chatted with Davidson, even treated him to a meal.

When they left the restaurant, the air was noticeably colder. He bade the Sheriff farewell and rushed to the train station, the German food not quite settled in his stomach. He was glad he didn't have to stay over, and would be back home in time to enjoy his wife's Irish cooking. Once he was settled on the train, he pulled out his little notebook and reviewed the few bits of information he had.

Brown died Friday early evening according to McKenzie, but his body wasn't found until mid-morning Saturday. He'd been left out in the open, so why wasn't he discovered earlier? Maybe the cold weather had led the coroner to be mistaken about the time of death. The only possible suspects were the tramps and his own brother. He believed the story the tramps relayed, and Jonathan hadn't even arrived in Toronto when Brown had been killed.

The amount of blood around the body left no doubt in Hodgins' mind that Brown died at the school. Someone must have heard the shot. The area around Ketchum School was quiet and the sound of a guns firing would have carried. Either he'd missed speaking with one of the neighbours or somebody lied. Reading back over the interviews with the people around the school, Hodgins realized one of the houses on Bishop Street had been empty the first time they checked with the neighbours around the school, and he hadn't gone back. He made a note to try the house again and to check with Barnes to see if any of the homes he visited also had no answer. Hodgins closed his notebook, then dug out the lunch Cordelia packed, hoping the biscuits would help settle his stomach.

CHAPTER TEN

When Hodgins arrived back at Station House Number Four, Barnes practically knocked him over in his rush to speak with the detective.

"Slow down, lad. Let me get my overcoat off and a cup of hot tea. Whatever it is can wait another few minutes."

Hodgins stood in front of the wood stove briefly, enjoying the heat emanating through the vents. After hanging his overcoat on a nearby peg, he went into the back and fixed a cup of tea. He noticed Barnes pacing in front of his office when he came back out front.

"All right. You look like you're about ready to burst. What is it?"

Barnes followed Hodgins into his office. "While you were away, a wire came in from Montréal. Apparently, a man walked into one of their police stations and confessed to killing Brown. They're already on the way here with him. Should arrive around 11:30 tonight."

"Well, that saves us a lot of bother. We can

concentrate on something else if we've got the killer. Jonathan will be happy to hear that bit of news, too. Strange how that man just up and confessed. Why flee to another province, someplace we're not even looking, and go to the police? He's not someone we've been searching for, whoever he is. Probably would've gotten away with it if he'd kept his gob shut."

"It is puzzling, sir." Barnes sat opposite the detective and laid a paper on the desk. "Here's the wire. Guess you made the trip to Berlin for naught."

Hodgins finished his tea and leaned back. "Suppose. I wasn't totally convinced those two were guilty anyway. They could've travelled a lot farther if they wanted to escape getting caught. Pleasant enough chaps, and Sheriff Davidson said they'd been there before and had no trouble with them. Need to confirm their whereabouts, just in case. Brown wasn't overly large, but he was strong. Not convinced one man could subdue him, and it could just as easily been three men arguing, not two. The argument may not even be relevant."

Hodgins asked Barnes to fetch a few of the other constables before they left. Barnes corralled four of them before they had a chance to leave. They all crowded into Hodgins' office.

"I know the weather's getting bad, but I need you to

visit the farms north of the city first thing tomorrow. Get yourselves horses from the livery and bundle up. I need you to find the farm where two tramps did some work last week. Young couple, wife's with child. About a days walk from the city. Might be a bit further. Don't go too far out, and for God's sake, if the weather gets worse, turn back."

Hodgins gave them a description of the tramps and sent them home. He retrieved the wire from Boston to re-read the incident between Jonathan and Janel Brown. Not a lot of detail had been provided. The end of the wire said details would be sent by post. Hodgins wasn't certain he wanted to read it when it arrived.

"Barnes, I believe I'll go see what my beautiful wife is fixing for supper. It's past your time as well. I'll meet the train tonight, personally."

* * *

After supper, Sara played in the sitting room, so Hodgins didn't get the opportunity to speak with Jonathan about the wire, but did mention the prisoner coming in on the train.

"Looks like you've been given an early Christmas present," Hodgins said. "We'll know more after I interview him. I'll get him settled into a nice cold cell tonight, then interrogate him first thing."

The evening dragged on, but the time finally came to

meet the late train. Hodgins was surprised when he opened his front door and encountered a foot or more of snow.

"Blast." He turned up the collar on his overcoat and ran up the street to where a carriage stood. He slipped a few times but managed to stay on his feet. The driver was brushing snow off one of the black horses. Hodgins ran his hand over the other horse to clear the snow from it's back and to hurry the driver along.

"Done for the night, sir. Have to find another."

Hodgins showed his badge. "One more trip. Need to get to Union Station. Wait for me. I'll be coming back with two more passengers after the train arrives."

The train was a half-hour late. The horses stomped their large feet and snorted, anxious to get moving. As the train pulled out, Hodgins led the Montréal policeman and his prisoner to the waiting carriage. The two men were groggy, barely able to stay awake. The officer said little, speaking in broken English. "The train, how you say? Wobbly?"

Hodgins smiled. "I believe you mean rickety." He wiggled his hand up and down. The officer nodded.

"Oui, rickety."

"I'm afraid the cab ride won't be much smoother, but at least it's quiet."

The officer got in first. Hodgins helped the

handcuffed prisoner up, seating him beside the Montréal policeman before settling on the seat opposite. Both the prisoner and accompanying officer were half asleep and dozed off in the carriage, despite the bumps and cold.

Hodgins studied the prisoner while he slept: a toad of a man with a receding hairline and bulging eyes. Hodgins wondered how he could have over-powered Brown. When they arrived back at Station Four, he once again asked the driver to wait, offering him the comfort of the police livery. The officer from Montréal asked if he could spend the night in one of the empty cells as he was leaving on the first train out and didn't want to go back out in the cold to find a room.

"No need to sleep in a cold cell. We have a small cot in the back, near the pot belly stove. Nice and warm. You can help yourself to tea, and you'll find some biscuits in a tin."

Once the prisoner was locked up, Hodgins showed the officer where he could sleep.

I didn't get your name," Hodgins said.

"Jean Beaudoin, Sargent De Police." He extended a hand as he yawned.

"Albert Hodgins. Thank you for coming so quickly."

"Ah, my son, he is Albert." He yawned again.

"I'm keeping you up. Make yourself comfortable."

Hodgins pointed to a shelf over a small sink. "Tea and biscuits are up there. Good night."

Hodgins hurried to the livery, anxious to climb into his own bed. He couldn't stop thinking about the prisoner. There was no way he could've dragged a dead body alone, especially so far, and in the snow. The area where the bloodied branch was found had to be at least three hundred feet from the school. He must have had help. Could he be wrong thinking the tramps were not involved?

As the streets were deserted at such a late hour, Hodgins arrived home in no time. The driver spoke sharply when he halted the horses.

"Yer home, sir. And that's where I'm headed myself."

Feeling guilty for detaining the driver more than two hours, Hodgins gave him a generous tip, earning him a nod and smile.

CHAPTER ELEVEN

Once again Hodgins woke to find himself behind his time. It was almost nine when he hurried into the kitchen. Jonathan sat enjoying a cup of tea with a constable, but not Barnes. That new constable again, Harry? No, Perry. Hodgins raised an eyebrow when he recognized the lad.

"I hope you're not here to tell me there's another body at the school."

"No, sir. Not that I know of. Inspector sent me in to find you. Wants you at the station right away."

"Tell him I'll see him when I can. I have a prisoner to interrogate. Tell him we may have caught the killer."

"Yes, sir." The constable rose to leave.

"Finish your tea. It's cold outside."

The constable remained standing and gulped down the contents of his cup, then scurried out the door after thanking Cordelia.

"That should keep the Inspector satisfied for a little while. I suspect he wants an update for the Chief Inspector and Gruger. I've been putting it off for too long. Hopefully, after interrogating the man brought in last night I'll be able to tell him we have the culprit." He turned to his wife. "Delia, I'm famished. Fix me up a large helping of eggs and sausages if you don't mind. Meanwhile, I'll just start with some of these." Hodgins uncovered the basket that sat on the table and took out two of the steaming hot biscuits, then, as usual, slathered them with her homemade apply jelly.

"Shouldn't you be hurrying along?" Cordelia remarked.

Hodgins took a large bite of his biscuit before answering. "Mouth watering, my dear." He took another bite. "I have a prisoner that needs questioning. Can't do that properly on an empty stomach now, can I? As long as the constable tells the Inspector that we may have the killer, he'll be content enough to wait."

Jonathan and Cordelia exchanged puzzled looks. It wasn't like Hodgins to be so unconcerned.

"Hurry along Delia. I'd like to have my breakfast before lunch time." He winked and shoved the rest of the biscuit in his mouth.

Delia smiled and went over to the cold box for three eggs and some sausages. Jonathan made himself another cup of tea. "This chap, he went all the way to Montréal

311

before confessing?"

"Yes. Strange that, don't you agree? Why travel all the way to Montréal? Why the devil didn't he come to one of the stations here in Toronto?"

"Who knows how someone's mind works? Maybe sitting on the train, his conscience got the better of him. Maybe he's a simpleton. I'm certain you'll beat it out of him."

Hodgins glared at his brother. "I do *not* beat my prisoners. I realize that's a common practice, but in my experience, all it does is make an innocent man confess just to make it stop. Then the real culprit gets away. I strongly urge all my men not to resort to extreme force. Unfortunately, I can't stop them unless I'm in the room with them. I'll admit I've hit a few myself, but I've never beaten anyone."

The conversation stopped when Cordelia sat a plate loaded with scrambled eggs and sausages in front of her husband. She cleared the dirty tea cups off the table, washed and put them away while he ate in silence. The scent of the sausages didn't even rouse the sleeping dog. When Hodgins finished, he took his plate to the sink, kissed Delia on the cheek, then turned to Jonathan.

"Once your family is settled in after the long train ride, what's say we go out and cut down a tree? This will be our first Christmas in our new house and we must have the biggest and best tree we can find. I have Sunday off. I'll hire a cutter sleigh and we'll head out to the country after church. Stop somewhere for a bite to eat. Make a day of it. Did you have a chance to look at that bit I tore from the paper about Rip van Winkle at the Opera House?"

"I'm certain the children would enjoy both that and cutting a tree," Jonathan said.

"Yes, that sounds lovely, dear," Cordelia added.

"Speaking of children, where's Sara?" Hodgins asked.

"She's gone skating with her friend Lucy. She was ever so excited about cutting down a tree and wanted to make certain her friend knows all about it."

"Do you have anywhere in mind to find a nice tree?" Jonathan asked.

Hodgins tapped the side of his nose and smiled. "Can't give away any secrets. I'll try not to be late," he said, heading for the front door.

∗ ∗ ∗

Hodgins stood outside the interrogation room, watching the suspect through a rip in the curtains. The fabric wasn't thick, but it allowed privacy when someone felt it necessary to get rough or to hide the identity of a witness. The man sat hunched over the table, sweat beading on his brow despite the chilly weather. Somehow, he seemed even smaller than the night before.

"How the hell did a man of such a small stature overpower a street-wise and strong man like Brown?"

The constable standing beside him shrugged in reply. Hodgins had been thinking about that all the way to the station. He watched the man fidget in the chair. Nervous sort of chap. How could he pluck up the courage to murder anyone? He opened the door and went in, taking a seat on the opposite side of the table.

"Mr. Towers, I understand you've confessed to killing someone in Toronto. Is that correct?"

Towers drummed the edge of the table with his fingers, staring at a scar on the tabletop. "Yes," he whispered.

"Tell me what happened. Why did you kill him? Start from the beginning."

"Made me angry, so I shot him." He stopped after just one sentence.

"And" Hodgins prompted. "Made you mad how?"

"Um, owed me money. Said he didn't have it so I shot him."

"I see. And after you shot him, did you check to see if he had your money on him?"

Towers nodded. "Checked his pockets. Empty."

First lie.

"Where did you shoot him?"

"In the school yard."

"No, I mean where on his person."

Towers scrunched his face as though trying to retrieve a memory. "Head, shot him in the head."

"Funny that," Hodgins said. "His bowler never even fell off."

"Put it back on him."

Second lie.

The questioning continued for over thirty minutes. Hodgins would ask a question and receive little more than a one-sentence answer. His frustration grew along with the serious doubts as to Towers' guilt.

"Tell me again, where in the head did you shoot him?"

"Left side, like the paper said."

Hodgins slammed his palms on the table and stood, his chair scrapping the wooden floor. "I knew it." Towers had not told him anything that hadn't already been in the newspapers. "You odious little toad. You're not guilty of anything except wasting everyone's time. I ought to lock you up for interfering in our investigation."

Towers slunk down in the chair and almost slid under the table.

"Constable," Hodgins yelled. "Get this worthless

piece of shite out of my sight." Hodgins stepped back, sending his chair toppling over.

The door opened and the constable who brought Towers up from the cells entered. "Want me ta lock him back up?"

"No. Throw him out. He's no more guilty that I am. What a waste of time. I'm sure the police in Montréal won't be pleased to know one of their own wasted two days for nothing. Is Sergeant Beaudoin still here?"

"Left about an hour ago."

Hodgins slapped his hands on the table again, leaning towards Towers. "I don't want to see you in my police station ever again. Do you understand?"

Towers nodded and without waiting for the constable to escort him, bolted out the door and through the station house. Barnes grabbed him when Towers rushed past.

"Let him go," Hodgins said. "Nothing more than an attention seeker."

Barnes released him and the man hurried out into the cold. Hodgins slammed the door to his office and kicked his chair before sitting. Barnes lightly tapped on the glass and waited. Hodgins hesitated before waving him in.

"Why did you let him go, sir?"

"That little toad just wanted some attention. Suppose it made him feel important. Read about it in the paper and decided to confess. God only knows why. Now we're back where we started. The only suspects are those two tramps and my brother, and I don't believe any of them are guilty. We've hit one dead end after another. Someone has to be lying and I don't want to believe it's my brother. Maybe I was wrong to dismiss the tramps so soon. Just because they were pleasant doesn't mean they didn't do it. What about the search for the farm couple. Any luck?"

"Four constables went out first thing. Two have already returned. Schancy came across a doctor who thinks he knows the couple. He's going back out with a fresh horse to find the farm. Should know soon if it's the right one."

"Hope it doesn't take long. The wind and snow started again a little while ago. Don't want to have to send out a search party for my men. Feels like it's going to be bad when it hits. With any luck it'll wait until after my sister-in-law arrives." He checked the time. "I best be going home. Entire family's going to meet the train. Imagine, four adults, three children, armfuls of gifts, and one very large dog, all under one roof. May have to evict a few mice to make more room."

"I envy you, sir. This will be the first Christmas without my pa. We've been invited to the Halloway's for Christmas dinner, but I dare say it won't be as lively as your home is bound to be."

"Why don't you and your family drop by, if you've no other plans? Christmas Eve maybe, or Boxing Day?

Barnes' solemn face lit up. "Why that's right nice of you, sir. I know Ma isn't planning anything, but I don't know about Violet. She may have plans that she hasn't told me about yet."

"By all means, bring your fiancée and her parents."

Barnes blushed, but smiled. "Haven't asked her yet."

Hodgins waved a hand dismissively. "She'll say yes, don't you worry about that."

"Are you certain Mrs. Hodgins won't mind? No offence, but your home isn't terribly large."

Hodgins laughed. "We'll fit everyone in somehow. Delia won't mind. She loves a party. I'll mention it today. Besides, she'll have Jonathan's wife, Elizabeth, to help." He rose from his chair and walked to the office door. "Let me know when Schancy has news. I'll go upstairs and give the Inspector the bad news about Towers before leaving to pick up Jonathan's family. Train's due at two. If anything new turns up, I'll either be at Union Station or at home."

Hodgins stopped at Grand's livery on Bay Street before going home to reserve two of their best carriages. The two-seat cabriolets just wouldn't be near large enough for everyone and their baggage.

CHAPTER TWELVE

"Six more people?" Delia faced Hodgins, hands on her hips. "How am I supposed to fit all those people around our table?"

"Doesn't have to be a sit-down dinner party. Just friends and family enjoying some time together. I didn't think you'd mind. Are you terribly angry? Nothing's set. I can always un-invite them."

Delia's mouth opened in horror. "Albert Hodgins, don't you dare un-invite them. And no, I'm not angry. You just caught me by surprise. Now that I think about it, it would be nice. Let me mull it over." She looked at the tall clock in the hallway. "Is that the time? Gracious, we'll be late meeting the train." Delia rushed upstairs to make sure Sara was getting ready.

"You're a lucky man," Jonathan said. "My Elizabeth would have had fits if I sprang something like that on her."

"If they were coming tonight I'd get a right earful for certain. At least there's no date set so she has almost two weeks to plan and shop. She actually enjoys all the fuss and bother. If there was a possibility she could plan parties for a living, I'm positive she'd do just that."

The brothers moved into the sitting room to wait for the carriages to arrive. Scraps padded along and flopped in front of the fire, all four legs sticking out. Jonathan reached down and scratched top of Scraps' head.

"Must be exhausting laying around the house all day. I'd have taken him for a walk earlier but the weather was too nasty."

Hodgins poured them both a whisky and they sat in the chairs by the fire. Jonathan leaned back and stretched out his legs.

"I suppose you've got this murder all wrapped up, what with that chap confessing."

Hodgins threw back his head, downing the whisky. "No, afraid not. Turns out he just read about it. Don't understand why some folk feel the need to confess to a crime they didn't commit. Especially when it results in a dance at the end of a rope."

Jonathan stared at his whisky, fingers silently tapping the glass. "Does that move me back to the top of the suspect list?" He looked up at his brother without raising his head.

"No." The word came out slow, as though he still gave it thought. "I'm at a loss. The two tramps seem to have a witness for their whereabouts. Just waiting for confirmation. Looks like I'll have to head back to Aurora, once the weather clears."

Delia and Sara were half-way down the stairs when someone knocked on the door. Sara ran to open it before anyone else. Two carriages sat in front of the house; one led by a pair of chestnut horses, the other by a pair of greys.

"Hurry, Daddy, Uncle Jon. Get your coats. We'll be late."

"We've plenty of time, Sara." Hodgins pinched her nose. "Get your coat and hat on. Bundle up. It's going to be a cold ride."

Sara grabbed Jonathan's hand and dragged him out the door before he had time to button his coat. "I'll ride with you, Uncle Jon. Keep you from being lonely." She raced out to the street and the driver of the greys helped her up.

"There you go miss. Here's a warm wool blanket for your legs."

Cordelia and Hodgins got in the other carriage and the horses made their way down Avenue Road, across Bloor to Yonge, then down to Union Station. The train was just pulling in when they arrived. Jonathan looked up and down the platform, searching for his family.

"There they are." He pointed down the platform and

waved. "Elizabeth!" He stopped a porter and helped him load a cart with their trunks and boxes.

"Is this all?" he joked. The baggage cart was so full the porter had to give it an extra shove to get it going. The cart slide sideways on the freshly fallen snow that begun just before the train pulled in. Another porter rushed to sweep off the platform while Hodgins reached out, preventing the cart from hitting Cordelia.

"I thought I'd finish the Christmas shopping here."

Hodgins noticed his brothers' sarcasm was lost on Elizabeth.

"Children, I want you to meet your Aunt Cordelia and Uncle Albert. And this lovely girl must be Sara." She gave her children a gentle push. "Cora, Freddie, this is your cousin Sara."

"I've so many things planned for us to do," Sara said. "We'll have so much fun."

"Don't you have any other children?" Freddie asked. "Just a girl?"

Hodgins laughed. "Sorry, but you'll have to make do. We men are rather out numbered. At least Scraps is a boy."

"Who's Scraps?" Freddie asked.

"We have a dog and he's ever so large," Sara answered. "He a very clever dog. Saved Daddy's life."

Freddie's eyes widened "Gosh, no fooling?"

"No fooling," Hodgins said.

As they followed the porter out to their carriages, a burst of steam shot out from the train, causing Elizabeth's skirt to wrap around her legs. "Can we please get away from this disgustingly dirty train?"

Hodgins heard a tiny giggle escape from Cordelia. He'd forgotten how prissy Elizabeth could be. It seemed she'd gotten worse. No wonder she and Jonathan separated briefly.

"Why don't we get everything in the carriages and I'll tell you all about our hairy hero after we get home," Hodgins said.

CHAPTER THIRTEEN

When they arrived home, Hodgins and Jonathan helped the drivers unload the baggage and parcels that filled both carriages. Cordelia showed Elizabeth and the children their rooms, leaving them to unpack and settle in, then headed to the kitchen. She had planned an elaborate meal to welcome her in-laws and wanted to get it started.

Earlier in the day, she'd purchased a large roast, big enough to last for several meals. There were still a few carrots, beets, and potatoes left from her modest harvest a few months earlier. Even though her husband had dug out a patch in the back, it wasn't nearly large enough to grow sufficient quantities to see them through the winter. At least she'd been able to save some of the household money to put towards a few Christmas treats.

The men stayed out of the everyone's way and resumed their conversation in the sitting room.

"Do you think you'll find anything useful up in Aurora? You mentioned that ropemaker. Could someone from there be responsible?"

Hodgins refilled his glass with whisky before sitting down.

"I honestly don't know. I had hoped to get back up there today to talk to more people. My list of suspects is rather short."

"Don't remind me." Jonathan laughed nervously.

"It's not funny, brother. How am I to remain impartial? I can't step aside. I've been directed to handle this personally. I don't want my older brother to be guilty, and the thought of someone randomly killing people around the city is terrifying."

"Just be thankful it's only one person and not a string of them. I give you my word, I did *not* kill Brown, but I'd like to shake the hand of the man who did."

"From what I've read in the report the Boston police sent, I imagine quite a number of people would join you in a que for that. Feel sorry for his wife. She'll have her hands full with three little ones."

Jonathan choked on his whisky at the mention of Janel Brown. "You've met her?"

"Yes, when I went up to Aurora, Tuesday."

"You have to admit she's a beautiful woman. Won't be unwed long, I'm sure."

"Not many men are willing to take on a widow with

children, especially young babies. But yes, I agree, she's a looker. Even disheveled and tired as she was, her beauty was evident." Hodgins reached over the arm of his chair and sat his empty glass on the floor. "She's got freckles across her nose, much like my Delia, and she's the most intriguing shade of green eyes. Yes, I'm sure she'll be wed again. Hopefully she makes a better selection next time."

Freddie charged into the room and dropped to his knees beside the resting dog. Scraps' tail thumped against the rug and he rolled over on his back.

"May I pat him, Daddy?" he pleaded.

"You'll have to ask your uncle. It is his dog after all."

Freddie turned to Hodgins, hand hovering over Scraps' belly.

"Go ahead. When the girls come down, why don't you all go into the yard and play with him?"

"Oh, that would be splendid fun." He giggled as Scraps licked his hand, then laid beside the dog and stroked Scraps' belly while waiting for Cora to finished unpacking. It wasn't long before the girls came down. The children put on their coats and boots and ran out the back door with Scraps leading the way into the yard.

Jonathan retrieved the newspaper from the mantle and gave part of it to his brother. "No more talk of murder, at least not today."

"Agreed." Hodgins took the pages and settled back in his chair.

* * *

Hodgins watched as Cordelia sat in front of her mirrored dressing table, removing the pins from her hair, placing them in a small porcelain dish.

"It's been a most tiring day, Bertie. I'm certain to fall asleep as soon as my head touches the pillow, if not sooner." She picked up her silver-handled brush and began the nightly ritual. Fifty strokes down the left side of her waist-long red hair, and fifty down the right, followed by a single loose braid, tied with a ribbon.

Hodgins hung his jacket in the armoire, then unbuttoned his shirt. Cordelia watched his reflection in the mirror of her dressing table.

"You've seemed troubled all evening, Bertie. Is it the man found at Sara's school? You haven't spoken much of it."

Hodgins sighed and sat on the edge of the bed. "I don't know what to do. Jonathan is at the top of my suspect list, such as it is. If he was anyone else, I'd have him in my jail."

Delia stopped braiding and turned to face him. "Jonathan? How can you possibly think he's responsible? What haven't you told me?"

"It's been difficult to speak about it with him in the house. Where do I start?"

"At the beginning, naturally." Delia finished braiding her hair and joined him on the edge of the bed. "Why do you think Jonathan is responsible? Surely not because he had a dalliance with the man's wife?"

"He didn't have a dalliance, at least he said it went no further than a few comments. It's everything. He knew Brown before, fired him for theft, tried to get familiar with his wife, was beaten up by Brown and his associates, and Jonathan's business card was found on the body. Is it a coincidence Brown was murdered just when Jonathan came to town?"

Delia thought for a moment, silently ticking off items on her fingers. "Didn't you say this Brown fellow was murdered early Friday evening?"

Hodgins nodded.

"But Jonathan arrived just before midnight on Friday."

"That's the only reason he hasn't been arrested. But I've been thinking about that. I didn't actually see him get off the train. I've been putting off confirming it. If it were anyone else, I'd have asked to see his ticket and checked with rail employees."

"Didn't you tell me earlier there was an envelope of

money in Brown's pocket? Could an associate have done it and been scared off before he had time to search his pockets?"

"The thought crossed my mind. Brown had quite the collection of dubious associates. I need to make more inquires. If the weather clears by Monday, I'll be taking the train back to Aurora to ask around."

But if Brown is from Boston and only recently moved up here, who would he know well enough to want him dead?"

Hodgins thought a moment. "Good point, Delia. It generally takes a lengthy hate to want to kill someone."

"Could it simply be mistaken identity?"

"Why, I hadn't even considered that. It was dark, difficult to make out features. I suppose he could have been clubbed from behind, then shot. But why not leave him in the trees? Why go to the bother of dragging him over to the school? It's as though he was placed there for a reason. Trouble is, I can't for the life of me figure out what that reason is." He sighed. "More questions than answers I'm afraid."

He kissed her cheek. "I think it's time you retired for the night. You look like you're ready to drop. With three children in the house, you'll need all the rest you can get."

As Delia crawled under the flannel blankets she

muttered, "Don't forget about the dog. He'll be extra rambunctious," the final word slipped out, barely more than a whisper.

CHAPTER FOURTEEN

The storm hit its peak overnight and continued all through Saturday before going on its way, leaving everything covered in clean, white fluff. When Hodgins looked out Sunday morning, at least three inches of snow clung to the bare branches of the maples and oaks, and the evergreen branches drooped under the extra weight. He heard Delia fussing in the kitchen and turned away from the upstairs window. He dressed quickly and went down to light the fire in the sitting room. The back door latch clicked, followed shortly by a not-too-gentle slam. Curious, he went into the kitchen and found Delia staring out the window. Peering over the top of her head, he could see Scraps running around the snow-family the children built the previous evening. They were buried up to what would be their knees, if they had any. Scraps ran circles around them, then rolled in the snow, knocking one of the smaller snow people over. The head landed on the dog, sending him in more circles.

"I'd better get him in before he's completely covered.

That shaggy coat will take forever to dry." Hodgins went into the small enclosed back porch and called the dog. The breeze that came in didn't have the same bite to it as the last several days. When Scraps spotted his favourite human he raced to the door. Hodgins had an old blanket ready and managed to wrap the dog before the beast's hairy paws soaked his suit jacket and vest. After rubbing the dog down as best he could, they both went inside. Scraps went straight to his blanket by the wood stove.

"Look at all those tiny balls of snow on his undercoat. That blanket will be soaked once they melt," Delia remarked.

"Packing snow. I'd better get a start cleaning the front walk. It's going to be the devil to move. With all this snow, the buggies and carriages will have trouble moving. It feels quite mild, though, so what say we walk to church? It's not that far and will probably be quicker."

* * *

After church, the children rushed to change out of their Sunday clothing, anxious to go looking for a tree. Hodgins broke the news when they came back downstairs, "I'm sorry Sara, but it will have to wait for another day. There's just too much snow. Plenty of time yet."

Sara pouted. "But you promised we'd get the tree today."

"Sara," Delia scolded. "Don't speak to your father like that. He can't control the weather. When the roads clear, we'll go and cut a tree. Now, why don't you and your cousins make some decorations?"

"Can we string popcorn?" Freddie asked. "I helped Mama last Christmas."

"I'm afraid we don't have any corn for popping just yet, but we've lots of coloured paper and glue. Why not make some chains after lunch?"

Once everyone was fed and the dishes put away, Albert and Jonathan retired to the sitting room to read and stay out of the way. The children busied themselves cutting strips of paper and gluing together chains, tree forgotten. Delia took Elizabeth into the sewing room to show her the dresses she was making for Sara. Scraps' head rose and he suddenly bolted off his blanket and raced down the hall, wagging his tail and barking. Someone knocked on the front door.

Hodgins rose to see who it was while Jonathan went to the bay window. "Looks like you're going to work."

Hodgins opened the front door to let the constable in.

"Sorry to disturb you, but there's been another murder." Barnes gulped several times, trying to catch his breath.

"Not at the school again, I hope?"

"No. This one was left in the laneway right behind the station house, sitting up and blindfolded, just like Brown."

"I can tell by the look on your face there's more to it."

Barnes reached into his pocket and pulled out a card. He hesitated before handing it over.

"Damnation!"

"Problem brother?" Jonathan stood behind Hodgins. "Afternoon Constable."

"Someone's left a body near my station house." He held the card up so Jonathan could read it. "This is your new business address, is it not?"

* * *

The detective and his brother once again stood beside a metal table in the coroner's office. Hodgins placed a hand on Jonathan's shoulder and faced Dr. McKenzie. "Sorry to disturb you on a Sunday."

McKenzie waved his hand, dismissing the comment. "Just like last time. He'll look like he's asleep. Except for a small hole over the left eye."

Jonathan swayed and his brother supported him.

"Steady on. Ready?"

Jonathan took a deep breath and closed his eyes.

"Ready as I'll ever be."

McKenzie lowered the sheet to expose the man's head. "Recognize him?"

Jonathan opened one eye and glanced down. "Yes. It's George Roberts. Associate of Brown." He turned away. "He's one of the men I fired for theft."

"That was before you moved. Why would he have your new card?" Hodgins asked.

"They were printed in advance. He could have taken one before I had the books checked."

The detective turned to the coroner. "Doctor, do you know when this Roberts fellow died?"

"Can't pinpoint exact time because of the cold, but he couldn't have been there long, else someone would have found him sooner."

"True. It's a popular shortcut, especially for some of my lads. One of them would have seen a body on their way in or out if he'd been left last night. Let me know when you've finished your examination. It can wait until tomorrow."

Hodgins turned back to his brother. "I need to speak with the person who found him. Are you well enough to make it home?"

"I'm not a baby, Albert. I'm perfectly capable of making my way back to your house."

He took a step towards the door and swayed again, reaching for the doctor's desk for support. "Think I'll hail a hansom."

Hodgins stood with his brother until an empty cab came. He recognized the driver. "Take my brother to my home, will you Peter? He's not feeling well." Hodgins chuckled as he walked to the station.

* * *

The station house was almost empty when Hodgins arrived. Most of the officers were out on their beats, except Barnes, who looked up when the front door opened, and one of the new recruits. A young couple in their early twenties sat at the constable's desk. Both looked to be in shock, the young woman sobbing.

"That the couple who found him?" Hodgins asked Barnes.

"Yes, they were out for a stroll after church. Decided to take a shortcut down the lane and found him. They've made a statement, and I've sent someone to fetch their parents."

"Fine. Bring me their statements." He went into his office and removed his overcoat. Barnes rushed in as Hodgins pulled the chair away from his desk.

"It's rather short." Barnes handed the sheets to Hodgins.

"Understandable." He sat down and indicated for Barnes to sit as well. "Give it a day or so and talk to the young man again. See if he remembers anything new." He read through the statements. "How much snow was on the body? It doesn't say."

"Snow? Didn't notice any. Is that important?"

"Is it important? Of course it is. Dr. McKenzie can't give us a very accurate time of death because of the cold weather. When did it stop snowing?"

"Sometime early this morning I believe." Barnes snapped his fingers. "Of course. If the body had been left during the night it would have been completely covered."

"Good man. Knew you'd figure it out."

"Wish I was as quick as you, sir. Just not smart enough I suppose."

"Balderdash. You're more than smart enough. Leaps and bounds over most of the constables here. Sergeant, too, but I won't admit to ever saying that."

Barnes seemed flustered, turning bright pink, but smiled broadly. "Th-thank you, sir."

"No need to thank me. Wasn't me who gave you your brains. Now, I need you to send another wire to Boston. Dead man is an associate of Brown. Name's George Roberts. And I'll need another sketch done. Storm's passed, so I'll be going up to Aurora tomorrow and I'd like to take a sketch of this Roberts fellow."

Hodgins stood and handed the reports back to Barnes. "Supposed to be my day off. If you find out anything important, you know where to find me. But *only* if it's something that can't wait until tomorrow."

CHAPTER FIFTEEN

Sweat dripped down Hodgins' back as he trudged through the deep snow. Not too many had ventured out that morning, except to go to church, so it hadn't been trampled down much. The snow crunched and squeaked under his boots and he cursed himself for not taking the trolley. He waved at Mr. Halloday, who stopped sweeping his walk when he spotted him. Hodgins hurried up his own walkway, not wanting to be delayed by his chatty neighbour.

The sounds of giggling children and Scraps' loud, deep bark came from the back of his house. With the children out of the way, he thought it would be the perfect opportunity to have anther talk with his brother.

After hanging his coat in the hallway, he looked in the sitting room for Jonathan, but it was empty. Pots and dishes rattled in the kitchen, so he followed the sound. He found Cordelia and Elizabeth chopping the vegetables for their evening meal.

"Ah, your tasty Irish stew. Can hardly wait." He

kissed his wife, then turned to Elizabeth. "Where might I find that brother of mine?"

"Out there." Elizabeth pointed at the window.

Hodgins peered over her shoulder and spotted Jonathan helping the children build a snow fort. Discussion pushed aside, he smiled. "Looks like fun. Think I'll join them."

* * *

Hodgins rose early and tried not to disturb his wife. He tip-toed to the window to see if any more snow fell overnight. The light from the gas streetlights cast a soft glow over the road, looking much the same as when he arrived home the previous evening. Hodgins jumped when a hand touched his shoulder.

"I didn't mean to startle you. Is something the matter?"

"No, Delia. Just checking the weather. Looks like a fine day for a train ride. I need to speak with Brown's widow again, and Jonathan, if I can get him alone. Somebody's not telling me everything."

"It's chilly. Come back to bed. It's too early to catch the train." Delia took his hand and gave it a gentle tug. "I think there's something you're not telling me. What is it? Is that second body connected to the first?"

"I can't sleep. Go back to bed. I'll tell you later."

"Why don't we chat over a cup of tea? I'll never get back to sleep now." She picked up their dressing gowns from the top of the chest at the foot of the bed and held out her arm. "Put this on Bertie. And don't forget your slippers."

Careful not to disturb anyone else in the house, Cordelia went into the kitchen and Hodgins started a fire in the sitting room. Cordelia joined him, carrying a tray with her Winter Rose teapot, two matching cups, and a plate of biscuits and cheese. She sat it on a small table beside one of the chairs and poured out the tea. Once they were settled, she inclined her head, indicating she was ready to listen. He let out a deep sigh and began.

"The second body was an associate of Brown's. And he had one of Jonathan's business cards in his pocket. Shot in the head, just like Brown. If Jonathan wasn't my brother…"

"But he's been here, with us. How could he have shot that man? And he wasn't even in Toronto when Brown was shot. Oh Bertie, you don't really believe he's involved, do you?"

He shrugged. "I don't know what to think. People change. I haven't seen him for over a decade. The policeman in me says he's high on my suspect list. He knows both men. He has a bad history with them. And I

341

don't know for certain what happened between Jonathan and Janel Brown. If it was just a few comments, as he says, why such a change in her demeanor when she realized I'm his brother? That look on her face was pure hatred."

"Well, when put like that, it is suspicious." She thought for a moment. "I suppose he could have hired someone, or taken an earlier train."

He laughed. "That's my girl. Thinking like a detective."

Hodgins picked up one of the biscuits and a piece of cheese, but didn't put them in his mouth. "I hate to ask, but would you mind doing a bit of snooping for me?"

Cordelia's face lit up. "I'd love to help, you know that. You've never asked me to do anything before. Is it dangerous?"

He feigned shock. "Dangerous? You sound as though you welcome it. Are you that discontented?"

"Bertie, how can you suggest such a thing." Cordelia smiled. "It does become rather tedious at times, though. Cooking, cleaning, sewing. A change is most welcome. What sort of snooping would you like me to do?"

"When you're tidying up, would you mind going through Jonathan's things? Look for anything unusual. See if you can find his train ticket."

Delia clapped her hands. "Oh, how exciting. Now,

how will I get him out of the house?" She placed a finger on her chin and tilted her head, thinking. "Maybe I can ask him to take the children out to cut down a Christmas tree? I know you wanted to do that, though. Would you mind terribly?"

"No, that's a rather clever idea. I don't know when I'll have the time now, and the children were rather disappointed when I cancelled yesterday."

"I know I should feel horrible going through his things, but it's so exciting."

The clock in the hall struck seven. "Gracious, is that the time? Sara can stay home from school again today. Even though arrangements have been made for Cora and Freddy to attend with Sara until winter break, there's no need to send them off right away. They've only just arrived. And today would be a perfect time to cut down a tree."

"I'll stop at the school and let them know not to expect the children until tomorrow. Now, we'd best get dressed. It's going to be a busy day for everyone. Oh, and tell Jonathan to go where Father used to take us for our tree. Best spruce in the area. If you find anything of interest, be certain to bring it to the station immediately. I never thought I'd say this, but I hope to God I don't see you."

As they ascended the stairs, Hodgins asked what excuse she'd give for not going with them.

"It's almost Christmas Bertie. I'll simply tell them I need to wrap presents and don't want them spying."

* * *

Rather than going to his station house after stopping at Ketchum School, Hodgins walked further up Davenport to see if anyone was home at the previously empty house on Bishop. Unfortunately, whoever lived there still wasn't home. He went to the house next door to inquire about their neighbours on the corner, only to be told they'd moved a few weeks earlier.

CHAPTER SIXTEEN

It was almost 8:30 when Hodgins arrived at Station Four. The Northern Railway train to Aurora was scheduled to depart at 9:15. He went straight to Barnes' desk without bothering to remove his overcoat.

"Barnes, is there a copy of the morning paper about?"

"Yes, sir." Barnes didn't make any attempt to fetch it for him.

Everyone became quiet and stared at Hodgins. He held out his hand. "I'll read it on the train."

Barnes reached down and opened his desk drawer, then slowly pulled out the paper. "I'm sorry," he whispered as he handed it over.

Hodgins rolled up the newspaper and shoved it in the pocket of his overcoat before heading for Union Station. Fortunately, an empty cab approached so he hailed it, enjoying a surprisingly quick ride down to Simcoe Street. The train just pulled in as he arrived, leaving only a short time for him to purchase his return ticket and settle down. He chose a seat in the corner, hoping no one would join him. Curious as to the reaction back at the station, he pulled out the newspaper. The story was on the front page.

"Damn!"

The woman sitting across the isle gasped, then turned to face him. "Sir, there are ladies and children present. I would appreciate it if you'd watch your language."

"Terribly sorry, ma'am. I do apologize."

Slightly red-faced, both from embarrassment and the headline, he went back to the paper and re-read it.

DETECTIVE'S BROTHER WANTED FOR MURDER

Below was a less-than-flattering sketch of Hodgins. As he read through the half-truths, he noticed no source had been listed as to who gave the interview. He puzzled over how the reporter knew about Jonathan's involvement. He hadn't told anyone about the business cards even though they were mentioned in his station's report. Someone must have spoken to the reporter, but why? When he returned, he'd be sure to track down that reporter and provide the correct information. He continued reading.

> Highly regarded Toronto detective, Albert Hodgins of Station House Four on Wilton Avenue, has a murderer as a house-guest.

A string of obscenities flew from his mouth, a little louder than expected.

"Really, sir. I must insist you conduct yourself in a

better manner."

Once again, he apologized, then looked around the train at the other passengers. Beyond the glares of women with small children, he spotted several men at the opposite end of the rail car. He moved down, apologizing again as he passed the shocked women. He noticed a newspaper among the parcels one of the women had and hoped she hadn't read it and recognized him. He slipped into the seat behind the business men. They were discussing the lead story in the paper.

"Corrupt coppers, the lot of 'em. I'll wager a days pay that Hodgins fellow gets his brother off and frames some innocent chap."

"I don't know," a second one said. "I went to school with Jonathan. Wouldn't hurt a fly. You know as well as I do those reporters make up a lot of their stories."

Hodgins smiled, trying to place who the man was that knew his brother. He'd only glanced at them, but the one by the window seemed familiar.

"Think I'll look up Jonathan. Haven't spoken to him in years."

"Hmm... you may be right," the first man said. "But I do know for a fact some coppers ain't above a bribe or two. Did you know this Detective Hodgins fellow?"

"Not very well. He's a few years younger, but I can't

recall him ever getting into the same mischief as the rest of us."

Hodgins felt a little less angry, and hoped other people wouldn't believe the rot that was printed. Trying to push the story from his mind, he returned to the paper and read the rest of the news as the train pulled out of the station. The men in front of him changed the subject, talking instead of their day's business.

A little over an hour later the men left the train at the Richmond Hill stop and he got another glimpse of their faces, but still couldn't place the one who knew Jonathan. The rest of the ride to Aurora was uneventful and he exited the train forty minutes later. His first visit was to the Widow Brown. She was still rather hostile towards him upon opening her door.

"What is it Detective? I've only just buried my husband and I am rather busy." She held the door open only enough to talk to him. He wasn't sure if to keep the cold air out, to hide something, or simply dissuade him.

"Please, I only need a few minutes of your time."

She considered his request for a moment, then opened the door fully. "If you must." She stepped back to allow entry, indicating for him to go into the same room as before. A fire blazing in the stone fireplace, instantly warming him up. There were crates and trunks everywhere, except on the chairs. Rather than sitting, he stood by the fire.

"Moving?"

"Yes. There's nothing here for me now. I'm going back to Boston soon. What is it? I'm rather busy as you can see." She lowered herself onto one of the chairs, but remained perched at the edge.

"As I said, I'll only take a few minutes. It's about your friend, George Roberts."

She appeared surprised when his name was mentioned. "I wouldn't say he's a friend, exactly. What about him?"

"He's been murdered."

Janel didn't seem shocked by the news. "Oh, is that all? If the only reason for your visit was to tell me that, you've wasted a trip. It's no concern of mine."

"Yes, well, I was hoping you could tell me why he was here, in Toronto. Did he have business with your husband?"

"Yes, they were partners. Have been for years. Can't tell you what scheme they were planning. Something in the city."

That last comment confused Hodgins. "If they were planning something downtown, why live so far north? That just doesn't make any sense. A two-hour train ride isn't a very convenient get-a-way."

Janel gave the detective a look of disgust. "You didn't know my Tony. Despite his faults, he loved me and the children. We moved here because there's so much space. If we'd moved into Toronto we'd be crammed into a tiny flat. Probably dirty, too. We wanted to raise our children better than what we were."

He nodded. "You're right. I didn't know your husband at all. And I completely understand wanting to raise your children in a small town."

Hodgins had seen both the good and bad sides of Toronto. He shuttered at the thought of what his circumstance would be like if he hadn't come from a respectable, middle-class family. He couldn't imagine life without Cordelia and Sara. Janel cleared her throat, bringing Hodgins back to the present.

"Do you know of anyone here that your husband associated with? Any friends or maybe another partner in this scheme?"

He recalled the young man at Campbell's rope factory and how quickly he came up with the Brown's address. He flipped through his notebook to recall the name and see if Janel mentioned him. Before he could find him, she answered.

"Well, there was Ace. He came here a few times, but

Tony preferred to meet him elsewhere, usually at one of the hotels." Hodgins looked up from his notebook just in time to see the hint of a smile disappear from her lips.

A knock at the door interrupted their chat. She pushed herself and her unborn child off the high-back chair. Hodgins rushed over to assist, but she shook off his hand.

"I'm perfectly capable of getting up myself." She eased her child-laden body off the edge and pushed up on the arms of the chair.

He thought she was amazingly large for seven months and wondered if she might be carrying another set of twins. For her sake, he hoped not. The person at the front door knocked two more times before Janel managed to waddle the short distance.

Hodgins remembered when Delia carried Sara. Right up to the end she refused his help, despite the struggle to do the smallest thing and she hadn't been near as big. He imagined Brown had had his hands full with Janel. He could see a fair bit of his Delia in her. Must be part Irish. Janel returned with an elderly woman.

He helped the woman over to one of the chairs by the fire while Janel sat on the other, glaring at him. It was clear she didn't want him around any longer. He ignored her and introduced himself.

"Oh, a policeman. I do hope you catch the scoundrel who murdered poor Mr. Brown. Decent people aren't safe anywhere these days."

"We're doing all we can, ma'am." It seemed obvious to him that Mr. Brown's occupation wasn't well known. "Are you a relative?"

"No, just a neighbour. Poor girl needs someone to help now that's she's all alone." She looked around the room. "Are you moving my dear?"

Hodgins intended to inquire about her relationship with Jonathan, but he didn't want to raise the question in front of the neighbour. "I'll leave you to your visit. We'll let you know when we've made an arrest. Can you give me your new address?"

"Nothing's settled yet. I'll leave word at your station before I leave."

He excused himself and headed to the main core of Aurora, stopping at the hotel on the corner of Wellington and Yonge. It was almost across the road from Campbell's and probably a gathering place for the workers. He sat at one of the tables in the dining area. A server was at his side before he had time to remove his coat.

"Cottage Pie, if you have it, and a pot of tea."

He asked about Brown and Roberts, showing him the sketched of the two dead men, receiving only shrugs and vague answers. The staff admitted they'd been in a time or two, but claimed to know nothing of their business.

Once Hodgins' meal was finished, he walked down one side of Yonge Street, stopping at the various shops, inquiring about the two men, and someone called Ace. Hodgins continued to show the sketches of Brown and Roberts, but no one recognized either. He was relieved he didn't have to stop long at the blacksmith's as the sickly-sweet smell of seared hooves turned his stomach.

He got the same negative responses at each place of business. He crossed the road and turned back north, receiving the same reaction from each shop-keeper. One of the clerks at Doan's General Store recognized Janel Brown, but couldn't provide any information other than she was a regular customer and not terribly social. Frustrated, he continued up Yonge Street to Campbell's to have another chat with Wally. Maybe he knew who Ace was.

"Mr. Campbell, sorry to interrupt your day, but I'd like to speak with Wally again."

"Sorry, but he's sick. Damn fine time, too. He's the only one strong enough to make the ship ropes. Order's due next week. First time making ropes for ships and if I deliver on time, there could be more."

"Must be this cold weather. Few of my men are ill as

well."

As Hodgins turned to leave, Campbell grabbed his arm.

"You don't think Wally had anything to do with the murder you're looking into, do you? He seems to be a good lad. Strong, but not much brains. Wouldn't hurt anyone."

"No, but he knew the man and I hoped he could provide some information. I'll come back in a few days."

Frustrated and a little dejected, Hodgins made his way to the train station. He picked up a local paper to fill the hour before the next train was due. After arriving at the station, he sat on a bench near the wood burning stove and reviewed the meagre notes he'd accumulated, pondering over the notation that Wally had visited the Brown's home a few times. He was about the same age as Janel, at least ten years younger than Anthony Brown. He was also strong and rather good looking. Could Wally have paid visits when her husband was away? Had she been unfaithful? She'd been extremely angry at Jonathan's advances. Yes, he was older, but he'd always had girls vying for his attention at school. And he was a successful businessman. Had she rejected one man for another or was he reading too much into it? He'd gauge Wally's reactions when he got to speak with him. Maybe he'd at least know about Ace, and what his relationship to Janel Brown was.

Since Hodgins had little information to review, he put the notebook back in his overcoat pocket and opened the newspaper to see if the local news was any better than Toronto's. He found more talk of the compulsory voting bill, something also found in the Toronto paper. Hodgins smiled as he read the account of a speech made by the MP for North York on his recent visit to Aurora. Apparently, it didn't go well as the audience laughed at Mr. Dymond's comments. Hodgins laughed out loud when he spotted the notice for the County of York's coroner, Dr. Strange. He couldn't imagine anyone being stranger than his own Dr. Hamish McKenzie.

He left the paper on the bench when the train pulled in. The cars were almost empty so he had his pick of seats. Again, he moved to a back corner. When the train pulled into the Richmond Hill station the same men he'd overheard on the way up boarded. The one who knew Jonathan spotted him and came over.

"You're Jonathan's younger brother, Albert, I believe? The detective."

"Yes. You were one of Jonathan's classmates, but I'm afraid I don't recall your name."

"Eustace Billings."

"Ah, Billings. Your family owns one of the largest medical equipment suppliers in these parts."

"That's correct. And if today's business went as well as I think it did, we'll be number one in no time. Mind if we join you?"

Hodgins waved his hand towards the seats opposite. "By all means. I'm guessing these men are in business with you?"

"Where are my manners? May I present Timothy Grainger and David Perkins. My top salesmen. I've been trying to acquire a small company. Who better to sweet-talk the owner into selling than two such convincing salesmen?"

The three men laughed heartily and Hodgins smiled and nodded, figuring they were little better than con-men, or simply bullies. To Hodgins, they had the appearance of thugs rather than salesmen. Only Billings seemed comfortable in his suit, as the two salesmen continually tugged at their collars and loosened their ties.

Billings became serious and leaned towards Hodgins. "I read that ole Johnny has himself in a spot of bother. Nothing to it, I hope?"

"Newspaper reporters. You know what they're like." Hodgins had a vague recollection of a less than flattering story about the Billings Pharmaceuticals a while back. He raised an eyebrow and looked directly at Billings when he spoke. "Don't always get the facts straight, do they?"

Billings touched the side of his nose and winked. "Spot on there old chap. Twist the facts so much they're barely recognizable. I was saying to my associates just this morning there's no way Jonathan could be responsible for it. Why, I recall one time in school several of us were rough-housing and someone, don't recall who, ended up with a bloody nose. Jonathan damn near fainted." He paused and laughed. "If Johnny were to kill someone more likely than not, you'd find him passed out along side the corpse."

Hodgins remembered the two episodes in the coroner's office and almost blurted it out, but decided not to make his brother appear too weak to an old school mate. He simply agreed, and they all laughed at some length.

"At least he has an alibi for both murders," Hodgins remarked once they'd composed themselves.

"Both? You man there's been another?" Billings asked.

"Yes. I suppose the other hasn't made it to the papers, yet. Didn't see it in the morning edition. He was home with me when that one happened."

"And he was at the Red Lion when the first took

place."

That statement caught Hodgins off guard, but he managed to avoid appearing surprised. How many more things was Jonathan keeping from him? He didn't want to discuss it further so he changed the subject.

"Afraid I can't go into much detail about the case. You understand. Tell me, what have you been up to, besides the family business? Do you have a family of your own?"

Hodgins half-listened and politely smiled and nodded the rest of the way to Union Station. Between Billings and his two salesmen, Hodgins now knew more about medical supplies than he cared to. They parted with the promise of a visit from Billings before Jonathan returned to Boston.

Once Hodgins arrived home, he dragged his brother outside, barely giving him time to button his overcoat.

"Just when where you planning on telling me you arrived in Toronto before I met your train?" Hodgins took long strides as he walked along the street.

"Slow down. How did you find out?" Jonathan hurried to catch up to his brother.

"You grew up in Toronto and still have old friends here. You were seen. The Red Lion of all places. If you didn't want to be seen, why go to a public place? You have no alibi for Brown's murder now. Come to think of it, you don't really have one for Roberts' either. You could easily have snuck out of the house while we were asleep."

Jonathan grabbed his brother's arm and pulled him to a stop. "Albert, surely you don't believe I had anything to do with either man's death?"

"I don't know you any more. You've been in Boston for a long time and have some questionable associates. Your card was found on both bodies. If you were me, would you not think you guilty?"

Jonathan stared at him in disbelief, mouth open slightly. "I can see how it looks, but I haven't changed that much. I swear on my children's lives, it wasn't me."

He paused before answering, mulling everything over. Finally, he sighed and put a hand on Jonathan's shoulder. "I believe you, but not because you're my brother." He smiled. "As someone recently pointed out, with your constitution, we'd probably have found you passed out alongside the bodies. What say we go back home where it's warm?"

Once they settled in front of the fire Hodgins continued their earlier conversation.

"Someone must be framing you. You've been out of the city for a decade, so why would anyone here be murdering people and trying to blame you?"

Jonathan shrugged. "I can't recall anyone that I

angered ten years ago, at least not enough to murder innocent people over." He snickered. "Not that Brown or Roberts are exactly innocent of much."

"That's just it. The two murdered men are from Boston. It has to be connected to your business somehow. Could there be someone with a grudge against them who knows you've had a run in with them? Get rid of his enemies and blame someone else."

"Afraid I can't think of anyone. Wish I could."

Hodgins remembered his short conversation with Janel Brown. "Know a chap by the name of Ace?"

"Odd name. Can't say I've come across anybody that goes by it."

"Give it a think for a day or two." He rose from the chair. "Smells like it's about time to eat."

CHAPTER SEVENTEEN

Excitement grew as the time to erect the Christmas tree neared. Even though many people with children waited until the little ones had gone to bed Christmas Eve to put up the tree, Hodgins preferred to enjoy it earlier. Both Cordelia and Sara agreed. Without being asked, Sara, Cora, and Freddie cleared up after dinner and even washed the dishes. Hodgins and his brother went out back to where the tree leaned against the house.

Albert grabbed the tree with one hand and stood it upright for a better look. "Red Spruce, just like when we were children. One of my favourites. Father's too."

"It is a nice tree. Not many left though. Shame. Is there another area where they grow?"

"Not that I've found. Maybe farther north. Now help me get this thing into the porch so I can nail the boards to the bottom."

After about a quarter hour, the tree stood in front of the bay window in the sitting room.

"Little shaky, isn't it?" Jonathan observed.

"Got that covered. Check the edge of the inside sill."

Jonathan peered behind the tree and tried to see what his brother was talking about. "All I see is a nail."

"Watch and learn, big brother." Hodgins pulled a length of string from his pocket, put a slip knot in one end and tightened it over a nail in the sill on one side of the tree. Then, he wrapped the string around the trunk, then fastened it to a nail on the other side.

"If it falls, it won't go far. It's the first tree with the dog and I don't know if he'll leave it alone."

"Brilliant idea. I'll have to try that myself next Christmas. Freddie managed to knock it over once last year."

"May we decorate now, Daddy?" Sara and her cousins stood behind them, holding the paper chains they'd been making.

"Yes, you may." He stood aside as the children rushed to the tree.

"It's larger than last year's." Cordelia and Elizabeth stood in the doorway. "At least a foot taller. I'm not sure our star will fit on the top," Cordelia said.

"Too late to cut it shorter now. If it doesn't fit it'll just have to sit near the top. A bit of string will hold it in place. Got plenty." Hodgins patted his pocket.

"Do you have any store-bought ornaments?"

Elizabeth asked.

"Yes, but I'm afraid to put them on just yet. Look how Scraps is sniffing around the tree. He might break them. I think I'll wait until Christmas Eve and put them on before lighting the candles." Cordelia turned to her husband. "Bertie, can you help me get them down from the attic?"

Hodgins knew Cordelia had put them away herself and didn't require his assistance, but she winked, indicating she wanted to get him out of earshot. She waited until they were in the attic before she spoke.

"I went through Jonathan's things, but I'm afraid I didn't find his train ticket. I did find this, however."

She reached into the pocket of the apron she still had tied around her waist and handed him a folded napkin. He opened it and saw it had the emblem for the Red Lion, along with writing. Jonathan's barely legible handwriting. He could only make out a few words: Aurora, Brown, and Roberts.

"One of the words may be Inn, but I can't make out which inn. And here, it says twelfth or possibly thirteenth. That coincides with Roberts' murder."

"But when was he at the Red Lion?" Cordelia asked.

He looked up at her. "I'll tell you about that later. I don't suppose you discovered this someplace where it would have easily been found cleaning?"

"No, it was in a pocket."

"It's already come out that he was at the Red Lion. But if Jonathan isn't forthcoming with any more details, I'll have to figure out a way to let him know we have the napkin, as I may have to put it with the other evidence. Things have a habit of falling out of pockets. I can say you found it on the floor while cleaning. Now, where are those ornaments we came up here for? They'll come looking for us if we don't go back down soon."

* * *

The Chief Inspector had been out of town, so the Inspector hadn't been badgering Hodgins for any further updates. Out of courtesy, Hodgins let the Inspector know what his plans were, and promised another update before the Chief returned. Hodgins waited a couple of days before taking the train back up to Aurora. The constables that had been off nursing their sour stomachs had finally returned to duty, so he hoped Wally suffered from the same illness and might have returned to the rope factory. Unfortunately, he was still off.

"Damn inconsiderate of him to be sick." Campbell paced across his tiny office. "That big order for the shipping company needs to be sent soon. If Wally isn't back right quick it won't be ready. I pride myself on always delivering on time. Not easy to find someone with the muscles to turn the larger ropes. Maybe it's time to convert to steam power. At least those blasted machines don't bugger off."

Hodgins pulled a card from his pocket and handled it to Campbell. "Let me know when he's back."

Campbell took the card and tossed it on his paper-covered desk. "You don't believe Wally had anything to do with this other dead man, do you?"

"Just want to ask him a few questions. He knew Brown, so maybe he also knows Roberts. I'm hoping he can tell me more about them."

Hodgins remembered the sketch of George Roberts he had done up and took it out of his overcoat pocket.

"Ever seen this man around?"

Campbell examined the sketch before handing it back. "Sorry. Doesn't look familiar."

Hodgins left the ropemakers factory, not certain where to go next. If Brown and Roberts both worked as labourers for Jonathan, maybe one of them had found employment somewhere in town. As he had no idea where anything was, he listened for any sounds that might direct him. He heard a fair bit of racket off to the west, so he walked down to Wellington Street and turned right. He discovered not one, but two, plow makers. He stopped first at Wilkinson's as it was on the same side of the street. No one there admitted to knowing Brown, Roberts, or Ace, so he crossed to the south side and entered the Fleury Works.

He discovered both Brown and Roberts worked there briefly, but had been fired. Unlike at Jonathan's business, they hadn't been let go due to theft, but rather for incompetence. Somehow, the two men had managed to render a large quantity of plows useless.

The foreman clenched both hands at the mention of the two men. "Fell apart right in the foundry. Can you imagine if that had happened after shipping? They were due to go out west that day. No one would've ever bought from us again. What have they done now? Ruined someone's business I suspect."

"No. They've managed to get themselves murdered."

The foreman laughed. "When you find the chap what done them in, let me know. I'd like to buy him a drink."

Hodgins smiled. "I think you might have to wait in line for that honour. Don't suppose you know anyone who goes by the name of Ace?"

The foreman shook his head, but a nearby worker butted in. "I think I might know who you mean. Fellow over at Campbell's goes by Ace."

Hodgins cursed and thanked both men, then turned

back to Campbell's. He stopped the first employee he encountered.

"Where can I find Ace?"

"Off sick."

Hodgins spotted Campbell towards the back of the long building and yelled to get his attention. The two men met mid-way down the building.

"I understand you employ someone who goes by Ace."

Campbell looked surprised. "Why, that's Wally. Already told you he's still off."

Hodgins berated himself for not asking about him earlier. "Why is he called Ace?

"Full name's Wallace. Ace for short.

"Wally. Wallace. I should have figured that out myself." This business with Jonathan must have him more rattled than he realized. Was it a coincidence that Wally, Ace, was sick at this particular time? Hodgins remembered the half-smile from Janel Brown.

"Tell me, when exactly did Wally become ill?"

Campbell thought for a moment. "Why, right after your first visit. He finished the day, but hasn't been in since." He wrung his hands. "You don't think...?"

Hodgins nodded. "Yes, I'm beginning to believe he's somehow involved. I don't suppose you can vouch for his whereabouts the evening of December 4? It was a Friday."

Campbell smiled. "Yes, I can actually. I treated my workers to a night out for all their hard work this year. Sort of a Christmas party, at the hotel on the corner, the Queen's."

Hodgins pulled out his notebook and started writing. "Are you absolutely positive he was in attendance the entire evening?" He made a note to check the train schedule. Two hours down, murder someone and two hours back. Longer if he went by horse. He already knew the answer before Campbell spoke.

"It's a long trip down to Toronto. I'd have noticed such a lengthy absence."

Hodgins closed the little black book. "Yes, I totally agree. Maybe it is nothing more than a coincidence. I'd like to check on him myself through. Could you give me his address?"

Hodgins followed Campbell to his office and waited while he wrote out the address and provided directions. Wally lived on Tyler Street, right at the corner of Tyler and George Streets. It didn't take long to walk there.

No one answered his knock. He tried several times, but the only sound was the brass knocker against the thick oak door. Hodgins walked around, peering in each of the windows. He didn't spot anyone in any of the rooms on the ground floor. He was looking in a window at the back of the house when a hand touched his shoulder. He jumped, knocking his head against the glass.

CHAPTER EIGHTEEN

An elderly gentleman stood behind Hodgins, chuckling as Hodgins rubbed his head. "May I help you, young man?"

Hodgins showed his badge. "Looking for Wally. He's not been at work for a while. Are you his neighbour?"

"Bin living next door for 'bout ten years. Seen my fair share of folk coming and going from this house. 'Fraid you've missed the young buck. Headed out with a large trunk, oh, two, maybe three days ago."

"Don't suppose he said where he was going?"

"Only saw 'im through the winder. Why don't you come inside out of the cold and have a proper chat. Wife's just made a batch of oatmeal cookies. Tell you everything I know about young Wally Caster."

Both Mr. Gardiner and his wife knew quite a bit about Wally, most simply gossip. The one interesting tidbit was the fact that Wally originally came from Boston and spoke about going back soon. He hadn't been in town more than four months. Could he have gone back to the

States? The puzzle pieces started to come together, but a large gap still needed to be filled in. Two cups of tea and three cookies later, Hodgins headed back to the train station.

* * *

Before going home, Hodgins made his way to Station House Four up on Wilton. He left instructions not to be disturbed, then transcribed his notes onto several sheets of long paper. It was late when he arrived back home and the children were all in a bed. Cordelia cut two thick slices of bread and several pieces of the roast she'd warmed for dinner. She'd managed to stretch it out longer then anticipated.

Jonathan sat in the sitting room reading the newspaper, Elizabeth in a chair beside a small table containing a hurricane lamp. She'd moved it to the edge to better catch the light, the candle inside illuminating the needlework she'd brought with her. Cordelia left them alone and stayed in the kitchen with her husband while he ate.

"There are so many seemingly connected pieces of information that just don't completely fit together. It's so frustrating." He took another bite of his beef sandwich then washed it down with a sip of tea.

"Tell me what you know so far." Cordelia poured

herself some tea. "Maybe you'll discover something as you speak."

"Well, as you know, my dear brother is at the top of my list, even though I truly believe him innocent. He knew both victims and did have problems with them in the past. Then, there's the two tramps, but we have witnesses to confirm where they were at the time of Brown's murder. Can't connect them to Roberts' as they're still in Berlin, and at the Sheriff's. Can't have a better alibi than that."

He rose and went over to the wood stove and cut a piece from the apple pie that sat on top, still warm.

"Funny thing. Brown's wife is packing up, planning on returning to Boston and someone I spoke to about Brown up in Aurora has disappeared. Seems he's also from Boston."

"You don't think there's something between this man and the Widow Brown, do you?"

"I must admit it crossed my mind. She's a beautiful young woman and the missing man, Wally Caster, is young, strong and quite handsome. He was at a party when Brown was killed, though. The only person whose whereabouts can't be confirmed is Jonathan."

"Don't be ridiculous. Jonathan was on a train when Mr. Brown was killed, and right here in our own home for the second murder."

Hodgins swirled around the remnants of his tea. "Found out the other day Jonathan actually came into the city Thursday night. That's why he had the napkin from the Red Lion. Never had a chance to tell you. As for George Roberts, Jonathan could have snuck out while we were sleeping."

Cordelia gasped. "Oh Bertie, how can you think such a thing?"

"I don't believe it, but others will. I'm missing something and if I don't figure out what, Jonathan may very well hang.

* * *

When Hodgins arrived at the station the next morning he had a wire sent to Boston inquiring about Wallace Caster, then made a cup of tea and shut himself away in his office to think. "Who could have killed both men and why were they framing Jonathan?" He mumbled to himself. "Whoever it was, was doing a damn fine job of making Jonathan appear guilty. How could anyone know when he wouldn't have an alibi? It has to be someone nearby."

He tore a clean sheet off his pad of long paper, listing the people he needed to follow-up with, or make further inquires about.

At the top he wrote down the two tramps, Curly and Scotty. Beside their names he indicated that he'd confirmed their whereabouts.

Next, Jonathan. Hodgins tapped his pencil while thinking. What could he write that had been absolutely confirmed? He started jotting points.

Arrived mid-night Friday – No

Red Lion early Friday evening – confirmed

Opportunity to kill Brown? – probably not

At home when Roberts was killed? – unknown

He moved on to Ace/Wally

Opportunity to kill Brown? – No

Whereabouts when Roberts was killed? – unknown

Relationship to Janel Brown? – unknown

Hodgins couldn't think of anyone else to add to his list. He re-read it and put little stars beside Ace/Wally. So far, he hadn't found out much about him. Another visit to Aurora was needed. But first, he had to set that reporter straight and provide the public with the facts, such as they were.

He started to put on his coat when the inspector opened the door, slamming it behind him. The glass rattled in the frame. The inspector had Monday's paper in his hand, and threw it on Hodgins' desk.

The tick over the inspector's right eye told Hodgins he wasn't simply angry, he was mad as hell, and that was never good. "Just now finding time to catch up on the paper and saw this. Why isn't he in jail?" The inspector jabbed his finger over the interview on the front page. "Who the hell spoke to the reporter anyway?"

"I don't know, and Jonathan's not guilty. I picked him up at Union Station myself at almost midnight the day of the murder, and he was at my home when the second occurred." He stood with his hands clasped behind his back, fingers crossed. He hadn't lied, just omitted a few details.

The inspector jabbed at the newspaper again. "Fix this. Now."

"Yes, sir. I fully intend to track down that reporter and correct the interview. Someone is framing him and I intend to find out who and why."

The inspector harrumphed. The tick over his eye slowed, and Hodgins relaxed, a little. "See that you do, else you may just find yourself reporting to Barnes." He turned, yanking the door open, letting it bang against the wall. Hodgins watched the door swing back, too stunned to grab it before it slammed shut.

Barnes knocked on the door and entered without waiting for a reply. "What's got the inspector in such a state? Haven't seen him that angry since... well, never."

Hodgins leaned back against his desk. "Bugger wants me to arrest my brother. If I don't arrest someone soon, he threatened to bust me lower than you."

"But I'm the lowest rank, sir."

"I know. Now, I need to you do something." Hodgins reached into his pocket for his notebook. "Go back to Davenport and speak with the folks around the school again. Maybe they've remembered something new. I need to go see that damn reporter."

Hodgins walked over to Yonge Street, took the trolley down to King Street, and then walked east. The newspaper office was at number twenty-six. Fortunately he'd recognized the reporter's name. Chatwick. Always hanging around the stations across the city looking for a scoop. Hodgins stormed into the newspaper office, but most of the desks were empty. He waited a quarter of an hour, pacing and fuming, until Chatwick finally appeared.

"Detective Hodgins. So glad you're here. Was just about to track you down. Hoping to interview you about these murders. Find out how you feel, what with your brother being a murderer and all."

Hodgins thrust the newspaper at Chatwick. "This is a load of shit and you know it. I expect the next edition will have a full retraction, complete with the *facts*, not that rot you printed Monday."

Chatwick shrugged. "Only printed what I was told. How would I know it wasn't the truth?"

"Next time you have a story that involves me or any of the men at Station Four, you talk to me before you print it. Unless you don't want anything from us in future. Imagine, no more police reports from my turf. Hmm, that might make us look rather good. No crime in my area at all."

Hodgins smiled at the expression on the reporter's face as it changed from smug to shock.

"Then again, if you'd like an exclusive when we find the man responsible...?"

"An exclusive?" Chatwick motioned Hodgins to an empty desk. "Tell me what you'd like me to print. It'll be in the evening edition."

Chatwick opened the desk drawer and pulled out several pieces of clean white paper. He stacked them neatly beside something shrouded with a cloth. Chatwick removed the cloth and tossed it behind his shiny, new Remington typewriting machine.

"I wish we had one of those contraptions at the station," Hodgins said. "Make the paperwork at least tolerable." He looked around and noticed several desks had a covered machine sitting on them.

Chatwick barely acknowledged Hodgins' comment. Instead, he picked up a single sheet and wove it through the roller. "Ok, shoot." His hands hovered over the keyboard waiting for Hodgins to start.

Hodgins told him about Jonathan's arrival, stressing his innocence, all the while staring in amazement as Chatwick picked away with two fingers. "Damn noisy thing."

"You get used to it. Maybe one day every office will have typewriting machines."

"City's too cheap," Hodgins remarked.

After correcting all the lies and half-truths, Hodgins went back home to talk to his brother. He didn't want Cordelia or Elizabeth to overhear his questions so he rushed Jonathan into a hansom and went west to The Miller Tavern. Fortunately, it wasn't busy. They found a quiet table in the corner and ordered two beers.

"It's time you told me everything. The inspector expects me to arrest you, and frankly, I don't blame him. I need to know about every incident that took place in Boston, no matter how trivial."

Jonathan shrugged. "I don't know what else to tell you."

"This is becoming tiresome. There has to be something. I won't judge you, but I need to know. Somebody's killed two men and is trying to have you hung for it. Why?"

Silence.

Hodgins slammed both hands on the table top, causing Jonathan to jump, and several nearby conversations to stop. "You know it takes very little to try my patience. Do you want me to put you in jail? The inspector would love that."

"No. Dear God, no." Jonathan picked up his beer, downed it, then signaled for another. The server nodded, stopping to clear several tables as she made her way to the bar. She returned with his beer, spilling a little when she placed it down. One quick swipe with a dirty rag and she was off to the next table. Jonathan finished the second before continuing.

"There's a reason I didn't check on Brown before hiring him and his friends. Some of my dealing have been... slightly around the law."

"How slightly? Am I going to have to let the authorities in Boston know?"

"Nothing too serious. I may have forgotten to list the occasional item on shipments going in and out of my warehouse."

"And I suppose it also slipped your mind when the taxes were collected?"

"It's possible."

"What else? I can't see anyone murdering people over that."

"I owe people money. The wrong kind of people, if you know what I mean. A lot of money. They probably think I've done a runner and may come looking for me."

Hodgins opened his notebook. "Give me their names and I'll see what I can find. If the Boston Police are interested in them, you may have to testify, so you might want to let Elizabeth know."

"She's not like your wife, Albert. I don't believe she'll take the news well."

"Would you prefer she found out as you were being dragged out of the house, in front of the children? I strongly suggest you sit her down and tell her everything."

Jonathan buried his head in his hands. His voice was muffled, but Hodgins understood his words. "I've been so stupid. Tell me what to do and I'll do it."

CHAPTER NINETEEN

Jonathan sat in front of his brother's desk at Station House Number Four, waiting for Albert to return with the promised coffee. Word had been left not to disturb them. Hodgins paused as soon as he came out of the back room. He could see Jonathan slouched in the chair, elbows on his knees, hands cradling his head. That wasn't the strong, over-confident big brother that moved to Boston with his new bride all those years ago. The man sitting in that chair was practically a stranger, and up to his neck in trouble. Hodgins went into his office with two cups and the entire pot of coffee. The inspector walked by and nodded when he spotted Jonathan.

"Right. First, you're going to tell me every sordid detail. This will be an official report so no half-truths or omissions. Then, you're going home to tell Elizabeth. You'll have to come up with something to tell the children, too. They may not read the newspaper, but the other children will hear their parents talking. Unless you intend to keep Freddie and Cora locked up inside until you return home to Boston, they'll need to be prepared. Understand?"

Jonathan nodded, poured some coffee into one of the cups, then began. Almost two hours passed by the time he stopped. Hodgins had several pages full of names, dates, and shipments.

Hodgins sat back and flexed his sore fingers. "You realize you could see a lot of jail time for this? Unless…"

Jonathan leaned forward. "Unless?"

"I wired those names you gave me earlier to the Boston Police. I'll include the new ones you just provided. If they express interest in them, maybe we can make a deal. You would have to testify in court back home and it'll do irreparable damage to your reputation and business."

"I'd have to move and start over. I don't know if I can do that."

"Once word gets out, and it will, you'll probably have to move anyway. No point in dwelling on it until we hear back from the authorities. They may have little interest in it."

"They'll be interested. The authorities have been after these people for a couple of years. I'll do whatever I have to. Moving is a better option than hanging. If they'll make a deal, I'll testify. It could get ugly."

Hodgins checked the time. "The children won't be

home from Sara's friends for a bit. Go home and tell Elizabeth. Maybe include Delia too. She's level-headed and will help calm Elizabeth. She can also help figure out what to tell the children. I'll take Delia and Sara over to the in-laws after dinner so you can have the house to yourselves to tell the little ones. Freddie may not understand, but Cora's bound be to quite upset."

Jonathan took a deep breath and ran his fingers through his hair. "You're right. I'll do it now. I'll fill Cordelia in, even though I suspect you've already told her most of it. Then the three of us can sit and discuss it." Jonathan stood, slipped into his overcoat, pulled his shoulders back, then walked confidently out the door.

* * *

Hodgins glanced at the somber faces around the breakfast table. Now that Jonathan's shady business dealings were out in the open, everyone seemed afraid to speak. Cora's eyes were red and swollen. Not a surprise as he'd heard her crying during the night. Sara fidgeted, unsure what to do or say. They'd told her about Jonathan's troubles on the way home from Cordelia's parents. Only Freddie seemed unaffected.

Cordelia tried to make breakfast as cheery as possible, softly singing a familiar Irish tune. Despite hard feelings between Hodgins and Delia's mother, Euphemia, he always admired her beautiful singing voice. Along with her red hair and freckles, Cordelia inherited that same voice from her mother. Hodgins caught her attention and shook his head. Delia acknowledged him with a nod and stopped singing before putting the breakfast on the table.

"Jonathan, as soon as I hear back from the Boston Police I'll send for you. Won't be able to decide on the best thing to do until we know more."

Cora burst into tears again and ran from the table, knocking the chair over. Scraps barked, then trotted after her. Sobs drifted into the kitchen from the sitting room. Freddie started crying and ran towards the front of the house to join her. Elizabeth rose, but Jonathan put his hand on her arm.

"I'll go. It's my mess. I'll try to explain it again. No matter what the outcome, there'll be no more side deals. I promise."

After he left, Elizabeth pushed her pancakes around the plate. Without looking up, she asked, "What's really going to happen to him?"

Her words sounded flat. Hodgins was unable to tell if she was upset or fed up. Were they headed towards another separation? Or something more final?

"I honestly don't know what will happen. As I said, we need to know what the authorities in Boston want.

Whatever the outcome, it won't bode well for his business. It's certain to be in the papers both here and in Boston. The only people who would want to deal with him would be criminals. However, if he testifies, even the crooks won't bother with him." Hodgins omitted the reminder Jonathan was still a suspect in two murders.

"His business will be ruined. None of our friends will ever speak to us again. We'll have to move."

"Why not move here?" Delia suggested. "Jonathan can stay in the import/export business. Toronto Harbour is just as busy a port as Boston."

"Oh, that would be wonderful," Sara said. "Cora is so nice. Please Aunt Elizabeth?"

"We'll see dear. There's much to discuss." Elizabeth pushed her plate away. "Excuse me. I need to check on the children."

"Well that was a pleasant meal." Hodgins popped the last bite of biscuit in his mouth, then finished his tea. "I need to get to the station." He kissed Delia and Sara before leaving.

As he put on his overcoat, he watched his brother and family in the sitting room. Freddie sat in front of the fireplace with Scraps, Elizabeth on the settee, Cora's head resting on her mother's shoulder. Jonathan stood staring out the bay window.

* * *

One of the sergeants brought a wire to Hodgins about an hour after he arrived. "Boston Police, sir."

Hodgins read the wire, then called Barnes in. "Fetch my brother, will you? Don't bother with the trolley, grab a hansom. Sharpish."

"Right away. Is something wrong?"

Hodgins smiled. "Not at all. Good news for a change. Now off with you."

Three quarters of an hour later, Jonathan raced into his brother's office. "Albert, what is it? Barnes said it was good news."

Hodgins waved the wire. "Boston authorities. As I suspected, they only want the men at the top. If you co-operate, they won't press any charges against you. I'd advise you pay the back taxes you omitted."

"That's a relief, but what about those two bodies? I won't go to jail for smuggling, but I may still be dancing on the end of a rope." Jonathan leaned forward. "You have to find the person responsible. I swear I didn't kill anyone."

"Can you give me any names to confirm your whereabouts Thursday, December 3? You were seen at the Red Lion. It's only a few blocks from where Brown's body was found, so you need to account for every second, from the time you arrived Thursday night, right through until I met you at the train station. How long were you there? Where were you before I met you at the station Friday evening?"

"You know I came in a week before my family to do business. That's what my meeting at the Red Lion was. I just came in a day earlier than I told you." Jonathan provided the names and addresses of the two men. "They cancelled after that story in the newspaper. I stayed overnight Thursday at the Red Lion. Staff there can vouch for me. My meeting was at five Friday evening. Had to come in Thursday as I couldn't catch the train that arrived Friday afternoon. Spent the entire day at the Red Lion, reading, chatting with the owner and staff. The meeting took longer than expected and I barely made it to the station before you arrived to pick me up."

"And I'll swear you never left my house when Roberts' was killed. Even if you by-passed the squeaky step, Scraps would have made a fuss and woke everyone. I'll send Barnes over to the Red Lion for statements."

Jonathan leaned back and grinned. "Well, I've nothing to worry about then, do I?"

"I'm confident saying you won't hang, but someone is framing you, and doing a damn fine job of it. If he doesn't succeed in getting you convicted, what else will he do? He might make it more personal. Could come after you."

"Or my family? Please, don't mention that to Lizzie. She's upset enough. She was even blathering on about moving here."

"Been meaning to talk to you about that. Delia mentioned it at breakfast and Sara got all excited about it. You already know once word gets out about your shady dealings your business will suffer. Would you consider moving back here?"

"I don't know. Maybe. Not a priority at the moment."

"Of course not. Think about it though. Now, shall I wire Boston and tell them you'll work with them when you arrive back home?"

Jonathan sighed. "Yes, I suppose you'd better. After the beginning of the year. Anything else?"

"No. Send Barnes in on your way out."

* * *

Barnes returned a few hours later with statements from the staff as well as from the owner of the Red Lion.

"Quite an interesting place. First time I've been in. About what I expected. Could use a better decorator, though. Place is littered with anvils, jackplanes, and even an old beer barrel. Why, they've even got a sheep's head mounted over the brick fireplace. Only nice thing was the dog." He pulled out his notebook and told Hodgins what he'd found.

"I spoke with several of the employees and they all recall seeing your brother drinking with two other chaps. One woman," Barnes flipped through his notes. "Sally, said he was there when she came on shift at six p.m." Barnes looked up at Hodgins and smiled. "The barman can't say one way or another when Jonathan left, but all the ladies remembered him."

Hodgins nodded. "Yes, he's always been popular with the women. Fortunately, he never took advantage of it." His thoughts drifted to the Widow Brown. "At least as far as I know."

"He came in late Thursday and spent the night. Owner said Jonathan stayed there all day Friday chatting to the staff, settling into the dining room around 5:30. Two men joined him for a meal and they stayed until about 10:30."

"Not proof positive he's not guilty, but it's enough to cast doubt. So, who are we left with?"

Barnes shrugged and shook his head. "No one we know of. Maybe someone involved in this deal of Brown's?"

"Problem is, the only person I know of is Roberts, and he's dead too. Mrs. Brown said she knows nothing of the business, but she could be lying. I got the impression she wasn't totally heart-broken over his death, and she seemed fed-up with his dealings. Before I informed her of his death, her response was a somewhat frustrated 'what has he done now?' or something similar."

Hodgins leaned back in his chair and twisted the end of his moustache. "I wonder…"

"Sir?"

"I need to mull a few things over. It's getting late. We'll continue this in the morning."

Hodgins rose and removed his overcoat from the peg. "Write up a report and get proper statements signed by the staff at the Red Lion. We'll need them if Jonathan goes to trial. Say, have you given any thought to coming over one night with your sweetheart? I think we all need a good old knees-up to brighten everyone's spirits. We're both scheduled the day off on Christmas Eve. Bring your family and hers. Delia and Elizabeth can put out a spread of cold meats and sweets. Who knows? Maybe we'll have something to celebrate by then."

CHAPTER TWENTY

Hodgins and Cordelia took a advantage of an unusually quiet house, relaxing in the two stuffed chairs by the fireplace. "A Christmas Eve party? That's sounds perfect. All our families together." Hodgins watched as Cordelia muttered and counted on her fingers. "Mother and Father can come in the afternoon, or before luncheon. Between Elizabeth, Mother and myself we can have everything ready by the time Henry and his family arrive. I assume the Halloway's will be coming, too? Can't have Henry without his sweetheart and her family." She stopped and wagged a finger in his face. "There will be no talk of Jonathan's connection to the two men."

Hodgins put his hands up. "I promise, I won't mention it. Only jolly discussions. Speaking of my brother, where is he?"

"Oh, an old friend dropped by and they went out to dinner. Billings I believe he said."

"Ran into him on the train the other day. Said he'd stop in to see Jonathan. If what he said on the train is true, at least Jonathan has one person on his side who's not related."

"Sit down and have some tea." Cordelia placed two cups on the kitchen table and filled them. "Dinner's almost ready, and the house is quiet for a change."

He sat beside his wife and took a sip of hot tea. "I thought there was something different. Where's Elizabeth and the children?"

"She took them skating."

Hodgins looked around. "Scraps too?"

"Yes. It's such a nice day they decided to go to the pond instead of the rink. That way Scraps could join them. I expect they'll be returning soon. I've gotten ever so much done this afternoon." She turned slightly to face him. "Are you any closer to finding out who murdered those two men?"

"No, but we found several witnesses to vouch for Jonathan's whereabouts for Brown's murder, and I'll swear six ways to Sunday he never left this house at the time of the second one. I'm confident we've enough to keep him out of jail and away from the noose."

Hodgins reached across the table and took a biscuit from the covered basket before Delia could slap his hand away. "Bertie, you really must stop eating so much. I don't think I can let your trousers out any further."

"I'll walk Scraps more often. It's worth it." He broke off a large piece of the biscuit and stuffed it in his mouth. "There's something different tasting about this."

"A recipe of Elizabeth's. Do you like it?"

"Not a good as yours but a delightful change." He ate another piece before continuing. "I'll be taking the first train back to Aurora tomorrow. I'm certain Brown's widow knows something, or that Wally bloke. She's packing up and he's already scarpered. I'd like to get this settled before Christmas, or at least by the end of the year. Jonathan has to go home right after the new year and testify. I don't want this hanging over his head. Even proven not guilty, word's bound to get out. I really hope he decides to move and put as much distance as possible between himself and the men he was dealing with.

* * *

It was going on eleven the next morning when Hodgins arrived back at the Brown residence. The coat pegs inside the door were empty, and the knick-knacks on the hall table were gone. He looked down the hall past Janel. The pictures were gone, too. She indicated for him to go into the sitting room where they spoke previously. Almost everything had been packed up. "Moving so soon?"

"I'm leaving tomorrow. I do wish you'd stop bothering me. There's nothing more I can tell you.

Hodgins leaned on the fireplace mantle. "Oh, I believe there's plenty you can tell me. You mentioned Ace last time I visited. That's young Wally Caster. Funny thing, he up and left town without a word. Headed back to Boston I believe." Hodgins only guessed at that, hoping Janel would say something to confirm it.

He reached over and read the tag on the nearest crate. "Same place your belonging are headed. Just how well do you know Wally?"

Janel placed her hand on her growing bulge. "What are you implying?"

Hodgins feigned surprise. "Why nothing at all ma'am. I was just making a casual obser—" He stopped, cocked his head, and starred off to the left, trying to recall something.

"Am I correct in remembering you said you're seven months along?"

"Yes, that's right."

"We received a rather lengthy report from the Boston Police. Listed many of your husband's stays in their jail. His most recent incarceration lasted only a few months. He was released mid-July, only five months ago."

"You're quicker than Tony. Took him two months to figure out the dates."

"Did he find out who fathered the child? Confront the man and end up dead, perhaps?"

Janel laughed. "No he was too stupid to see what was right under his nose."

Once again, her earlier half-smile popped into his mind. "Wally."

"Very good, Detective."

"But he didn't kill your husband. I know that for a fact."

Janel turned and casually strolled over to an end table with a single drawer, half-hidden by a doily. Hodgins heard the drawer slide open, then close. When she turned back towards him, a small Derringer was in her hand, pointed straight at his chest.

He held up his hands. "Hold on. I'm not going to arrest you for having another man's baby. Please, put the pistol down."

"I know you're an intelligent man, Detective. Surely you must have figured it out. Why else would you come here?"

He took one step closer. "I know you couldn't have killed anyone. Woman your size and condition would never have been able to drag a dead body into those positions. And your husband was dragged a fair distance. I'm sure if I asked around I'd find people to confirm Wally was here in town when Roberts was killed as well. Again, I'm asking you to put the gun down." He took another step.

Janel raised her arm, pointing the gun at his head. "Stay put. I need to think."

Hodgins gambled on his instincts. "Who'd you hire?"

She smiled. " See? I said you were intelligent. Tell me, do you treat your wife with respect? I image you do. Not like Tony. He treated me as a maid and housekeeper. Said I was too stupid to understand any of his plans. Well I showed him. I planned this." She waved her arms around. "All this was my idea. I wanted to start a new life with Ace, Wally. He's young, attractive and honest. Everything Tony wasn't."

"Does Wally even know it was you who arranged all these killings?"

"No." It was barely more than a whisper. Did she regret what she'd done, or did she think Wally would leave her if he found out? She lowered her arm, gun pointing at the floor. Hodgins took another step.

"But why kill Roberts? Surely you could have gone away and not killed him?"

"Your brother insulted me. Treated me like one of those trollops. Word got around he was planning a trip to Toronto to visit his brother, so I convinced Tony it would be a good idea to move here. So many more people to fleece. First, Ace moved and found a job. Tony had business cards from when he worked for your brother, so I made certain to take them. After we moved, I accompanied Tony into the city one day. While he made arrangements with Roberts I went shopping. Shopping for a hired killer. It wasn't difficult to find someone to kill both and leave the business cards. My revenge against your brother for treating me like a common tart."

She stopped pacing and pointed the gun again. "Unfortunately, it seems like I'll have to take care of you myself."

The safety release clicked. Hodgins flinched. He was too far from any of the piles of boxes and crates to dash behind. His gaze fixed on her hand. It started to shake. He held his breath, waiting for the shot.

CHAPTER TWENTY-ONE

One of the babies cried causing Janel to turn towards the hallway. Hodgins made his move. Three long strides and his hand clamped over her wrist.

"No!" Janel screamed. Hodgins squeezed her wrist, forcing her to drop the pistol.

"Afraid you won't be meeting Wally any time soon."

"You can't do this," Janel yelled. "You're ruining everything." She beat his chest with her free arm.

Hodgins kicked the gun away before grabbing her flailing arm. He couldn't simply throw her to the floor and risk harming the unborn child. He looked around, searching for the twine she used on the boxes. Distracted, he didn't see her bring back her leg.

"Damn."

Janel kicked his shin. Hodgins loosened his grip. It was just enough for her to break free. She shoved him, knocking him into a chair then ran down the hall and out the back door.

Hodgins didn't think she'd get far as she only wore

house shoes and didn't have a coat or shawl. He limped down the hall and looked out the still open door. A trail of footprints headed north. The second baby began crying. He couldn't leave them alone. The snow would reveal Janel's hiding place, so he hurried next door to fetch the neighbour to watch the twins.

Hodgins tracked Janel through her yard and onto a neighbouring lot. Her footprints disappeared around the corner of a house. He followed and found himself on Wellington Street. The area was covered in tracks, making it impossible to tell which way she went. Hodgins turned west, hoping Janel went towards the main part of town. He only got a few feet when he heard yelling. It sounded like, "get out of my yard." Hoping it was Janel, he crossed the road and headed toward where he thought the voice came from.

A few houses down he spotted tracks leading around a house. He heard someone pleading for help. Janel. Hodgins rounded the back of the house just as she was being allowed in.

"Stop. Toronto Constabulary." Hodgins ran to the door. Janel tried to push her way into the house, but the lady blocked her way.

"Don't want any bother with the law." She backed into her house, closing the door, leaving Janel out in the cold.

Janel dropped to her knees, shivering, cradling her belly. "Please, don't let anything happen to my baby."

Hodgins removed his overcoat and draped it over her shoulders, then led her to the train station. He gave a quick explanation to the station agent, who locked her in his office. Hodgins wired his station, then went back to the Brown's home to fetch a coat for Janel and ask the neighbour to mind the babies until someone came for them.

* * *

When the train arrived back in Toronto, Janel was taken to the hospital, a constable left guarding her door. She wasn't outside long enough to get frostbite, but the doctor wanted to keep her a day or two, just to make sure the baby was unharmed.

Hodgins hung his overcoat on a peg by the front door and joined his family in the kitchen to fill them in. "Well, I'm glad that's over with." Jonathan rubbed his throat. "I was beginning to feel the rope around my neck. I'd still like those boxing lessons, though."

Elizabeth rushed over to Hodgins and threw her arms around him. "Thank you Albert. I'm so relieved." She kissed his cheek then stood beside her husband. "We discussed it last night. As soon as Jonathan testifies we're going to sell the house and move here."

"I told her the children can stay here and get settled into school permanently," Cordelia said. "I know I should have spoken to you first, but I didn't think you'd mind."

"Of course they can stay here. Probably best if they're not around during the trial." He turned to Elizabeth. "You can wire the school tomorrow to have their records transferred."

Elizabeth looped her arm through her husband's. "Jonathan, maybe we can start looking around after Christmas for a suitable location for you to start over? Might be able to get you set up by February. House too."

Jonathan looked out the kitchen window at the children playing in the back with Scraps. "Maybe a dog as well?"

"One thing at a time dear. I'm sure Sara will share for awhile." Elizabeth peered over his shoulder. "Wherever would we find another dog like Scraps anyway?"

"As you said, one thing at a time." Delia reached for Elizabeth's hand. "This Christmas is going to be extra special. Come, let's start planning the Christmas Eve party."

CHAPTER TWENTY-TWO

The next three days exhausted everyone as they hurried to finish all the preparations for the party. Sara and Cora made the invitations and personally delivered them. Every room on the main floor had been decorated and was ready to be filled with family and friends. Cordelia's mother would make the plum pudding and mince pies, which would be warming on the wood stove while they consumed their main meal. Elizabeth prepared a large bowl of chestnut stuffing, while Cordelia took care of the roast goose. Along with the goose, they'd also have cold sliced roast beef and chicken, apples, oranges, boiled potatoes, and wine.

Sara and Cora wanted to make gilded walnut, raisin, and nut garlands, as well as popcorn balls for the tree and hallway. Since they were having a party, Cordelia agreed and added the necessary items to her shopping list. Once the girls had used all their supplies, they started baking sugar cookies and sweets. Freddie's job was to keep Scraps out of the way. He didn't need to be asked twice to play with the dog, especially as they let him test the cookies.

The day before the party Albert went to his in-laws and, with the help of Cordelia's father, brought over the pianoforte. Its rectangular shape fit perfectly between the fireplace and the Christmas tree. The little pale-blue piano had tiny pink and yellow roses painted along the top, connected with vines. A wreath had been painted in the centre of the music holder. Hodgins knew Delia missed being able to play whenever she wanted now that they weren't living with her parents. Maybe he'd look for one after his brother and family were settled.

Constable Barnes arrived late-afternoon with his mother and younger sister. His sweetheart Violet Halloday and her parents arrived shortly afterwards. As soon as Barnes introduced his family to Jonathan's he scampered across the room to be with Violet. Hodgins watched as Barnes slipped his arm around her waist. He figured they'd be married by spring, and knew another party in his home was inevitable.

Despite Hodgins' best efforts, talk soon turned to the recent murders.

"Imagine," Cordelia's mother said. "A young woman having her husband murdered just so she could be with her fancy man. And to frame Jonathan for it. Disgraceful, not to mention those two babies and another on the way.

Any idea what will happen to them?"

"She'll remain in jail until her baby comes, then it will be put up for adoption. Normally, she'd hang for her part in the killings, but she's given us the name of the man she hired. I expect the judge will give her life in prison instead, Hodgins said.

"Her twins have already been taken to the St. Paul's House of Providence. Most likely they'll be parceled out separately. Not many would welcome two little ones at once." Barnes shook his head. "Imagine. Having a sister and never knowing it."

"I think we should take them, Daddy." Everyone turned to Sara. "I wish I had a sister. I was ever so sad when Mommy lost the baby."

"Heavens, you remember that?" Cordelia asked. "You were only five."

"Oh, please, can we have the babies? I'm old enough to help take care of them."

The guests all remained silent, enjoying the unexpected conversation.

Hodgins and Cordelia exchanged a look. Cordelia smiled. "Your father and I will have to discuss it Sara."

"Cordelia, how can you consider such a thing?" her mother asked. "The babies of a murderess?"

Sara squealed and clapped her hands. "Oh, please,

Daddy? Babies for Christmas. I already know what we can name them. Holly and Ivy."

"As your mother said, we'll have to discuss it." He winked at Cordelia before turning back to Sara. "Why, they may not think us suitable parents after they see how we've raised you."

Mr. Halloday cleared his throat. "I've a sort of announcement to make myself. I say, I'd like to make an announcement."

Hodgins turned towards Barnes, thinking the young constable couldn't wait and he'd already asked for Violet's hand. Barnes shrugged in answer to the unspoken question.

"I've been in correspondence with my sister. She's planning a tour of Europe in the New Year and I've arranged for my daughter, Violet, to accompany her. They'll be gone four, maybe five months. Splendid opportunity for her to learn art and culture from several different countries. Rub elbows with the higher echelon. My sister is acquainted with many high-ranking people abroad."

"F-f-f-five months?" If at all possible, Barnes' jaw would have landed on the hardwood floor. He moved across the room and stood beside the detective, whispering. "I can't ask her to marry me now. What if she

405

meets a count or something?"

Before Hodgins could reply, Violet rushed over. "Oh, Henry. Isn't this the most exciting news? London, Paris, maybe even Cairo. All those magnificent art galleries." She stopped as she noticed the look on his face.

Hodgins watched in amusement. Her expression changed continually as she worked things out in her mind. Finally, her eyes widened, the joyful look gone.

"Henry! I promise, I'll be absolutely miserable without you. It will feel like years. I wish you could see it all with me."

Barnes tried to smile. "No, you'll enjoy your adventure. I forbid you to be miserable. Promise you'll write often."

"Every day. I promise."

While the young couple discussed the next several months, Hodgins wove his way through the crowd to the sitting room doorway and took the tray of sweets from Cordelia.

"Poor Henry." Cordelia tsked and shook her head. "Mrs. Halloday was telling me just the other day about her sister-in-law's trip. Now I understand her comment about eligible young noblemen. How could they even think about sending her away to find a husband when they know how much in love those two are? I thought they liked

Henry."

"Poor Henry indeed. He asked me not to say anything, but he was planning on proposing after Christmas. He just told me he won't now. He's going to be a bugger to work with until she returns. For his sake, she'd better come back without a count in tow."

Hodgins put the tray on the side table and they rejoined their guests, now crowded around the pianoforte. His mother-in-law played Silent Night while Barnes stood by the crackling fire, alone.

ABOUT THE AUTHOR

Nanci M. Pattenden is a genealogist and an emerging fiction writer, currently working on a collection of detective stories set in Victorian Toronto.

She has completed the Creative Writing program at both the University of Calgary and the University of Toronto.

Nanci currently resides in Newmarket with her fluffy cat Snowball.

nanci@nancipattenden.com
www.murderdoespayink.ca
www.nancipattenden.com
@npattenden